Gun Shy

Lori L. Lake

Quest Books
a Division of
RENAISSANCE ALLIANCE PUBLISHING, INC.
Nederland, Texas

ISBN 1-930928-43-2

Second Edition
First Printing 2002

9 8 7 6 5 4 3 2 1

Cover design by Mary D. Brooks

Published by:

Renaissance Alliance Publishing, Inc.
PMB 238, 8691 9th Avenue
Port Arthur, Texas 77642-8025

Find us on the World Wide Web at
http://www.rapbooks.biz

Printed in the United States of America

Musical Lyric Permissions

Acknowledgements

Never-ending thanks to my publisher and friend, Cathy LeNoir, and to my dear partner in crime, Barb "Captain Doc" Coles, for giving me the opportunity to work out a second edition of this book. Thanks also to Barb's life partner, Linda Daniel, for support and venerable advice.

Grateful appreciation to the fine graphic artists who have so generously shared their *Gun Shy* art with me: L.J. Maas, Encarnación, and Mary D. Brooks.

To Ann Reed, one of Minnesota's finest singer/songwriters, heartfelt thanks to you and Lin Bick for generously allowing me the use of your lyrics. I hope that many readers will go out to www.annreed.com and order your wonderful music.

Thanks to my "First Editor," Day Petersen, for advice and inspiration and to Barb Coles for managing to edit this and read through it at least ten times. You're a trooper. For beta reading, proofing, and galley reviewing: Erin Linn, Elizabeth "Buff" Seymour, Dr. Joy, Ruth Boetzel, Carrie Carr, Jan Trumbo, my judicious friend Norma, Pat Smith, Nann Dunne, Kim Miller, and Betty Crandall.

Best love to Angela Reese, my talented "Websister" who created and maintains my website.

To Mary "MaryD" Brooks, Web Goddess Extraordinaire, for working through so many drafts of the new cover for this second edition and for *Under The Gun.* You made them match so nicely!

To all the Fans and Bards in the Xenaverse: you are a determined and creative group who have inspired me to no end. Special thanks to Bacchae, Sobbie, and KatLyn.

For law enforcement research, thanks to Officer Erin Linn; Police Sgt. Mike Maloney; Reserve Officer Rose Madison; and Dr. Sue, who educated me about post-traumatic stress disorder in cops.

Love and appreciation to: all my sisters and their families; the Hamerski family; Marie Sheppard Williams; the original Tuesday Night Writer's Group: Lee, Carolyn, Susan, Monica, Liz, and Marie; MaryAnn Howard; Denise Karamafrooz; Mo McKinney; Peg Thompson and Beverly Zawacki. Thanks to teachers who have stuck by me all these years: Jan Burgess, Coach Petersen, Art Nanna, Anna LaCompte, and Anna's late husband, Albert, for always believing in me, even when I didn't.

But above all, I am very grateful (and thank God!) for Diane. As I've said before, she had to live with a crazed madwoman while this was being written, and then, with all the totally unexpected fallout. It hasn't been easy, but as they say, third time's a charm.

Lori L. Lake
August, 2002

Still for Diane
Forever and Always.

Chapter
1

The gold and white squad car swung around the corner onto Como Boulevard, no headlights and little sound but tires squeaking on hot pavement. To the left, in the heart of the city of St. Paul, was Como Lake, a small body of water only half a mile in diameter. The street ran parallel to a walking and biking path that ringed the lake. To the right sat a row of darkened homes up on a slight slope, which were heavily shaded by huge elm and oak trees.

The police car paused four houses away from a white, two-story stucco home. Officer Desiree "Dez" Reilly turned off the air conditioning and powered her window halfway down, staring intently at the stucco house. With a weary sigh, she listened for the nighttime noises over the engine of the car. The neighborhood was silent, almost too quiet. She should hear crickets, but all was still. She cut the engine, picked up her flashlight, and stepped out of the car, shutting the door so it clicked quietly. As she strolled along the sidewalk, the hum of nighttime insects started up, and she stood in front of the stucco house, waiting, listening. Somewhere down the street came a faint bass thump of music as a car passed through the intersection and faded off into the distance. Otherwise, no one was out.

Her eyes scanned the street and the houses with practiced speed. Nothing seemed out of place, but someone had reported the sound of a woman screaming and had pinpointed the noise as coming from the house in front of her. A string of residential break-ins had occurred over the last two months, all centered in this area. Even more disturbing was that in three of the seven cases, a woman had been raped. Cops at roll call were beginning to toss around the words "serial rapist." It was enough to make Dez take notice, living as she did within a mile of the lake.

Outside the air-conditioned car, the August humidity seeped

into her pores through the short-sleeved blue uniform shirt, through the bulletproof vest, and through the white cotton t-shirt she wore, adding to her fatigue more than she thought possible. She took a deep breath of the dank air and felt herself sweating. August in St. Paul was no fun, but at least the mosquitoes weren't after her. Yet.

She was tall, lean-hipped, and broad-shouldered with long black hair caught up in a French braid. She walked with a confident stride across a strip of grass, over the sidewalk, and up the cracked walkway to the house, pausing periodically to listen. There were six stairs to the porch, and the first floor windowsills were slightly above her eye level. The front windows were dark, but a shaft of golden light shone from an open second floor window around the corner of the house. Leaving her flashlight off, she strode around to the south side and paused for a moment. Now she could hear angry muttering, the sound of an urgent, high-pitched voice, and then a frantic scream quickly muffled.

Dez heard a ripping sound, and then deep-throated laughter. A male voice growled, "Stop it! Stop fighting or—"

"No, you stop it. Get out of here!" a woman's voice shouted.

"Oh, shit!" the man's voice growled. "You move, I cut her throat. Got it?" In a different tone, he hollered, "Get her!"

That was all Dez needed to hear. She touched her shoulder mic and called for backup as she ran toward the back of the house and around to the other side, visually checking the doors and windows until she found what she suspected: a sliced window screen leading into what she thought would be the dining room.

Hearing another scream, she flicked on her shoulder mic again and advised the dispatcher to hurry the backup team. In a hoarse whisper she said, "This sounds bad. I think there are at least two male suspects and one, maybe two, female victims." In the background she heard far-off sirens, and as her skin crawled, she felt an uncharacteristic compulsion to do something and do it now. A loud crash startled her, and she hit the shoulder mic again. "I'm going in. Tell 'em to follow quick as possible—north side window."

Hooking her flashlight on her belt, she hoisted herself up over the windowsill headfirst and tumbled into the darkened house as quietly as she could. Scuttling across the floor on her hands and knees, she moved toward the faint light of the doorway and peeked around the corner. *Stairs, where are the stairs?* She rose and silently inched around the corner out of the dining room. She grabbed the flashlight off her belt, feeling the metal warm against her palm, then clicked it on and unholstered her gun.

****

Jaylynn Savage realized she was tired when her watch chimed eleven. She had spent the entire evening in the air-conditioned college library cramming for her summer term finals, and visions of Constitutional Law danced in her head. She persisted for another ten minutes, then gave up when her vision kept blurring. Running hands through short white-blonde hair, she hoped the political theory exam would go well in the morning, but she just couldn't study one more minute. Going over and over the material was no longer productive. Since the library closed at midnight anyway, Jaylynn decided to head home. She packed up her books, said hello to friends on the way out, and exited into the humid summer air.

Jaylynn liked to say she was five-and-a-half feet tall, but that was only if she was wearing shoes with an inch heel. A slender build, lightly tanned skin, and sun-bleached blonde hair were evidence of time spent outdoors. Her face, framing warm hazel eyes, was full of youthful innocence and of something else perhaps best described as contentment.

As she strolled away from the library, her legs felt strong, but fatigued, from the five-mile run she'd taken earlier in the day. She walked slowly from the library to the bus stop, going over First Amendment issues. *That's one area of the exam that I'll ace. I know that cold.* She thought about how glad she would be to finish this final class. Perhaps she'd have time to write poetry again.

The bus deposited her half a block from the rented house she shared with two friends. Cutting up the alley, she let herself in through the kitchen door. Jaylynn loved the old house she and Tim and Sara lived in. Not only was it situated right across the street from Como Lake, but it was also enormous. Every room was spacious with tall ceilings, ornate woodwork, and walk-in closets. She shut and locked the door quietly so as not to awaken Sara. Her other roommate, Tim, wasn't home yet. She could tell because his beat-up red Corolla wasn't parked out back. She tossed her keys on the table and crept up the stairs.

Sara must still be up, she thought as she turned the corner on the landing. The lamp in her roommate's room cast a faint patch of light that slightly illuminated the top stairs. She thought of her friend sitting on the couch, studying in the spacious master bedroom and she smiled, but then an acrid smell, like body odor, assaulted her senses causing Jaylynn to squinch up her face and frown. When she heard a thud and a ripping noise, she paused on the stairwell, heart beating fast for reasons she didn't understand. She eased up the last two stairs and peered silently around the doorway into her friend's room.

Sara lay twisting on the floor in the wide space between the twin beds, her hands taped together. A huge figure in a dark gray sweatshirt and black pants straddled her waist, muttering and threatening. He held a knife in one hand and a silver strip in the other. Sara screamed as he tried to put the duct tape over her mouth. She shook her head furiously, whipping around her long brown hair and causing it to stick to the tape. Her assailant slapped the side of her face and she screamed again and struggled, tears running down her cheeks, as he forced the strip of tape over her mouth.

He said, "Stop it! Stop fighting or I'll—"

Without a thought, Jaylynn pushed into the room. "No, you stop it. Get out of here!"

"Oh, shit!" He rolled aside and spun around, grabbing the girl on the floor by the neck. "You move, I cut her throat. Got it?"

He wore a tan nylon stocking over his head, obscuring his face and making his features look distorted and diabolical. He glanced towards the shadowy area behind the door and said, "Get her!"

Jaylynn turned to see a smaller man, dressed like the first and also wearing a nylon mask. She screamed, a loud, throaty bellow. He was no taller than she, but was much stockier and held a wooden bat in one hand. As she screamed again and backed toward the door, the smaller man grabbed her by the shoulder and arm. He dragged her onto the twin bed near the door and shoved her so hard that she bounced when she hit the mattress. She saw the baseball bat coming at her face and rolled to the side to avoid it. It hit the wall with a resounding crash. As he dove toward her, Jaylynn got her feet up, knees to her chest, and kicked him in the torso, sending him sprawling against the opposite wall and to the floor. Before she could roll off the bed, he was up. He dove on her again, the bat in one hand and a hank of her hair in the other.

Jaylynn shrieked and growled, kicking at him and swinging wildly, some of her blows connecting solidly. He stumbled back from the bed, panting. Getting a better grip on the bat, he advanced on her again. "I'll kill you, bitch!"

Footsteps pounded on the stairs, then a husky voice shouted, "Police!" A flashlight beam shone down the hall. Jaylynn's attacker turned toward the doorway and she saw him swing the bat. It struck an arm coming low through the doorway and she heard a clatter. Jaylynn rolled off the bed. She yelped when her knees hit the floor and then she looked up to see a blue-clad figure dive into the room and roll. Instantly the cop was back up.

Dez winced when she saw the bat descending, but it was too late to pull back. She felt an explosion of pain when the bat connected, and her hand involuntarily turned and opened. Her Glock flew from her grasp and skittered behind her. She knew she didn't have time to find it in the hallway and instead burst into the room shouting in rage.

The beefy man with the knife let go of Sara and pulled himself to his feet. His partner, wielding the bat, rushed Dez, only to be met by her right elbow slamming a solid blow to his face. He dropped the bat and staggered back, cradling his face. Jaylynn took the opportunity to kick him behind the knee and he screamed in pain and fell. She looked for Sara, caught her eye, and saw her friend's look of terror. Jaylynn gestured, pointing toward the closet, but when Sara tried to rise, the big man shoved her, knocking her back to the floor. The bound woman made a high-pitched noise as she squirmed away and slid halfway under one of the twin beds on the far side of the room.

The man with the knife came at Dez in a rush, but out of control. She got the flashlight up to block the downward lunge of the blade and then kicked at his groin with her steel-toed service boot. Enraged, he yowled but kept on coming, managing to slice downward through her shirt to imbed the knife in her vest. She knocked aside his knife arm and gave him a right elbow to the chin, sending him off balance, and then punched him in the side of the head with the flashlight. As he went down, the other man regained his footing and picked up the bat. He swung high and Dez ducked to a squat, then launched herself to head-butt him across the room. He hit the bedside table and smashed the lamp to the floor. Sara squeezed further under the bed to avoid being landed on.

Dez extricated herself from the little man's grip as Jaylynn sprang across the room and wrenched the bat from his hand. She whacked at his head. Though he raised his arms in defense, she nailed him solidly on the collarbone, feeling a surge of adrenaline when he roared in pain. She stepped back, tripping over the big man's leg as he rose, cradling his bleeding head. Scrambling on all fours, Jaylynn crawled across the carpet, up and over the twin bed near the door, and dove into the hall. *I've got to find the gun. Find the gun. Find the gun.* It repeated like a chant in her head. She spotted it on the landing three stairs below and picked it up, surprised to find it much lighter than she expected. She realized she didn't know how it worked. Was there a safety?

As Jaylynn came back through the doorway, she saw the woman in blue whirl, graceful and deadly in the same motion. Every time an attacker came at her, she used quick left jabs and kicks to flatten one, then the other. The larger man wailed in a high-pitched voice and tried to get up. The cop nailed him in the side of the head with a vicious roundhouse and then kicked him in the chest.

"Stay down," the cop shouted. The smaller man lay on his side, heaving with exertion. The officer handcuffed his wrist to the bigger man's ankle, then jumped clear of them and, with her left hand, dragged Sara out from under the bed and toward the closet across the room.

Jaylynn stood in the doorway holding the bat and the black gun. "Here," she said, offering the weapon to the police officer. She kept the bat for herself.

The tall, dark woman turned, her face white despite the exertion. She seemed enormous to Jaylynn—not fat, just solid and very powerful. Later, Jaylynn would remember the feral smile of satisfaction on the cop's face and consider that she might be a very dangerous woman. But at that moment, as she looked into steel blue eyes for a heartbeat, she felt as though she knew her, and a thrill of recognition coursed through her mind. The blue eyes narrowed as they met her own, and for a brief moment, Jaylynn wondered if the woman recognized her, too. But of course she couldn't know her. The cop hurried across the room and snatched the gun from Jaylynn.

Sara whimpered, and Jaylynn moved further into the room. "Sara! Sara, are you all right?"

"Wait," Dez said. She held the Glock in her left hand and stood over the two panting men. "Don't move. I'd be so *very* happy to shoot your fuckin' heads off if you move a single muscle." Dez could hear the sirens coming, their whining becoming more insistent as her backup drew nearer. She glanced at Sara and made a quick motion with her head toward Jaylynn. "Get her outta here," she growled. "Now! Into the hall. And be sure to stay clear of these two jokers. Wouldn't wanna have to blow their brains out, now would we?"

Jaylynn wanted to tell her it was perfectly all right with her if the cop emptied her gun into their sorry carcasses. Instead, she leapt to Sara's side and helped her to her feet. She pulled her out into the hall where her friend sank to the floor sobbing. Jaylynn slowly pulled the duct tape off her mouth. She was still trying to loosen the twisted tape from Sara's hands when the backup officers burst into the house.

****

The house was surrounded with spotlights and curious onlookers. Police ran in and out of the stucco home as a tremendous commotion, both inside and outside, engulfed the neighborhood with noise and light. After a few tense moments, Dez relinquished her guard role and let the backup cops take charge. Once the suspects were properly cuffed, she stepped over and pulled the nylon masks off their heads. Two white males, in their early twenties, neither very handsome—especially in light of the damage she was glad she'd inflicted. The bigger man was bruised and bleeding from three gashes in his brows. His ear bled a trail down his neck. The slimmer man bled profusely from a cut below his left eye. At the moment, they were both sullen and angry as they sat on the floor muttering and cursing her. The backup cops read the two men their rights before dragging them out of the room and down the stairs.

Dez's right arm throbbed painfully as she eased down the steps, passing the emergency medical team coming up the stairs for the injured young woman. A stream of cops crowded through the front door to take a look at the two suspects, both of whom Dez suspected were responsible for the neighborhood's recent rapes.

The living room, now flooded with light and activity, was furnished with overstuffed chairs, a fluffy sofa, an upright piano, and a futon couch. Four oak bookcases full of neatly ordered books stood along one wall. Movie posters covered most of the other walls: a black-clad Schwarzenegger from *The Terminator*, Jackie Chan in a flying kick, Geena Davis pointing a gun, and Stallone hanging from a cliff. Dez walked through the room, past a Bruce Willis *Die Hard* poster, and out the front door. As she stepped wearily down the front stairs, a thin man dressed in khaki slacks and a tan t-shirt ran up the walkway.

"Where's Jay and Sara?" he asked her breathlessly, running his hand through his red hair.

"Inside." Two paramedics maneuvering a stretcher came up the walk towards her, and she navigated the last two stairs and stepped over onto the grass, gesturing to the young man to do the same. "Who are you, sir?"

"Tim Donovan—I live here." He started to push past, looking back at her, his face pale and stricken. "Are they...uh...okay?"

"Yup, I think so." Dez continued down the walk, suddenly feeling a bit sick to her stomach. As she moved along, she tried to flex her forearm, but it hurt too much. She looked at her watch: 11:58. *In two minutes my shift is over. Good timing.* She headed over to the ambulance to have her arm looked at.

Tim took the stairs two at a time and blasted into the house just in time to nearly mow over the EMT's and his two roommates.

"Sara, Jay, what happened?"

"Oh, Tim!" Sara fell into his arms weeping.

"Excuse me, sir," the EMT said as he gently grasped Tim's shoulder. "Please, we need to transport her." The medic turned back to Sara. "Come along, Miss. Let's take you in for a little look-see and make sure you're okay." He helped Sara onto the stretcher and covered her with a blanket.

"I'll go with her," Jaylynn said.

"Only room for one, ma'am," the EMT said. He strapped Sara down and nodded toward his fellow medic, and they moved the stretcher toward the stairs.

Jaylynn turned to Tim. "One of us needs to go with her, but we need to close up the house, too." She pointed at the open window at the top of the stairs.

"Here, Jay," Tim said. He shot a hasty look toward the stairs as the EMT's rounded the corner and disappeared. Digging in his pocket he pulled out his car keys. "Take these. You drive over, and I'll go with Sara now." He turned and took the stairs down two at a time.

"Wait, which hospital?" she called out after his departing back. He paused, looking back at her impatiently as she said, "How do I know where to go?"

A patrolman standing behind her in the hall touched her arm. "I'm Officer Milton. I've got a lot of questions for the report. Why don't you follow me over to the hospital?"

"There you go," Tim said. "I'll see you over there." He disappeared down the stairs.

"I have to lock up the house," Jaylynn said to the cop.

"Good idea," said Officer Milton. "I'll help you with the windows."

Jaylynn collected her things and locked all the doors. As Officer Milton escorted her through the yard, a white van pulled up, and two men piled out of the vehicle. One shone a bright light in her face while the other man held a microphone and shouted questions at her.

The reporters did double-steps on the lawn next to Jaylynn and Milton as the officer tried to hurry them down the walk. "Can you tell us what happened?" one reporter asked in a breathless voice.

Jaylynn said, "I came home to find two men in our house attacking my roommate. They tried to get me, too, but before they could, a cop—" She stopped and looked around the yard, letting her eyes come to rest on the various police cruisers. "It was a woman cop. I don't know who she is, but she nailed both of them even after losing her gun. It was incredible, a sight to behold!" She looked up at Milton. "Who was she, Officer? Where'd she go?"

"Reilly," Milton muttered.

"Who?" Jaylynn said, but the reporters had already heard.

"Reilly? Desiree Reilly?" one of the men repeated excitedly. "Reilly was the officer? Oh, this is going to be a *great* story. What else can you tell us?"

"That's it, folks," Milton said as he pushed past them. "You know the channels to go through." He took hold of Jaylynn's elbow and rushed her down the walk. Wordlessly, he helped her into Tim's Toyota, then got in his cruiser and slammed the door. He turned on his lights, but not his siren, and pulled around the other police cars parked haphazardly along the street, slowing to wait for Jaylynn to catch up with him. Jaylynn looked back at the scene. Neighbors stood in tight little bunches watching from the front stoops of their houses. She waved as she passed the couple on the corner and they hesitantly waved back, not quite sure who she was.

****

Dez's forearm swelled so quickly that before she even arrived at the hospital, the paramedic had to immobilize the forearm with an inflatable splint. "It's likely broken, you know," he said.

"That's what I'm afraid of."

At the emergency room they led her through the crowded waiting area and toward an examining room. She didn't want to look around, but she couldn't help herself. The last time she had been here was for Ryan. Even now her eyes filled with bitter tears, and she bit her lip to try to control her thoughts. She hated this place, didn't want to be here. She considered turning around to leave, but before she could, the nurse on duty was at her heels ushering her into the ER and onto a table. The nurse helped her unbutton and remove the bloodied and tattered blue shirt, and Dez pulled at the Velcro on the bulletproof vest. The nurse picked up a pair of trauma shears.

Dez said, "Hey, no! These things are expensive."

"Do you keep them if they're sliced open like that?" The nurse pointed to the big cop's left breast. Dez looked down, surprised to see an 8-inch gash. "It's easier to cut it away. Otherwise I might hurt you," the nurse said, a question in her voice.

Dez shrugged her shoulders. "Don't worry."

The nurse put down the shears and ripped away at the Velcro straps on the vest as Dez looked around. The emergency room wasn't all that big, with six bays, three on either side of an aisle that ran up the middle of the area. Her overall impression of the room was that it was filled with a lot of pipes and tubes and contraptions, and the dominant colors were white or dull silver. She thought it smelled like some sort of cleaning fluid. Dez sat on the exam table closest to the door. In the back corner, furthest from the door, an elderly woman lay hooked up to oxygen and strands of other tubes. With eyes closed, her hands fluttered across the chest of her pink robe as a technician fussed over her. *Heart attack*, Dez thought. *That's what that looks like.*

The nurse managed to get the vest loosened and off. She pulled at Dez's t-shirt.

"It's just my arm. No need to strip naked is there?"

"I need to be sure you're not hurt anywhere else." The nurse pulled the curtain around the bay.

Dez frowned. It occurred to her that if she hadn't realized her vest was shredded, then the nurse probably thought she might not know about other injuries. "Here, check me over." Dez lifted her shirt with her left arm and the nurse ran her hand across her back, down her abdomen. "I think I'm fine. Really. I'd tell you if I was hurt anywhere else."

The nurse nodded as she helped pull the t-shirt back down. "Can't help it, Officer. They'd have my head if I missed anything." She leaned down and untied Dez's black work boots and slipped them off. "Step out of the slacks, too. Stand up. Here, I'll help you." She laid the blue pants over the exam table and checked the big cop over, then handed her a nearly translucent sheet to put over her bare legs. "Just sit back up there." Once she was situated, the nurse got out a blood pressure cuff and strapped it on Dez's arm, checked her pulse and blood pressure, and shone a light in her eyes. The tall cop bore the exam patiently.

"Okay, you're doing fine," the nurse said as she removed the cuff. "Let's go ahead and get you dressed again, and I'll have the doctor come in as soon as possible." They worked together to get her re-dressed as Dez cautiously held her right arm.

The nurse whipped open the curtain around the area and tried to catch the attending physician's eye. When that failed, she sighed and her brown eyes looked tired.

Dez asked, "Been a long shift, huh?"

"Yes, and I've only been here four hours. It's been quite a night. As soon as he checks you over, we'll get you across the hall to radiology."

From outside the tiny box of a room where the x-ray machine was kept, Dez sat on a bench and observed the arrival of the victims of the evening's melee. Paramedics rolled a weeping Sara into the ER, followed closely by the red-haired man who stutter-stepped alongside the gurney in order to hold the hand of the young woman. Moments later, Jaylynn came running in, Officer Milton at her heels. Not long after that, a middle-aged woman appeared in the doorway and was ushered over to the partly curtained area.

When the x-rays were done, the nurse gave Dez an ice pack for her forearm, and she was led back into the emergency room where she eased herself onto the exam table.

"Hey, Milton," Dez called out to her fellow officer as he finished talking to the young woman on the gurney and flipped his notebook closed.

He looked up and nodded, then strode toward her and smiled. "Reilly. You're hurt, huh?"

"Arm. Guy hit me here." She lifted the ice bag and gestured toward the middle of her forearm. "Think it's busted—maybe I'll get lucky and it'll just be a bad bruise, but I have a hunch it's broken."

"Tough luck, but hey, you did good tonight."

"Yeah, I'm glad for them."

Their backs were to Dez, but she could see the red-haired man with his arm around the feisty blonde woman. Dez's face took on a puzzled look as she stared at her. *Where have I seen her before?* She surveyed the lean legs and khaki shorts, the hot pink tank top and the well-rounded hips and shoulders. Short white-blonde hair topped a long, regal neck. Dez wished the woman would turn around so she could study her more closely.

She couldn't see the girl who had been attacked, though she could see an older woman leaning over her whom she assumed to be the young woman's mother. Dez heard a soft murmur of reassuring words being spoken to the girl. The doctor and another nurse swept past Milton and headed for the bay where the brown-haired girl lay. The nurse stopped for a brief moment and waved the two onlookers away. It was clear that the blonde woman tried to protest, but the doctor reached up and pulled a curtain around the bay to shut them out. They stepped back and Milton called out, "C'mon, people. Let her mom handle this for a bit. They'll take good care of her. Come out and wait with me."

Jaylynn and Tim looked disappointed, but they headed toward the door, both focusing on Milton. The young woman glanced briefly at Dez and did a double take. "You! It's you." She stopped in front of Dez, close enough to put her hand on the big cop's knee. "What happened to you?" Behind her the red-haired man stepped up to peer over his friend's shoulder.

Dez shrugged as she felt herself start to blush. She lifted the ice bag again to display her swollen arm, which was also beginning to show the pale outline of a wide bruise.

Puzzled, Jaylynn said, "How did you...how did that happen?"

"Little guy hit me with the bat when I first came in the room."

"But—but, how did you do that—stop them, I mean—with your arm like that?"

Dez shrugged again and knew her face was fully crimson.

Jaylynn said, "Well, that was totally exhilarating. It was amazing to see! You were incredible."

Dez mumbled, "Not really. Actually, you did half of it. If you hadn't kicked them a few times, I would've been in worse trouble."

Dez's nurse returned just then. "All right, all right," she said.

"Enough with the visiting. I've got work to do. Out. Out into the waiting area." She shooed them out, waving at Milton, too.

Dez put her hand on Milton's sleeve to hold him back. "Before you go, what are their names?"

"Don't know the young man yet, but I'm gonna question them now," he said. He flipped open his memo book and thumbed down a few pages. "Her name's Jaylynn Savage, and that one over there," he nodded toward the bay in the corner, "she's Sara Wright."

"Thanks," she said, and then the nurse demanded her attention to tell her the doctor would be in shortly to set her arm and have it casted. *It's broken,* Dez thought. *That's just great. Three or four weeks of desk duty. Just what I need. Shit.*

****

Jaylynn and Tim settled into the waiting room among a conglomeration of sickly and unhappy people either waiting to be seen or waiting for some loved one.

"She didn't look so good, did she, Tim?" Jaylynn said.

He fidgeted and said, more sharply than he meant, "Well, she just survived a beating and a near rape. What do you expect?"

"No, I don't mean Sara...the cop. I meant the cop."

"Oh yeah, her, too." He reached into his back pocket and pulled out a comb to nervously style his hair.

Jaylynn winced, remembering the dark-haired cop's battered arm. *And to think I didn't even notice what happened! How could I have been so blind? I remember him hitting her with the bat...but now that I think about it, of course she wouldn't escape unscathed. In bat versus arm, the bat always wins.*

Tim put his comb back in his pocket. "I don't know what would have happened if I had come home and found you both being raped. Or dead. Oh, God." Shaking, he took a deep breath and put his head between his knees, messing up his hair.

Jaylynn draped her arm across his back and leaned down to speak in his ear. "That didn't happen, so don't even think about it. It's all right, Tim."

He sat back up and shivered. "Keep reminding me, okay?" He got his comb back out and repeated the styling, his hands shaking.

It took almost an hour before they learned the hospital would keep Sara overnight for observation. Until then, they sat in the waiting room watching wounded people being hauled in and scores of cops coming and going through the ER entrance. Jaylynn wondered if every cop in St. Paul had stopped by the hospital to check on Officer Reilly.

She turned the events of the night over and over in her head.

What if she hadn't come home when she did? What if Sara had been killed? She shuddered. What if both of them had been killed? What if the cop hadn't shown up when she did? Too many "what-ifs." Jaylynn looked over at Tim. His head was tipped back against the wall and he was asleep, his hand in hers. Just then the glass door leading to the exam rooms opened and the woman cop emerged, followed by a nurse. She carried her blue uniform shirt and a gray vest in her good hand. In the thin tank t-shirt her broad shoulders were nearly as white as the cast that covered her right arm from knuckles to elbow. She and the nurse went to the main desk and spoke briefly with the clerk who handed her a white prescription bag. Jaylynn watched as the tall woman tried to sign something with her casted right hand, then gave up and switched to her left hand, which she held awkwardly above the paper on the high counter.

Two patrol officers rose from the uncomfortable waiting room chairs on the other side of the room and strolled toward the woman cop. The male officer was young, his bleached white hair in a buzz cut, and he wore golden wire-rimmed glasses. He swaggered over, his bow-legged stride confident and sure. Taking shorter paces next to him was a smaller, wide-shouldered Latino woman. Her short-cropped hair was jet-black and she was probably in her late thirties. The male cop came up behind the wounded woman and gave her a mock blow to the lower back, and she turned. A slow smile crossed her face and she smacked him in the stomach with the back of her good hand as the shorter, black-haired woman slid her arm around Reilly's waist. She said something in the injured woman's ear, which must have been serious because the tall cop looked down at her cast and nodded grimly.

That Reilly sure is tall, thought Jaylynn. She towered a good foot over the nurse and was maybe six inches taller than the other woman cop. Without the bulk of the vest she looked slimmer than she had during the fight. Jaylynn admired her lean hips and very wide shoulders. From behind, she was as broad-shouldered as a man, except that with her brunette hair French-braided so beautifully, it wasn't likely she'd be mistaken for one. The big officer slung his arm across her shoulders, and as the three moved to leave, Jaylynn could see how tired the injured cop looked.

"Hey," Jaylynn said over the low din in the room. She almost didn't expect to be heard, but Dez looked at her and gave her a quick nod.

"Wait a minute," Jaylynn heard her say to the two cops and then she strolled toward her and the sleeping man. Jaylynn stared at Reilly and was captivated again by the bluest, steeliest eyes she'd ever seen, eyes that bored right through her. Her heart beat faster and she choked in a short intake of breath, tilting her head slightly to the side to try to take in the strange, almost disturbing glimpse of something familiar yet forgotten. She extricated herself from Tim and rose to face the woman in blue. She reached out for Dez's left hand saying, "Thanks for what you did," and squeezed the bigger woman's hand and then reluctantly let go.

"No problem. It's my job."

Jaylynn smiled and gazed up into tired but warm blue eyes. "I hardly think getting your arm broken is in the job description."

Dez shook her head. "Not usually." She took a deep breath and turned to go. "Good luck to your friend in there, Ms. Savage. She's going to need a lot of support."

"We'll take care of her," Jaylynn said. "Thanks again."

"Yup. See ya around." Dez turned and made her way out the door as Jaylynn peered after her thoughtfully. *Nice looking woman.*

Jaylynn and Tim finally got home after two in the morning. The house was a little spooky to her, but she was so tired that she fell into bed, taking only enough time to set her clock for her nine a.m. final. If her professor asked any questions about arrests or searches and seizures, she was sure she'd have some good examples from tonight.

Chapter
2

Dez stirred awake the next morning to the thump-thump sound of her downstairs neighbor, Luella Williams, beating a broom handle on the ceiling. She looked at her bedside clock: 6:40 a.m. She didn't think three hours of sleep was going to cut it, but her landlady had given the signal, and from the warning, Dez knew she'd be on her way up the stairs. Luella lived downstairs in the two-story house, and she and Dez had grown close over the nine years Dez had lived there.

Groggy from the pain pill she had taken in the middle of the night, Dez rolled out of bed, barefoot, still wearing her duty slacks and a t-shirt. Her arm throbbed mercilessly. She opened the apartment door just as Luella, in all her plump, elderly blackness, rounded the newel post below with newspaper in hand. Dez leaned against the doorjamb waiting for her to climb the last of the stairs.

"Good Lord, Dez!" Luella said. "Sorry if I woke you, but you're on the news again. What have you done to yourself now?" She shuffled toward the door with her pink bedroom slippers skiffing on the hardwood hallway floor, her flowered robe swirling around her, and her silver hair in wild disarray. What Dez liked best about her landlady was the indomitable spirit that animated her deep brown eyes. Luella had a good-hearted smile always full of love and compassion for her moody tenant.

Dez looked at her casted arm and shrugged. She pulled the door open wide and Luella entered and dropped the folded newspaper on the tiny kitchen table. She stood looking at Dez with a frown on her face. The injured cop sank down into a seat at the dinette table as Luella reached over to smooth dark hair off her forehead and let her hand rest there for a moment. "You feel like you've got a fever, gal." Dez did not respond, so Luella moved over to open a cupboard.

"What are they saying on the news?" Dez asked as she watched Luella set the teakettle in the sink and fill it with water and then put it on the stove to heat. Dez stood, reaching with her good arm, and took out a wicker basket of various teas from the top of the cupboard and set them on the table. Then both women sat and gazed at one another.

As Luella fingered the packets of tea, she said, "Channel 5 is calling you a hero. Channel 4 asks why the police didn't catch the criminals sooner. Channel 11, as usual, did a more in-depth story. They say you caught two rapists—in the act, too."

"Not exactly. I got 'em before that happened." Dez shifted in her chair, not sure what to do with her casted arm. She set it on the table, but that felt awkward and made it throb. She moved it to her lap. It still throbbed. *Oh well. Guess I'm going to have to get used to that.*

Luella picked up the newspaper and unfolded it to the bottom of page one. "Check this out. One of them stinkers has welched on his buddy already, even told the cops that they'd done four other rapes, so it looks like this is a good collar for you. It's a pretty decent story—see?" She handed the paper to Dez, who winced immediately upon seeing the headline: *The Life of Reilly: Tragedy and Triumph.*

"Geez, what a stupid headline." Dez dropped the paper onto the table and looked away.

"You might not want to read it right now, Dez. They go into detail about...you know...about Ryan's death and everything." The older woman hesitated when she saw the pain in Dez's eyes. "But according to the paper, this was a great collar. You captured two very nasty guys, and since they gave each other up already, I think it's safe to congratulate you."

Dez was relieved. From what she'd seen, she knew they had enough evidence to convict the two men of assault, but if they didn't have criminal records, which she suspected might be the case, they could have gotten off easily. Of course there was always DNA evidence from the other attacks, but sometimes that didn't work out in court either. Much better that they'd turned against each other.

Luella gestured toward Dez's arm. "Is that broken?"

Dez nodded. "One of the jerks hit me with a bat. I can't believe I didn't really feel it until later." Which was actually a lie. She had known immediately that something was wrong because she had no grip in her hand, but she decided Luella didn't need to hear about that. "It'll be a good three or four weeks, I guess, before I can go back on regular duty." She shook her head in exasperation.

"Just what I need now."

Luella reached over and covered Dez's good hand with her soft fingers and patted her. "A little bit of rest might be just what you need after what you've been through lately. You look exhausted, and you've been pushing yourself like there's no tomorrow. Ever since Ryan—"

"Yeah, I know," Dez said abruptly as she stood up to check the teakettle, which was hardly warm yet. She leaned back against the counter and tried to cross her arms, but that sent a shooting pain up her arm, and she suddenly felt nauseated. She moved back to the chair and sat, allowing Luella to reach out again and stroke her pale arm with her soft, mahogany-colored hand and pink fingers.

Dez said, "I'm sorry, but I don't think I can take you over to Vanita's house today."

"Big deal. She can get off her fat butt and take a cab. You're always running us around."

"That's no way to talk about your sister," Dez said in mock seriousness. "Look at the bright side though. You won't have to iron for me for a couple weeks."

"No more chores for you for the rest of the summer either."

"Not much summer left. Wish I'd mowed yesterday."

"Oh, don't even worry about it. I can hire out the lawn," Luella said.

With a sudden fierceness Dez said, "For crap sake! I suppose I won't be able to play guitar for weeks."

Luella gazed at her grumpy friend and nodded. "Could be. You heal fast, though." Then she clucked and frowned. "But right now you don't look so good, little missy." An understatement. Dark circles under Dez's eyes paired up with lines of pain across her forehead. "You look beat. And *when* was the last time you ate?" Luella's voice was full of accusation.

Dez gave her a half smile and a shrug and then got up and took the teakettle off the hot burner with her good hand. She got two mugs down from the cupboard, one at a time, and set them on the counter.

"Here. Let me do that," Luella said. "You sit down there." In the absence of protest from Dez, Luella got the two mugs of tea ready and shuffled back over to the table where she added three spoons of sugar to hers. She lowered herself into the dinette chair, took a big sip, and said, "You're nothing but skin and bones, Desiree Reilly. You need decent food to recuperate. I'll be making up some good stuff for you today. It's not like you'll be able to cook. And besides, that so-called healthy stuff you eat isn't enough to nourish a squirrel." She reached for the sugar bowl and proceeded to heap another teaspoon of sugar into her lemon tea.

Dez had to smile. Luella was from the old school of red meat and potatoes, rich desserts, and three squares a day. Dez had long ago ceased to eat fatty foods, beef, or pork, but she didn't skimp. She ate plenty of grains, poultry, eggs, fish, vegetables, and fruit. She certainly ate enough to keep 175 pounds on her muscular six-foot frame.

"You're going to let me help whether you want to or not," Luella was saying. "I'm not going to stand by this time while you waste away. For once you've got to..."

"Okay."

"...take better care of your—what?"

"I said okay. Whaddya got for breakfast?"

The speed at which Luella rose belied her 74 years. As she hustled toward the door she said, "Fresh made jam and toast, pancakes, fruit. You want a little bacon or ham?"

"Everything but the meat sounds great."

As Luella made her way down the hallway, Dez could hear her: "I'll let you off this time, but you need good meat to heal. I think we'll be having roast beef tonight..." Skiff, skiff, skiff. Luella's arthritic knees navigated the stairs. "...and some nice roasted potatoes to go along with it...and fresh juicy corn..."

Dez stood up and got out some protein powder and a shaker cup. She drizzled water into the cup with the powder and shook it vigorously with her good hand, then sat down to drink it.

She knew she couldn't ask for a better landlady. She and Luella had an arrangement that worked for both of them. Dez kept up the yard and lawn, fixed anything mechanical that she could, and helped with heavy spring cleaning. In return, Luella did her wash and ironed her uniforms, looked out for Dez, and served as a loving mother. The arrangement had evolved over the last nine years until Dez was as fond of Luella now as she would be of her own mother; that is, if her own mother were still speaking to her.

****

Good as her word, Luella brought up a tray of breakfast treats. She sat drinking tea at the dinette table while Dez tried to eat. The food was excellent, but she had no appetite. After she ate what she could, Luella cleared everything away. She smoothed the hair off Dez's brow and brushed her warm lips across her forehead. "You go get some rest, honey," she said. "I know you haven't had much sleep. Call me if you need anything." She shuffled to the door balancing the tray carefully.

"I'll get the door, Luella." Dez stood and saw her out, then shut the door and turned to face the empty apartment. She was so terribly tired, but when she went to lie down, sleep would not come. She lay on her back, light slicing in through the small window high above the bed. Her mind raced, and she couldn't help thinking about all the violence she had witnessed lately. She had been a cop for almost nine years, and she'd only been in minor altercations, usually just scuffles with people who didn't want to be arrested. Those periodic chances to flex her muscles she had actually enjoyed, not minding busting a few heads if it was needed. But she had never broken a bone, never been seriously injured.

Then all of a sudden, in the last fourteen months, there had been a rash of attacks on cops. Two officers had been shot to death by a crazy man who didn't even go to trial but instead went straight to the mental hospital. Murders of civilians in the city had doubled, and she'd been to far too many bloody crime scenes lately. Worst of all, her partner, Ryan Michaelson, had died, and now she'd been wounded by last night's attackers.

The department shrink had told her after Ryan's death that it was normal to be upset about these things, and Dez had eventually admitted she wasn't sleeping well. The shrink gave her instructions: don't go to bed until sleepy; if sleep doesn't come within about twenty minutes of lying down, get up and do something else until sleepy; get up on time, regardless of whether she'd had enough sleep. She'd tried all these things with no success. When she mentioned it to the counselor, the word depression came up, setting off major alarm bells. The doctor spent time talking about it and the types of medication that could help, which scared off Dez completely. She resolved not to be depressed and, the next time the topic came up, she told the shrink she'd finally started getting good sleep again. She attended the mandatory six sessions with the department psychologist, and that was it. She never went back.

But here it was, nearly three months since Ryan's death, and still, no good sleep. Instead, her mind busily spun through traumatic events, tried to rewrite what actually happened, though she knew it was futile. The only good thing about last night was that she had enjoyed subduing the two rapists, had enjoyed the solid sound of her fist and feet on flesh. At least after this altercation she felt a sense of grateful relief—nothing at all like the feeling of helplessness she had experienced after capturing Ryan's killer. She would have liked to have beaten that man to death, make him pay for what he'd done, but she didn't get the satisfaction. Ryan was dead, and that man was still alive. It made her angry to think about it.

She banished thoughts of Ryan from her mind, tried to breathe deeply, to let her thoughts float away. Instead, her monkey mind

took a few more twists and turns and brought other painful images
to mind: a tall, willowy, red-haired woman with laughing eyes and a
deep tan standing on a rock in front of the water of Lake Superior;
sitting in the low light of a banked campfire in the Boundary Waters
Canoe Area; lying here in this very bed. The eyes, the smile, the
presence: Karin. She put her out of her mind as best she could and
turned over on her side, annoyed and restless. She tried to settle
her cast somewhere comfortable and ended up placing it on a
pillow, her arm tucked close to her side. She tried not to think of
Karin, but the more Dez willed her from her memories, the more
stubbornly the redhead stayed.

It was the oldest story in the book: older woman woos the
younger, treats her special, gets her in the sack a few times, has fun
for about three months, and then when commitment was at hand, it
was "so long, been nice knowing you." Dez was totally smitten,
ready to plan a life, move in together, and spend the rest of her days
at Karin's side. The Day Of The Dumping, as she had come to
think of it, she showed up at Karin's place as planned. They had
made plans to go out to dinner, but as usual, they skipped the plans
and wound up in bed, a trail of clothing dotting the hallway from
the front room to the bedroom. Karin was inventive, passionate,
and beautiful. Dez couldn't get close enough to her. They lay in
the brass bed after making love, and the phone rang.

"No, don't go," Dez said. "Just let it ring." She wrapped her
arms tightly around Karin, laughing and teasing her.

Her lover struggled. "Let me go," she said coldly. She pushed
Dez away and struggled out of the bed, pausing to grab her robe,
but before she could get down the hall, the answering machine
clicked in. A woman's voice, a husky, trash-talking woman's voice,
filled Dez's ears. In the middle of the message, Karin picked up,
and Dez didn't hear the rest. She lay wide-eyed in the bed trying to
understand why a woman was calling her lover, *her* Karin, and
begging to come over for sex and shrimp cocktail.

Dez was shocked at the change in Karin when she returned to
the room. Karin held a handful of clothes and tossed them on the
bed. "It's been fun," she said, "but it's over."

"What?" Dez sat up in the bed, pulling the covers around her
to try to stave off the ice-cold shock invading her body.

Karin began pulling on her own clothes. As she slipped on
jeans she said, "You had to know this wasn't going to last forever."

"But—but—I don't understand. Why?"

Karin sighed and squeezed her eyes shut. "Dez, please don't
tell me you're going to make this difficult. Get up and get dressed.
Go home. The party's over." She pulled a sweater over her head
and smoothed it down, then stood with one hand on her shapely

hip, a look of disinterest on her face.

Dez was shaking too hard to get up. She reached over for her t-shirt and slipped it on over her head. "This was all a game for you?" She couldn't keep the disbelief from her voice.

"No, no, it wasn't a game. It was just—good fun. Like sports. A little action here, some fun times there." She gave a jaded laugh. "Don't tell me you ever thought this was something meaningful?" She laughed uncomfortably.

Dez fought back tears as she untangled her clothes and tried to make her fingers work to put them on. She stood and slipped on her jeans, then turned to face Karin. In a low voice she said, "Yeah, I thought we had something good going here." With an aching plea she couldn't hide she said, "Are you seeing someone else, that other woman?"

Karin let out a deep breath. "Of course," she sighed. "I thought you knew. Never stopped seeing her. She's not the jealous type."

"How would I have known?"

Karin shrugged. "Just thought maybe someone from around the department would have said something. I may have a bit of a reputation."

"No. No one said," she whispered.

And how could anyone tell her anything? She had done all she could to distance herself from Karin, to hide from others the fact that she was a lesbian. Perhaps people might wonder, but she didn't think so. It was a secret she kept to herself, and no one in the department would have known, except that Karin seemed to have had very effective radar. She'd played the seduction game to the hilt and Dez fell for it completely. A wave of anger washed over her, then a feeling of physical revulsion. She grabbed her things and stalked out of the house.

The next six weeks were nearly unbearable. After a week, she didn't care about Karin's other lover. She went to Karin and told her she would look the other way, but Karin had laughed at her, said the break was final and that it was over. Every day at work, Dez had to see Karin at roll call. Every day was a misery.

Then two things happened. First, Ryan asked her to partner with him in a two-man car, and second, Karin accepted a position with the Bureau of Criminal Apprehension. Out of sight, out of mind. With the woman gone, Dez could finally begin the process of sorting out her feelings. She had never considered herself a particularly violent person, but in this case, she found herself wanting to hurt or maim Karin. The images came to her in dreams: Karin, beaten and bloody, begging for forgiveness, falling off bridges to the rocks below, shot repeatedly. Dez was filled with a hatred so strong she felt sick to her stomach at times. But slowly it abated. As the winter days grew longer and spring beckoned, the injury that had felt like a death wound began to heal. After nearly eight years, she still bore the invisible scars, but she wasn't dead. She had survived, and never again would she let that happen to her.

Ryan had brought light into her life, his laughing presence a balm to her pained soul. Without even knowing the kind of medicine he was dispensing, he had taken her into his heart and made her a friend. With Karin assigned across town at the BCA, the constant reminder of her smile, of her shapely legs, of the passion they'd shared faded into the background. Dez had dated a few other women since then, but no one that stuck, nobody who was particularly special. In the past year, even before Ryan's death, she hadn't wanted to go out with anyone at all. It didn't seem worth the effort, and she tried hard not to think about there being an emptiness in her life. At one time she had wanted a lover, a life partner, but she was younger and naïve then. These days she no longer thought about it.

Now Dez was left with those old images and memories only when she slowed down long enough that they could intrude, uninvited, upon her. Nothing like what occurred with Karin would ever happen again. Never again would she have to face her coworkers while feigning good humor and pleasantness when, deep inside, a pain festered and burned. A wall went up, a rule was made: all cops are off limits.

Chapter
3

Jaylynn closed her second blue exam book and wrote her name on the front of it. She stifled a yawn as she set the little essay pad aside and opened the first blue book to go over her essays one last time before turning them in to the professor. Pausing to add punctuation where needed, she read carefully through her answers to all five questions. Satisfied, she closed both blue books, picked up her backpack, and got up to turn in the exam. The proctor took them without even meeting her eyes and stacked them in the corner of his desk.

She felt like she was sleepwalking her way out the door and across the campus to the parking lot where Tim was to pick her up. She looked at her watch. Fifteen minutes early. She stopped and sat on one of the many benches in the Commons, closed her eyes, and let the warm morning sun bathe her face. It was going to be another hot day, but at ten a.m. it had only just begun to heat up.

A honk sounded from the parking lot and she peeped open one hazel eye and spotted Tim's faded red Corolla. She rose wearily and made her way over.

"Hey there," he said. "You're early."

"So are you," she said as she dropped her backpack onto the front seat and slid in next to it.

"Yeah. I've seen you write—five miles a minute. So I figured you'd be done early, and I want to get over to the hospital and see when they're gonna let Sara go."

He gunned the car and sped off down the street. Jaylynn leaned back against the headrest and closed her eyes.

"How'd the test go?"

Without opening her eyes she said, "Fine. I think. Nothing

unexpected. Gotta get at least a B."

"Ah, that's nice."

They rode the rest of the way to the hospital in silence, parked, and found their way to Sara's room.

Sara was asleep, her brown hair splayed across the pillow and her face turned slightly toward the light streaming in the window. Tim and Jaylynn crept in quietly, but as soon as they neared the bed Sara awakened with a start, her eyes wide. "Oh, God, you scared me."

Jaylynn moved to the far side of the bed, and she and Tim both reached simultaneously for Sara's hands. "Don't worry," Tim said. "It's just us chickens." He leaned down and gave her a kiss on the forehead.

Jaylynn studied her friend's pale face as she leaned against the bed. She stroked Sara's arm and squeezed her hand tight. "So, how're you feeling this morning?"

In a grouchy voice, Sara said, "I didn't get a wink of sleep. I can't wait to get out of here. I've never been checked on and awakened so many times in my life. And when I *did* fall asleep— geez!—what rotten dreams. How bad do I look?"

Tim said, "You look beautiful, as usual."

Sara shook her head wearily and turned to Jaylynn. "The truth now," she demanded.

Jaylynn studied her friend's face. "Double black eyes are on the way. Your chin is gonna be black and blue for days, and that wallop on your temple...oh girl, does that hurt?"

Sara reached up and touched her forehead. "They kept shining lights in my eyes all night. I guess they thought I had a concussion."

"Where's your mom?" Jaylynn asked.

"She'll be back at two when they release me. She stayed until about seven this morning, then went home to sleep a few hours."

"Two!" Tim said, outraged. "Damn. When I called this morning, they said you would leave sometime after ten."

"Well two *is* sometime after ten, Tim," Sara said. She gave him a playful poke to the stomach.

Jaylynn smiled and thought to herself what a good sport Sara was. She didn't know how she herself would handle it if she were in Sara's shoes. Then again, she too had been attacked...but somehow it wasn't at all the same. How could she ever admit to Sara that the experience was completely different for her than for her friend? Already, since last night, she'd relived it in her dreams, and she had thought through it over and over during her Con Law exam. She kept seeing the intense and powerful officer in a flurry of kicks and punches. She remembered the heavy feel of the wooden bat swinging in her own hands, the weight of the black gun. So fast. It had all happened so fast, in a thirty second jumble of sounds and sensations. When she slowed it down in her mind and remembered the sequence of events, she was astonished at how much had happened. She couldn't quite get her mind around it all.

Jaylynn stopped leaning against the bed and sank down on it, still holding Sara's hand. Sara was saying, "When I get home, I want to sleep for about fifteen straight hours."

"No problem," Jaylynn said. "I'm going to collapse in my room, too."

Sara winced and took a deep breath. "Jay?"

"Yes?"

Sara looked down at the covers and then squeezed her friends' hands. "I can't go back and sleep in that room—at least, not right away. I just can't." Tears welled up in her eyes.

Tim leaned his hip on the edge of the bed so that Sara was flanked by two very concerned friends, both talking at once. She let them soothe her for a moment and then went on. "I'm wondering if maybe we could switch rooms, Jay?"

Jaylynn shrugged and nodded. "I'll be getting the best part of the deal. I get a huge room, and you get the little one. It doesn't have as much closet space, you know?"

Tim said, "I'd give you my room—"

Sara cut in, "No way. No thanks. I'm *not* sleeping in the attic. I don't care if it *is* nice up there. It's too creepy for me." She squeezed his knee and made him jump. "Besides, you've got it set up so nice with all the lava lamps. I wouldn't want to wreck your love nest."

Jaylynn said, "As long as you don't mind—just remember though, the phone won't go that far. What about those long distance calls from Billy Boy?"

Tim said, "That's no big deal. We'll just get her a longer cord." Glad to have something useful to do, Tim stood and with enthusiasm said, "We'll go home and switch things, won't we, Jay?" He looked at her for confirmation and when she nodded, he said, "A new room coming up in a jiffy."

"One more thing," Sara said. "We've got to do something about those downstairs windows."

****

By the time Mrs. Wright brought her daughter back to the house, Jaylynn and Tim had switched Sara's and Jaylynn's rooms. Jaylynn's queen-sized bed, dresser, bookcase, desktop PC, and computer desk went in the master bedroom with plenty of room to spare. Sara's twin beds fit in the smaller room with no problem, but the couch couldn't go, so Jaylynn found herself the proud possessor of a solid orange, over-stuffed sleeper sofa.

Sara's mother stayed for an hour or so helping her daughter get settled and then left, saying she would be back later that night. Jaylynn slipped into a night shirt and shorts and fell onto her bed exhausted. She slept through the afternoon and into the early evening, and when she finally did awaken, it was only because of hunger pangs. She shuffled downstairs to the warm kitchen and ate two bowls of Wheaties as the final light of the day faded away and the cricket noises of the night began. She put the milk and cereal away and went back to her room.

As she lay down on her bed in the dim light, a muffled scream rang out. She was up and across the room in an instant. "Sara!" Jaylynn took three strides down the hall and breathlessly smacked open the closed bedroom door.

She found Sara sitting up in bed, a sheet tangled around her legs and her eyes wide. Tears ran down her face. Jaylynn moved over to the bed and wrapped her arms around her friend. "What is it? Bad dream?"

Sara nodded. Jaylynn pulled the shaking woman closer and stroked her hair. "Shh. It'll be okay. You're safe now."

"I don't feel real safe."

"That'll pass. It'll take a while. It hasn't even been a day yet. Here, roll over on your stomach. Good God, it's hot in here." She rose and opened the window to allow the slight breeze into the stuffy room. Sara turned over and put her head on her arms. Jaylynn came away from the window and slid down on her side next to the brown-haired woman. With her left arm supporting her own head, Jaylynn used her right hand to rub soothing circles on Sara's back. Gradually Sara's tears subsided, and she lay quietly, her head turned toward Jaylynn.

"When I was a little girl," Jaylynn said, "I used to have a lot of bad dreams. Remember that movie *Alien* with Sigourney Weaver in it? I still remember her—Ripley, I mean. She was the main character stuck on a space ship with those awful aliens from the pods. I watched it on TV when I was about nine. Big mistake. I dreamed of those horrible devouring monsters every night after that. Drove my parents crazy. My dad was *so* mad that I'd watched that. I bet I woke up at least twice nightly, night after night after night for a couple of years. Then my dad's sister, Auntie Lynn—she and my dad are who I'm named for—anyway, she came to stay with us one summer a short while after my Dad died. She slept in my room right across from me every night for three months. The first time I woke up screaming, she crawled into my twin bed—pretty much just like this."

Sara gave an embarrassed chuckle. "I'm sorry to be such a coward."

"Oh, no. You're not at all." Jaylynn smiled warmly at Sara and smoothed the hair out of her friend's face. "That's funny because what you just said is exactly the same thing I told Auntie Lynn. Here's what she told me. You are a willing participant in your dreams. They come *from* you and they come *to* you. She asked me what I was dreaming about that was so scary."

"Do you remember?"

"Oh yeah. I have several varieties."

"Have?" Sara asked incredulously. "You still have them?"

"All the time. I think I can remember three main kinds. In the first one, I am running and running, and every time I look back I see those terrible alien pod monsters chasing me and getting closer and closer. The faster I run, the heavier I feel until I just can't run any more. I scream, but they just keep coming until I'm surrounded, then they try to rip me to shreds."

"Gross. I'd hate having nightmares like that!"

"Just wait, there's more. I have this other horrible one where I'm trapped in a really tall building and I can't get out. I'm way up high in the penthouse, and it's a hundred stories down. The door is locked, the only way out is the window, and fire keeps burning closer and closer. I scream and scream for help, but nobody comes. I crouch in the window, but I can't jump because I know I'll fall a couple hundred feet and be dashed on the pavement below."

Jaylynn stopped rubbing her friend's back and closed her eyes. "In the third dream, I *am* falling. I've almost always been pushed off the side of a really tall skyscraper. One of the alien monsters waits below, jaws dripping with blood and guts. I grab for a ledge, a post, anything. But I can't avoid falling off the edge of the damn building, which I have *no* idea why I was near since I am so totally scared of heights. I scream my head off, and luckily I always wake up just before I hit the bottom. Ew! I gotta say that's about my least favorite dream." She shuddered.

"So how come *you* aren't waking up screaming every night?"

"Auntie Lynn taught me something. She told me to think of a hero, someone to protect me, and then while I'm dreaming, call for help and they'll come. We spent half the night listing out all the qualities I'd have in a hero and then she had me visualize her."

"Her?"

Jaylynn laughed. "What can I say? Even at ten I wanted a woman hero."

Sara rolled onto her back and scooted over a bit. Jaylynn did the same and the two roommates lay shoulder to shoulder on the twin bed, sides touching. Sara reached down and took Jaylynn's hand. "If I was gay, I swear you would be exactly my type, Jaylynn. Sometimes I wish I was."

"Oh, but Mr. Bill would be so very disappointed. Have you called him yet?"

"No. I will. I'm too tired right now. He'll be upset. It's the middle of the night in Germany anyway. I'll wait until the regular time we talk tomorrow." She gave Jaylynn's hand a squeeze. "So tell me, after you created this wonderful woman, what did you do with her?"

Jaylynn laughed. "I let her save me pretty much every night. My hero was tall—or taller—than most men, broad-shouldered, strong, fierce, and really resourceful. Pretty much the opposite of me at ten. She wore an entire suit of black leather, kinda like Arnold did in *Terminator II*, and she rode a lightning fast silver motorcycle. Under her helmet, she had long beautiful black hair that I could comb, and she had so many space guns and knives and martial arts weapons that nobody crossed her. She'd kick their ass from here to eternity."

Giving Sara's hand a squeeze, Jaylynn went on. "When I was eleven, my mom even made me the parts for a little space suit out of sheet metal. Mom sewed the metal parts on black sweatpants and a black sweatshirt. It was really cool. I wore it for Halloween. I should get out the pictures for you. I was pretty tiny then, so it was really cute. I wanted so bad to have a Space Invaders B.B. gun, but she was afraid I'd shoot some neighbor kid's eye out. I tried to swipe some paring knives from the kitchen, but my mother almost had a heart attack. I had to use a cardboard gun she made and I colored."

"You wanted to be an alien chaser like Ripley?"

"Hmm...no, I wanted to be prepared when those aliens showed up and tried to eat me."

"What was the point of the Ripley character then? Just for kicks on the side?" Sara giggled, then flinched when Jaylynn poked her in the ribs.

"Very funny, Sara!" Jaylynn paused and her voice took on a soft, dreamy quality. "She wasn't really Ripley. She didn't even look like Sigourney Weaver at all. I don't know how to explain. I wanted to be an equal with My Hero, be as brave and strong and true as she was. I spent a lot of time at night thinking about her."

"What was the point of this little exercise," Sara asked as she grinned and elbowed Jaylynn back, "besides giving you something—or should I say *someone*—to fantasize about?"

Elbowing her friend again, Jaylynn shook her head and bit back a smile. "Well, it took many nights, but every time I had a bad dream, Auntie Lynn would get in bed with me, have me close my eyes, and then ask me to tell her what happened. As I told her about the scary parts, she'd ask me to imagine My Hero and how she could save me. So I'd lay there and visualize all these fantastic feats that she would do. And then Auntie Lynn would listen, maybe add a few suggestions, and then say, 'Good. Now go back to sleep and dream that same dream again—only this time, call on your Hero. She's a part of you. Use her.' And Sara, it worked. It really works, even today."

"Hmm. Interesting," Sara said. "You really still do this, even now?"

"Cross my heart—maybe once or twice a week. Even though the dreams are scary, I don't mind them so much any more because she always appears. She always rescues me. My dreams have truly become odd little adventures. Weird, but exciting, too." Jaylynn paused for a moment. "And there's one more thing," she said thoughtfully. "And anybody but you would think I'm crazy, but— that officer from last night, you know? Reilly? She fits the bill. Give her a giant Uzi and dress her up in a space suit...I'm telling you, she could be My Hero."

Sara turned over on her side and leaned up onto her elbow. "How convenient," she said dryly and tried to hide her smile.

"Hey! What's that supposed to mean?"

"How convenient for *you.* But I can tell you for a fact, I would not be imagining some six-foot kick-ass police woman. I'd go more for the Antonio Banderas type. He could have a sword all right, and an Uzi, too, for all I care, along with that sexy Zorro costume."

Skeptically, Jaylynn said, "Are you serious? You sure you wouldn't rather have that incredibly beautiful brunette Zorro fell in love with? Catherine Zeta Jones?"

"Oh no, no, no. Not my type at all. Antonio—now *he* would fit my bill."

"You'd pick him as a hero?"

"Absolutely."

"Okay, Sara. If you're serious. Let's talk through this."

"You mean talk about what happened last night?" When Jaylynn nodded, Sara swallowed, took a deep breath, and said, "I'm not sure I can."

"Yes, you can. I'll stick with you. Let's go over it step by step, and let's rewrite it with Antonio coming in at every step to save the day. Trust me, this really works. I'll be right here for you. Will you try?"

Sara nodded, a grave expression on her bruised face.

"Okay then, how did it start?"

****

Jaylynn sat on the couch cross-legged and barefoot in shorts and a t-shirt. At Sara's request she hadn't opened the main floor windows, but she had the oscillating floor fan on high. She munched on a bowl of salty popcorn as she watched a *Star Trek: Voyager* rerun. It was after midnight when Sara crept into the house and Jaylynn was waiting for her. She leapt up from her position on the couch and greeted her friend enthusiastically. Reaching down to pick up the remote and flick the TV off, she asked, "How was your first night back at the video store?"

Sara double-checked the lock on the front door and said, "Okay, I guess. They were all really nice. One of the guys stuck by me at the register a lot." She plopped down on the couch and Jaylynn re-seated herself sitting sideways on the couch facing her roommate. The bruises on Sara's face had mostly faded, with the exception of two bluish half-moon circles under her eyes, which continued to fade a little more as each day went by.

Jaylynn held out the popcorn bowl. "Want some?"

Sara said, "Nah—I'm not up for it right now. Maybe later." She ran her hands through her hair and lifted it off the back of her neck. "I've never missed a whole week of work like that. It's hard to get back in the routine." She sighed and gave Jaylynn a puzzled look. "Something's up. What's your news?"

Exasperated, Jaylynn asked, "How can you *always* tell?"

"I don't know—I just can. You get this gleeful look about you, Jay, like something really cool happened."

"Something cool did happen. You are looking at a proud—and probably successful—applicant to the St. Paul Police Academy." Jaylynn couldn't help but laugh uproariously when she saw the look of disbelief and surprise on her friend's face. "I know, I know it sounds incredible, but I went down to the Police Department today and talked to one of the Lieutenant Commanders, and he called the POST Board right from there."

"What's the POST Board?"

"The Peace Officers Standards and Training Board. I guess they've had a tough time filling the last few classes of officers, and by the end of the year, they'll have almost a third of the police force retire. Right now, employers are begging for workers, including the police. Since I have a college degree with solid law and psychology majors, I'll probably get in. They're starting background checks tomorrow."

"But you were accepted to law school. I thought you wanted to be a lawyer?"

"I still may. But I think this will be great experience. And the surprising thing is that if they do expedite the paperwork like they said they would, I'll start the week after next! And after the initial orientation and screening, I'll even get paid."

Sara looked at her thoughtfully. "I have a hunch your mother is going to be very surprised. Are you sure about this?"

"Yeah. Why do you ask?"

"Well, Jay, it's not like you to be quite so impulsive. I—I guess—I'm just really surprised, that's all. You sure you want to jump right into something like this?"

"Sure, why not?" She gave her friend a puzzled look. "You don't think it's a good idea?"

"No," Sara said forcefully. "I didn't say that. I just wondered if you had thought it through. What possessed you to go down to the Police Department anyway?"

Jaylynn felt sheepish to admit it, but she told her friend the truth. "Actually, I wanted to talk to Officer Reilly."

"Oh, *I* see." A smile crossed Sara's face, which she quickly stifled.

Jaylynn got a fierce look on her face and picked up the popcorn bowl from her lap and smacked it onto the coffee table. "What's that supposed to mean?"

"Nothing. Nothing at all."

"Then get that smirk off your face!" Sara started to giggle, and Jaylynn turned red. "It's not what you think. *She* tried to talk me out of it, too. She even held up her cast and told me broken limbs were run-of-the-mill experiences."

"And you didn't believe her—or what?"

"Sara, I want to learn all about police work. After last week— well, it's just fascinating to me, that's all. I think it's a career I'd enjoy. There's excitement, but also structure. And if I find it isn't perfect for me, then I've always got my deferred acceptance to law school. Plus, it'd be a good job to have if I do go after a law degree. Either way, it's a perfect solution, don't you think? I was going to have to get a job sooner or later anyhow."

"Gimme some of that popcorn." Sara snagged the bowl when Jaylynn slid it down the coffee table. "If your heart is set on this, then that's great. I was just curious. At least you look good in light blue." When Jaylynn gave her a puzzled look, Sara went on, "You know—police blue? It's a good color on you."

Chapter
4

The fall class of Police Academy recruits milled around the track oval awaiting the arrival of their instructor. They had started with sixteen in the class, but already three had dropped.

The breezy and sunny autumn weather made it a perfect day for footraces. Jaylynn and her fellow rookies had been told to warm up by jogging the three blocks to the high school track, and they arrived in a pack. After running wind sprints in the center of the oval, Jaylynn sat on the grass and did some hurdler's stretches.

"Hey, Savage," said Dwayne Neilsen. "You gonna stop to stretch out when you chase after the bad guys?" He sneered at her, his rugged face affecting a look of superiority. The three other young men who had become his buddies in the first three weeks laughed along with him, and one of them said, "Sure hope you never have to lift anything heavy on duty. Probably have to stretch those pecs, huh?"

Jaylynn smiled sweetly at the four men whom she had begun to call the Four Stooges behind their backs. They were all a bit above average in height and had indeed excelled at the weight-lifting component of the physical fitness tests. But here she knew she was in her element. Paula Marshall came to sit nearby and stretched her legs out, too. She rolled her eyes at Jaylynn when the Four Stooges weren't looking.

Of the eleven men and two women, Jaylynn was the smallest. At five foot five, she was at least three inches shorter than everyone else, including Marshall, but as she stretched her legs, she looked around and appraised the fitness of her cohorts. She decided some of them were likely to be fleet of foot, especially Mahoney and Schmidt. But none of the Four Stooges worried her. She just hoped Marshall would be able to keep up.

Their instructor, Sgt. Vernon Slade, finally strolled on the field. Like the rest of them, he wore navy blue shorts and a gray sweatshirt that read SPPD on the front. Slade was a lean man in his late twenties, with a gaunt face and piercing brown eyes. His brown hair was cut short on the sides, but it was longer on top and puffed to the side in the wind. In one hand he held a stopwatch. In the other he held a silver whistle, which he used to blow one short, sharp shriek. "Okay," he said. "Listen up. I'm going to set a pace, and all of you will follow. This is *not* a race, but you all have to keep up. I'll line you up, and each of you is to follow three yards from the person in front of you. Not four yards. Not two yards. How many yards?"

"Three, sir!" they said in unison.

"When I blow the whistle, the person at the end of the line sprints to the front and falls in *behind* me. Got it?" When everyone nodded, he called off the thirteen names. Jaylynn found herself sixth in the pack with Marshall two behind her.

Sgt. Slade began an easy lope around the track. After a minute had passed, he blew his whistle and the man at the back cut outside the group and sprinted to the front where he dropped in behind the sergeant. The whistle blew again, and along came Neilsen, one by one followed by the others until it was Jaylynn's turn. By then the group had traveled half a mile, and Jaylynn's legs were feeling warmed up and strong. She cut to the front and fell in, waiting patiently for her turn again.

By the time the group hit the fourth round of sprints, they had traveled nearly eight laps around the 400-meter track and had begun to lag and spread out. "Come on, people," Sgt. Slade hollered over his shoulder. "Get a move on!" Jaylynn admired the sergeant's fortitude. He was obviously a regular runner. Only he and two men, besides herself, continued along without a lot of panting and groaning.

After the sixth round of sprints, Slade dodged out of the line and turned around, continuing to run backwards. "Mark my pace," he said, as he slowed. The group gradually decreased speed and came to a stop. Jaylynn caught sight of Neilsen and his Stooges, bent over and gasping for air.

Slade said, "Everybody warmed up now?"

"Yes, sir!" they huffed.

"All right," he said. "Next exercise." A harmony of groans erupted. "Anybody here have a problem with that?"

"No, sir!"

"Line up again in original order. On my mark, you will take off one at a time and run one lap. If the person behind you passes you, then you will run again."

Tweet! The first man took off. Slade waited for five seconds to pass on the stopwatch, and then, *tweet!* The next man sprinted away. Five more seconds...five...five...five...and then it was Jaylynn's turn. She followed a shy recruit named Oster, and she could see that he would never catch the man ahead of him. She ran smoothly, glancing back as she rounded the first turn. Mahoney was behind her and she caught his eye for a moment. He shot a glance at Oster. She didn't know why she knew it, but she could tell Mahoney wouldn't push hard enough to catch her, and that meant that she could back off on Oster who was struggling. At the next turn she looked back again and no one was threatening to catch anyone.

One by one they each crossed the finish line and slowed up until the thirteen recruits stood waiting for the next drill.

Sgt. Slade, a half-grin on his face, nodded at the group. "I see," he said. "*Esprit de corp*. Hmmph. Guess we have to raise the stakes." He put his hand to his chin and considered for a moment. "Line up again. New rules: anybody who *doesn't* pass the guy in front runs again. And if you get passed, you run again. Let's go."

"Sir," said Mahoney. "What happens to the person running first? Denton, I mean. He doesn't have anyone to catch."

"Luck of the draw, Mahoney. If Denton can hold you all off, he's done for the day."

They lined up, and the sergeant whistled Denton off. At five-second intervals the whistle blew, and then it was Jaylynn's turn. She didn't have any trouble catching up to Oster and passed him after the first turn. She ran loosely and effortlessly, not straining at all, but on the last turn Mahoney caught up with her. They ran abreast for the last 30 yards, and then he pulled ahead at the very last.

She concentrated on catching her breath and waited until the sergeant said, "Denton, Mahoney, Vell, Chin, and Sprague— you're all out. The rest of you line up and be ready to go in sixty seconds."

Jaylynn was still winded, but she was amused to see that only one of the Four Stooges, Sprague, had managed to get out of the next race. Then she spent the next minute focusing on her breath, letting her muscles relax. She shook out her legs and kept walking. She looked at Oster, lying on the grass gasping. "Oster," she said quietly. "C'mon. You can do it." The red-faced man looked up at her from his sprawled position, a pained expression on his face, and shook his head. She stuck out her hand. "C'mon. Just put one foot in front of the other." He accepted her hand and let her help drag him up.

"On your marks," Slade shouted.

The eight hustled over to their spots. Jaylynn was now fourth, and Marshall followed her. The Three Stooges brought up the rear. She easily caught and passed Oster and drew near Pike, but couldn't quite catch him. She crossed the finish line well ahead of the remaining six, none of whom had managed to pass the others.

When the last runners stumbled over the line, Slade said, "Pike and Savage, you're out." He put his hands on his hips and faced the six other sweating, heaving runners. "What am I gonna do with the rest of you? Tell you what. You have a choice, each of you. You can either take four laps right now, or select any one of those who are out and challenge him or her to a race. Laps or race. Schmidt?"

"Laps."

"Oster!"

"Laps, for sure, sir."

"Marshall!"

"Laps, sir."

"Neilsen!"

The Head Stooge directed his patented sneer toward Jaylynn. "Sir! I'll take Savage."

"You will, huh?" With a twinkle in his eye, Sgt. Slade said, "You sure about that?"

Neilsen smiled broadly revealing large white teeth. "Yes, sir."

"What if you lose?" Slade asked.

"Oh, come *on*." Neilsen said confidently.

"If Savage beats you, then you run the mile anyway."

"No problem." He turned to his buddies. "You guys up for this?"

Slade cut in. "That's for *me* to determine." He looked at Grainger and Fuller, but they were already assenting. "Okay then," the sergeant said. "Line up."

Jaylynn didn't have long to get her head into the race. She had watched the entire interchange thoughtfully as she formulated a plan, which was something she had always attempted to do whenever she competed. Running another 400 meters full out didn't appeal to her, so she decided to run smarter, not harder.

The three men slapped hands and lined up in lanes one through three, and she took the outside lane by default.

Slade said, "Stay in your lanes, people, until that white line outside the first turn. Understand?" When they all nodded, he said, "All right. On your marks...get set..." and he blew the whistle.

The three men took off gleefully, one of them even making a whooping noise. Jaylynn settled into a restrained pace for the first 75 meters and, as she expected, fell behind. When the three men came tearing out of the first 100-meter turn, Neilsen was narrowly in the lead and she was fifteen yards back. She made up ground on

the straightaway though. She felt some fatigue, but she calculated
that she still had plenty of strength for the final 200 meters.

Vaguely, Jaylynn could hear distant shouts, but her eyes
focused on the back of Neilsen's legs while her mind played out the
chant she often fell into when running a race: *I can do it I can do it
I can do it...* She could see the three men slowing slightly, their
strides shortening and becoming more labored. Though she would
have rather waited for the straightaway, halfway through the second
turn she eased out of the inside lane to pass Grainger and Fuller.
And then she was right behind Neilsen's over-sized, muscular legs.

I can do it I can do it I can do it... She reached down and
summoned up the fiery ball of energy that was sapping her breath
and causing her legs to burn, and she willed herself into a strong
kick. Thighs pumping, calves straining, arms flashing, she pulled
past a startled Neilsen, and continued to chew up the last 50 meters,
beating all three men by six seconds and at least twenty-five yards.

As she crossed the finish line she heard a click and then she
slowed, her legs flaming, and her lungs near bursting. For the first
time of the day she was so winded that she bent over and gasped for
breath.

Marshall took her arm as Sgt. Slade strolled over, a funny look
on his face. "Savage," he said, "you just broke the new recruit
record for the 400 meters. 58.5. Not bad."

A jubilant Oster smacked her on the back and said, "After-
burners—that's all they saw." She stood up straight and shook her
legs out, still winded.

Neilsen, Grainger, and Fuller were also doubled over,
wheezing. Slade blew his whistle. "Okay, all of you who selected
laps, get going. You've got exactly ten minutes!" When the Three
Stooges didn't immediately move, Slade said, "Hey, you three—get
a move on it!"

They looked up, shocked, but were gasping too hard to speak.

Slade said, "Get your rears in gear, gentlemen. Your ten
minutes are ticking away."

****

Later in the locker room at the training center Marshall said,
"Jaylynn, I hope you didn't make enemies of those idiots."

Jaylynn finished pulling on street clothes and reached for her
hairbrush. "I don't care." She brushed her damp hair out of her
face then waved the brush toward Paula Marshall. "They've been
rude since day one, as though they have more right to be here than
you or me. I refuse to let them win."

Marshall picked up her gym bag and gave Jaylynn a serious

look. "I hate to make enemies."

"They were already your enemy, if you want to look at it that way. They're selfish, mean-spirited, and juvenile. I'm not going to do any less than my best, even if it makes them look bad." She tossed the brush into her own bag and zipped the top closed. "Think I should dry my hair? How windy is it out there?"

"It's not bad," said Marshall as she waited for Jaylynn to follow her. "Hard to believe it's already October though."

"No kidding. In a week we start our field training. Amazing how fast this is going."

****

Dez sat on the end of the locker room bench, her back against the far wall and one foot up on the bench. Fully dressed in her uniform, she held a hand gripper, which she squeezed together rhythmically. She considered how much the gripper resembled the handle of a hedge clipper without the blades. After twenty squeezes she stopped and rested her hand a moment, then did another twenty squeezes. And another.

Five full weeks had passed since she had broken the radius in her arm and tonight would be the first time back on evening patrol. Relieved to be healed, she was more than ready to get back to the street. She stood and tossed the gripper on the top shelf in her locker, grabbed a bottle of water, then closed the door and locked up. With one last adjustment to her gun belt, she strode off and up the stairs to the roll call room. She knew she was good and early, but she was anxious to get back on the job. She decided desk duty was not something she wanted anything to do with again—not for a very long time.

She ambled down the long hall, by the main entrance, and strolled past the Lieutenant's office. The duty sergeant looked up. "Hey, Reilly," he said.

"Hi, Belton."

"Lieutenant wants to see you."

She stopped. "Why?"

Belton shrugged.

She crossed her arms and stepped closer to him, her eyes narrowing. "Am I in trouble again?"

"Have you busted into any crime scenes lately without backup?"

"No." She gazed at him intently.

The sergeant crossed his arms, too, and grinned at her, his ebony face gleaming in the fluorescent light. "So go on in, Reilly."

She stepped past the beat-up desk and poked her head in the

open door. Lt. Malcolm looked up. "Afternoon, Reilly," he said.

"Afternoon, sir. Heard you were looking for me."

"Yeah, come in and sit down. Shut the door."

Dez did as she told and sat in the ancient solid wood visitor's chair. She shifted in the uncomfortable seat and put her elbows on the armrests.

"We've got thirteen new recruits coming our way and, God knows, we need the new blood. How long we been running short on this shift?"

"Since way before I got injured."

"Do you realize how many guys are retiring April 30th?"

Dez looked down at her hands. "Yes, sir. I think over thirty."

"Forty-three, Reilly." The Lieutenant leaned back in his tattered leather chair and pulled at his mustache. "I want to see these new cadets trained properly, and you know the new Chief is expecting miracles. She's going to personally watch this class of recruits—says she wants to be sure her new training protocol is followed." He sat forward, put his arms on the desk, and picked up some papers. "I didn't expect Stevens to go out on paternity leave, but his wife had the baby early and needs help for a while. So I'm assigning you his Field Training Officer duties."

Dez started to say something, but he cut her off. "Reilly, I know you haven't been an official FTO before, but I really need you now. Tour III doesn't—in fact, none of the shifts—have enough experienced vets, and we're getting a bunch of these rookies in rotation. They've gotta ride with somebody, and you're one of my best. Will you do it?"

With a sigh Dez said, "Of course, sir." She wanted to roll her eyes, but instead kept a steady attentive gaze leveled at her superior.

"Thatagirl. Thanks. I'll make sure you get a commendation for the extra work."

Lt. Malcolm was only in his mid-forties, not old enough to be her dad, but a little too old to be a brother. He had always been respectful toward Dez and, though some of the other cops made fun of him, she never minded his old-fashioned sayings like "thatagirl" and "okey-dokey." She appreciated the fact that he had always treated her fairly and gave her a shot at many challenges. "What's the plan?"

"New bids are coming up for January. Between now and then we're gonna cycle the recruits through the three Tours. I want you to ride with one from the first group, then the second group, then the third, and then I need you to stay with one of the ones who bid for our shift until he or she is settled in."

Trying to hide her exasperation she said, "But sir, you're talking *months*."

"Yup. Maybe six or eight—at least until some of them can be trusted in one-man cars alone." He nodded solemnly. "It'll be worth it in the long run because they'll get really good training. And I hear that this group is darn talented." He tapped his temple with his forefinger. "Got some smart ones this time. Might not have gotten very many new recruits this round, but they're supposed to be bright."

"When's this start?"

"Next week. In the meantime, here." He tossed her a folder and a sheaf of papers. "Go over the protocol, memorize all the Chief's new rules and regs, and check the folder to decide who you want to select."

"*You're* not assigning the recruits?"

"You pick who you want, Reilly. I'll assign the rest." He flexed his hands and began to systematically crack his knuckles, one finger at a time. "I'm giving you first choice. Seems only fair since you aren't getting any warning. All the other FTO's have been prepared for weeks. Besides, I know you've had it tough lately— just thought it was only fair to let you decide since I am asking this as a favor."

Dez knew she wouldn't have had a choice and that it really wasn't a favor at all, but she was grateful for the respectful way the Lieutenant coerced her into doing the extra duty. She rose. "When do you need this stuff back?"

"When shift starts?"

"*Tonight!*"

He grinned. "Yeah." Looking at his watch, he said, "That gives you seventeen minutes to make copies. Go on. I'll see you in a few." He spun in his chair and rolled backwards to his file cabinet. Leaving him pulling files, she headed toward the copier. While the machine auto-copied the eighty pages of training rules and regs, she opened the folder and shuffled through thirteen slim packets of paper. The information was filed according to who was performing best—on top of the stack—to the worst—on the bottom. Leading the pack was a 27-year-old named John Mahoney, and then came Savage, Vell, Schmidt... Dez stopped and flipped back: Jaylynn Savage. She didn't forget many names. Twenty-four-year-old female, bachelor's degree from the U of M, resides on Como Boulevard. *Damn!*

Dez hadn't thought much about it when she got two phone messages from the young spitfire who had helped with those two serial rapists. She hadn't called her back but had, instead, passed the messages on to the Lieutenant. Then the young woman had shown up at the station, and Dez had taken exactly sixty seconds to discourage her from applying to join the force. The small woman had seemed energetic and intelligent, and the big cop didn't believe she'd be all that interested in police work. Dez hadn't thought she was serious. *Surprise, surprise. The young woman followed through after all.* She thumbed through the report to see that Savage excelled at the written work and was leading the class in many categories, including basic law, investigative procedures, records/forms/reports, authority and jurisdiction, and communications. Her weapon work was not at marksman level yet, but showed steady improvement, and her unarmed self-defense appeared to be good and improving. Physically, she was noted to be in excellent condition.

The copy machine finished the job and clunked to a halt. Dez lifted the cover and copied Mahoney's dossier as well as Savage's, and then looked quickly through the rest. She reviewed the last recruit, the one rated thirteenth in his class. Oster. Average in the written work, average at weapons, slightly below average for a male in unarmed self-defense. His physical condition was noted as mediocre, but improving. In the area for notes, however, Dez read the following: *This cadet has a great deal of desire to join the force. He displays courage and esprit de corp. Though originally expected to wash out, he has shown remarkable fortitude and perseverance. V. Slade.*

Dez knew Slade to be a good teacher and a fine cop, and after a moment's hesitation, she copied Oster's paperwork, bundled the originals back in order in the folder, and returned to the Lieutenant's office.

He looked up and smiled at her. "Well?"

She said, "Mahoney," and Lt. Malcolm nodded. "Savage." He inclined his head again. "Oster."

"Oster! Isn't he the cellar dweller?"

She leaned against the doorframe with a slight smile on her face. "He is. I got a hunch about Mr. Oster though. Sounds like he should have washed out, but he hasn't. If he *should* be kicked, then you know I'll do it. But if he can grow, then he'll be a worthwhile project."

The Lieutenant shook his head. "You've always got the dangdest rationale for things, Reilly, but go ahead. And thanks." He looked back down at his paperwork, and she turned to leave. "Reilly!"

She glanced back. "Yes, sir?"

"Not a word about this, okay? I'll have all the assignments made, your choices included."

"Thank you, sir." She headed off down the hall with her sheaf of papers thinking that she had a difficult task ahead of her and that there was no doubt it would be a giant pain in the ass.

Chapter
5

Jaylynn dressed in the required clothes for the night's work: black oxfords, black jeans, a black t-shirt with POLICE emblazoned on the back in orange, and a dark blue patrol jacket with no insignia sewn on yet. Sgt. Slade had provided each of them with a black baseball cap, also bearing bright yellow letters spelling out POLICE. She looked at herself in the mirror and the first thought that came to mind was Cat Burglar. She strapped a bulging but compact fanny pack around her waist and got in Tim's beater to drive down to the police department.

She was amazed at everything she had learned so far. They had learned to march, stand at attention, salute, and perform like a well-organized military unit. She knew First Aid and CPR, and she had training for how to deal with all sorts of catastrophes: gas leaks, explosions, live wires, broken water mains, radioactive materials, and toxic chemicals. She knew how to shoot, use a baton, search suspects, put on cuffs one-handed, and subdue someone much bigger than she was using the rudiments of judo, boxing, and karate. She had memorized so many procedures and policies, statutes and ordinances that her head felt packed full of data. She was ready for the street.

At the end of the first six weeks in Police Academy, Jaylynn was aware of two indisputable facts. One: John Mahoney was a nearly perfect cadet and would undoubtedly be first in the class. And two: Dwayne Neilsen hated her guts.

She was nervous about the next stage of the training, but she was more bothered about being around Neilsen. She had now handily surpassed him in every classroom topic and nearly every physical fitness category. He could lift much more and carry heavier loads, but pound for pound, ounce for ounce, she was just as strong and fit. For her audacity in seeking to excel, he never

stopped picking at her. He and his friends made sport of her every
moment that they were away from the instructors. She was relieved
to get a change of scenery, even if she was still likely to have to deal
with him in the classroom three days a week.

From mid-October to mid-November, in addition to the
classroom training three days per week, she'd have field observation
on three weekdays with only Sundays off. After that, if she made
the grade, she'd go into six weeks of Tour Rotations for more
observation and a gradual shift into taking on responsibilities. In
January, the course work would be over, and she'd become a full-
time St. Paul police officer on probation.

Her first two weeks of observation were on Tour I, the
graveyard shift—also known as Dog Watch. She didn't look forward to staying up all night. She'd never been able to stay awake
much past two a.m. in her life, and during the entire five years she
attended the University she'd never pulled an all-nighter to study.
She didn't have a lot of time to adjust to the odd hours, so the first
night when she showed up at the main stationhouse she had
managed to sleep only two hours in the early evening. She
wondered if she could stay energized from nine p.m. to six a.m.

She arrived at the main station forty-five minutes early,
considerably before Vell, Chin, and Sprague appeared. Entering
through the front door, she found the place brimming with cops and
citizens coming and going, everyone talking at once. The entrance
led into a large room with a high ceiling. A thirty-foot-long counter
spread out directly ahead. At one end on the far right there was a
gate with an officer posted nearby, seated on a tall stool. In front of
him was a plastic sign: "Information and Complaints." The entire
area was painted in two tones of blue with several framed landscape
prints hanging on the walls. To the right and to the left of the
entryway were long benches, resembling pews, upon which a variety
of people sat waiting. Despite the obvious effort at creating a
restful, pleasant environment, the station smelled as musty as a
damp cave.

Jaylynn strode toward the counter and caught the eye of the
officer at the complaint desk. He stared impassively as he watched
her approach. His crew-cut hair and lack of a neck made her think
he must have been a football player in his earlier days. She held up
a plastic card. With a toss of his head, he directed her to the gate at
the end and pressed a button somewhere under the desk to release
the latch. Jaylynn pushed through and let the wooden gate slap
shut behind her.

"Here, I'll take that card," the desk sergeant said. He opened a
drawer behind the counter, fished around a moment, and then came
up with a blue card. "Don't lose this," he said. "This mag card

works out back at the staff entrance. If you do lose it, report it right away and we have to re-key everything. The brass does *not* take kindly to that." He watched as she tucked the card into her fanny pack. "This your first night?"

She smiled and said, "Yes," and stuck out her hand. "Jaylynn Savage."

He took her hand into his crushing grip. "Finch. Bob Finch. Nice to meet ya."

"Thanks," she said with a broad smile.

"Head on back to the briefing room—you know where that is?"

She nodded. Sgt. Slade had given them all the nickel tour earlier in the week, so she knew her way around. He pointed back over his shoulder and turned his attention to the desk where an elderly woman was now standing, demanding his immediate attention.

Jaylynn took her first walk alone down the hall, past the comm center, past the watch commander's office, and to the stairs that led down to the briefing room, also called the roll call room. Beyond it lay stairs down to the department gym, outfitted with scads of excellent weight equipment she looked forward to using. Beyond the first set of stairs lay another smaller flight of steps that led down to the men's and women's locker rooms which were also connected to the gym. She moved slowly down the small flight of stairs to the locker rooms. She wouldn't be assigned a locker until the middle of November when she went on rotation. Still, she went in to look around.

When she entered the large gray room, she saw that the rest rooms were to the left and around a corner. Five bright blue stalls sat in a row across from four sinks and an entire mirrored wall. Through a glass and metal door there were also two enclosed showers and a small sauna. The rest of the locker room was large and square with a main aisle running down the middle from the door to the far wall. On either side of the aisle, four sets of over-sized bright blue lockers jutted, the only color in the otherwise gunmetal gray room, and there were backless wooden benches, embedded into the concrete, sitting in front of each of the locker rows.

The room was unnaturally brightened by multiple rows of fluorescent lights. There were no windows whatsoever. At present, no one was in the room, and all Jaylynn could hear was a quiet drip-drip-drip echoing from the bathrooms. She went into one of the stalls to use the facilities, and when she was done washing up, she went back upstairs to the roll call room and sat down. Seconds later, Vell walked in dressed identically to her.

"Hey, Vell," Jaylynn said with a rakish grin on her face.

"How's it feel being dressed like a cat burglar?"

The first two weeks of Tour I graveyard observation went well, though Jaylynn was exhausted by the third day. Despite sleeping from the moment she hit the bed in the morning until late afternoon, she could not get used to Dog Watch's late night hours. It occurred to her that if she had to work that shift, she'd never make it—so much for her police career. She hoped to go on Tour III swing shift once her training was over.

Jaylynn also kept watch for the black-haired cop, but she hit the streets before Tour III ended, and Jaylynn's shift ended hours after all of swing shift had gone home. It wasn't until she started riding days with Officer Culpepper, also known as Cowboy, that she ran into Desiree Reilly—literally. After she and Cowboy ended their tour early one day, they returned to the station. She pushed open the door to the police entrance only to find six feet of scowling electricity staring down upon her. Jaylynn came to an abrupt halt, stock-still and tongue-tied.

"You're in an awful hurry," the tall woman said. Her police cap was tucked under one arm, and she had a paper sack in one hand and a quart bottle of water in the other.

Cowboy pushed the door open further and squeezed past the two of them. He said, "Dez, honey, how ya doing?"

She gave him an amused glance, but instead of answering said, "This rookie giving you any trouble, Cowboy?"

He stopped and smiled, running his thick hand through short white-blond hair. "Nope. She's picking it all up nicely." He turned and moved away. "See ya tomorrow, Savage."

"Bye, Cowboy," Jaylynn managed to squeak out, but he probably didn't hear her. She turned her attention back to the piercing blue eyes inspecting her face.

The big cop said, "Guess I'll be seeing you week after next."

"Oh?" Jaylynn asked, a surprised look furrowing her brow.

"Yeah. You drew the short straw and got me for Tour III observation and then for field training. Didn't the Lieutenant tell you?"

"No, I think we're getting information on a need-to-know basis. Are you sure?"

"Yup."

The cop slid a foot forward, and Jaylynn became aware of the fact that she was blocking the door. She stepped aside to let Dez Reilly pass. "Hope you have a good night," Jaylynn said.

"Yeah. You, too."

Jaylynn watched as the long-legged woman ambled out toward the parking lot full of police cruisers, reached a vehicle, and disappeared into it. The rookie let the door swing shut and restrained herself from running down the hall, screaming maniacally, but she did allow herself a happy grin as she went to sign off shift. Only a few more days with Cowboy, and then she'd do the two weeks of Tour III observation in the company of Desiree Reilly. And if she heard the policewoman right, she was planning on being Jaylynn's FTO, too. Now she could hardly wait to get home and tell Sara.

****

The first thing Jaylynn noticed once she got in the passenger seat of the squad car was that Officer Reilly wore silver reflective sunglasses until the sun was down and it was so dim that the streetlamps clicked on. Only then, almost as an afterthought, did the veteran cop slip the glasses off and tuck them into her shirt pocket. Out of the corner of her eye, Jaylynn noticed how the veteran's eyes constantly scanned the area, intently examining every passing person, every car, every movement.

Jaylynn watched the early evening gradually shade from gray to darkness. The nightlife emerged like moles creeping out of deep holes. There were a lot of people out in the cool, crisp air. At present there was no snow on the ground and, though it was only 28 degrees out, there was no wind. With just a warm jacket, any seasoned Minnesotan on the street would be comfortable tonight.

Jaylynn racked her brain for something to say to the taciturn woman beside her, but her earlier attempts at conversation had met a brick wall. The quiet FTO didn't offer comments, and she answered any questions in the sparest of language. They'd been in the car for over two hours, getting out only three times so far to check on an underage smoking call and two reports of possible domestic disputes, both of which turned out to be unfounded.

Despite the calm demeanor, Jaylynn thought Reilly was like a tightly coiled spring, with waves of tension radiating from her. She was silent, though it was anything but silent in the car. In addition to the regular dispatch noise on the radio, the car's AM/ FM radio quietly played a top 40 station. Then the cell phone rang and Reilly picked it up and listened. Her eyes narrowed, punctuating periods of silence with terse statements: "Yes, sir...Mmhmm...Okay, thanks." When she hung up, she said, "Savage, our meal break isn't until nine. Can you last that long?"

"Sure," Jaylynn said. "I brought a couple snacks here." She pointed to her fanny sack.

"Me, too," the big cop said, gesturing to the paper sack she'd set on the seat between them.

Dispatch came over the radio, and Reilly picked it up to

respond. Jaylynn frowned. *How had Reilly known to answer that call?* She was too embarrassed to ask. Already she had relegated the two radios to background noise, but she could see that she shouldn't do that—at least not the dispatch radio anyway. She needed to listen to it all the time, but how did she do that while conversing—if you could call what they'd just had a conversation. She also did not know what dispatch had been asking their unit, but it didn't cause the veteran cop to speed off to any call. They continued to drive down University Avenue, occasionally taking a side street and then coming back to the busy thoroughfare.

Jaylynn ventured forth a question, "How long have you been on the force?"

"Eight and a half years."

"And you like the job?"

"Yeah."

The quiet officer turned off Snelling Avenue onto Thomas, slowing when she saw a glut of cars parked and double-parked in front of a ramshackle house scattering streams of light from all windows. Small knots of people stood on the front porch and on the lawn, tiny points of orange light giving evidence to all the cigarettes being smoked. Other partygoers made their way through the gathering and up the stairs to enter the house. Reilly wheeled the car past, rolled down her window, and meandered on around the block casually. She approached the house again and parked across the street.

From the passenger seat Jaylynn could hear the pounding of the bass. *Looks like a really good party going on—probably a bunch of Hamline University students.*

Reilly said, "Just follow me in and don't say anything." She got out of the car and Jaylynn hastened to open her door and get out. She put her hands in her pants pockets and cut across the street, literally following the long strides of the big cop. Every step brought them closer to the shrieking, pounding sound of Metallica. The crowd quieted and parted when they caught sight of them, and three men in the front yard began to back off and sidle away. By the time the two women hit the top of the stairs, most of the occupants of the porch and yard had miraculously disappeared, leaving three women and a man who came up the stairs behind the officer and the cadet.

Before Reilly could ring the bell, one of the three women, a perilously thin person really no more than a girl, shouted over the musical din, "Can I help you, officer?"

"Yeah, you can either turn the noise down or break up this party. Are you the owner of the house?"

She nodded. "I rent this place, yes." The woman dropped her

lit cigarette on the cement stair of the porch and ground it out with her foot. She pulled at the screen door to the house and stepped in, holding it open so that her companions and Reilly and Savage could enter. Letting loose of the door, she moved over to the stereo system and turned the music off.

The woman smiled brightly and said, "Would you like something to drink, Officer?" She raised her eyebrows and leaned toward the kitchen. Meanwhile, behind them, Jaylynn heard the screen door open and close, open and close, as some of the partygoers quietly departed. Still, dozens of young men and women remained in the kitchen, on the staircase, and on the couch and chairs.

Dez narrowed her gaze and gave her a withering look. "No, thank you, ma'am." She raised her voice and said, "This is your one and only warning, people. If I get one call from dispatch, I'll be checking ID's and arresting you." She narrowed her eyes and looked at the owner. "You, miss, you get the violation tag, the fine, and the report to the college that you disturbed the peace." She paused a moment and breathed in, her eyes covering every square inch of the room. "And that better not be anything more than cigarettes burning in here. Got it?"

The thin woman nodded solemnly.

"We're outta here then." The big cop turned and ushered the cadet toward the door. Jaylynn grabbed the cool metal of the screen doorknob and turned it, bursting out into the crisp air. She bounded down the stairs and over to the car. When they got in, she was surprised when Reilly turned to her and said, "We'll be back before the evening's through. Just wait and see."

"Why do you say that?"

The car roared to a start and Reilly pulled away from the curb. In a thoughtful voice she said, "Because she's not the only occupant of the house. I don't think she can control all those people. If it's that loud this early, it's only gonna get louder. Plus there's too many kids coming and going. So she's gonna end up getting tagged."

It was the most information Jaylynn had gotten out of the woman all night, and she jumped on the information. "So how many calls like this do you generally get?"

"Anywhere from two to twenty, depends on the time of year."

"Because of the weather?"

"Nah...more the status of the students. Weekends, holidays, certain school events. There's a lot of colleges around here." She steered the car back onto University Avenue. "Hamline kids aren't so bad. Saint Kate's girls are pretty rowdy, but the worst by far are the spoiled rich kids all around St. Thomas. Bunch of rotten troublemakers. Got plenty of money for drugs and alcohol, not to mention supersonic stereos, and a lot of them think they own the world."

She followed a dented gray Chevy Nova that pulled into an Amoco convenience store/gas station. The Nova parked on the side of the store in the regular parking spaces, while Reilly parked at one of the four gas pumps.

"We need gas?" Jaylynn asked.

"Nope. Get out."

The occupants of the gray Nova hadn't noticed the police car. They opened their car doors and staggered into the store. The veteran and the cadet strolled behind. Reilly moved up behind the young man and woman as they stood in front of the soda pop case. The man wore jeans, tennis shoes, and a red and brown plaid shirt under a jean jacket. The woman was dressed just the same, except her plaid shirt was green and blue. Both of them were close to Jaylynn's height. The young woman reached into the refrigerator case and pulled out a liter-sized Mountain Dew, and the pair turned and halted, looking up at Dez with fear on their faces.

"Good evening, folks," the tall officer said.

They mumbled greetings, and looked away from her, at one another and around the store.

"You two been out partying?"

Jaylynn watched the thin man suddenly begin to quiver as he tried to shake his head no. She could see both kids' eyes were vacant and glassy.

The big cop said, "You got any ID?"

The girl pulled a driver's license out of her back pocket, but the boy shook his head.

"You better not be driving," Dez said to him.

"No, sir, I mean no, ma'am," he said.

In a low menacing voice, Dez said, "You better not be jerking me around."

"No," he said, a note of desperation in his voice. "Honest. I'm not."

"What's your name?"

"Arnie Jensen."

"You go to school around here, Mr. Jensen?"

He nodded. "St. Thomas."

"And you don't even have any school ID?" She handed the license back to the girl.

"Not on me, officer." His speech was slow, but he was trying hard not to slur. He swallowed and took a gulp of air. The girl tucked her license back into her pocket and stood sullenly holding the cold bottle of Mountain Dew.

Dez said to the boy, "Hmpf...I'll bet you're not 21."

The boy did not respond.

The tall cop stared at him for a few seconds. "Where do your parents live?"

"Duluth."

"You play any sports?"

He spoke in a slow mumble now. "Hockey."

"How would you like me to call up your parents and tell them that their son is stoned out of his mind and should be taken home? How would you like me to contact your coach and let him know about this little incident?"

The boy's eyes nearly bugged out of his head, and suddenly his voice was much clearer. "I wouldn't like that at all. Please, please don't do that."

Jaylynn marveled that the boy was still on his feet since his legs seemed to be shaking so badly. The contrast of his black hair against pale skin made him look unnaturally pallid. She looked up at the tall woman beside her and realized the cop was enjoying the confrontation. Her eyes sparkled and she seemed to be working very hard to maintain a stony face. She turned to the girl and said, "I would suggest you leave that car of yours right out there and either walk home or call for a ride. If I see you drive that car out of this lot, you're goin' downtown for a fun night in jail."

Now the girl's eyes nearly bugged out. She set the liter of Mountain Dew down on a stacked display of Valvoline motor oil. "Can we go?" she asked.

The tall cop inclined her head slowly, nodding while she fixed a mean stare on the two. As if a starter's gun had gone off, both plaid-shirted kids bolted for the door, the boy looking back only once. Jaylynn saw them walk around the side of the building to the Nova. The girl reached in for something and then locked up the car. Without a backward glance, they took off down the street.

Dez picked up the sweating bottle of pop and returned it to the cold case. "I'll be back in a second," she said, and she disappeared around the corner to the rest room.

Jaylynn watched the boy and girl as they ambled away from the gas station. The girl's gait was steady, but the boy lurched along. The second time he stumbled, the girl took his arm and leaned into him. They turned the corner and that was the last she saw of them.

The rookie hadn't been one to get wasted in high school or college. She'd been a "good kid" and hadn't gotten in much trouble—at least not trouble anyone had ever caught her at. She smiled thinking about all the small parties she'd been at where everyone had mostly sat around drinking beer or wine and playing Trivial Pursuit. She'd always enjoyed staying sober enough to converse—not to mention being lucid enough to laugh about intelligently funny things. She'd never liked hangovers anyway, and from what she could see, both those kids were going to feel rotten in the morning.

Dez reappeared next to her, startling her from her thoughts. The tall cop flashed a glance toward Jaylynn. "You want a pop or something?"

"Sure." Jaylynn stepped to the cold case and pulled a glass door open. She snagged a Pepsi, and then watched as Dez picked out a quart bottle of Chippewa Spring Water.

When they got to the counter, the big cop waved her away and pulled out her own wallet. "I'll get this," she said. "You can get the next round."

In a pleasant voice the counter clerk, a grey-haired man with a significant five o'clock shadow, said, "You running my business outta here again, Reilly?"

"Yeah, can't be helped. Buncha drunk college students. They'll be back to get that car." She pointed to the gray heap out the side window. "You'll get some business from them then."

He said, "Why don't you go ahead and take that on the house?"

"Thanks, Mr. Fisher, but this is your livelihood." She offered him some bills. He rang up the purchase, took two pennies out of the penny dish by the register, and handed her even change.

"Thanks for keeping an eye on this place," he said.

"No problem. See ya later." She twisted the cap off the bottle as she turned towards the door, her long legs eating up the distance in four steps. Jaylynn scooped up her Pepsi and strode quickly behind her. They got back in the car, and the rookie took a swig of her pop.

"No matter what," Dez said, "pay for everything wherever you go. Some guys take stuff on the house. Don't do it, Savage. It's too short a step to being on the take."

Jaylynn nodded. "Okay," she said. "By the way, would you mind calling me Jaylynn—or just Jay, if you want. I'm still not used to everyone calling me Savage." She giggled and said, "Makes me sound like a brute."

"Okay," Dez said. "Eat if you want now. We may not get much chance later." She opened her paper sack and drew out an item wrapped in wax paper. Jaylynn unzipped her fanny pack and pulled out a package of Hostess chocolate cupcakes. She started picking at the cellophane as Dez's wax paper opened to reveal a sandwich, thick with turkey or chicken. Dez saw her peering at the sandwich in the dark. "Want half?" she asked.

"Oh no, that's okay," Jaylynn said. "I'll just eat this."

"A cupcake won't stay with you long, Savage—I mean, Jaylynn. Here, have half. I've got three more in the bag."

The rookie accepted the sandwich and said, "You brought *four* sandwiches?"

"I usually do." She took a big bite and while chewing said, "I don't always eat the bread, but I need the protein."

Jaylynn nodded as though she understood completely, though she had no idea why Dez would need four sandwiches. She took a bite and found the turkey to be cool and moist, even if it was all too dry for her taste. "What's on this?"

"Turkey. Nutty oat bread."

"That's it?"

"Yeah. You don't like it?"

"No, no, it's good," she hastened to say. "The turkey is nice and tender."

"I try to spice up the meat because I don't put on mayo or anything like that."

"I see," Jaylynn said. "Want one of these cupcakes?"

"Sorry. Never eat sugars after six. But thanks." She popped the last of the sandwich in her mouth and swiped her hands on her pants legs, then started the car. "Okay, let's get back at it." She pulled out of the parking lot and swung onto the dark street. "I think we should take a look at that little party over by Hamline again." With gusto she said, "Won't be long before we get to arrest a few people. That ought to liven up your night."

From that moment on, Jaylynn noted that Dez's demeanor toward her changed. All of a sudden, for no apparent reason, the tall cop began to talk—rather, she gave information, and lots of it. She explained what she was doing and why. She gave advice. She quizzed the rookie about procedures and laws. In short, she made the nights of observation fly by, and every day when midnight approached, Jaylynn was sorry to have to knock off and go home. By the time the ride-along observations were over, she was enthusiastic about getting into her regulation uniform and assuming her duties.

Chapter
6

Dez Reilly sat at a desk in the Reports Room putting the finishing touches on FTO reports for Oster, Mahoney, and Savage. They had performed adequately—or better—during their initial rotations with her, and she was recommending to Lt. Malcolm that all three be advanced to official rookie status after the first of the year. She slid open the metal drawer on the rickety desk and pulled out a stapler to tack the pages of each report. Rising, she scooped up her bottle of spring water and the reports and headed off down the hall to turn them in.

The watch commander's office was next to Lt. Malcolm's, and as she passed it by, she saw it was decorated with red and white Santa mosaics, pictures of misshapen Christmas trees, and yards of red and green chains made of construction paper. Every year, Commander Parr's five kids trimmed the office he shared with the other commanders, and every year Dez was amazed at the sheer volume of bad art.

The duty sergeant looked up from his report and greeted her. Belton, a slim black man in his fifties, had always gotten along well with her. She gave him the stack of reports. He said, "Hi, Reilly. You working Christmas Eve?"

"Yeah. I took Christmas Day off, but I'll be here tomorrow. And New Year's Eve and Day, too."

He shook his head. "Glutton for punishment, huh?"

She shrugged. "What the hey. I'll use the double time money for something special—maybe get myself a facial or something."

He frowned and looked up only to see the twinkle in her eyes. He stifled a grin and said, "Try the pedicure. My wife swears by it."

She nodded solemnly. "Pass these on to the Lieutenant for me, okay?"

"Will do. And Reilly?"

She paused. "Yeah?"

"Merry Christmas."

"You, too, Sarge. Hope you have a nice holiday."

She turned away, catching a whiff of evergreen smell that reminded her of Christmas trees and reindeer. She headed off down the hall to the back entrance to get some fresh air, realizing she had grown to dislike Christmas. She paced outside in the late afternoon light, her hands behind her back. *Don't wanna be a grinch though,* she thought. She didn't hate the holidays, but she was grateful when they passed. The only thing that made Christmas bearable was Luella. Her landlady always had her clan of family and friends over starting on Christmas Eve, and the celebration extended for several days after, with people coming and going, bringing presents, sharing holiday food. Dez was glad that her apartment was separate, though. She could get away when she needed a break, or she could choose to hang around the pack of laughing, jovial people who showed up for the cheer and good food.

Other than Luella's shindig, Dez attended no festivities. Her father was dead, she didn't speak to her mother, and she had no idea how to contact her younger brother. Family had not been in her picture for a number of years, and she liked it just fine that way.

An old red Toyota rolled into the parking lot and stopped a dozen feet away, the occupants unaware of her leaning against the side of the building. She watched as Jaylynn and the red-haired man from last summer turned toward one another. Jaylynn leaned over and gave the man a brief kiss, then launched herself out the passenger door and hustled through the chilly air and into the back entrance.

Dez shivered. The red-haired man backed up the clunking car and made his way out of the parking lot, not noticing that the big cop was staring daggers at him. She exhaled a big breath of air and watched as it clouded white smoke in front of her face. Full of tension, she stomped over to the door and went in, making her way downstairs to the roll call room.

The big cop sat on a metal folding chair near the back of the silent briefing room and took a long pull from her water bottle. Checking her watch she noted it was nineteen minutes until roll call. She set the water bottle on the floor and closed her eyes. Starting with her feet, she began to systematically tighten and release her muscles until she sat motionless and relaxed. A tiny squeak caused her eyelids to snap open, and she saw Jaylynn standing uncertainly in the doorway.

The younger woman said, "Sorry. I didn't mean to interrupt."

"You're not interrupting." The big cop straightened up in her chair and stretched neck muscles that still felt tight.

Jaylynn strode into the room and sat in the chair next to Dez.
"So you have big plans for tomorrow?"

"The usual."

The rookie suppressed a grin with difficulty. Getting any
personal information out of the reserved woman was next to
impossible. She'd already learned that prying didn't work; the tall
cop just retreated further underground. So far, the only tactic that
yielded results was to overflow Dez with her own personal details
and then occasionally the tall woman volunteered something.

Jaylynn said, "I guess I'll have quite the phone bill this year.
I'm staying in town, so I'll have to call my family. Lucky I can go
hang out with Sara's folks, and of course Tim has the house decorated to the nines." She paused, giving the big woman opportunity
to speak. Out of the corner of her eye she watched Dez take a swig
of her water. It occurred to her that the other woman used those
bottles of water like some people used cigarettes—as a distraction.
Dez didn't appear to be listening at all, so when the dark head
swung toward her and penetrating blue eyes bored into her, she was
taken aback.

Dez said, "Where does your family live?"

"Seattle."

The tall cop nodded slowly. "Why don't you fly out for
Christmas?"

"There isn't really enough time."

"You could have taken some extra days. The sergeant would
have worked it out."

Jaylynn smiled warmly. "I wanted to stay. I didn't want to
miss any training. Besides, they'll all be here over spring vacation
in a few months, so I'm looking forward to that."

Dez took another drink from the bottle. "You're off tomorrow
though, right?"

"Yeah, I think we're planning on eating about six different
meals at various places. I'll be a couch potato by shift time, so I
didn't want to have to work."

Just then Oster shot into the room. "Hey guys," he said
enthusiastically. "How you two doing?" He clapped a meaty hand
on the rookie's shoulder and sat next to her, two chairs away from
Dez.

Dez tossed him a glance and nodded. Jaylynn said, "Things
are going okay. What are you doing for the holiday?"

Oster crossed his arms across his chest and with a smug self-
satisfied look said, "I'm givin' my girlfriend the biggest diamond
rock I could afford and hoping she will say yes."

Dez watched as Jaylynn gasped and socked the smiling man in

the arm. Then the rookie threw an arm around him and gave him a hug. "I am so happy for you, Mitch! I just know she'll say yes. Who could resist you?" She sat back in her chair, eyes shining, and then gave the blushing man another punch in the upper arm. "Where you going on your honeymoon?"

"That's totally up to her," he said. "If she'll marry me, we'll go anywhere she wants. I think she'll pick Hawaii though."

Dez said in a low tone, "Hope you're packing away a ton of dough, Oster. Hawaii ain't cheap."

Oster leaned forward in his chair. "Ever heard of charge cards, Reilly?" He grinned as he sat back and beamed at the rookie. "Jay, I don't think I've ever been so happy in my life. I've got this great job that I really like, and I think I'm gonna marry Donna." He did a little chair dance but stopped when a clatter of footsteps came down the stairs and some of the other officers filed into the room followed shortly by the duty sergeant.

Dez casually turned her attention to Oster, staring at him over Jaylynn and out of the corner of her eye. She frowned. For some reason Oster's happy news had rankled her. She wanted to smack him. She turned away and focused on the sergeant's updates.

Dez's sour mood persisted through the shift, which was eventful, though routine. She and Jaylynn broke up the same kind of bar fights, arrested battling spouses for the same kind of domestic disputes, and answered the same kind of noise complaints as any other night. The only difference was the proliferation of seasonal red and gold and green splattered all over every home and business. By the time midnight rolled around Dez decided she did indeed feel like a grinch.

When they returned to the station, Jaylynn headed straight downstairs after signing out. Dez took a detour to the property room and dropped off a watch they had found on the street. Sooner or later, perhaps someone would come looking for it. She threw her empty plastic water bottle in the trash in the hall and headed down the stairs, meeting Jaylynn coming up. The younger woman carried a gym bag and had changed into tennis shoes, blue sweat bottoms, and a big bulky coat.

"Have a good day tomorrow," Jaylynn said in a tired voice.

"You, too. See you Saturday," Dez said. She squeezed past the rookie and made her way into the locker room, unbuttoning her shirt as she drew near the locker. In front of her bright blue metal storage locker sat a small square package, wrapped in red, blue, and green striped paper and adorned with a golden bow no bigger than a walnut. She bent over and picked it up, hefting the lightweight present and recognizing immediately that it was a CD. She pulled a tiny card off the front, ripped open the envelope, and read it: *Merry*

Christmas, Dez. Thanks for all your help during my training. I can never thank you enough. Love, Jaylynn.

She tore away the wrapping paper and uncovered a disc by someone she had never heard of: Lisa Stansfield. Crunching up the cellophane and colorful wrapping paper, she walked over to the garbage and tossed them in. She felt bad. This was a kind gesture from the rookie, and she knew she had been such a grump all night that Jaylynn couldn't have enjoyed the evening. Oh well. It wasn't her job to entertain the new recruits.

She changed clothes and gathered up her things and trudged upstairs to the Lieutenant's office. The duty sergeant was away from his desk, so she tapped on the frame of the open door, and Lt. Malcolm looked up, startled. "Hey, Reilly. You have an okay shift?"

"Yes, sir. Went fine." She gestured at the compact disk in her hand. "My assignee, Savage, left me a Christmas present. I understand from the rules that FTO's aren't supposed to—"

Waving his hand through the air, he cut her off. "Yeah, yeah, she mentioned it to me, and I gave her the okay." He smiled at her. "Will a ten buck item cause you to give her a good recommendation if she doesn't deserve it?"

"No."

"That's exactly what I figured. So don't worry about it."

"Yes, sir."

"Have a good Christmas, okay? I'm off the next few days, so be good." He smiled at her.

"No problem. Merry Christmas to you, too, sir." She turned and hiked down the long hallway and out into the icy air to her truck. It was snowing again, small frozen clumps, and the recently plowed streets were already covered over. She started the engine, then popped in the CD as she wheeled out of the lot. A funky bass and percussion beat began, and she listened to the smooth jazzy voice singing about searching for and finding love. Dez frowned. *Happy music. Everybody's so goddamn happy.* She accelerated down Dale Street, her eyes taking in every movement, every light. The song continued, the powerful voice sexy and self-assured.

She reached over and ejected the CD, one-handedly tucking it back in the case. The singer seemed to have a terrific voice, but she couldn't take any more sappy happy stuff. Completing the rest of the drive home in silence, she parked in the garage out back and plodded up to the house which was alight, golden streamers of illumination causing the stucco house to look a little like a Christmas ornament. Dez didn't notice. She plodded through the swiftly accumulating snow, climbed the back stairs, and with a weary sigh crept up to her apartment.

****

Right on time, Tim was waiting for Jaylynn behind the police station. She tossed her gym bag in the back seat and climbed in front.

"How was your night?" Tim asked.

With a sigh she said, "Not bad, not good, not really anything. Yours?"

He gave her a wide smile and peeled out of the lot. "The chef gave me a bottle of Cabernet and the boss slipped me a card with a hundred bucks in it."

"Tim! That's great."

"And we have a new maitre d' who started last week. Kevin. I just met him, and oh my, Jay, he is so sweet. Whoo-wee!"

She rolled her eyes. "Do tell."

"Blond. Slender. Beautiful blue eyes. About twenty-five. He looks *fantastic* in the tux. My heart skips beats just thinking about him."

"Is he available? Hell, is he gay?"

"Oh yeah. He for sure registers on *my* gaydar. I invited him to come share the Cabernet with me, and he accepted! He hasn't got any family here in the Twin Cities, so I hope you and Sara don't mind if he comes along. Hey!" He reached over and turned up the radio. "Have you heard this new song? It's just fabulous. Listen."

A nice driving bass beat started and then a sultry female voice singing about a cool, mysterious blue-eyed woman. Jaylynn couldn't help but smile a bitter little smile. Sounded exactly like Dez. "Who is this?"

Tim said, "I couldn't believe it—Blondie! Remember them from back in about grade school? I saw her—Deborah Harry—in a movie a while back and she's older than my mom. But man, what a voice."

Jaylynn agreed as she continued to listen to the quick beat of the song. *I think I'll be buying that CD*, she thought. She shifted uncomfortably in her seat as they pulled up to the house. *I wonder if Dez will like Lisa Stansfield?* She was one of Jaylynn's favorite musicians. She liked how the woman could go from jazzy tones to upbeat funk to solid love ballads. All three of her CD's were just so sexy and full of emotion. She couldn't help but feel happy listening to even the saddest of the songs.

They got out of the car and she grinned as Tim nearly danced up the snow-strewn walk to the back door. It was hard to feel sad or out-of-sorts around him. He had a way of cheering a person up without even knowing he was doing it. She decided there was no use fretting about things she had no control over. Smiling as she felt the cool snowflakes on her face, she took his arm and they high-stepped into the house.

****

In the middle of the week following Christmas, Jaylynn had her final classroom meeting with Sergeant Slade and her fellow rookies. The tests were over, the rigorous physical regimen was complete, and all thirteen recruits were scheduled to move on to the next phase of training.

Slade said, "You're all done with the 'grin and wave' part of this training. Now you get down to the real thing. For the next six weeks, you'll all work closely with your FTO's, and you'll be expected to perform with exemplary skill. Think about what you're doing. Use your best judgment. Talk to each other and share information. And please feel free to call me or come by the western precinct any time. I have an investment in your successes."

After class, each recruit shook Slade's hand and filed out, everyone talking and animated as they departed. Jaylynn hung back and waited for the others to leave. She shook Slade's hand. "You've been an excellent teacher," she said. "I've really appreciated what you've done for all of us."

"Savage," he said, "I know for a fact that you're going to be a very good cop. You've got a lot of talent."

"Thank you, sir. But could I ask you a question?"

"Sure! Any time. My door is always going to be open for you. I hope to hear great things from you in years to come." He looked closely at her face. "Hmm, what is it?"

She wasn't sure how to put it, so the words just tumbled out. "I'm working with an FTO who's like, perfect, sir. She can handle anything. She walks in a room and just by looking at people she can control the situation. She intimidates the hell out of anyone moving. I walk in the room and people don't even *notice*. How am I going to be a good cop when I don't have that kind of presence at all?"

He pursed his lips and squinted at her, then nodded. "Your FTO is Desiree Reilly, right?"

"Yes."

"You're right. She's imposing. She's a lot bigger than you. She's gotta be—what?—six, eight inches taller?"

Jaylynn nodded.

"Bad news, Savage. I don't think you're gonna grow any taller." He grinned at her as she gave him a rueful look. "Seriously," he said, "you're *never* going to work a room like she does. You're not the strong-arm type, and you look far too sweet to be able to threaten and compel the way she can."

Jaylynn let out a sigh of defeat and sat down in one of the desks. "That's what I *mean*, sir. What am I going to do?"

Slade swung a leg over the desk chair in front of Jaylynn and settled down facing her and the rear of the room, his arms resting on the chair back. "You obviously don't realize that you have something Reilly will never have."

Startled, she looked at him, her hazel eyes intent. "Sir?"

"Use your *own* talents, Savage. You have a whole different set of skills, and they're just as effective as Reilly's tactics."

Jaylynn was confused. How could she be as physically imposing, as daunting as her FTO without those same skills?

His brown eyes looked at her sympathetically as he reached a hand over and tapped her forehead twice with his forefinger. "Use this."

"But, Sarge, she's also very smart. She's got it all."

At that, a hearty chuckle burst out of Slade. "Savage, it's so apparent...hey, you're totally overlooking the obvious. You've got a God-given gift of quick wits and fast talk. Use your head. Use your mouth. You'll never bully your way out of bad situations. You're gonna *talk* your way out. And believe me, that's every bit as effective. You go out on patrol now, and instead of thinking about all the ways you don't measure up to Reilly—or anyone else for that matter—think about how you can use your own particular style. Be loud. Be flashy. Be yourself. Will you do that for me?"

Jaylynn sat feeling a little bit stunned. She felt like a dummy, but at the same time, a bubble of gleefulness rose inside her because what Slade was saying felt exactly right. All her life, what she lacked in stature she had always had to make up for in cleverness or perseverance or sheer dint of will. Why would this job be any different?

She rose from the desk smiling. "Thanks, Sarge. You've given me a lot to think about." She reached for his wiry hand and when he stood up, she gave him a little half-hug, too. "I'll check in with you every so often."

"You make sure to do that, Savage."

She picked up her bag and with a smile headed out the door feeling lighter than she had for days. She didn't look back, so she missed the shake of her instructor's head and the bemused look of respect he cast her way before he gathered up his own things and got ready to leave.

****

New Year's Eve was always a hopping night, and Dez figured it would be busy what with everyone on earth wanting to party hardy 'til the dawn rolled in. She had reluctantly offered to let Jaylynn drive and, to her dismay, the rookie agreed with excitement. The big cop hated riding along, but she also knew Jaylynn needed experience behind the wheel, so she sat in the passenger's seat, arms crossed, feeling exceedingly crabby.

The first six hours of their shift had been spent dealing mostly with drunks: drunks on the street, drunks in bars, and drunken brawlers beating on their wives in their own homes. When Dispatch put out the next call—another threatening drunk—Dez snapped a reply at the Dispatcher, her temper frayed at the edges from the repetitiveness of the situation.

When they arrived in front of the Castlewalk Bar on University, another unit was already there. Neilsen, the surly rookie from Jaylynn's class, was just getting out of the car with his FTO, Alvarez, with whom the rookie had ridden her first observational rotation. Two men stood blocking the doorway to the bar, but both appeared skittish. Another man, a scrawny mope in his late sixties, stood several feet away from the bar door screaming to be let back in. His tan jacket was tattered, and his jeans, greasy with age, drooped on his hips. Dez exploded from the cruiser as Alvarez and Neilsen approached, and the three closed in on the screaming man.

Jaylynn got out of the car, shivering in the cold breeze. She was glad the streets were cleared of snow and ice. Even after five years in Minnesota, she still didn't like to drive on ice. As she came around the nose of the car and stepped up on the sidewalk, Alvarez said, "Hey there, sir. Can we help you?"

The drunk wheeled around, saw the three huge officers, and fumbled in his jacket. All three cops pulled weapons, but not before the staggering man revealed a dull Bowie knife. He began to wave it out in front of him as he teetered and lurched. "Get the hell 'way from me. I had 'nough of p'lice brut—brut— you know..." He took another step and shook his head from side to side as though he were dizzy.

All three officers trained their guns on the swaying man. They looked up, startled, when Jaylynn shouted, "Wait! Stop! Yoo hoo. Hey, Mister!"

This distracted him. He wheeled her way and squinted. Now the four officers formed a box around the drunk. She could see he was inebriated beyond the point of fully understanding what was happening. She opened her hands and held them up, palms out. "Sir. No need to be afraid of me. I won't hurt you."

"A little girl cop?" he asked. He brandished his knife her way, his back to the other officers.

Jaylynn looked over his shoulder at ice-cold chips of blue and gave Dez the slightest toss of her head. "Mister, I may look little, but I'm the boss of those three right now. Look at them." He cast a nervous glance over his shoulder. "Officers, back up," she said. "Give this man some room."

The three officers took two steps back, though Neilsen had to be waved back by Alvarez.

"See?" She smiled at him. "They'll follow my orders. Now listen. Nobody's gonna hurt you, but you gotta give me the knife. Then how 'bout you and I go get a nice nightcap?"

"Say," the wobbling man said. "You're kinda cute."

"Thank you." She gazed across the sidewalk and smiled at Dez who didn't seem to be seeing any humor in the situation. Turning her attention back to the man she said, "What's your name?"

"Denny."

"I'm Jaylynn. Glad to meet you, Denny." She stepped close enough to see tendrils of steam coming out of the man's mouth and wafting around the steel glint of the knife. Her three coworkers tensed and stepped forward. She gave them a stern look. "Well?" she asked. "Is that any way to treat a lady, Denny—waving a knife at me? Is that your style with the girls you date?"

"Oh no, I c'n be a gentleman," he slurred. "I'll put it away."

"I'd like to get a better look at your knife," she said suggestively.

"You would, huh," he mumbled, leering at her. "Here." He turned it in his hand so that the handle faced her, and she moved one step closer to accept it from him. Before she could pull it away, her colleagues had him. Neilsen cuffed him and shoved the old coot, screaming, over to his vehicle. Jaylynn handed the knife to Alvarez.

"Nice work, Savage," he said. "It's good to see you doing well." He turned and walked toward his car. "See you later when the next drunk call comes in."

Jaylynn stood near the car, feeling elation flood through her body. Slade was right. Maybe she couldn't bully her way through a situation, but she *could* bluff and use bravado with the best of them. She hadn't felt anger or uncertainty, and she hadn't been a bit afraid just now. She had reacted, and it felt so natural that every atom in her body was alert and singing throughout the entire altercation. She felt wonderful.

And then Dez grabbed her sleeve and strong-armed her over to their car. The tall cop opened the passenger side, gesturing for Jaylynn to get in.

"Hey!" the rookie said. "I'm driving."

In a low voice, the big cop growled, "Not anymore you're not. Gimme the keys."

Jaylynn pulled them from her pocket and handed them over, stepping into the car, brow furrowed, and her heart pumping faster now than it had during the confrontation with the drunk.

Dez went around to the other side, and in a whirlwind of motion started the car, threw it into reverse, and squealed away from the curb. Once the car accelerated to the speed limit she said in a stiff voice, "What the hell did you think you were doing?"

Jaylynn turned in her seat and looked at the side of Dez's face, pale in the moonlight. "Let me get this straight. I just subdued a drunk, and you're mad about it?"

"No," she said in tense but measured tones, "you just put yourself at risk."

"Oh, come on! The three of you would have shot that man to death if he'd made the tiniest move. I've never felt so safe in my life."

"I'm the senior officer. You take orders from me. You don't tell a crazy drunk you're in charge unless you are."

Jaylynn knew she should feel cowed and put in her place, but she didn't. Instead, a streak of stubbornness rose up in her. "I *was* in charge. At that particular moment, I was in charge, and it was appropriate. We four worked as a team. I never lost sight of him or any of you, and I never compromised anybody's position, much less my own. It was by the book." She twisted in her seat to face forward and crossed her arms tightly over her chest.

Dez didn't respond at first. When she did finally speak up, she said, "You're in training, Savage. There's still a lot you don't know."

"You're the Field Training Officer, but respectfully, I beg to differ. How exactly do I get any training if all I do is hang back and watch *you* handle all the calls? How do I gain your trust if I never show you I'm trustworthy?" When she got no response to that, she fired her last parting shot. "Fine. Go ahead and put it in your report to the Lieutenant, and I'll deal with it with him." She turned away and looked out the window.

Dez lapsed into silence, which was broken only by yet another dispatch for—what else—a fight at a bar. At that call and the remaining few for the night, Jaylynn hung back and let Dez handle everything, taking direction as it came, and following the instructions precisely.

When they returned to the station at the end of Tour III, she couldn't wait to get out of her uniform and go home, but before she could sign out and hit the stairs, Lt. Malcolm came around the corner.

"Hey, Savage," he said. "I hear you did a nice job tonight with some drunken pirate."

She glanced over her shoulder at the glowering form behind her. "How'd you hear that, sir?"

"Alvarez gave you high praise." He clapped her on the back. "Good job to both of you," he said, including Dez in his smile. "Keep up the good work." He started on down the hall then tossed over his shoulder, "Happy New Year, ladies."

"Happy New Year to you, too, sir." Jaylynn couldn't help herself. She turned and gazed pointedly at her FTO, only to find the blue eyes gentle and thoughtful. She cleared her throat, but she couldn't think of a thing to say, so she stepped past the big cop and headed for the stairs.

Dez took a moment to sign out, stopping to think in the hallway before descending slowly down the steps. She hated to admit it, but maybe the rookie had been right tonight. If Jaylynn were Ryan and the whole thing had gone down the same exact way, wouldn't she have congratulated him for his quick thinking? *Hmmm...so why was it any different with the rookie?* One hand on the stair railing, she paused on the last step and thought back to the night's scene. She closed her eyes and remembered the crisp breeze in her hair, sensed the eyes of the two men standing at the tavern door. Knees bent, heart beating madly, she sighted down her arm, over the barrel of her gun, keeping the laughing, hazel eyes in her line of vision.

Fear. She had been afraid. The man waved the shimmering knife, and he was going to use it on Jaylynn. Some badly dressed loser drunk, stinking of booze and out of his mind, threatened her partner. From somewhere, deep in the far recesses of her memory, a vision of fire, blood, and pain leapt out at her. *Not again. I can't lose a partner again, especially not this one.*

A sudden, intense pain clutched at her chest, and for a moment she thought she might cry. Dez opened her eyes and shook her head vigorously. She decided she must be even more fatigued than usual. Taking the last step down, she walked toward the locker room. *This must be about Ryan more than anything. I feel she is under my protection—sort of like I was under his protection and he was under mine.* She reached for the locker room door only to have it pull open away from her.

"Uh—hi," Jaylynn said. "Sorry." She opened the door wider and stepped back to allow the bigger woman to pass. She had already changed into jeans and was wearing a huge, dark brown down coat. She held a pair of brown mittens in one hand.

"Hey, can we talk?" Dez asked.

Jaylynn shrugged and waited for the taller woman to pass. Then she let go of the door and followed her over to the lockers. Dez removed her gun belt and hung it in her locker, then straddled the bench and looked up. She fell into searching hazel eyes and felt her stomach drop right out from under her. Looking away, she discovered she was glad to be sitting down because she didn't understand why her legs suddenly felt shaky. A feeling of déjà vu struck her, and from out of nowhere a thought popped into her head: *she's the one.*

The tall cop pinched her eyes shut and shivered, gooseflesh rising on her arms. For the briefest moment, she felt sick to her stomach, but it passed and she looked back up at the younger woman. Taking a deep breath, she cleared her throat and tried to focus on a spot right over the rookie's left shoulder. In a low, quiet voice she said, "Listen, Jaylynn. I was too hard on you tonight. I questioned your judgment, and I shouldn't have. You caught me totally by surprise. I—I was wrong."

Jaylynn had a hard time keeping her jaw from dropping open in amazement. The great Desiree Reilly was apologizing. The rookie was so stunned she blurted out the first thing that came to mind. "You pulled rank on me."

Dez winced a little and looked away. She nodded her head twice then returned her gaze to the young woman standing above her. "You noticed that, huh." It was a statement, not a question. She nodded once more. "I'm not saying I won't do it again, but I'll try not to unless it looks like an emergency, okay?"

"I think you should let me drive for the rest of the month."

Dez found a giggle pushing its way up from her diaphragm, but she stifled it. Holding back a smile, she said, "How about just tomorrow night?"

"Oughta be for at least a month."

"Don't push your luck." With a twinkle in her eye, Dez said, "How about for the rest of the week?"

In her best Seven of Nine voice, the rookie said, "That would be acceptable."

Dez rose from the bench and reached out to poke the smaller woman in the stomach with her knuckles. "You haven't been wearing a bulletproof vest, Jaylynn."

"No," she hesitated. "I haven't gone to buy it yet."

"You've got the department voucher though, right?" When the rookie nodded, Dez went on. "You really should wear one. They're a big help in an attack. I'd have been less concerned out on the street tonight if you'd had one on. Besides, they're good protection in car crashes."

Their eyes met, and Jaylynn smiled. "I'll take that as a challenge. I'm a perfectly good driver."

"I'm sure you are."

Jaylynn turned to leave, but Dez's voice stopped her. "By the way, Jay, thanks for the CD last week. That was nice of you."

Jaylynn was flustered for a moment before she realized what the big cop was referring to. "Oh, you're welcome. Hope you liked it."

"Yup." She turned back to her locker to finish changing, leaving Jaylynn to wander out of the locker room with a surprised but pleased look on her face.

Chapter
7

New Year's Day found the two cops fatigued and bored. In contrast to the previous night, all was quiet. There weren't even any good parties to bust up. When a call came at nine p.m. reporting a suspected shoplifter at work in the Target store, Jaylynn floored it and zoomed up to Hamline. She pulled into the parking lot and parked the car near the front entrance. As she stepped out of the cruiser, she heard a shout.

Dez reacted exactly as Jaylynn did. They both focused on the man just outside the glass sliding door who was shouting, "Stop! Thief! It's him." He pointed. A slender Asian man cut across the parking lot and headed for the street.

Jaylynn slammed the door shut and was off like a shot. Legs and arms pumping, she felt the adrenaline surge and hurdled the pile of snow in the parking strip. Her feet came down solid in the street, and she zeroed in on the fleeing man who was heading around the back of a large office building across the street. To her right and slightly behind, she heard Dez's breath. "I'm left," the rookie shouted, and peeled off around the front of the building, while Dez went in hot pursuit around the back.

Jaylynn poured on the speed and passed the front of the office building just as the man came around the side followed by the tall cop. Seeing the rookie, he veered away and headed down a grassy embankment toward the freeway. Jaylynn scampered down behind him, skirting a pile of snow and feeling warmed up and ready to fly. Now she turned on the speed and narrowed the distance. She knew Dez was close behind, and trusted that if she herself fell trying to get the guy, then her partner would clean up after her.

The rookie grabbed the sleeve of the man's jacket and stuck a leg in front of his shin as she passed him. He tripped and fell hard, rolling once onto his side. He was panting as she turned around and jogged back, and then Dez was cuffing him and pulling him up. The tall cop patted down the wheezing man and removed a Walkman, four unwrapped CD's, and a pack of batteries from his pockets. She handed the merchandise to Jaylynn and jerked the man's arm. "Let's go, buddy boy."

Jaylynn fell into stride with Dez, noticing that her partner was much more out of breath than she. The big woman looked down at her and said, "You never mentioned you were a sprinter."

"Oh. Yeah. Why?"

"That was a good run, Jay."

"Why, thank you."

Dez shook her head and turned away, dragging the young man along.

That was the most excitement that cropped up for the evening. The rest of the shift dragged along as they cruised darkened streets and listened to the radio. Jaylynn wasn't sorry when midnight rolled around. She was more than ready to go home and catch some sleep.

The rookie didn't even bother to change clothes. In a hurry, she tossed her patrol jacket and hat in the locker, grabbed up her down coat, and bid Dez goodnight, heading out to the parking lot to wait for Tim. She passed through the rear police entrance, followed by Dwayne Neilsen. "Hey, Neilsen," she said, then paid him no attention as she scanned the parking lot for the beat-up Toyota. So she was startled when Neilsen took hold of her arm and forced her another ten steps and around the corner into a darker area by the side of the building.

Still clutching her arm he said, "I suppose you think you're pretty cute after last night with that drunk."

"What? Take your hands off me."

He tightened his grip and raised his right hand to shake his finger in her face. "You bitch. If you think I'm gonna stand aside and let you make me look bad..."

"I'm warning you," she spat out, "let go of me or I'll report this. I've put up with your shit long enough, and now I'm—"

"You'll what?" he said, venom in his voice. "Ha. I'm bigger than you and—"

A white hand appeared from out of nowhere and removed the finger shaking in Jaylynn's face. A deep low voice she recognized said, "And I'm as big as you, asshole. Why don't you pick on someone your own size?" The grip on Jaylynn's arm loosened. Surprised, she watched as the snarling man whirled and tried to free his hand. He kicked out at the tall woman. She neatly sidestepped, then nailed him in the forehead with an elbow. He dropped to his knees, and she twisted the hand she held in a death grip until it was behind his back and she stood behind and over him.

Grabbing him under the chin with her free hand, she tilted his head up so that she could see into his face. "Can you hear me?" she asked.

He closed his eyes. "Yes."

"This is gonna be reported. That's a done deal. How I report it is up to you." She jerked his neck and jammed her knee into his upper back, still kinking his arm upward so hard that he grunted with pain. "Savage," she said. "Stand in front of him and say your piece."

Jaylynn didn't know exactly what Dez meant, but she moved around in front of Neilsen and looked down at his flushed face, the veins on his forehead standing out in the dim light. "You've been nothing but rude and cruel. And for no good reason," the rookie said. "I put up with the teasing, but this has gone too far. You touch me again or make trouble for me, and I'll make sure you get fired."

He choked out, "What are you gonna do now?"

Dez abruptly let go of him and he fell face forward. He caught himself on his hands and rose to his feet, a look of hatred on his face. He towered over Jaylynn, but he was only about two inches taller than Dez. The big cop got right up in his face and stared him down. "I'll tell you what we're doing now. We're all going back into the station and you're gonna tell the Lieutenant you lost your temper with Savage, and then you'll apologize. It's that, or I'm writing you up."

"You hit *me*," he said. "I think I'm the one who should—" A withering glance from the dark woman shut him up. He brushed off the knees of his pants and ran a hand through his short hair, but he followed them in and did what Dez demanded, though not with much conviction. Jaylynn thought Lt. Malcolm was pretty savvy though, so she wasn't surprised when he asked Dez to stay behind as the two rookies filed out of the room.

On the way out the door, Jaylynn asked, "Dez, before you leave, may I have a word with you?"

The tall cop nodded. "I'll look for ya in a few minutes."

Jaylynn headed downstairs to the locker room, several strides behind a very angry Neilsen. She figured she had a couple of minutes, so she stripped out of her uniform and tossed the blue shirt and pants in the department laundry. Pulling on jeans, a t-shirt, and a sweater, she thought about what had happened. One thing she knew for sure, she'd never want to be the object of the tall woman's ire. She was one ferocious fighter when she got mad.

The rookie didn't turn around right away when she heard the locker room door open, but when she did, she found her protector standing cross-armed and lounging against a locker in a posture of arrogant confidence. Her black hair glinted under the fluorescent lights and her eyes shone bright blue.

Jaylynn smiled at her and said, "I don't mean to sound ungrateful, but I was handling things just fine out there."

This obviously surprised the other cop. She straightened up and frowned. "He was attacking you, Jay."

"He was doing the same bullshit he's been doing since day one at the Academy. I had it under control. He just needed to whine."

In a menacing voice, Dez said, "He was threatening you. It looked like he was going to hit you."

"I don't think so."

"Well, he'll think twice about it in the future now."

"Yeah, if you didn't make it *worse* for me."

"You won't be seeing all that much of him. Lt. Malcolm is assigning him to the other sector from here on out."

"Oh great! Now he'll really be plotting to show me up."

In a dangerous voice, Dez said, "He better not or I'm bouncing his ass outta here."

"Don't you see, Dez? He's just an insecure jerk. But he really does want to be a cop, and he might turn out to be a good one—who knows?"

"Character is everything in police work. He doesn't have any. Men who hit women don't deserve to be cops."

Jaylynn grinned. "What about women who hit men?"

"Nobody should hit anybody."

"Spoken by the Perennial Pounder who just left a goose-egg the size of St. Paul on the guy's forehead."

Dez crossed her arms and gave Jaylynn a serious look. "You think I overdid it, huh?"

"Just slightly. Look, I'm not ungrateful. In fact, for a moment, I really enjoyed seeing him on his knees, unseemly as it is for me to admit it."

Dez snickered. "You couldn't have enjoyed it half as much as I did. I wanted to beat the crap out of him."

"Thank you for not doing that."

"You're welcome."

"I better go now. I'm sure Tim is wondering where I am."

"I'll go with you just to make sure Neilsen's not hovering in wait for you."

"No, no!" Jaylynn stomped her foot. "It's *fine*, Dez. I'll see you tomorrow." The rookie turned and marched out of the locker room. Dez watched her go, a thoughtful look on her face, and then sighed. She decided she still had a little too much energy, so she went back to her locker and unlocked it. *Time to do some sprints*, she thought. If she was going to keep up with a certain blonde-haired spitfire, then she had better put some effort into it. She pulled out her running clothes and changed.

Chapter
8

Dez worked out alone in the weight room. At midnight on a Friday night after Tour III ended, she usually had the place to herself, which was just how she liked it. After hoisting three 45-pound weights on each side of the leg press, she got down into the contraption. This exercise always made her feel like a turtle on its back. She took three deep breaths, forced her legs to press the weight up, and released the safety. Coupled with the 75-pound weight of the press carriage, she was lifting 345 pounds. She didn't stop at ten reps but kept straining, pressing the load up and down, until she could go no further without her lungs and legs exploding. She let the weight down with a clang and felt the misery of the burn fading away, then started another set, and another.

She punished herself. Every day. Once she had felt joy in working out. Now she worked her muscles to the point of exhaustion, hoping each night would find her so physically tired that sleep would attack her in the same way she attacked the weights in the gym. Each night she was disappointed.

It had been seven months since the death of her partner in June. She still had difficulty thinking of him as dead. Gone. Never to ride with her again. His absence was a vicious rip in the fabric of her everyday life. She hadn't been a cop long when he became her one true friend on the force, the only guy not the slightest bit upset that she was a better marksman, a black belt in karate, and more physically imposing than many of the men in blue. Though four inches shorter than she, Ryan had been five feet, eight inches of solid muscle. He wore health and good humor like a mantle about him, and she loved partnering with him in the two-man cars. She was just as surprised as most of their peers when he asked her, the quiet and dour rookie, to try riding with him after his partner retired. Later, when she asked him why, he said he'd had a hunch that he'd enjoy working with her more than with the male rookies who were cocky, wisecracking showoffs. "I like riding with women," he'd said. "A lot of the guys are fun, but after a while, I get tired of them talking sports and lying about sex all the time. Women bring up interesting subjects. It makes the shift go by quicker."

But now he was dead at age 38, leaving behind a stunningly beautiful wife and two grade school aged kids, all of whom looked to Dez with such sadness and anguish that she could hardly bear to visit. Soon, she should go see Julie again, play with the little boy, Jeremy, who was also her godson. She would talk to the second grader, Jill, about horses and new songs on the radio—but the thought of it made her nearly sick with the weight of grief and responsibility. She'd been through this before at age nine when her police officer father died, but she found this was different. Somehow back then she had been better able to insulate herself from the pain. Strange that now she was older, she didn't seem to have the fortitude she'd had as a child.

Dez extricated herself from the leg press and returned the weights to the rack, moving on to the calf raise machine.

It was Ryan who'd gotten her interested in weightlifting in the first place, the one area at which he could beat her—at least for a while. He spent many years bodybuilding and competing in local shows, and he told her she had a great physique. "Totally sculptable—you could win shows!" was what he'd said, embarrassing her to no end. She resisted at first, but he talked her into working out with him after their shifts, and she never regretted it. Most days after swing shift ended, they met in the gym to lift together. Whether they'd had a boring, frustrating, or exciting evening, hitting the weights at the end of the night was a good way to relax.

Not anymore.

Dez finished the calf routine and decided to call it quits. She flexed her forearm. It felt stronger—still stiff—but not painful. It would be a while longer before she regained the muscle she'd lost while in the cast, but she was pleased with the progress she'd made since August.

She toweled off as best she could, stepped into sweat bottoms, then pulled a jacket over her baggy sweatshirt. Grabbing her sports bag she cut down the hall and past the Roll Call Room. She was surprised to see Jaylynn sitting there, feet up on the desk, reading a magazine. She almost passed by, but as she neared the doorway, the younger woman looked up.

"Oh hi, Dez," Jaylynn said.

Dez paused and looked at her watch. They had been off shift

for an hour and a half. "What're you still doing here?"

"Tim's tied up. I'm waiting for him to call." She gestured to her cell phone. "I thought he'd be here by now. If I'd known it would take him an *hour*, I'd have taken a cab home."

Dez hesitated a moment, then said, "C'mon, I'll drop you off on my way."

"But if he calls..."

"You'll have the cell phone with you. Just make sure you leave it on."

"Oh, right. Okay." She bent down and picked up a backpack, put on her down coat, and followed Dez out to the parking lot.

As usual, Jaylynn shivered when the cold Minnesota air hit her. "Aren't you cold?"

Dez hit the keyless entry for her Ford 150 pickup, and the interior lights popped on. "Not really. I'm so overheated from the workout, it'll be half an hour before I cool down."

"Must be nice." Jaylynn stepped up into the pickup. "This is such a cool truck. Must be real new."

"Yup." It had been Ryan's, a new purchase he had delighted in. He had special ordered it with an oversized storage unit in the bed, a bench seat in the front, and the extra cab space so all four members of his family could ride with him anywhere. She bought it from Julie a few months earlier when she had learned Ryan's widow was selling it. Sometimes when she wasn't thinking of her old partner, she thought she could smell a faint whiff of his aftershave wafting through the truck. For that reason alone she was glad she'd bought the vehicle.

The rookie admired the interior, running the palm of her hand over the sturdy texture of the dark red seats. "Bet it's great to have the extra cab. You've got lots of room for storage or extra riders."

"Mmhmm."

Under the parking lot lights, Jaylynn could see both the interior and exterior were a dark cranberry red, a deep, rich shade which matched Dez's sweatshirt.

Dez drove directly to Jaylynn's house and pulled up in front. Every light in the house was on.

"Having a party?" Dez asked.

"No. Ever since the—the attack, Sara has been leaving all the lights on until Tim or I get home. She's stopped parking out back— see, her car's out here." Jaylynn sighed. "She's still having a very tough time, mostly nightmares and panic attacks. Actually, we're worried about her."

"What's she gonna do if you and Tim move?"

Jaylynn looked perplexed. "We're not moving, not any time soon anyway." She reached to open the door. "Want to come in?"

"Nah. It's nearly two. I better get home."

"Okay, see you tomorrow." The rookie got out, shut the door, and trudged up the front walk feeling those icy blue eyes at her back. When she got the front door open, she looked back, and sure enough, the Ford truck hadn't moved an inch. She gave a brief wave and disappeared into the house.

****

January in Minnesota is a cold, unforgiving time, with dangerous wind chills and low temperatures. No squad car could keep out the cold enough for Jaylynn. The rookie didn't think it was any mistake that the North Pole explorer, Anne Bancroft, made her home in Minnesota. The rookie thought it might be possible that she herself could survive in the sub-zero North Pole weather after five years' practice in St. Paul. She hugged her arms tighter around the front of her and retracted her neck deeper into the turtleneck she wore under her vest and shirt.

All night long her throat had felt scratchy and she knew she was fighting a cold, which she hoped to avoid. She'd taken extra doses of vitamin C and worn an additional layer of cotton long underwear over the silk long underwear she usually dressed in. Once shift was over, she planned to hunker down in front of the TV, swathed in blankets, and eat hot chicken soup and crackers. Then she wanted to sleep for about twelve hours. In the meantime, it was just a matter of staying warm and dry. She looked over at Dez, marveling that the bigger woman never ever seemed to get cold. *I need to find out how she does that,* thought Jaylynn. *Gotta get the recipe for whatever heat elixir she's using.* She smiled to herself and turned her attention toward scanning the snowy streets around them.

Dez pulled up in front of a squalid-looking takeout restaurant called *The Cutting Board.* Despite the fact that it was nearly ten p.m., Jaylynn could see a horde of customers through the giant plate glass surrounding three sides of the building. Sitting near the front windows were four empty booths sporting bright yellow vinyl that was cracked and split. The rest of the place was furnished in various shades of orange, gold, and olive. The whole effect was one of near-neon proportions. Jaylynn reached over and whacked the tall cop on the upper arm. "Kind of a 60's throwback here, huh?"

"Yeah, but it's good," Dez said in a cranky voice.

They got out, and Jaylynn shivered in the winter wind as she walked swiftly toward the restaurant. She hastened to push open a heavy brown door and join the crowd milling around inside. Moist warm air circulated, soothing her throat for the first time all day.

The aroma wafting from the kitchen was heavenly, a spicy smell of meats and sauces and hot oil. A black man with wild gray hair like Don King's stood behind the counter shouting out orders and ringing things up. Through a window-sized aperture behind the cash register, Jaylynn saw at least four people hustling around in the kitchen. Periodically somebody hollered "Order up!" and an arm extended through the opening with a shopping bag stapled shut at the top.

"What do you want?" Dez asked.

"What have they got? Where's the menu?"

"They make anything: deli sandwiches, barbecue, fried chicken, everything with side stuff. Actually, you never know exactly what you'll get. It changes every day. If you fight your way up to the front you can see the list on the counter of what's served for today."

"What do you usually order?" She slipped off thermal mittens, and pulled a crinkled five-dollar bill out of her pocket.

Just then a deep baritone voice resonated, "Well, good evening, Officer Reilly. Your usual?" Heads turned, and the crowd parted from the cash register all the way back to the officers.

"Yes, Otis. And something for my partner here." She looked at Jaylynn, one eyebrow arched.

It seemed as though everyone in the restaurant was staring at her and Jaylynn felt a blush rise warming her face all the way to the roots of her blonde hair. But she smiled and said, "Fried chicken. I'll try that."

Otis said, "White or dark?"

"Little of both please."

"Coming right up." In a rich, booming voice, he blasted out the order over his shoulder toward the kitchen. Jaylynn handed over the crumpled bill, and Dez strode forward through the gulf of customers and handed it to Otis along with two other bills.

"No need, Officer. Always on the house for you," he said with a smile on his face.

She smiled back at him. "You'll go broke at that rate. Your kid needs it for college, I'm sure."

"In that case..." The cash register went ching-ching, and he shoved the bills in and slammed the drawer shut. Dez turned and strolled back toward the booths, and Jaylynn followed her. No sooner had they gotten settled than a man in a white apron scuttled out and delivered two over-sized paper sacks. Dez lifted one bag, hefted its weight and then passed it over to Jaylynn. She ripped the staples apart on the other smaller bag, then tore it open and took out one bundle wrapped in wax paper. Meanwhile, Jaylynn began pulling out packages and opening them. She had a chicken breast, a thigh, coleslaw, a Styrofoam cup of mashed potatoes with melted butter, two pieces of Texas toast, and some plank-cut fries. Dez was half done with her sandwich before Jaylynn even got all the items unwrapped.

"What have you got there?" Jaylynn asked.

"Sandwich," Dez said with her mouth full.

"I can see that. What kind?"

"Third-pound turkey, lettuce, tomato on wheat, no spread."

"Blech! Least they could have done is give you some mayo. You want some of my stuff here? I know I can't eat all of this."

"Didn't want mayo. I like it just like this."

"You and your bark and twig bread." Jaylynn turned her nose up and shook her head a bit, and then ripped into her chicken. "Oh, this is great!" She closed her eyes. "Nice flavor." Chew, chew. "Really moist." She opened her eyes and took another big bite. "This is delish."

Dez arched an eyebrow. "You can spare me the commentary. I've had it before, so I know how good it is."

"Then how can you resist it? It's just so—so—heavenly. And these fries!" She popped a plank in her mouth, chewed furiously, then gripped the plastic fork and took a taste of the mashed potatoes. "Wow! These aren't fake spuds. And that's real butter, too."

She dug into the potatoes as Dez watched her with amusement.

"Are you aware that you eat food like most people have sex?"

"Food is the next best thing to making love," Jaylynn said, her mouth full. She looked up at Dez. "Don't you think so?" She gave the veteran cop her regular intent look and stopped fussing with the chicken to hear her answer.

Dez laughed nervously. "I never thought of it that way. Maybe." She rolled up the wax paper and stuffed it in the paper bag, then crunched that up into a tight ball. Jaylynn went back to scooping mashed potatoes out with a plastic spoon while Dez sat patiently and stared out the window into the dark night.

****

On Martin Luther King Day the skies were dark and cloudy, but it never snowed throughout any of the festivities that took place across the precinct. Despite the holiday, the police were out in full force making their presence known so that no hate crimes or crimes of stupidity were committed. Four years earlier on MLK Day, Dez remembered when pranksters had burned a cross on a black family's lawn. It took 72 hours to run down the jokers, and for three days a very nice family of five existed in terror, worried that the KKK or some other white supremacy group had earmarked them. It turned out that the stupid youths who had committed the crime didn't fully understand the significance of the burnt cross—which eased the fear and panic for the family and for the neighborhood.

Unfortunately, family troubles didn't take a holiday, even on MLK Day. They spent almost ninety minutes out of the car taking four children, ages six, five, three, and two, to the juvenile authorities after another unit arrested the mother for driving while under the influence of drugs.

When they got back in the car, Jaylynn said, "God, that's a lot of kids to have at age 20."

Dez said, "I sure wouldn't want four kids under age seven."

"No, that'd be a handful. Just my two little sisters were a stretch for my mom. And I feel like I half raised both of them. I was 14 when Amanda was born and then almost 16 for Erin. After diapers and feeding and babysitting for them, I'm all mothered out. Maybe I'll change later on, but I really don't know. How 'bout you? Ever want kids?"

"Me? Nah. I'm sure not interested in giving birth."

"Me neither. Pain is not my friend."

Dez snorted, "Mine either."

"You ever think about settling down, getting married?"

"Not much. I don't see myself marrying."

"No hot prospects on the horizon for me either. My mother would *love* to rush me to the altar, but it's not happening any time soon." Jaylynn sighed and looked away. *Not unless they make a law where I can marry a woman*, she thought as she winced out a smile.

"What are you smiling about?"

"Nothing. Just considering something." She paused to think. "I grew up all my life wanting to find someone special who'd stick with me through thick and thin. Somebody I wouldn't need to be married to because the commitment would be obvious to anyone who looked."

"And?"

"I guess I've never found anyone that faithful." She thought of Sandi in high school with whom she'd been madly, hopelessly, and platonically in love. Sandi, who was now married to the best middleweight wrestler on their high school team. Then Dana, her first lover in college who'd gone off and slept with a good-looking drunken basketball player on the women's team—and she hadn't been the slightest bit penitent. And Theresa: she was a whole other story. Theresa didn't want anybody to know about their relationship, not even have the slightest suspicion, and she'd insisted on dating men, "just for appearances." When Jaylynn learned she was sleeping with one of the guys in the other dorm, she'd flipped out, and that was the end of that. Since then, she'd avoided dating, preferring to focus on her studies and hoping she'd find "the real deal" sometime, somewhere.

Dez looked over at the rookie who had suddenly lost her sunny disposition. "There *are* people who are that faithful," Dez said. Not in her own personal experience, but she knew what Ryan and Julie had. And Crystal and Shayna. Luella and her late husband. In her own bizarre way, even her mother had been faithful to Dez's father all these years. Maybe it wasn't healthy, not the way her mother had held off kind and caring suitors, but maybe there was something to be said about being so in love with one person that no one else ever measured up. Could two people really commit to one another so wholly and totally that nothing and no one would ever come between them? Dez thought she herself could. It was other people who were the problem.

Jaylynn said, "I sure as hell hope you're right."

"If it's true and you ever find that," Dez said, "better grab on and hold tight. Somehow I don't think it happens very often."

Jaylynn didn't argue with her.

Chapter
9

Early as usual, Dez sat at a round table for eight. The other thirty or so tables sprinkled around her were not yet occupied, though she could see several of her colleagues out in the foyer. She had chosen a spot in the center but toward the back of the hall, and she had seated herself immediately upon arriving, not trusting her nerves if she were standing out front with her peers.

The Fraternal Order of Police sponsored two major gatherings each year: a barbecue in the summer and a February banquet. Each event was a chance to honor retirees, celebrate family connections, and see the brass let their hair down. This year, however, it would also serve as a eulogy of sorts for Ryan Michaelson. The thought of that caused a block of cold ice to expand in Dez's chest, making her short of breath. She honestly did not know how she would make it through the evening, but she had promised Ryan's wife, Julie, she would be there for Jill and Jeremy. It was her duty, so she sat on the hard chair and waited, trying to remember to breathe and wishing she had worn something cooler than the black wool blend jacket and slacks and long-sleeved silk blouse she had selected.

Officers she ordinarily saw in uniform began to trickle in wearing suits or sports jackets. She nodded at Belton as he, his wife, and their two sons seated themselves at a table nearby. She watched Lt. Malcolm as he spoke respectfully to Commander Paar near the rear door. One of the commander's children, a girl of about four, held onto her father's big white mitt with both of her hands and swung lazily from side to side, her head tossed back and brown hair dangling. She wore a black and white plaid jumper and white leotards with shiny patent leather shoes. Dez remembered wearing exactly the same sort of outfit when she was that age. The sight of the little girl and her dad made her wistful for her own father.

She caught a flash of white hair and blanched upon seeing a tall, regal looking man bearing down on her table. Taking a deep breath, she steeled herself and rose, trying to calm seriously frayed nerves. She met the man's gray eyes with a level gaze. "Hello, Mac," she said.

He came to a stop at her table, his double-breasted gray suit crisp and handsome, the silver buttons shiny in the fluorescent light. Standing before her, hands clasped in front of him, was Xavier Aloysius MacArthur, "Mac" to his friends and fellow officers. Mac had been one of the finest watch commanders the St. Paul Police Department had ever known. He had also been her father's very best friend, and her former mentor. The burden of the history they shared weighed heavily upon her. She wished she could feel pleased to see him, but she did not.

"Dez," he said kindly. "How are you?"

She nodded slowly. "Fine, Mac. Just fine." She didn't know what else to say to him and knew he felt the same toward her. It had been like this between them since she was age 22. He had been so proud of her when she joined the force, had taken her under his wing. He drilled her, offered reams of advice, and gave her assignments no woman usually got. She blossomed under his tutelage. She knew she was his favorite and that it rankled some of her peers, but he was like a father to her and she refused to apologize for it.

And then when she began dating Karin, her mother had, as Colette Reilly said, "spilled the beans." Dez never understood why her mother had found it necessary to tell Mac she was gay, and things had never been the same since. Mac, an old-fashioned Irishman who'd attended twelve years of Catholic school, couldn't reconcile the sexuality issue with the young woman he had very nearly raised as his own after his best friend, Michael Reilly, died. He became formal, proper, withdrawn from her. In some ways the estrangement had been more painful than going through the death of her father when she was younger. She missed her father, that was true; but sometimes she ached to talk to Mac again the way they used to. But it was not to be. Despite the rift, he still had the grace and dignity to always greet her respectfully.

"I've thought about you often lately, Dez," Mac said, fumbling for words. "I remember what it was like to lose your dad..." He paused, looking over the top of her head as though searching for a teleprompter. Tucking his hands in his pants pockets, he said softly, "I'm sorry about Ryan."

The lump in her throat was so large that she didn't know how she did it, but she choked out, "I know, Mac. Thanks."

He stood a moment longer, then removed both hands from his

pockets and patted her gently on the shoulder. "See you around, kid." Turning on his heel, he strode toward Commander Paar, and Dez watched him reach out and shake the other man's hand, then squat down to see eye to eye with the little girl clutching her father's leg. At that point, if Julie and the kids hadn't appeared in the doorway, she would have fled the banquet and never looked back. But before she could escape, Jeremy caught sight of her and wormed his way through the people and past the white-draped tables to launch himself into her arms. Grinning gleefully, he wrapped his little legs around her waist and his arms around her neck. She held the squirmy body, taking in his clean, little boy smell, and feeling an ache in her heart that would not leave.

"Dez," he said, cradling her face in his hands. He stared intently, his eyes twinkling. "You missed Valentine's Day."

"No I didn't, sport. I sent you a present."

"But you didn't see the humongous heart I made for Mom."

"I'll have to come by soon and see it then, huh?" He nodded at her, his face ruddy red and happy. She looked into the bright blue eyes of the kindergartner, eyes so like his father's. She felt the tears well up and willed them to go away. Glancing past Jeremy, she saw Julie and Jill, hand in hand, had arrived at the table, and she saw that Julie was also struggling with tears. Setting Jeremy down, she forced a smile and reached a hand over to cup Jill's pale face. "Hey, Jill. How are ya?"

"I'm good, Dez," she said in a solemn voice. She looked up at her mother, a worried expression on her face, and the tall cop searched out Julie's eyes. The slender woman let go of her daughter's hand and enfolded Dez in a fierce hug.

"Hey," Dez said gruffly, "we'll get through this, okay?"

Julie nodded against Dez's shoulder. In a choked voice, she said, "I'm glad you came. I didn't want to either, but the kids...the kids need to stay connected." She stepped back and smiled, blinking back tears. "All right. Let's sit." She gestured toward the table.

Just then, Dez saw Julie's eyes widen with pleasure, and the big cop shifted to look over her shoulder. She was engulfed in a big hug from behind and knew instantly from the smell of Timberline aftershave that it was Cowboy. Wrenching herself around, she fake-pummeled the huge man with a series of punches to the mid section. She said, "Charles." Left punch. "Winslow." Right jab. "Culpepper." Left hook. "The Third." She started a right roundhouse, but he caught her fist in his hand.

"Desiree Marie Reilly, The First, I could crush you in an instant," he said, a huge grin splitting his face.

"You just try it, mister," she retorted. It was like a shot of adrenaline to see his happy face, and her spirits lifted even further when she spotted Crystal and Shayna heading her way. She pulled her fist from Cowboy's warm hand and watched Crystal swagger toward them, dressed in a brown pantsuit and multi-colored blouse.

"Hey, *chica*," Crystal said. "What's up?"

"Nothing. You're gonna sit with us, right?"

"For sure," Shayna said. "I don't know most of the rest of these clowns." She cast a skeptical look around the banquet hall, frowning as she scanned the crowd. She turned her attention back to the group and reached a hand out to Julie. "Hi there," she said. Julie returned the greeting warmly and then helped Jeremy get his chair pushed in.

Dez always thought Shayna looked like a plump and slightly cynical Oprah Winfrey. She stood about two inches taller than Crystal. Her dark hair was a mass of tight curls and she usually wore some sort of huge dangly earrings. Tonight she sported a pair of shiny golden disks, nearly three inches in diameter. In a serious voice, Dez said, "Hmmm...pretty," and reached over to touch one.

In a dry voice, Shayna said, "Crystal, honey, your pal here is fingering the merchandise again."

Cowboy hooted, and Dez's face flushed as she attempted to defend herself. "I was just checking to see if those teacup saucers were as heavy as they look."

"Light as a feather, hon." Shayna gave Dez a droll look and then said, "So, is it a rubber chicken dinner or what?"

Dez shrugged. "I don't know, but I'm not eating it. Whatever it is, you can have mine."

"Ooh girl—then you can finger my earrings any time!"

Crystal reached over and took hold of her partner's forearm. "Quit flirting," the Latina said, her eyes shining with amusement. She looked over at Dez and said, "Can't take her out anywhere anymore."

Dez blushed some more as the group of them settled in at the table. Shayna had a way of keeping Dez totally off balance, and though it could be irritating at times to the big cop, tonight she was happy for it. She took her seat again between the kids, with Julie on the other side of Jill, and Crystal, Shayna, and Cowboy rounding out the group of seven. The room had filled up, and Dez thought it was awfully warm. She reached up to slip her jacket off and sensed someone over her right shoulder. Turning, she heard him clear his throat.

"Uh—hi Dez," came a tentative voice.

"Oster," she said, surprised. He stood awkwardly behind her, wearing tan slacks, a crisp white shirt, and a tweed sport coat.

"Would you mind if I joined you?" Nervously, he gestured

toward the empty seat between Jeremy and Cowboy.

Cowboy rose and gestured to the seat next to him. "Jump right in." Towering over the table, he stuck his hand out for the shorter man to shake. "I'm Culpepper—better known as Cowboy. Good to meet you, Oster. Jeremy and I were going to need some reinforcements what with all these pushy women, so we're glad you're here." He looked around the table with a smirk on his handsome face as Julie, Shayna, and Crystal all protested loudly.

Oster let go of the big man's hand and said, "Call me Mitch."

Cowboy nodded as he folded himself back down into his seat.

Dez pulled Jeremy's chair right up next to her own and reached over to pull the eighth chair out. "Here ya go, Mitch. I thought most of you rookies wouldn't attend tonight."

"Why?" Mitch asked, his serious brown eyes looking at her quizzically.

"Oh, I don't know. Savage and Mahoney were on duty tonight. Figured you would be, too."

"Nope," he said. "Thursdays and Fridays are my nights off."

She nodded, and then her attention turned to a small hand that tugged on the sleeve of her blouse. She leaned down so Jeremy could tell her about the rabbit he and his classmates were raising at school. Oster was on his own to present himself around, though he already knew Crystal. She heard Crystal introduce the rookie to Julie and Shayna, and then the brass was getting settled up at the head table. The Chief tapped the microphone and the noise in the room began trailing off. The evening program began with the Chief's remarks. Dez whispered to Jeremy that it was time to listen, and the boy nodded, slipping his cool hand into her larger one and leaning against her side. And that's the way she got through the evening: hanging on for dear life to a six-year-old.

****

Saturday night, a morose Dez got in the car, and Jaylynn could tell something was wrong. She tried to give the other woman an opportunity to talk about it, but every conversation she started was met with noncommittal grumbles or curt answers. Jaylynn said, "How was the banquet last night?"

"Fine," was all Dez said. Jaylynn gave up and sat quietly watching the afternoon light fade away into early evening. They patrolled for another two hours and then handled two citizen complaints before getting a more urgent call from dispatch.

"Shit," Dez said.

"What?" Jaylynn wanted to kick herself for not paying close enough attention to the dispatcher. She hadn't caught the details, though she had heard the address.

Dez hit the lights, sped up, and took the next corner at high speed. "It's a rape call. I hate these calls the most. Put on your latex gloves, Jay. You might need 'em." She pulled out a plastic package from her own breast pocket and set it on the seat beside her.

They arrived at an apartment four-plex and hustled up the walk to the security door. In the distance, a siren wailed.

"Ring the bell for number two," Dez said. "Let's get in there before the paramedics arrive and see if we can get any information now—maybe get a lead. Otherwise, we'll have to work around the rape counselor at the hospital, and that'll slow us down."

The buzzer sounded and Jaylynn pushed the door open. She led the way down the hall as Dez donned her latex gloves. They hurried to the second door on the left, which they found was ajar. She banged on the doorframe loudly. "Police."

A tiny whimper from inside said, "Come in."

Jaylynn pushed the door open and eased her way in, her heart beating wildly. What she found shocked her. Facing her, a very young woman, maybe only 17 or 18, knelt between a ratty sofa and a coffee table clutching a phone receiver. She was dressed in a skirt and a ripped blouse with blood spattered on the front. Her hair was a mess and there was blood streaming from a cut along her eyebrow. Tears poured down her face and mixed with the blood. She set the receiver back on the cradle with a shaky hand.

Jaylynn drew near and knelt on one knee beside her, putting a gloved hand on the girl's shoulder. "Hey," she said. "I'm Officer Savage. You're safe now. Can you tell us what happened?"

The girl glommed onto her leg and began sobbing wildly. "He raped me. He hurt me and hit me—he just kept hitting me!"

Dez's low voice sounded from above Jaylynn's head. "Who did this to you?"

"I don't—I don't know his—" she hiccuped, "I don't know his name. He lives in the up—upstairs apartment."

Jaylynn said, "What's your name, honey?"

"Kristy South."

"And how old are you?"

"Sixteen."

"Where are your parents?"

"They're at work," the girl sobbed.

Jaylynn patted her back. "Shhh, it's okay." She felt tears come to her eyes and she couldn't will them away.

"What does the man look like?" Dez interrupted, as she made notes in her notebook.

The question brought on a fresh wave of tears.

"Hey, it's all right," Jaylynn said. "What do you remember about the guy?" The girl burrowed closer to her and pressed her face into Jaylynn's chest, making a mess of her uniform front. Jaylynn paid no attention. "Tell us what he looks like and we'll make him pay for doing this to you."

"Brown hair, brown eyes, I think."

"How old?" Dez asked.

"I don't know...old like my parents."

"Good. That's helpful. How tall was he?"

"Taller than me, but not much."

"How tall are you?"

"Five-five."

"His race?"

"White," the girl said.

"What was he wearing?"

The girl looked up over Jaylynn's shoulder and told Dez, "Jeans. Black shirt. And—and—Nikes, red and white ones. He had a brown bomber jacket." She started to get up. "I need a tissue."

Jaylynn got to her feet still holding onto the girl's arm. "You sure you're okay, Kristy? Here, you sit there on the couch. I'll get you a tissue."

On shaky legs the girl sat back on the rumpled sofa. Jaylynn crossed the room and grabbed a box of tissues off the bookshelf and brought them back. She took two herself and placed the box on the coffee table in front of the girl. She wiped her own eyes and blew her nose, then squatted back down in front of the girl and put a hand on her knee.

Dez hit her shoulder mic and reported in to dispatch, giving a description of the assailant and requesting backup.

The phone on the coffee table rang and the girl leaned forward to pick it up, then pressed a number and hung up. They heard a far-off buzz and then the clumping noises of the paramedics coming down the hall.

Dez asked quickly, "Kristy, how many apartments are there upstairs?"

"Two. Mrs. Leopold lives in one and the man just moved in the other."

"Which apartment does Mrs. Leopold live in?"

"The one with the bird on the door."

A knock sounded and Dez walked back to usher in the EMT's.

Jaylynn said, "The paramedics are going to take good care of you. You'll be safe with them, hon. I need to call your parents. How can we reach them?"

"I already called my mom," the girl wailed in a high voice.

"She's coming home from work now." She grabbed more tissues from the box and pressed them to her eyes. Jaylynn stood up, tears on her face, and stepped away to allow the EMT's access to the girl. Just then, she heard a breathless voice down the hall calling out, "Kristy! Kristy!"

Dez stopped her at the door.

"I'm her mother—I need to see her," the woman said wildly.

"Ma'am, she's going to be okay."

"Where is she?"

"Listen," Dez said, in a low, authoritative voice. She made the woman look her in the eye. "You need to be calm now. You need to be strong for her. She's scared, but she's okay."

The woman covered her mouth with her hand looking for all the world like she was going to burst into hysterics.

Dez said, "You can do this, can't you? Because the paramedics are gonna take her to the hospital to be checked. They'll probably let you ride in the ambulance with her if you're *very* calm."

Mutely, the woman nodded, her face pale and solemn.

"If you'll wait here just a moment, ma'am, they'll bring her out in a minute." Once the EMT's wheeled the girl out into the hall, Dez wrote a last note and then slipped her notebook into her pocket.

Jaylynn stepped out the apartment doorway, following the medics.

"Savage," Dez hissed under her breath.

With a start, Jaylynn looked away from the scene in the hallway to see that Dez was livid with anger.

"Quit crying," Dez whispered sternly. "Wipe away the tears."

A shudder of revulsion ran through Jaylynn, but she complied, swiping her face hastily along the sleeve of her blue shirt. The paramedics prepared to move the girl out to the ambulance followed by the mother who was making a valiant attempt at calmness.

Once the mother, daughter, and paramedics were through the glass front door, the big cop grabbed Jaylynn's arm. Bending down close to the rookie, she said angrily in a muted voice, "Cops don't cry. The public expects us to be sympathetic, to be understanding, but we goddamn don't cry. You understand? No tears on duty."

Before Jaylynn could respond, the backup squad arrived, lights flashing, and pulled up on the parking strip. In the flashing lights outside, Jaylynn saw two cops get out of the vehicle, but she wasn't sure who they were. Dez went out the front door and down the stairs to confer with them briefly, and all three turned and moved up the steps toward Jaylynn. She opened the door for them. Without a glance at the rookie, the tall cop strode through followed by the two men, one of whom headed into the apartment. The second officer and Dez hit the staircase near the front door, taking steps two at a time. Jaylynn trailed behind in shock, feeling sick to her stomach. She was afraid she would start crying anew, but she forced herself to concentrate on navigating the stairs. When she got to the top, Dez was halfway down the hallway, waiting, gun in hand. So was the other officer. Across the hall, the other apartment door sported a life-like stuffed cardinal perched on a skinny piece of wood.

"Are you ready for this?" Dez whispered accusingly, looking back at the rookie.

Jaylynn nodded and unholstered her weapon.

They stood on either side of the doorframe, backs to the wall, she and Dez on one side, the backup cop on the other. Dez rapped on the door with the butt of her gun. "Open up! Police."

Jaylynn held her breath and waited. No noise. Then across the hall, the door opened a crack and a diminutive old lady peeked out. She saw the officers holding their guns and smacked the door shut. Jaylynn looked at Dez, and they both holstered their weapons.

Dez stepped over and tapped on the door. It opened two inches.

"Yes?" a wavering voice said.

"Sorry to bother you, ma'am, but have you seen the man who lives across the hall?"

"He went out some time ago. He came dashing down this hall, ran in, and then slammed the door on his way out. Why?"

Dez said, "We need to talk to him. If he comes back, will you please call 911?"

The old woman opened the door wider. She looked rattled, but she craned her neck upwards at the policewoman and said, "Why certainly, Officer. What's he done?"

"I can't say, ma'am, but if he returns, stay in your apartment and don't talk to him. Just call 911, tell them where you live, and explain that the man in apartment 3 has come back. They'll send a squad car over. Do you know his name?"

"No, I don't. He just moved in recently."

"Okay, ma'am. Here's my card. If you have any questions or any information about him, call and leave me a message. I'll call you back."

Mrs. Leopold took the card reluctantly and tucked it into the pocket of her housecoat.

Dez said, "Thank you, ma'am. Oh, and one more thing: can you give us the phone number or address for the manager of this apartment?"

****

Jaylynn said nothing all the way back to the car. She got in and sat silently as Dez called dispatch and reported what she had learned from the little old lady. Then the veteran got out her notebook and made a few more notes before starting up the engine and pulling away from the curb. She gave a little wave to the other squad as they drove off in the opposite direction. In the dim light of the dashboard, Dez wasn't able to make out the rookie's expression, but she knew Jaylynn was upset. She sighed. "Hey, should we swing by the station and get you a new shirt?"

Jaylynn said, "No, that's okay."

"That blood is going to set. You won't be able to get it out."

"I don't care."

Dez hesitated for a moment and then plunged in. "Jaylynn, rape calls are pretty awful." No response. She shifted in the driver's seat. "You think I'm cold and hard-hearted."

"Yeah. That about sums it up."

Dez grimaced, struggling to decide what tack to take. "When you respond to a call like that, it's—well, it's not personal at all. You have to put all thoughts of your own feelings out of your head."

"That's inhuman."

"No, it's not. You have a job to do, a specific job. Of course you're concerned with the victim's health and safety, but after that, your job is to get information we can act on. Get descriptions; take note of the crime scene. What did you get for notes?"

Jaylynn shrugged and didn't answer.

"We're lucky the sergeant didn't show up and check on us."

"But that girl needed more than two impersonal cops standing there interrogating her and making perfect notes."

Gently, Dez said, "And that girl is getting that right now from medical and psychological doctors. That's their job. Our job is to help catch the asshole who did this, and the way we do that is by gathering information as quickly as possible and then acting on it. I was harsh with you in there to shock you out of your feelings about that kid. When you go to these types of calls, you can be mad. You can be furious. And of course you'll be upset. But *don't* show it. You can't show weakness at a time like that. The victim is looking to you as an authority figure who will protect and help."

"What about support? What about gentleness and kindness?"

In a frustrated voice, Dez said, "You can still be supportive and kind, but you just goddamn can't cry!" In a much quieter voice, she added, "You cry later. Cry all you want."

"Do you?"

Dez was taken aback. "Well...sure. Sometimes. Not so much

anymore." She sighed. "In nearly nine years I think I've seen a version of just about everything. After a while, you realize it's the human condition. There's misery and suffering and bad luck galore. I couldn't possibly cry enough for everything I've seen."

Jaylynn crossed her arms over the bloodstained uniform. In a soft voice she said, "I don't know if I can do a job where I don't get to have my feelings."

"You can have your feelings, Jay. You just can't show them under some circumstances." Dez cleared her throat and hesitantly said, "By the way, you did everything else right tonight. You were supportive. You kept her calm. You got her to focus on telling us what we needed to know."

In a tight, controlled voice, the rookie said, "It's good to know I wasn't a total failure."

"Listen now, you're taking this too seriously. Everybody goes through the same thing."

"Okay, fine. Let's not talk about it anymore. But you can't stop me from going to the hospital to check up on her tomorrow."

"Geez! I'm not an ogre, for God's sake." Dez hit her turn signal and took the next corner fast enough to cause the tires to squeal. "Listen to me. You act like you think I don't care. Well, I do. It's just that we've got a job to do tonight. As soon as we're off duty it's okay if we go back to being human beings."

"It doesn't seem right not to be a human being on the job!"

Dez didn't answer. She remembered feeling much the same way when she first started, but unlike Jaylynn, she was able to mask her emotions much easier. "You wear your heart on your sleeve."

"So?" Jaylynn asked accusingly. "Tell me exactly what is wrong with that?"

Dez didn't answer right away. She couldn't figure out any other way to phrase what she thought without being blunt and offending Jaylynn. She thought about the fact that most of the job was all about control. It was about exercising power responsibly. It was about keeping a tight rein on all emotions: anger, sadness, fear, even happiness. Emotions could be used against you. Neutrality and distance—those were the goals, neither of which the rookie possessed. It was clear to Dez that Jaylynn would impulsively jump into any situation, emotions charged, and running ninety miles an hour. She didn't know if she could train the young woman out of that response. As her FTO, she had to somehow succeed, though, or Jaylynn's days as a cop would be numbered.

Dez rolled down the car window and let in a blast of chilly air. Reaching over to the dash, she turned up the dispatch radio one notch. After a moment, she clicked on the side lamp and double-checked the vehicle hot sheet. Finally she asked, "What time are you going to visit that girl?"

"Why?"

"Just curious."

"Are you saying you would go, too?"

"Sure. If it makes you feel better. But we'd have to go awful damn early. I'll bet they'll only keep her overnight and then send her home first thing in the morning. Tell you what. You hit the sack right after shift. I'll come by and get you at nine."

"All right."

Dez could tell the rookie was still unsettled, but there was nothing more she could do or say. She knew that it was these kinds of things that would either make or break a young recruit. She hoped Jaylynn would persevere. She remembered her first rape call vividly. She had been in training with a male officer, Mickey Martin, who was more at a loss than she. He expected her to take care of everything having to do with the woman—and she only had the book training on what to say, what to do. It was made worse by the fact that the woman was beaten half to death, but conscious, crying, and angry. Dez had been stunned and sickened by the physical violence visited upon the woman.

She looked out the window, her eyes constantly surveying the dark streets. She didn't guess she had done much better helping Jaylynn through her first sexual assault call than Mickey Martin had done for her.

****

Jaylynn didn't feel well at all once she got home after the rape call. Her head hurt and her stomach was queasy. She desperately wanted to talk about what had happened, but Tim wasn't home, and Sara was just starting to get back to normal after the events of last summer. She knew if she tried to talk about the young girl, Kristy, then Sara would have nightmares. So she put on her best face and tried to act like everything was fine.

As soon as she entered the kitchen though, Sara said, "Hey there, Jay." She smiled at her friend and then did a double take. "Whoa! Bad night or what?"

Jaylynn shook her head. *How did she always know?* She was just thankful Sara only read faces, not minds. "Just a long night." She slipped out of her jacket and hung it on the back of the wooden nook chair, then sat down across from Sara, who was eating buttered toast and drinking tea while studying.

"Tea water is still hot."

"Okay." Jaylynn moved about the kitchen getting a spoon, mug, tea bag, and some hot water. She set the full mug down carefully on the table and returned to her chair.

"Want to talk about it?"

Jaylynn put her elbows on the table and her chin in her hands. It occurred to her that it wasn't only the poor young girl she felt bad for but also for herself. "This is a hard job sometimes. I like being able to help people and to sort out disagreements, maybe protect kids and old people. But then really bad stuff happens." She put her head in her hand and gazed into the warm depths of the sympathetic brown eyes across the table.

"You didn't see your first murder victim today, did you?"

"No. In a way I am more prepared for that than just for the daily indignities we come across. People can be so mean, so cruel to each other. It just hurts my heart."

"I don't know if I would want your job, Jay. I think I would find it depressing."

Jaylynn took a sip of the hot tea, relieved when it warmed her stomach and instantly relaxed the tightness in her abdomen. "Most of the time it's not really depressing. I'm starting to get to know shopkeepers and restaurant patrons and regulars at the bars. People are starting to remember me, too. Everybody knows Dez. I think most of the people we come across every day are not really all that bad, maybe just stupid idiots and petty crooks or people desperate for money—but not like murderers and rapists. I guess I can handle stupidity or bad decision-making, but calculated cruelty always gets to me."

Sara listened intently, as she always did, and Jaylynn couldn't help but feel a sense of gratefulness wash over her. She reached across the table and patted the brown-haired woman's hand. "Thank you for always listening."

"At least someone in the household has an interesting life," her roommate replied dryly.

Jaylynn tipped her head to the side. "How much time 'til Billy Boy comes back?"

"A very, very long time from now. It still looks like no sooner than October."

"I thought you had it down to the exact days, hours, minutes."

"I had to stop thinking of it that way. It was driving me crazy." Sara looked at her watch. "With any luck, he should call in about an hour."

"I wish you could just fly over to Germany and visit him."

Sara shook her head. "It just won't work. I'd like to, but I can't."

"Look at the bright side—he's done after October, and then you can get married."

"Believe me, I can't wait."

Jaylynn took a final swig of her tea and then rose. "I need to finish writing Auntie Lynn a letter, and I gotta get up early tomorrow, so I'd better head upstairs."

"'Night, Jay."

"Sleep well, my friend."

Chapter
10

Jaylynn sat quietly in the police cruiser, her eyes watching the nightlife intently as she thought about things. She felt tired, mostly from sleeping poorly and then getting up so early to go to the hospital. She had been glad that she and Dez had gone to see the girl. Kristy South's overwhelming helplessness from the night before had changed, overnight, to rage, and Jaylynn encouraged her to be mad as hell at the man who had raped her. Dez stood in the doorway and talked awkwardly with the girl's father, a portly, bald fellow who had a constant look of stunned disbelief about him. The mother and father were anxious about Kristy being released, and Jaylynn tried to reassure them that it always took the hospital more time than expected. She wrote her work voicemail number on a generic St. Paul Police Department business card and told the teenager to call her if she ever needed to talk.

The rookie wished she had gone home and taken a nap, but instead, she had cleaned house, made a casserole, and done laundry. The next thing she knew it was 2:30 and time to head to the station.

Now she sat in the chilly squad car and watched Dez out of the corner of her eye. She often marveled at how Dez's eyes rarely stopped scanning. Any time the tall woman stopped scrutinizing the world around her and let her eyes come to rest on Jaylynn, the rookie's stomach got butterflies. She was grateful it didn't happen all that often.

Dez turned a corner and rolled past the neon-lit street corner where they saw a dark-haired woman standing in front of a smoke shop. Tall and razor-thin, she was unseasonably dressed in a red mini-skirt, fringed halter top, and spangly red spike heels.

"Gotta be cold, huh?" Dez asked. "Last I checked the temp was only 38."

Jaylynn shivered. Even with the heat on in the car, she continued to feel the cold much more acutely than Dez.

Dez turned at the next corner. "I think we'll go around and
check on Miss Thing one more time."

As they approached again, they could see the hooker leaning
into the window of a big white Pontiac. Dez flicked the overhead
lights on and off. The driver of the white car suddenly floored it
and took off down the street, nearly knocking the prostitute off her
feet. She stumbled back on the sidewalk, pulled her skirt down with
one hand, and proceeded to give the officers the finger. Dez eased
the car up next to her and Jaylynn rolled down her window.

"You'd best go home, ma'am," Jaylynn said.

In a slurred voice, the hooker said, "Well, fuck you! He was a
friend of mine."

Dez leaned over toward the passenger side. "Yeah right.
We've heard that one before."

Jaylynn could see that the woman was much older than she
looked from the distance. Despite her long, lanky figure, her face
was tired and overly made-up.

"Ruined my night, you stupid bitches, can't get any yourself—"
Without warning, the woman spat at Jaylynn, catching her in the
face.

"Oooh, gross!" Jaylynn winced in disgust as she wiped her
cheek on her jacket sleeve.

Dez was out of the car before the prostitute knew what was
happening. The big cop grabbed hold of the scowling woman and
locked her arm behind her back, then forced her two steps back to
the wall of the smoke shop and pressed the woman face-first into
the brick.

The hooker let out a shriek. "Let me go, you bitch!"

"Is that any way to show respect for a police officer?"

"Fuck you," she said, hissing like a cat. She squirmed and
tried to kick Dez in the shins. The tall cop moved up close and
anchored her firmly in place by pressing one knee between the
woman's legs and against the wall. It also prevented her from being
stilettoed by the pointy high-heels.

"You just earned yourself a fun trip down to the station, lady."
The weight of the angry hooker suddenly sagged against Dez.

Once Jaylynn wiped her face satisfactorily, she got out of the
car, flipping her handcuffs off her belt. "Do we really want to run
her in, Dez?"

Before she could reply, Dez shouted, "Oh shit!"

Jaylynn pulled her weapon and held it steady on the woman.

"No, no," Dez said as she made a disgusted face. "She just
peed on my leg." Dez released the woman and stepped back only to

see her stumble. The poorly dressed woman turned. Pulling at the fringe of her halter top with blood red fingernails, she gave them both a vacant-eyed look and slumped back against the brick wall, just barely keeping her footing in the high heels.

"She's stoned," Jaylynn said, as she holstered her weapon.

"I'll say." Dez looked down at the thigh of her uniform slacks. A dark wet spot had spread all the way down to mid-calf.

"And you're gonna smell," Jaylynn said, trying to suppress a giggle as she pointed at the dark, steaming stain. Dez shot her a glare and stomped over to the squad car to call for an ambulance. By the time the paramedics arrived, the woman was alert and feisty, cursing and threatening as before. They had to strap her down on a gurney to take her away.

"Now that's a first," Dez said. "No adult has ever peed on me before." She opened the trunk of the car and searched around until she came up with a ratty olive colored Army t-shirt. "I don't know whose this is, but it's mine now. Get in and let's go." She put the t-shirt on the front seat of the car and sat on it.

"You're gonna ride around for," Jaylynn looked at her watch, "three more hours in that stench?"

"Hell, no." She turned on the car lights and hit the gas. "I'm going home to change."

"Why don't you go back to the station?"

"Haven't got any slacks there."

As they neared Dez's neighborhood, she asked Jaylynn to call them in for a break, and the rookie contacted dispatch.

Jaylynn had never been to Dez's house and wondered what it would be like. She didn't expect the neat, two-story stucco house they stopped in front of. Dez got out in a hurry. "Come on. You can come up and wash your face." She slammed the door and stalked away from the car.

Jaylynn followed Dez around to the back of the house and waited for her to unlock the door. They entered a hallway with a door straight ahead and a staircase on the right. Dez took the stairs two at a time. On the landing at the top, she watched as Dez navigated the low ceiling with practiced ease. The staircase and landing were tucked in the eaves, so even Jaylynn had to duck her head.

Dez unlocked a door, flipped a light switch, and stepped aside to let Jaylynn into a tiny kitchen, about twelve-by-ten feet square. The dinette table was just inside the door with a small CD player sitting on the side against the wall. To the left were a small closet, a refrigerator, a short counter containing a microwave with cupboards overhead, and a sink under a small window, which was hardly bigger than a porthole. Across the room were more

cupboards and a counter. A doorway to the right, straight across
from the entry door, led into another room. Jaylynn looked around
the kitchen and admired its compactness, so opposite of its owner.
The vinyl flooring was pale blue and tan, the cupboards shiny light
oak, and the counters navy blue. Everything looked new and clean,
the only thing out of place being a cereal bowl and spoon on the
sideboard next to the sink.

Dez tossed her keys on the table, removed her jacket, and hung
it over one of the dinette chairs. Jaylynn did the same and then
followed Dez through the doorway into another room not much
deeper than the kitchen, but three times longer. Taking up the left
half of the room was a double bed, two dressers, a valet chair, a
wardrobe closet, and a small bedside table. On the wall beyond the
foot of the bed sat a roll top desk, closed up tight. Over the bed was
another window similar to the one in the kitchen, though slightly
bigger. In the right half of the room on the far wall were floor-to-
ceiling shelves with a couch sitting not four feet in front of them. A
low-slung coffee table sat parallel in front of the couch.

Across the room on the opposite wall sat an entertainment
system, and next to it on two metal stands were two guitars. One
was a warm golden color steel-stringed acoustic, the other a shiny
red electric model with silver thunderbolts on the front. Beyond the
guitar stands to Jaylynn's right was another door. Dez pointed to it.
"Bathroom's right through there. Just grab any towel you want and
throw it in the hamper when you're done."

Jaylynn went in and shut the door. At least the bathroom was
roomy. On the right, the tub/shower was extra long and extra wide
and included a whirlpool. *Someone laid out some cash for that*, she
thought. The beige toilet and sink matched the tub, and the blue
and tan floor matched the kitchen floor. An open-front oak cabinet
was filled with neatly folded towels, sheets, and washcloths. Next
to it sat a narrow bureau, which was topped with a tray holding
various colognes, deodorant, and spray bottles. Another of the
porthole windows, much larger than the others in the kitchen and
bedroom, let in light from the streetlamp.

Jaylynn knew they didn't have a lot of time, so she pulled out a
royal blue towel, washed her hands and face, and dried off quickly,
tossing the towel into the wooden hamper as she left. Dez rose
from the couch, barefoot and wearing a red terry cloth robe. She
picked up her uniform slacks and held them at a distance. "Yuck."

"You're not gonna shower, are you?"

"You bet I am. I'm not spending the rest of the shift in this."
Dez paused in the bathroom doorway. "Make yourself comfortable.
There's iced tea in the fridge, and you can turn on the TV if you
want. Time me. It'll take me less than ten minutes."

Jaylynn went into the kitchen and opened the first cupboard to the right of the sink. Bingo. Glasses galore. She took one, opened the fridge, and poured herself some iced tea, then took note of the contents of the refrigerator: a door-full of condiments, milk, orange juice, a plate of leftover roasted chicken breasts, and tons of fruits and vegetables. Not a can of pop in sight and no greasy snacks. *Doesn't this woman eat anything sinfully delicious? Where's the butter? The cheese? There aren't even any eggs in there—just those little containers of liquid egg whites.* She smacked the door shut and headed back into the other room and sat on the couch to marvel at Dez's tiny home.

The entire L-shaped apartment was tucked into the eaves of the house, and she bet it wasn't more than 700 square feet. There were closets and drawers built into the eaves, so there was probably a lot more storage than it appeared at first glance. Somehow she would have pegged Dez to live in a large rambling place with a couple of big dogs, or at least a cat or two. She guessed she would have to revise her assumptions. Though small, the apartment was cozy and warm, and Jaylynn liked the solid blues, maroons, greens, and tan accents throughout the room. The double bed's headboard was dark mahogany, which contrasted nicely with the navy blue and forest green comforter. A matching quilt adorned the back of the wide couch. At the foot of the bed lay another quilt, this one maroon and blue, with a freshly pressed pair of slacks tossed partly over it. Dez's vest and other clothes were piled on the valet chair near the closet.

She looked past the foot of the bed at the roll top desk and resisted the urge to go over and investigate. She wondered if she would find all the clutter of a lifetime packed in there? Or would each of the little cubbyholes be as neat and tidy as the rest of the apartment? She wondered if Dez had a computer. She certainly didn't seem to live a very high-tech life.

Hmmm, the only thing missing here is anything at all of a personal nature. Where are the photos? None of the walls displayed any art—no pictures or knickknacks. Jaylynn wondered if Dez had only recently moved in. It sure looked like it, otherwise how could she be so neat? Jaylynn remembered when she and Sara had moved into Tim's rental house. Within two weeks the place was a mess, and it wasn't until the three of them sat down and bargained out a system for cleaning and picking up that the place had become the slightest bit organized.

She slid behind the couch and stood looking at the books, CD's, and videos on the shelves there. There were even about a hundred old vinyl record albums. Lots of nutrition and health books. Hundreds of CD's. She saw ones by artists she knew:

Melissa Etheridge, Stevie Nicks, k.d. lang, Everything But The Girl, Billie Holliday, Etta James, Sarah McLachlan, The Pretenders, Cris Williamson, and more. She also noted unfamiliar names: Lucy Kaplansky, Cheryl Wheeler, Leo Kottke, Richard Shindell, Kristen Hall, David Wilcox, Dar Williams, Elizabeth Cotton, Michael Hedges. Eight of the Indigo Girls' CD's—Jaylynn didn't realize they had so many. She moved on and looked through a huge collection of videos, most of which Jaylynn had never seen. She pulled one out and read the notes on the back.

True to her word, Dez emerged in short order, again dressed in the red robe. "I'm hurrying, so don't worry." She strode gracefully across the room to the valet chair and sorted through the clothes, picking up several items.

"I'm not worried." Jaylynn took a sip of her tea. "Hey, you've got a lot of good videos. I've never seen some of these."

"Go ahead and borrow any you like," Dez said as she dressed.

Jaylynn turned away to give her privacy. "Thanks a lot. Maybe I'll take you up on that sometime." She couldn't help looking over her shoulder, but when she caught a glance of Dez's ivory-colored back, she turned away in haste, then busied herself reviewing the video she held. "Here's one I always heard was good."

"Which?" Dez asked in a low voice as she pulled a t-shirt over her head.

"*Truly, Madly, Deeply.*"

"Yeah, that's pretty much one of my favorite movies of all time. Bring a box of hankies though." She picked up her vest and slung it around her shoulders, then fastened the Velcro. She pulled on and buttoned her shirt. Adjusting her cuffs, she moved toward the doorway.

Jaylynn said, "I'd love to bring the box of hankies over some time and watch it."

"Sure. Whenever. Come on, let's get back out there."

"You play guitar, huh?"

"Yeah, some."

"You'll have to play a little for me some time."

When Dez didn't answer, Jaylynn hastily returned the video and followed her to the kitchen. She set the empty glass next to the bowl on the drainboard, then put on her jacket and followed Dez out into the hallway and waited for her to lock the door.

That wasn't so bad, Dez thought. *No awkward questions. No muss, no fuss.*

"How long have you lived here?"

Oh no. Now it starts. "Going on nine years."

Jaylynn was ahead, moving toward the stairs, so Dez missed seeing her jaw dropping. "Wow, nine years. You sure haven't accumulated much stuff." *Or many people*, Jaylynn thought. *That was definitely a single person's pad.*

"Guess not. I don't need much stuff. I moved there right out of college and I've just stayed. I like the place."

"It's very nice."

"Thanks."

They thundered down the steps, Jaylynn in the lead, and she stopped with a start when she reached the bottom of the stairs and found a silver-haired black woman standing there, arms crossed over her ample bosom. She wore pink slippers, a flowered housedress, and a pink sweater around her narrow shoulders. Her silver hair was swept back and held in place with two silver combs. The twinkle in her eye was evident to Jaylynn, even though she'd never seen the woman in her life.

"You two sounded like a herd of elephants. How can two little gals like you make so darn much noise?"

From the bottom step Dez replied, "Sorry, Luella, but we're in a hurry."

"What's the rush?" Luella said, then turned to Jaylynn. "She never slows down much—even mows the lawn at a breakneck pace. Do you have to run to keep up with her?"

Jaylynn glanced back to see the warm smile on Dez's face. "Go ahead, Jay, tell her. I'll try not to get mad about it."

Jaylynn looked back at Luella. "Actually, I can beat her in a foot race. Maybe not for a long distance, but in sprints for sure. And the noise coming down the stairs was probably more my fault than hers. Sorry."

Luella moved toward her. She reached a soft brown hand out and patted Jaylynn's shoulder. "You must be her new partner, hmm? How long you been riding together?"

"She's been training me for about eight weeks, I think."

Luella looked over Jaylynn's shoulder and fixed a level stare at her tenant. "Well, Dez, nice of you to mention it." She made a tsk-tsk sound with her tongue. "Were you going to introduce us, or just let the poor woman wonder?"

Dez sighed and stepped down the last two stairs. "Luella, I just haven't—it's not that I—" She shrugged and rolled her eyes. "Jay—Jaylynn Savage, this is Luella Williams, nosy landlady, chief cook and uniform washer."

Luella flashed a mouthful of white teeth. "Chief cook...hmm...I like that. You eat the same gerbil food she does, Jaylynn?"

Jaylynn had no idea how to answer, so she was noncommittal. "I don't—I don't think so."

"Good. When are your days off?"

"Mondays and Tuesdays one week—Monday through Wednesday the next week. For now. Same as Dez's. Why?"

"Well then, why don't you just come for dinner Monday night and we'll have a decent meal. You like au gratin potatoes?"

"Love 'em!"

"How about steamed broccoli—maybe with a little cheese sauce?"

"Ooh, sounds yummy."

"Can you come about six?"

"Sure. I guess. You want me to bring something?" She turned her head to look at Dez. *Uh oh. Maybe that was the wrong answer.* Dez didn't seem any too happy.

"Oh no," Luella said. "That's not necessary. And Dez, if you could grace us with your presence, I might even make a baked chicken for you."

Dez didn't know whether to be mad at Luella or not. Why did they have to run into her tonight? She'd carefully avoided having any of the new trainees over. Things weren't like they used to be, back when she'd invited Ryan and Cowboy and Crystal and any number of other cops over for a big feast every month or so. They always congregated at Luella's and regaled the older woman with stories of their bravery and ability to leap tall buildings in a single bound. Dez hadn't thought about it, but it suddenly occurred to her that the old woman might miss it. The one time Crystal had brought up their raucous get-togethers, Dez had cut her off and said she wasn't ready for parties, not with Ryan so recently dead. Crystal had wrapped a friendly arm around Dez's waist and told her to let people know when she was ready.

How many months had passed? It didn't matter. She still wasn't ready.

Luella insisted on giving Dez a hug, and she shook Jaylynn's hand and saw them out the back door. They got back in the police car, the rookie shivering a little. Dez called and reported back on duty. She flicked the switch for the heater, even though she knew she'd be roasting in short order. Maybe she could turn it down a bit later when the smaller woman was warmer and not paying attention.

Jaylynn cleared her throat. "Dez?"

No answer.

"Dez, I'm sorry about that. I get the distinct impression you'd rather I had turned your landlady down."

Dez pulled to a stop at a red light and, with a practiced eye, surveyed the area. She avoided Jaylynn's eyes and said, "No, it's okay. She gets lonely. It'll be good for her. Forget about it."

The light changed and Dez proceeded slowly through the

intersection, keeping an eye on a car double-parked in front of the check-cashing outfit in the middle of the block.

The rookie said, "How come you have Luella do your laundry? I always see you hauling your uniforms out. I thought the department paid for that."

"Yeah, they do," she said in a grouchy voice. "But Luella does a much better job. Besides, she insists." Actually, Luella always made a big deal about the maintenance Dez did around the place, and if she didn't give her the laundry, Luella would cut the rent. Dez was well aware that her landlady already undercharged on the rent and that she couldn't afford to take less. So the big cop did all she could to keep the house up, and in return, Luella did all the wash and ironing.

Her thoughts were interrupted when, out of the blue, Jaylynn said, "So. What are you doing Sunday night after shift?"

Dez frowned. "Sunday night?"

"Yeah, I was thinking we could watch *Truly, Madly, Deeply*. Since I'm going to Luella's Monday, I know you'd be stuck with me twice in two days, but hey, I'll bring the hankies and popcorn? You supply the iced tea and video?"

Dez felt a moment of panic and was glad it was dark in the car. "Oh, I don't know, Jay..."

The radio squawked as the dispatcher called their squad number and followed it up with information about an assault in progress and the address. *Saved by the bell*, thought Dez. She made an abrupt U-turn and sped away at a faster rate than she really needed to. Jaylynn picked up the radio and answered the call.

For the moment all talk of Sunday night was forgotten.

****

Monday rolled around, and Jaylynn was excited at the prospect of going over to Luella's. She hoped Dez would be there, but even if she wasn't, the rookie looked forward to the visit with the older woman. Dez had told her not to worry about dressing up, so she had worn pressed blue jeans, a warm thermal shirt with a light blue sweater over it, and her light brown Doc Martens. It was still so cold out that she had on her thermal mittens and down coat.

She drove over, having borrowed Tim's beater, and arrived right on time. As she stood on the front porch, her senses were assaulted with mouth-watering smells. She rang the bell and Luella came to the door wearing pink slip-on slippers and a fluffy white apron over a belted dark blue dress. A splotch of red sauce stained the apron. She held a maroon mixing bowl in the crook of her arm, a wooden spoon poking out from some batter. "Well, there you are," Luella said as she unhooked the porch's screen door. "C'mon in. You can hang up your jacket right there on one of those hooks."

Jaylynn moved through the porch area, stepped into the house, and closed the door behind her. Luella resumed mixing the contents of the bowl and led her into the kitchen.

The rookie asked, "Whatcha got there?" as she gestured at the bowl.

"At the last minute I decided I had a hankering for cornbread, so I'm mixing it up. Think we should have 'em in muffin cups or little loaves?"

Jaylynn said, "Hmmm, either way would be great."

"Maybe I'll just make muffins. Then there's a chance that fool friend of yours would eat at least one." She set the bowl on the counter and bent down to open a low cupboard, then fumbled around until she got hold of a muffin pan and pulled it out. "Here, I'll let you grease this thing up." She gestured toward the can of Crisco on the counter. "Use one of those paper towels hanging there." She pointed to the dispenser on the wall.

Jaylynn took the pan from her and proceeded to grease each indentation. "You know, it smells good halfway down the block. What are you making?"

"We're having spicy pork ribs and those au gratins I promised you. I made some broccoli—with and without cheese sauce—and I have a little pie, too, for dessert." She reached over and took the pan from Jaylynn, set it on the counter and spooned twelve dollops of batter into the cups, scraped out the bowl, and put the pan in the oven. "Those'll be up in about 12 minutes, but until then, let's go sit in the dining room."

She slipped off the apron and hung it on the back of the kitchen door, then led Jaylynn into the other room where an elegant table was set.

"Ooh, what pretty plates," Jaylynn said. Standing next to the table she bent over and traced the tiny rosebuds and violets on the white background. There were three settings at the large table, one at the head and two others to its right and left. The other half of the table contained four sets of hot pads, ready to hold warming dishes.

"These came from my mother and father," Luella said as she pulled out a chair and sat. "Got 'em in 1945, right after the war. I started out with eight place settings, but I'm down to about six and a half now what with bowls or plates or teacups being broken periodically over the years."

Jaylynn sat. "At my house, we're still eating off the Melmac plates I brought with me to college."

"If you like beautiful dishes, I know a wonderful store reasonably priced. If you ever want to go buy a set, I'll come help you pick 'em out."

"One of these days when I set up my own house, I'll take you up on that offer."

"Good girl." She reached over to pat the young woman's hand. "Now tell me all about you, about how you became a police officer, and how you're liking it."

Jaylynn discovered Luella very easy to talk to. The kindly woman listened intently, yet her attention did not feel at all intrusive. The rookie told her about growing up in Seattle, winning a four year track scholarship to the U of M, and moving to snowy Minnesota five years earlier. When the timer went off and they got up to take the cornbread muffins out of the oven, she was telling Luella about choosing law enforcement because it interested her. "I thought I might be able to make a difference," she said, "like Dez has made a difference in so many people's lives."

Luella paused, holding the pan in her hand. "You think she does?"

"Well, sure," Jaylynn said, surprised.

The silver-haired woman set the pan on the top of the stove and closed the oven. "I wish someone would tell *her* that. I swear, no one is harder on herself than she is." She moved to the corner of the kitchen and picked up a broom, then held it up in the air and banged on the ceiling with the end of it.

Before she could set the broom back in the corner, Jaylynn heard a clump-clump noise and looked toward the back hallway. The door opened and a dark head popped in. "Hi, I'm here."

Luella said, "Come on in and join the party."

Dez appeared in the kitchen, hands in her pockets. She was decked out in red, white, and blue: blue jeans—Levi's, to be exact—a bright red, long-sleeved shirt, and brand new white Nikes. Her face betrayed no emotions other than curiosity as her eyes surveyed the kitchen, coming to rest on Jaylynn. She nodded and said, "What's up?"

Before Jaylynn could answer, Luella said, "It's about time you high-tailed it down here. Everything's ready, so you two go get settled." She shooed them out of the kitchen.

Jaylynn said, "Don't you need a hand?"

"Nope," the silver-haired woman said as she grabbed her apron from the back of the door. "You two just clear out and let the serving expert do her thing."

In the dining room they sat and Dez said, "She really is a serving expert. Wait'll you see what she trots out here with."

Jaylynn licked her lips and grinned. "I can't wait. I'm

starving."

"You know, Jaylynn, I've never met anybody in my life who was as hungry as you are all the time."

"Yeah, right. And *you're* not eating every three hours?"

"But I'm having totally healthy stuff."

She smiled warmly at the cranky woman. "Whatever."

Luella brought them each a glass of milk and then bustled in with a platter of pork ribs in one hand and a serving dish of seasoned chicken breasts in the other and set them on the hot pads. She went back and got a bowl of potatoes and a small container of brown rice. She carted in a double-dish of broccoli, one side with melted cheese and the other plain. The two cops watched in amusement as she hastened back and forth, coming in last with a wicker basket full of hot muffins. She sat down and reached a hand out to each woman. Jaylynn took a soft brown hand into her right hand and then stifled a laugh when the older woman gave Dez the evil eye. "Let the circle be unbroken," Luella said. In response, Dez sighed and reached her other hand across the table, surprising Jaylynn, who realized with a start that she should take Dez's hand.

Once the three women were clasping hands, Luella bowed her head and prayed, "Dear Heavenly Father, bless this food and bless these girls. May they both be kept safe in their daily work, and may the food before us refresh and fortify us all. We ask this in Jesus' name. Amen. Okay, girls, eat up. Jaylynn, you don't even have to think about eating that boring brown rice. That's for Miss Polly Purebred over there." She stood and moved to the other end of the table where she could supervise the passing of the dishes. Once they'd loaded up their plates, she took her own plate and filled it, then took it over and sat down. "Ahhh," she said. "I'm dang near famished."

Dez rolled her eyes. "I have at the table two of the biggest exaggerators on the planet."

Jaylynn laughed and almost choked on her first bite of au gratin potatoes. With her mouth full she said, "Luella, this is undoubtedly the best—no, the most stupendous—no, the most incredibly, fabulously, wondrous meal I have ever had in my 24 years on the planet."

Her conspirator grinned back. "I have never in all my livelong years had so much fun assembling a meal, especially knowing how unbelievably thrilled you two would be to partake in it." She looked at Jaylynn, smirking and giggling as she chewed, then kicked Dez under the table. "You got anything to add?"

"Good chicken," the tall woman said as she calmly forked up a piece and guided it to her mouth. The other two went off in a fit of laughter. Dez said, "I can tell already that you two are gonna be a problem."

"Why?" Jaylynn asked, batting her eyes innocently.

"At this rate, someone's gonna have to apply the Heimlich maneuver to one or the other of ya."

This caused more laughing. "C'mon," Luella said, "quit being so serious. What happened to your sense of humor?"

"Guess it's on hiatus." She took a bite of plain broccoli and gazed, deadpan, at her landlady. Luella met her gaze and narrowed her eyes to stare her down. A big grin spread slowly across the black woman's face until Dez broke down and smiled back. Then Luella reached down under the table and squeezed Dez's knee until she yelped. In a huff, Dez said, "Guess it's off hiatus now."

"Good thing," her landlady said. She picked up a rib and held it gingerly in her fingers. "Now Dez, honey, you *never* told me that Jaylynn was a track star."

"You never asked."

"Now how would I know to ask?"

Dez shrugged.

"You didn't know, did you?" the older lady asked.

Dez glanced over at Jaylynn who was coloring nicely. "I know she's a fast runner."

Luella said, "She went to the U on a track scholarship. How come you never found out about that?" She didn't ask accusingly but seemed to be trying hard to understand how Dez could have overlooked something so important. When Dez didn't answer, she said, "Brag on yourself a little bit, Jaylynn. Tell Miss Oblivious here what you've done—you must have a few records, hmmm?"

Jaylynn set her fork down on her plate, her face flaming. "Well, I went to nationals three times, and placed in the top six each time, but I never was able to win, place, or show."

Dez said, "What event?"

"400 meters, 200 meters, 1600 meter relay."

"You went to nationals for all three?"

Jaylynn nodded solemnly.

"That's good. What'd you have to do to get there—place in the top three in the state or what?"

"First."

"Are you saying you're the best sprinter in Minnesota?"

Jay chortled. "Not anymore, but I guess you could say I *was* back in my salad days. And I was never that great a *sprinter*—more middle distances."

Dez nodded and scooped up a cornbread muffin, absently splitting it open and eating half. Jaylynn watched the landlady's face light up in a smile, but Dez didn't notice.

Dez said, "I used to run the 400 meters—I always called it the puke race."

"I know what you mean. When you're done, that's exactly what you feel like doing."

"I never could break 60 seconds—hit it right on a couple times, but never got below."

Jaylynn grinned. "That's why I got to anchor the relay. Every once in a while I nailed a 56 or 57."

"Did you ever do any other events?"

"Oh, a little hurdles, some long jump, occasionally a little high jump, but those were never my specialties. Mostly I just ran my butt off. How 'bout you? You do any other events?"

Dez nodded. "Javelin, shot put, discus. They wouldn't let women do pole vault, but I liked it."

Jaylynn leaned forward, putting her elbows on the table. "I bet you were good, too. You've got some records yourself, don't you? Come on, 'fess up."

Dez set her fork down, pushed her plate away, and sat back in her seat. "Just in high school. Well, I guess I had the conference javelin record in college, too, but I never went to nationals or anything. I might have done better my junior or senior year, but I quit."

"You quit the team?"

"No, I quit college. I put in two and a half years, got bored with it, and applied to be a cop. As soon as I turned 21, I joined the force. So I never got my degree."

Luella said, "I keep telling her to go back and pick up some night classes, but she says she's not interested."

"What were you majoring in?" Jaylynn asked.

Dez gave her a crooked smile. "Little of this, little of that. Mostly law enforcement related, sports, a few music classes. What's your degree in?"

"I loved college. I took light loads during spring track season, but the rest of the year I loaded up and did quantity, not so much quality, so it's not like I was an A student or anything. I've got majors in political science, psychology, and English."

"Busy girl, weren't you?" Luella asked.

"I figured if they were paying, I might as well get all I could out of it. Of course it took me an extra year to finish, and my parents paid for that, but it was worth it, I think."

Luella stood and cleared a couple serving plates. "You girls ready for some pie?" Before Dez could make a comment, her landlady said, "I know, I know. You pass, right?" When Dez nodded, Luella said, "Fine, but no whining when Jaylynn and I sit here enjoying two pieces of succulent and tasty apple pie with melted butter and cinnamon sugar on top."

Dez looked at her in mock astonishment. "Who me? Whine? No whining from this quarter."

When Luella ambled into the kitchen, Jaylynn leveled her gaze at the veteran cop. "So, you took music classes?" When her question was answered with a nod, she went on, "What kind of classes?"

"Mostly guitar and music theory."

"Mostly?"

"A little voice."

"So you can sing! That's great."

Dez bristled. "I never said that."

"If you can sing at all, you're doing better than me. Sara has a beautiful voice, and she plays piano. Wish I could play an instrument." She picked up her fork and shoveled up the last chunk of potatoes on her plate. "Well, I guess I can carry a tune, but singing has never been my forte. Must be fun to be able to play and sing." She swallowed the au gratins and set the fork back down.

Luella entered the dining room carrying two rosebud plates loaded with generous pieces of steaming apple pie. "Dez, you should go up and get your guitar. Come down and play us that piece you wrote for my 70th birthday."

The tall woman's face flushed scarlet. "Oh no."

Luella lowered herself slowly in her chair. "Quit with the shy thing. I'm sure Jaylynn would enjoy it. Go. Get your guitar."

Dez stood, pushing the chair back with her heel. "I'm not singing."

Her landlady halted a big bite on its way to her mouth. "Fine. Then play me that nice melodic piece you've been working on."

As she stalked out of the room Dez tossed back, "That's not even finished."

"We don't care, girl. Just come back and entertain us." After she left, she said to Jaylynn, "You ever notice she's about as bull-headed as they come?"

Jaylynn smiled, her hazel eyes sparkling. "No doubt about that." They talked some more and ate the pie. "Luella, what work did you do before you retired?"

"Thirty-nine years at the telephone company. Worked my way up from operator to shift supervisor to head of customer service."

"So you had to deal with all the cranky people mad about their phone service."

"Um hmm. I really didn't mind it at all. But I finally retired about five years ago, and that's been fine, too."

Jaylynn popped another bite into her mouth and smiled. "This is just *wonderful* pie! I don't think I have ever had better. The crust is so flaky."

"I learned to make it from my momma. She was an accomplished baker." She spiked the last apple and popped it in her mouth. "I love pie, but who can eat a whole one? I'm so glad to have guests every so often so I can cook up things I never get to make for myself."

"Thank you for this great dinner, Luella."

"You're welcome, sweetie. Hmmm. Where's that ornery cuss got herself to? She should be back by now." She got up and snagged the milk glasses.

Jaylynn rose. "Let me help you with these dishes." The two women worked together and cleared everything away. Luella transferred the food to plastic containers while the younger woman rinsed and stacked dishes.

Luella said, "I just want to leave a lot of that to soak, so don't worry too much." She put her hands on her hips. "What's keeping that girl so long?"

Right on cue, Dez came down the hall toting her acoustic guitar. She stood uncertainly in the hallway looking into the kitchen. "I'll just go play in the living room and you two can listen from in here."

"Ah ah ah," Luella said. "Not so fast." She dried off her hands on her apron, slipped it off, and hung it on the door hook. "C'mon, Jay. Let's go relax in the other room."

They all trooped into the living room. Jaylynn sat in the wooden rocker. Luella lowered herself into the wing chair, and Dez perched on the edge of the couch.

"What do you wanna hear?" Dez asked in a resigned tone.

Jaylynn decided to let her two companions duke this one out. She smiled agreeably and settled into a steady rocking rhythm.

The landlady said, "Play that one tune I always like so much—you know, the one where you twang the notes."

"Bend? You mean bend the notes?"

"Yeah, that's it."

"Okay, give me a second. I have to go to an open tuning." She quickly adjusted the tuning pegs and Jaylynn listened to the guitar make a wow-wow-wow sound as Dez changed the tone of three of the strings. She put her ear down close to the guitar, strummed it a few times, made one more minor adjustment, then closed her eyes. She began to pick out a melody with the fingers of her right hand while simultaneously moving her left hand over the strings on the neck of the guitar. Her fingers bent and hammered the strings at the neck in a way that Jaylynn had never heard. What emerged was a melancholy combination of notes that reverberated and rang in such a way that it sounded like two or more guitars playing complementary fugues. The song traveled through three different movements but kept coming back to the same theme.

Dez plucked the last notes and then let them ring out and fade away. Only then did she open her eyes shyly. "That the one you wanted?"

Luella said, "Actually, that's not the one I was thinking of, but that surely was beautiful. Makes my heart feel full."

Jaylynn sat silently, thinking. *Wow!* She, too, felt her heart was full; in fact, she felt she could start crying. The piece was mournful, almost a lament. It brought to mind memories of her father, of being a little girl trying to understand why he had died and left her. On the verge of tears, she shook herself and rocked in the chair more with vigor. "That was remarkable, Dez. I liked it. What's it called?"

Dez frowned. "Don't have a name for it yet."

"I know," Luella hollered, "play that honky-tonk thing I like."

Dez nodded knowingly. "I know *exactly* which one you're referring to now." She took a minute to tune the strings back up, then stood up and dug in her pants pocket to pull out a black pick. Closing her eyes she started strumming a rollicking, slapping beat that soon had both women tapping their toes.

Jaylynn listened and thought about the contradictory sides she had seen of this woman. Head bashing, rough-and-tumble versus sensitive guitar player. Suspicious and untrusting versus intensely loyal. College dropout versus canny, streetwise strategist. Moody and grouchy versus gentle and obedient toward Luella. She studied her as she played guitar. Her blue eyes were closed tightly, the tip of her tongue peeking out between the straight white teeth. One foot tapped out the beat, and when Jaylynn closed her own eyes and listened very closely, she could faintly hear the tall woman humming the melody as her fingers flew over the strings.

The rookie opened her eyes and looked at Luella who was slapping her knee and grinning widely. The old lady tipped her head from side to side in time with the music and let out an occasional, "Oh yeah! Play it, girl!" which made Jaylynn laugh.

She glanced back at Dez only to find her staring intently at her. Eyes met and she felt the connection, the same exact gut reaction she had experienced the very first time she had seen the policewoman. It made her dizzy and short of breath. She blinked to shake off the light-headedness and Dez abruptly ended the honky-tonk tune and stood.

"Enough fun for one night."

"One more," Luella said. "C'mon, sweetie. Just one more, okay? Play my anthem, why don't you?"

Dez exhaled. She paused a moment and then sat down again. "Okay, but *you* have to sing it." She played a little intro and then nodded, and the old woman began singing in a true but quavery voice:

Lift every voice and sing
Til earth and heaven ring,
Ring with the harmonies of Liberty...

Jaylynn rocked contentedly to the even beat. She closed her eyes and took a deep breath as she enjoyed the song she had heard a few times before.

Let our rejoicing rise,
high as the listening skies,
let it resound loud as the rolling sea...

And then Luella slid into the chorus and, unexpectedly, a second voice joined hers, a smoky contralto singing the alto line.

Sing a song, full of the faith that the dark past has taught us.
Sing a song, full of the hope that the present has brought us.
Facing the rising sun of our new day begun.
Let us march on till victory is won...

Jaylynn peeked one eye open and through thick lashes watched Luella and Dez sing the next verses of the old spiritual in two-part harmony. Amazement wasn't even the word for her reaction. The word flabbergasted came to mind. She was totally flabbergasted—and filled with an intense longing so strong that her heart hurt. A lump rose in her throat and she fought back tears. In a way she envied the two women. They seemed so close. She longed to have met each of them much sooner, realizing now that there had been a gap in her life about which she had never even been aware.

The song came to an end and no one said a word as the notes from the guitar tapered off and faded out. Dez looked her way sheepishly, and to cut her apprehension, Jaylynn said, "You two could take that on the road!"

Luella smiled and said, "That's always been one of my most favorite songs. My father sang that to me when I was a tiny little girl. Usually brings a tear to my eye. Desiree, my dear, thank you for singing it with me."

"You're welcome," she said as she rose, holding the golden guitar by its neck. "I'll be back. I'm gonna take this upstairs." And she turned and sped out of the room.

"Wow," Jaylynn said, "she's got some kinda voice, doesn't she?"

"Yes, she does, and she doesn't share it with just anyone. I'm surprised she joined in, but I'm glad she did."

"Me, too. I can't get over it. Wow!"

The rest of the evening flew by as Luella continued to pry information out of the two of them, and suddenly it was after ten o'clock. Jaylynn looked at her watch and rose to say her goodbyes. She made her way out to the porch, took down her coat, and fished in the sleeves for her thermal mittens.

Luella stood in the doorway holding a large foil-wrapped package. "You be careful driving out there," she said. "Looks to me like it's snowing."

Dez stepped out on the enclosed porch and peered through the window. "That's just snow flying around off the roof. The street's clear." She leaned against the frame of the porch window as Jaylynn slipped on her coat.

Luella grabbed Jaylynn before she could zip up her huge coat. She snaked her arms into the coat and around the rookie's waist to give her a big hug.

"Thank you for the wonderful dinner, Luella. It was a great evening."

"God bless you, Jaylynn. You're a special girl. Let's do this again soon."

"Okay, sure."

Luella handed her the foil-wrapped surprise. "I know you'll enjoy this later. It's extra good for breakfast." Jaylynn slipped the package in a roomy coat pocket, and the landlady took the big mittens out of her hands so she could zip up her coat. "These look nice and warm."

Jaylynn said, "It's like wearing boxing gloves—makes it hard to drive—but I hate it when I get cold." She pulled her hood up. "Good night, Luella. Good night, Dez." Dez opened the front door and Jaylynn brushed by, smacking the tall woman lightly in the midsection as she passed. "See ya Wednesday at work."

"Will do," the tall woman said in a quiet voice as she shut the door.

All the way home, Jaylynn's mind raced. She thought Luella was one of the nicest people she had ever met. And Dez was—well, Dez was Dez. She had her own grouchy charm. Jaylynn pondered the attraction, for she could not avoid admitting it. She was attracted to—totally smitten with—the tall, dark-haired cop. But she didn't really understand why. Something like a magnetic force drew her to the other woman, and she felt helpless in its pull. She had a sense of déjà vu, too, that was so strong she couldn't believe that they hadn't grown up together or known each other at some time in their lives. But growing up on the West Coast precluded them from ever having met.   Maybe she had seen her walking around Como Lake, but then she thought she'd have a clearer picture of her. She definitely would remember that physique! So then she found herself wondering about dreams.   How could her Hero so closely resemble the taciturn cop? She wished she had more control over her dreams because if she did, she would actually like to question her Hero. She would ask, "Who are you, and did I make you up when I was little? Or are you real?"

When she arrived back at the house, she parked Tim's Toyota and hustled through the frigid night air into the warm kitchen. She pulled her coat off and hung it over the back of one of the chairs at the table.   She started to leave the kitchen and then suddenly remembered the treat in her pocket and reached in to pull out the foil-wrapped package. Before even unwrapping it, she could smell what it was. Apple pie laced with cinnamon and sugar. She smiled and took it up to her room with a fork and a glass of milk.

Chapter
11

Jaylynn thought that the old saying about March roaring in like a lion and going out like a lamb was true. She had thought January and February were cold, but today, the first of March, was colder than she could bear. It wasn't so much the temperature, which was actually only in the middle 30's. It was the stop-and-go rain and sleet and the nonstop wind that blew down the collar of her coat and into every warm fold of her body. She felt that all she'd done all evening was shiver, even with the heater cranked up. She checked her watch: 11:10. With a little luck, they'd make it through the last fifty minutes and head back to the station so she could go home to a nice warm bed and maybe some hot cocoa.

The dispatcher came over the radio reporting a car accident and, upon hearing the location, Dez hit the lights and siren. She pulled off onto a side street and reversed course. It was only a mile to the crash site and they arrived in short order. Jaylynn emerged from the car into a foggy, misty night where the cold bit through her clothes and made her shiver. The two-lane road, on a rise, was wet and slick from all the day's rain. A gravel shoulder on either side sloped down into wide fields where an occasional stubble of cornstalk poked up from wet ground. Even through the water, Jaylynn took note of the skid marks on the pavement, which dug into the gravel and into the short cropped grass as the hill gave way to the field.

Another cruiser was already on the scene. One officer lit flares to redirect traffic while the other crouched down in the hollow below the road, trying to make his voice heard over screams coming from a car upside down in the wet gully. The crashed vehicle was sunk down in a muddy depression, and shallow moving water surrounded the car. Jaylynn and Dez scrambled down the embankment to join the other cop who acknowledged them with a nod.

"Hello, Reilly, Savage."

"Hey, Coombs," Dez said. "What've we got here?"

Coombs stepped out of the ankle deep water to drier land next to them and tucked his cold hands under his arms. "Single car rollover. Four-door Ford Explorer SUV. Seems to be at least two occupants. I can't quite tell. The car is sitting upside down in maybe three inches of water. I stuck my arm in, tried to feel around, but the roof is crushed in too much. No way to pull these people out."

A piercing scream came from the car. "Help me! Help—oh God, help..." The voice trailed off into moaning and then all was silent.

Coombs shook his head. "I don't know what else to do."

Dez stepped back, then took three quick strides forward and abruptly leapt from the drier ground over onto the undercarriage of the overturned vehicle. Kneeling on cold metal, she leaned over the far side and saw that the driver's side was mashed completely into the gully. She couldn't even see the windows on that side. She turned and moved back to the side nearest her colleagues and squatted down. Leaning over the side, she kicked her legs back, and lay flat on the undercarriage, letting her head dangle over the side and into the broken-out rear passenger window. "Hey in there," she called out.

"Help me," came the plaintive cry.

"This is the police. We're here. We'll get you out."

"It's cold. Please...help me."

"We're working quick as we can. What's your name?"

"Cassie."

"Who else is in the car with you, Cassie?"

"Jordan and Francie."

"Who's driving?"

"Jordan."

"I can't see you very well," Dez said. Actually it was so dark she couldn't see anything in the car at all. "You're in the back seat, right?"

"Yeah. And it's cold."

How to ask the next question without scaring the girl? Dez decided being direct was best. "Are you able to crawl toward me?"

"No," wailed the girl. "I'm stuck."

"Are you upside down or not?"

"Yes, upside down."

Dez slid further over, bracing herself by grabbing something that felt like the axle, so that she could peer into the rear passenger window. Still she couldn't see anything. She pulled her flashlight off her belt and shone it on her own face. "Cassie." No answer. "Cassie, can you see me?"

"Um hmm."

"Okay, so you know I'm here, and we're going to get you and your friends out as soon as we can." She shone the light into the car and scanned the contents. The roof was compressed most in the front and on the driver's side. Dez couldn't tell for sure, but the two kids in the front seat didn't look like they could be alive. She couldn't see their heads at all, though she could see their torsos. There was no movement, and the roof was pressed into both bodies, so she didn't hold out much hope for them. The section of the car with Cassie in it was less crushed, but she could see that the girl was resting upside down on her shoulder and neck in a painful looking position. A couple inches of water pooled around her, and rivulets of blood dripped down her neck and face and into the water.

Too much blood, Dez thought. *We need to get her out of there.* "Cassie?" No answer. "Cassie!"

She stretched an arm in as far as she could and tried to grab the girl. She couldn't quite reach her. She pulled her arm back out. Using the flashlight Dez punched out the few remaining shards of glass in the rear window. "Hang on there, Cassie. Okay? You hear me?"

A quiet voice answered. "Um hmm. I'm...so...cold."

Dez raised her head. Across the way on the bank stood several figures. "Savage! EMT's here yet?"

"Yes, just arriving."

"We need blankets. We're going to need the fire department's jaws of life. Anyone call them?"

"Yeah," Coombs said. "I just did."

Two burly EMT's came over the rise and stumbled down into the gully carrying their tackle boxes of equipment. "Whaddya got there?" one shouted to Dez. A light rain began to drip into his face, and he wiped his eyes with a big paw.

Dez shifted from lying on her stomach to a kneeling position. She held up three fingers and said, "Three, I think, stuck in the car. We can only get to the one in the back seat." She stood and jumped off into the pool of water surrounding the car and waved the paramedics over. "We need to get in there and pull her out. Soon." She shone her flashlight in the window and gave a nod of her head.

The first EMT peered in, then stood up and nodded. "May have to wait for the Fire Department. No way can I get in there."

Dez said, "Me neither." She looked up the hill, but figured Coombs was also far too big. "Savage! Get over here." The rookie waded out into the water, cringing from the cold. She stepped on an uneven spot and staggered, but Dez grabbed her arm to help her regain her balance. "Sorry to do this to ya, but you're gonna have to crawl in there."

"Okay."

"You're gonna get pretty wet."

Jaylynn shrugged. She looked up as drops of rain fell, scattered at first, and then more heavily.

Dez said, "I'm not even sure you can squeeze in through the window, but I know I won't fit. I think you can do it if you get down to your t-shirt."

"Okay. What do I do when I get in there?"

"Unhook her seatbelt, work her free from what's holding her, and slide her out. If you get her close enough, we'll pull her out as carefully as we can."

Jaylynn took off her warm patrol jacket and handed it to Dez. She tried to hide the fact that her hands were shaking as she untucked her uniform shirt, unbuttoned it, and handed it over, too, then removed her bulletproof vest. Embarrassed, she pulled off her two layers of long underwear while Dez peered at her quizzically. That left only a scoop-necked tank top. She unhooked her gun belt and set it on the car. Lowering herself to her knees, she winced as the ice-cold liquid hit her legs and saturated her uniform pants.

"I'll help you in and out," Dez said as she piled all the clothes on top of the gun belt.

The two paramedics stood on either side of the window. Dez climbed on top of the car and lay on her stomach on the undercarriage, her head directly over the window, with her arms hanging down. Jaylynn poked her head through the misshapen window frame and squeezed her shoulders in. She grabbed at something that had the texture of wet plastic and then pulled until she felt herself lifted slightly by the back of her pants belt. The frozen metal doorframe dug into her thighs. With another tug, she was in far enough to feel the fabric of the car seat above her and the cloth of the jacket Cassie wore.

The cold water hit her chest and she nearly shrieked. Biting her lip, she pushed with her legs to leverage herself further into the opening and twisted halfway onto her side. She shivered as she fumbled around to locate the seat belt. Without warning the interior was suddenly flooded with light and she squinted. The rookie saw the upside-down outline of her partner's head in the window and looked back at the young girl, unconscious nearby.

Dez said, "Try to let her down real easy. Look, there's the latch for the seat belt. Kind of get under her and cushion her when it releases."

Jaylynn rolled onto her back, flinching from the chill of the frigid water. She squeezed under the girl's torso, further soaking herself, then reached up and pressed the red button. Released from the harness, the girl slid onto Jaylynn, emitting a groan and a mewling whimper before going limp.

A deep male voice said, "Is she stuck on anything? Can we pull her out?"

Jaylynn replied, "Yeah, I think you can."

Dez said, "Okay, you hang onto her, and we'll pull you out, okay?"

"Yeah. Go."

Jaylynn felt a vise grip on her ankles and she was dragged through the water toward the window. She clutched at the girl feeling the heavy weight.

She heard Dez's muffled voice say, "Let her go now," and the girl drifted away from her as though by levitation. "Let's get you out now, Jay." She was lifted again by her belt as Dez powered her, face up, through the window. She felt the edge of the window frame scrape across her chest and she put her hands over her face to avoid any sharp edges. It was like doing the limbo once she got her feet back on the ground. She wiggled and squirmed her way out into the cold rain with the help of Dez's strong hands.

Jaylynn said, "How is she?"

"We got her," came a deep male voice. The rookie stepped away, her feet numb, and trembled as she watched the two men carry the girl away. Outside the car, it was clear that Cassie was just a slender slip of a thing, hardly more than a girl. The burly men slogged through the water and up the embankment carrying the slight bundle and were over the top and out of her sight when she finally shook herself out of a daze and started toward dry land. There was a splash next to her and she looked up as Dez, holding her gun belt and shirts, took hold of her arm and guided her up out of the water. The big woman held out the silk long underwear shirt, then the cotton one. She slipped the Velcro vest over Jaylynn's head and helped her put on her blue uniform shirt, then wrapped the insulated patrol jacket around her shoulders.

"Quick," Dez said. "Zip this thing up." Jaylynn fumbled with the zipper with hands of ice. "Here. Let me do that." Impatient fingers pushed Jaylynn's hands aside and zipped up the jacket. Dez reached out and took the rookie's hands into her own warm ones. "Geez, your hands are cold. We've got to get you into the car and get the heat on."

Through chattering teeth the soaked woman said, "Aren't *you* cold?"

"Yeah, freezing! But I've had my coat on and I'm not nearly as wet as you." Keeping hold of one of the rookie's hands, Dez pulled

her up the embankment as firemen suddenly dashed past and down
to the car, dragging ropes and equipment.

The ambulance doors were just shutting Cassie in, and as they
hastened to their cruiser, the women watched it pull away, siren
blaring.

"Uh oh," Dez said. Lieutenant Andres stomped toward them,
a rapidly wilting unlit cigarette dangling from his lips. He had the
start of a day's growth of beard and his bloodshot eyes snapped and
flared at them. He held a hand up to stop them in front of the
patrol car.

"Reilly! What the hell did you think you were doing? Who
told you to effect a rescue?"

"Nobody, sir."

Jaylynn watched as Dez's face became cold and impassive, her
eyes small slits.

Andres said, "If anything happens to that girl, the department
could be liable."

"She was bleeding to death, sir," Dez said.

"You're not an EMT—how do you know?"

"I've got enough training to know *that*, sir."

"You patrol cops don't know shit." he said and continued to
harangue them, emphasizing departmental liability. Dez knew
Andres had never liked her and was probably squeezing his lucky
rabbit's foot with the hope that she made some sort of mistake for
which she would be found liable.

After a couple of minutes, Dez glanced over at Jaylynn and
then did a double take in concern. Shaking with cold, Jaylynn
stood dutifully, her lips nearly blue. Dez unzipped her own jacket
and slipped it off. "With all due respect, sir, Savage here is soaked
through. She could go hypothermic if we don't get her warmed up.
In fact, our shift ends in just a few minutes. With your permission,
I'm going to send her home to a hot tub."

Grudgingly he stepped aside. "There'll be hell to pay if you
screwed up, Reilly."

"Yes, sir," she said as she opened the cruiser door and stuffed
Jaylynn in. She covered the rookie's legs with her own coat, then
slammed the door shut and ran around to the other side. She got in
and started the engine, then pulled away in a spray of gravel.
"Fuckin' asshole."

"What?" Jaylynn asked. Her teeth chattered and she shivered
from head to toe.

"It figures my least favorite Lieutenant would have to venture
out on duty tonight." She cranked up the heat as high as it would
go. Once she was several blocks away from the accident site, she
turned on the siren and lights and floored it. "Maybe we should

have had the paramedics look at you."

Jaylynn shivered so hard, she was shaking. "I'm...okay...I'll...be...fine." She forced the words out.

Dez looked over at her, worried. She pulled up in front of the young woman's house, wrenched her door open, and flew around to the other side of the car to help the struggling woman get out.

"I'm fine," Jaylynn choked out. "Just need a hot bath."

"No no no," Dez said, as she steered her up the front walk toward the dark house. "You don't get a hot bath. You have to be rewarmed slowly. You can actually go into shock if you're hit with hot water—Jay? Jaylynn? Where are your keys? Your house keys?"

Jaylynn looked at her blankly.

Dez fished through the rookie's jacket, patted her front pants pockets. "Jay!" She leaned down and tipped the other woman's face up so she could look her in the eye. Jaylynn shook uncontrollably and stared, her eyes unfocused. Her skin was unnaturally pale, even whiter than Dez's. "Jay, do you have your house keys?"

"In...my...locker."

"Shit! You should have gone with the EMT's." Dez banged on the door and rang the bell. She waited, then took Jaylynn's arm and dragged her back to the car.

"I'll just go—take a hot bath—"

Dez paid no attention. She ripped open the passenger door and shoved the shaking woman in, not bothering to buckle her up, then ran back around to the driver's side. She hesitated long enough to crank up the heat before she peeled away. "Jay, listen to me. Don't go to sleep. You'll be warmed up soon. Come on, stay with me!" She reached over and smacked the trembling woman on the thigh. No response.

She screeched to a halt in front of Luella's and got Jaylynn out of the car. Twisting Jaylynn's arm around her own neck and with one arm around the smaller woman's waist, Dez pulled her along. Jaylynn stumbled beside her in a daze. Dez went right up the stairs and beat on the front door.

In a few seconds her landlady's nervous face peered out the side window, and then the front door popped open. She stood in her nightgown and fuzzy slippers, a pink wrapper pulled tight around her. "Why Dez—"

"Emergency, Luella. She's wet, probably hypothermic. I need your help." Dez grunted out as she half-dragged Jaylynn into the house.

Luella stepped aside to let them through. "What do you need, honey?"

"Need to borrow your guest room." Dez didn't wait for an

answer as she guided the lurching woman down the back hall. Over
her shoulder she said, "And will you go make some hot cocoa or
cider, something like that?"

"Sure," Luella called out. "There's extra blankets in the
bottom drawers of the dresser." She turned and headed for the
kitchen. "Two mugs of warm cocoa coming up in a jiffy."

Dez stumbled into the dark room and swatted an arm up the
wall to flip on the light switch. A lamp on a bedside table blinked
on and cast a warm glow on the pale tan walls, illuminating a small
room, neatly organized with a full-sized bed, maple dresser, and
kid-sized writing desk under the window. Dez moved the shaking
woman over in front of the bed and steadied her. She wrestled
Jaylynn's zipper down and slipped her jacket off, stripped away the
rumpled blue uniform shirt, then ripped off the Velcro strips of the
vest. The young woman's lips were blue, her eyes vacant and
drowsy. She leaned back against the edge of the bed.

"Wait. Don't sit yet. Help me out. Gotta get those wet things
off." She made Jaylynn stand, half-supporting her with one arm
while she reached back and pulled the bed covers open. Dez pulled
at the damp vest. She had to wrestle with it a bit, but she removed
it and then tugged the other three layers over the rookie's head,
finally stripping off the bloodstained tank top last. She undid
Jaylynn's belt and the water-soaked blue pants, slid them down, and
pushed her back onto the bed wearing only her bra and panties.
Dez fumbled at shoelaces until she got them untied and pulled the
duty boots off, then socks. The smaller woman's feet were like
frozen blocks.

"S-s-s-so cold," Jaylynn said as she shook uncontrollably.

"I know, I know. Lie down," she said in a gruff voice. "We'll
get you warmed up soon." Jaylynn tipped over to the side and Dez
took hold of her ankles and swung her legs up on the bed. She
pulled the covers over and tucked the smaller woman in.

Luella appeared in the doorway. She held an empty hot water
bottle under one arm as she unraveled the long cord of a heating
pad.

Dez moved closer to her landlady. In a low, worried tone she
said, "Maybe I should have taken her to the emergency room?"

"She's still shivering," Luella said, "so she'll be all right. It's
when you stop shivering that there's trouble."

"Can you keep an eye on her for a few minutes, Luella? I have
to return the squad car and sign us out, then I'll be right back."

"No problem, dear. Hurry up."

Dez disappeared from the room as the silver-haired woman
bent slowly and plugged the heating pad cord into the wall outlet,
then opened the bottom dresser drawer and tugged two wool

blankets out to spread over Jaylynn. She moved out into the living room to the thermostat and turned it up several notches. Returning to the guest room, she sat on the edge of the bed, humming to herself, her hand patting the shivering rookie. Before Luella knew it, the tall cop was back.

"That was quick," Luella said.

Dez said, "Speeding is one of the few benefits of driving a cop car."

Luella stood and inspected her tenant. Hands on hips she said, "Are you as wet as she is?"

"No. No, I'm fine."

"Don't lie to me, girlie. I can see you're wet. Look at those pant legs."

"Well, just my legs are wet. The rest of me is pretty dry."

Luella gave her a perplexed look and reached down to run her hand down to the knee of Dez's uniform. In her bossiest voice, she said, "You are too wet. Get those clothes off right now and crawl in there and warm her up. She's not gonna warm up quick enough without help, you know."

Dez said, "I was thinking maybe you could—"

"Are you nuts? I got the circulation of a penguin. Poor girl would probably freeze to death next to me. Go on. Get in. Here, toss these over the top of her." She helped Dez rearrange the two blankets, then said, "Hot chocolate ought to be done now, too."

Luella picked up the empty hot water bottle from the top of the dresser and shuffled out of the room, leaving Dez to strip off her own clothes and shoes and then go around to the opposite side of the bed. Jaylynn lay curled up on her right side facing toward the door, her arms clenched over her chest. Dez slipped under the covers and turned to her right side and scooted over. Before her skin even touched Jaylynn's, she could feel the chill radiating off, and she winced when the cold flesh touched the front of her legs. Jaylynn's back was a frozen block against her stomach, but she resisted the desire to recoil. Putting her arm around the smaller woman's middle, she moved as close as she could, tucking her head up over Jaylynn's left shoulder. The body next to her trembled violently, her teeth chattering so hard they made clicking sounds.

Luella bustled into the room with a TV tray and set it next to the bed, then left and returned with two mugs half-filled with steaming liquid, which she placed on the tray. She picked up the heating pad from the floor and went to the foot of the bed. "I'm going to tuck this under here on top of the sheet by your feet. I put it on high but it isn't all heated up yet."

Dez said, "Thanks Luella, you're a lifesaver."

"I'm going to go fill that hot water bottle too. How cold does her stomach feel?"

Dez shifted her hands to Jaylynn's middle and, a little embarrassed, pressed the flat of her hand there a moment. She said, "She feels pretty cold all over—maybe not quite as cold there."

"All right then. I'll be back in two shakes of a lamb's tail." She bent slowly and gathered up the clothes on the floor.

"Luella, you can leave those. I'll get them—"

"Don't you worry. Looks like some of this needs to be put to soak. I'll take care of it."

Jaylynn continued to shiver, but less violently, and Dez thought she could feel some warmth generating between them. Several minutes went by, and though Jaylynn wasn't shaking as much, her skin still felt like cold jello. More time passed and Dez began to worry. Quietly, because her lips were near Jaylynn's ear, she asked, "Hey, you feeling any warmer?"

Dez thought the smaller woman nodded, though she continued to shiver so she wasn't sure. "Jaylynn, was that a yes?"

"Um hmmm."

"As soon as the shivering calms down some, you think you can drink something warm?"

"I'll try."

"Your legs and back are a little warmer now."

Through gritted teeth, Jaylynn choked out, "Feels like I'll never get warm again."

"You will, just be patient."

"Where the hell are we?" she groused.

Luella stepped in the room just then carrying a bundle wrapped in a towel. "So, my dear, you're finally with it again?"

"Hi, Luella," she said miserably. "I think so."

"Here, take this hot water bottle and hold it on your tummy." She lifted up the edge of the covers and slipped the bundle under.

"Ohhhh, this is even warmer than Dez is."

Luella said, "That girl's like a furnace, isn't she? Dez, are your feet warming up?"

"Yes, Luella. My feet are fine."

"As long as you two are thawing, I may as well get together a little midnight snack. I'll be right back." She disappeared from the room before Dez could protest.

"Oh geez. She's gonna show up with a pile of food ceiling high."

In a muffled voice Jaylynn asked, "Would that be so bad?"

Dez nestled closer and lifted her chin up over Jaylynn's upper arm. "You're not shaking as badly now. I guess you're doing better, huh?" When Jaylynn assented, Dez said, "Think you could drink some cocoa?"

"Yeah."

Dez slipped her right arm under Jaylynn's neck and pulled herself up on her elbow. She snaked her left arm out from under the covers and hooked a mug. Carefully she brought it near. Jaylynn tried to reach for it, but Dez said, "No, just stay under the covers. I'll hold it for you."

Jaylynn lifted her head a bit and let Dez guide the mug to her lips. "Yum! This is great."

"Everything Luella makes is great. I'd weigh 300 pounds if I didn't fight her off daily."

Jaylynn let her head drop on Dez's arm. She shivered slightly and snuggled deeper. "I guess I'd weigh 300 pounds then. I couldn't refuse her."

"You'd probably only get to about 250 with the smaller build and all."

"That's comforting." Jaylynn pulled the covers tighter against her neck.

Dez set the mug back on the tray and picked up the other one, brought it to her lips and downed most of the hot liquid. "Whew, that is good. And it's not instant. She makes it from scratch."

"Dez?"

"Yeah?"

"Will you turn over?"

"What?" she asked, confused.

"On your other side. Will you turn over? My back is feeling better now, but my stomach and legs are freezing."

Dez flipped over and faced the wall. She flinched when the chilled skin touched her back, hips, and thighs, which made her break out in shivers. In a cranky voice she asked, "How can you be so cold and not dead?"

Jaylynn said, "How can you be so warm and not melted?" She pressed a chilly cheek to Dez's shoulder.

"Very funny."

Jaylynn shuddered again. "I'd be warmer without these wet underwear on."

"Yeah, me, too." Neither woman made a move to remove any more clothing.

Jaylynn slipped her right arm around the bigger woman's waist, placing her forearm against a taut stomach. With warm hands, Dez rubbed the cold arm and hand.

"Where's the hot water bottle?" Dez asked.

"Leaning on my back."

"Good. Here, I'm going to get the heating pad." She reached down and snagged the cord, dragged it up, and tucked it behind the smaller woman's knees then pulled the covers tight over them again and lay back down.

"Ohhh, that feels good. I can actually feel heat now. What a relief." An arm tightened around Dez's middle, and her hand came to rest just below the other woman's breastbone.

Dez looked down and realized she was beginning to feel heat she would not want to admit to. She swallowed and tried to still her beating heart. Glad she was not facing the chilled woman, she took a deep breath and resisted the urge to flee, saying, "You should have told me before you got so damn cold."

"I guess I didn't really notice until it was too late."

In a grumpy voice Dez said, "Now that you know what it's like, pay closer attention next time."

Dez felt a cold hand move down to the side of her stomach and pinch the muscle there. When she jumped, Jaylynn said, "I do believe you're in a compromising position here, Miss Big Shot Cop. Don't go getting grouchy on me or I'll have to tickle ya." She poked into the muscle of her companion's stomach.

"Hey!" Dez yowled, but Jaylynn's arm tightened around her before she could squirm away.

"I'm not warm enough yet."

Dez growled, "Be nice or I'll unplug the heating pad and leave you with that tepid hot water bottle."

"Yeah, right."

Dez turned over on her back. "You should drink the rest of that cocoa. I'm sure the 5-course meal chaser is coming any minute."

Jaylynn rolled onto her back, clutching the covers, and half sat up to grab the mug. She leaned on her elbow and sipped it. "I feel way better now, but I'm still cold. My feet are freezing."

"Here, put the heating pad on 'em." Dez sat up and reached to the middle of the bed until she found it. The blankets fell away as she leaned forward, revealing muscled shoulders and smooth ivory-colored skin.

"Dez!" Jaylynn said, "You're letting all the cold air in."

"Whine, whine, whine!"

From the kitchen a warbling whistle trilled. Jaylynn set down her mug. As Dez settled the heating pad against her feet, Jaylynn asked, "She's not *really* making a 5-course meal, is she?"

From her seated position Dez looked over her shoulder, a scowl on her face. In the golden lamplight, Jaylynn couldn't quite see the blue in her eyes. They actually looked dark and far away. "I guarantee you she is making some sort of full meal. I don't know how she does it." Dez sighed. "How are your legs and feet—you feel the heating pad now?"

"Yeah, but they're sure not as warm as the rest of me."

Dez stretched long arms under the covers and clamped hot hands on Jaylynn's left thigh, then kneaded gently down to her calf and back up. "Getting any circulation now?"

Jaylynn was grateful for the dim lamplight because a surge of warmth branched out starting somewhere in the pit of her stomach—or perhaps lower—and radiated outward. And then she felt the blush come on exactly when Dez leaned over more closely to give the same treatment to her other thigh.

"Does that help?"

"Yep, I'm definitely warmer." Jaylynn was relieved to hear the tread of the older woman in the hall. She rounded the corner into the room carrying two tall glasses of milk balanced in one hand and a pair of three-inch tall ceramic pink pigs in the other. Dez reached across Jaylynn and took the glasses from Luella's hand and put them on the TV tray. Jaylynn frowned as she looked at the pink pigs.

"Salt and pepper shakers," Dez said.

"Aren't they cute?" Luella asked. "I bought 'em years ago at an estate sale up the street. Two more minutes and I'll be back with some goodies."

"Nothing big for me, you know," Dez said.

"Um hmm," Luella said as she rolled her eyes and headed out of the room.

"Wait," Dez said. "Can I borrow a robe or shirt or something?"

Luella paused. "Why?"

"I want to run upstairs and get us some dry clothes."

Luella disappeared for a moment then popped back in the room. She handed Dez a worn green and red plaid wrap-around robe. "It was the mister's so it ought to fit you."

"Thanks. I'll bring it right back."

Jaylynn watched all of this with amusement. She wasn't used to anyone, not even the duty sergeant, ordering Dez around. Even more amusing was how meekly Dez took it from the older woman.

"Back in a second," Dez said. She threw the covers aside and stood, pulling the robe around her shoulders and tightening the belt before she turned around.

Jaylynn said, "I've still got the heating pad, but there's definitely a chill in the bed now that you've gotten out."

From the foot of the bed Dez glanced at her, a peculiar look on her face. "I'll be right back."

Jaylynn sank down under the blankets. She kicked her feet back and forth and felt the warmth of the friction from the heating pad and sheets. Even though her body was nestled in a toasty cocoon, she still felt chilled. She hadn't been kidding when she'd said it wasn't as warm without Dez.

She looked around the small room she was lying in. Plain and simple. Hardwood floors with a multi-colored braided rug next to the bed. The maple dresser matched the headboard. The window shade was open and a lacy valance hung at the top of the window frame. On the desk sat an 8 x 10 photo in a frame, but Jaylynn couldn't see the photo. Two of the pictures on the walls were of flowers: daffodils and jonquils in one, roses and bluebells in the other. The third picture hanging over the dresser was of two sweet children walking across a rickety bridge with a benevolent looking guardian angel hovering over them. The wide golden frame highlighted the gold of the children's hair and the angel's halo. All in all, it was a cozy room to warm up in.

True to her word, Dez returned carrying an armload of clothes and the plaid robe. She had changed into tan-colored wool socks, flannel sleeping shorts, and a loose black t-shirt that had a pink explosion on the front and read "Cherry Bombs Attitude Gear."

"Here," she said as she stood over Jaylynn. "Put this on." She handed Jaylynn a long-sleeved sleeping shirt. "Take off your wet things, okay?" She turned abruptly and sat on the edge of the bed facing away from the cocooned woman. Jaylynn sat forward and unhooked her bra, slipped it off, and then wormed her way into the shirt without ever taking the covers off. Over her shoulder Dez tossed a pair of red cotton shorts, soft and worn, and said, "Take the last of the damp stuff off and just wear these."

Jaylynn was more than happy to remove the wet underwear and slip on the shorts. They actually felt warm against her skin.

"Socks," Dez said. She stood and handed them to Jaylynn as Luella came around the corner bearing two plates.

"Now, Dez," Luella said. "You need to keep your strength up, so I went ahead and dished you up a plate, too." With fake menace in her voice, she ordered, "Get back in there where it's warm."

"All right," Dez said in a resigned voice. She moved around to the other side of the bed, got in, shifted upward against the headboard, and rearranged the covers over her lap.

Luella set the two plates on the TV tray, then pulled forks out of her robe pocket and handed them to Jaylynn, who passed one over to her glowering partner. Jaylynn paid no attention to her bedmate. She was intent on plates filled with buttered carrots, turkey, mashed potatoes, and a liberal splash of gravy covering half of each dish. Suddenly her stomach clenched, leaving her feeling weak. "I can't believe how hungry I am," she exclaimed.

Luella handed a plate to Jaylynn, who passed it to a reluctant Dez, then accepted the other for herself. The older woman beamed, then went over and got the desk chair and dragged it next to the TV tray. With difficulty, she lowered herself into the chair next to the bed and then watched as her young visitor lit into her plate like she hadn't had food for decades.

The gravy was succulent, spiced with pepper and something Jaylynn couldn't identify. "This is *so* good." She looked over at Dez who was dutifully eating the carrots.

"Now, are you girls going to tell me what happened?"

Between bites, the smaller woman told most of the story, though Dez took over for a while when it came to the parts Jaylynn was fuzzy about. After they'd explained, Jaylynn said, "I wonder how those kids are?"

In a low, flat voice, Dez said, "Probably all dead."

Jaylynn drew a quick breath. "What do you mean?"

Dez shrugged. "The kids in the front were crushed, I'm sure. And the girl would be lucky to live through that. Between her injuries and the cold—look how it affected you—well, she'd be lucky to live."

Jaylynn swallowed and sat back. "God, she was just a teenager. I hope she doesn't die."

Dez looked away and nodded. "Yeah. Maybe we got her out in time. Hard to tell." She set her plate on her lap. The carrots and turkey were gone, but not the potatoes or gravy.

Luella said, "I'm sure you two did the best you could. That's all anyone could ask. I'll pray for the girl tonight and tomorrow and perhaps God will see fit to give her another chance." She lifted her legs up to the edge of the bed and stretched them, leaning back in the chair. "Don't get old," she said. "Arthritis is just no fun at all."

Jaylynn set her plate aside on the TV tray. "Do you take anything for it?" she asked.

"Sure, but there's only so much can be done for these ancient legs."

A low voice said, "Couldn't have anything to do with the high fat diet." Luella ignored her.

Jaylynn elbowed Dez and pointed at her plate. "If you're not going to finish that off, may I?" Dez nodded, and the young woman snapped up the plate without a moment's hesitation. "This is just the *best* gravy."

With a sly grin Luella said, "Why thank you, dear. It's nice to be appreciated." She squinted her eyes and gave Dez a mock dirty look, which her tenant returned.

"Hey, I didn't do so bad, Luella. The turkey was great, as usual, and I did break my carb rule."

Jaylynn asked, "What's your carb rule?"

"No carbohydrates after six o'clock."

Luella shook her head. "Don't pay a lick of attention to her, dear. You go right on and eat like us normal folks."

Jaylynn shoveled in the last couple of bites, then said, "I'm pretty warm now, so I suppose I should get home."

But Luella wouldn't hear of it. She leaned forward and touched a moist palm to Jaylynn's forehead, smoothing back the white-blonde hair. "You still aren't all that warm. I think you should stay put. Besides, I've got some special breakfast goodies started. You need to stay and sleep. And you haven't got any clothes to go home in until I finish your laundry anyway."

"But it's the middle of the night, Luella," she protested. "I shouldn't be keeping you up. And you don't have to do my laundry."

"Oh, goodness, that's nothing. It's not like I sleep well anyway. And it's nice to have a little excitement every once in a while. Stop worrying yourself over it. I'm often up at this time." She looked at the gold watch on her wrist. "At midnight that talk show comes on that I like to listen to."

Jaylynn said, "Oh. What show?"

"I forget the man's name. He's somewhere in Colorado, and for two straight hours he talks to people about the government conspiracy regarding aliens."

Dez said, "Illegal aliens or outer space aliens?"

Luella said, "Definitely outer space. It's quite interesting."

Dez arched an eyebrow, flicking a look over at Jaylynn before she said, "Luella, don't tell me you believe in that stuff."

"Of course not, you fool," the older woman said with a chuckle. "But it's a laugh a minute listening to all the looney tunes who do." She ignored the teasing sigh of relief from her frowning tenant and lifted her legs off the edge of the bed, scooting the chair back. She stood, replaced the chair under the desk, and then picked up the plaid robe from the foot of the bed. "You just wake up in the morning when you want, and I'll fix you the mother of all breakfasts. You, too, Miss Health Nut. I'll make something you can eat, too. Now why don't you both get some sleep?" She shuffled to the door, hit the lights and went down the hall.

Jaylynn lay in the darkened room letting her eyes adjust to the faint light coming in the window. In the compact double bed, she was close enough to Dez to feel the heat the bigger woman exuded. She would have loved to move closer to that warmth, but something held her back.

A low voice said, "I can go up and sleep in my own place if you'd rather."

Jaylynn wasn't sure what to say. She opted for honesty. "That's okay. I'd like you to stay, Dez. You're keeping me warm, you know. Even from over there."

"Are you still cold? How about your feet and legs?"

"Not too bad. The food helped. I ought to be fine by morning."

"All right."

She felt the bigger woman turn away onto her side and rustle around trying to get comfortable. Jaylynn felt fatigue coming on very quickly, and she wafted along half-awake for several minutes. Dez continued to toss and turn furtively. Finally Jaylynn put a hand out and found Dez's hip. "Hey, if you're uncomfy, you don't have to stay. Do you need more room?"

"No. I just don't want to crowd you."

Jaylynn chuckled. "Oh please! I've got two little sisters who both crawl in bed with me every chance they get. I'm past the point of feeling crowded. Just relax, okay?" She turned on her side facing Dez, scooted over a few inches and snuggled into the bigger woman's side, settling her head against a warm shoulder and pressing her knees up to a toasty leg. "Good night," she said. No answer, but by then she didn't care because she was already asleep.

Jaylynn awoke a few hours later. The sun had risen and was casting rays of light through the window. She felt a thrill of contentment to find Dez pressed close behind, an arm around her waist and their legs entangled. She was warm and felt entirely protected. Shifting from her side, she looked back over her shoulder. Even in sleep the bigger woman scowled. For some reason, Jaylynn found that endearing. Settling back on her side, the arm around her tightened and pulled her closer. She took a deep breath and drifted back off to sleep.

Two hours later, Dez awoke to the sound of pans clanking far off in the kitchen. She was not amused to find herself wrapped around the rookie. It was all she could do to keep from leaping out of the bed. Instead she wormed away from the sleeping woman and slipped out, shaking her head with relief that Jaylynn hadn't realized she was being mauled. She wasn't sure how she would have explained herself. As she tiptoed out of the room, Jaylynn woke and said, "Hey you."

Dez stopped in the doorway. "You're awake. You feel rested?"

Jaylynn stretched and yawned. "Haven't felt this good in weeks. Bet my hair's a mess though."

In all seriousness, Dez said, "Yeah, you're giving Alfalfa a run for his money."

"Your braid is coming undone, too, so join the club."

Dez reached up to undo what was left of the braid, allowing her thick black hair to spill out over her shoulders. "I'll be back with some clothes," she said as she turned on her heel and disappeared down the hall.

Jaylynn grabbed the pillow from the other side of the bed, stacking it on hers, and reclined. She continued to snuggle in the warm covers. Being so cold the night before was almost like a bad dream, ethereal and hard to believe. In a few minutes, Dez returned fully dressed in jeans and a long-sleeved cotton jersey. Her hair was neatly brushed in its usual smooth French braid.

"Hey, no fair," Jaylynn said. "How'd you get tidied up so quick?"

Dez shrugged and tossed Jaylynn a pair of red sweat bottoms and an oversized blue and green wool sweater, then leaned against the doorframe with her arms crossed. Jaylynn pulled the sweater over her head. The waist was fine, but the shoulders bagged ridiculously. "Too bad you didn't run this wool thing through the washer and dryer for me. Maybe it would fit after it shrank."

"Sorry. Best that I could do."

"One good thing though—it's definitely warm." She pulled the red sweats under the covers and wrestled them on, then pulled the covers back up and leaned against the pillows. "It smells fabulous in here!"

Dez nodded. "She's in there creating sumptuous delicacies. Bet you're gonna love this."

"And you won't?"

"Like I said, I'd weigh 300 pounds if I let her feed me regularly."

"What's she making?" Jaylynn asked, an expectant look on her face.

"Oh, I can't spoil her surprise. She'll probably want to tell you herself. I'm not even sure how long she's been at it."

Alarmed Jaylynn said, "She hasn't been up all night, has she?"

"Oh no. She can whip up these two thousand calorie snacks in less than 15 minutes. Just wait and see. Are you gonna lie there all day or what?"

Reluctantly Jaylynn tossed the covers back and swung her legs over the side of the bed. Dez glanced down at her feet. "You want some slippers?"

"Nah, I'm good in these wool socks, but thanks."

Still slouching against the doorjamb Dez said, "So, no bad after effects from last night? You feel warm enough?"

"Oh yeah! But who wouldn't with such a great furnace emanating heat all night."

Dez stood up straight, trying to hide the blush that spread from her neck all the way to the roots of her hair. Before she could say anything, Jaylynn popped off the bed and put a hand on her forearm. "Desiree Reilly, that's a good thing. I'm thankful you exude heat like a pottery kiln. Sure made my life less miserable."

Dez ducked her head and shifted away, moving around to the other side of the bed. "You want to help me here?" She began pulling sheets and covers into place, smoothing the spread. Jaylynn took hold of her side and evened it up.

"How do I ever repay Luella?" Jaylynn asked.

"You don't. She wouldn't think of taking money. She loves to entertain and cook for people, but she's getting to the point where friends and relatives are old and infirm or dying off, so her circle is shrinking." Dez arranged the pillows, then picked up one of the blankets to fold. Jaylynn took the other. "She's a very social person, but all she's got left is her sister Vanita who lives on the other side of the lake near you. Neither one drives anymore, so I run them back and forth every so often. You'll have to meet Vanita sometime. They're like two peas in a pod." Dez opened the bottom drawer of the dresser and they put the two blankets away.

Jaylynn asked, "She never had a family?"

Dez stood and pushed the drawer shut with her foot. "Yes, she did." She stepped back and picked up the photograph from the top of the little desk. Jaylynn stood next to her and looked at an old studio picture of two adults and two boys. A stately black-haired, dark-eyed man sat in the upper left corner of the picture. His smile was wide, an obvious twinkle in his eye. He wore a dark suit with wide lapels and a black tie, and he was balancing a laughing boy of about six on his right knee. The boy was a miniature version of his father and was also dressed in a handsome dark suit. To the man's left sat a beautiful mahogany-skinned woman, her hair coifed high. She wore a flowered dress and long white gloves on elegant arms, one of which was steadying another laughing child in her lap. The second little boy was a toddler dressed in light-colored slacks, a white shirt with a high collar, and red suspenders. His head was turned toward his brother and they seemed to be sharing a moment of total hilarity while their parents attempted to fight back laughter themselves.

Jaylynn leaned closer to peer at the photo Dez held. She put an arm around the bigger woman's waist and leaned her head on her shoulder. "If that's Luella, she was drop dead gorgeous!"

"Yes, she was."

"She's still a good-looking woman now, but wow. Look at her." She studied the photo a moment longer, then said, "I bet she was a corker of a mom. What happened to her husband?"

Dez sighed and nervously stepped away from Jaylynn's embrace. She replaced the photo on the desk. "They all died in a house fire in the 60's—smoke inhalation. Luella was staying at her sister's to help with their new baby."

Jaylynn gasped and said, "Oh, that's *terrible*. Such a beautiful family." She paused a moment. "Now I know one of the reasons she seems to take a person under her wing."

"Wish I'd known her back then," Dez said. "I don't know how she ever got over it."

From the doorway came a voice, "I don't know how I got over it either." Both women looked up, startled. Luella gazed at them thoughtfully. "It was no doubt the worst thing that ever happened in my whole life. Every other rotten thing pales in comparison. But it happened thirty-five years ago." She looked at Dez. "It does get better over time. I'd have to say you never quite get over it, never forget, but after a while it feels like less a burden."

"Oh, Luella," Jaylynn said. "It brings a tear to my eye to think of it."

"Mine, too, at times," the older woman said. "But we've still got lives to live, things God set us on earth to do. You keep on keeping on, that's what you do." She picked up the two mugs from the TV tray near the bed. "A body's got to enjoy what the good Lord provides today because it may not be there tomorrow. I loved those little boys and their father, and I'm happy to have had them in my life, even if only for a little while. That's how I feel about things nowadays. People, too. They're only in your life a while, so live it up while you can."

She turned in the doorway and called back over her shoulder, "And speaking of living it up, come on in the dining room. As soon as the timer rings, apple panny-cakes will be on the way to the table, and you definitely need to see them all puffed up in their splendor and glory."

Jaylynn wiped a tear from her cheek with the back of her hand. She looked up at the passive expression on Dez's face, and when the tall woman met her eyes, Jaylynn said, "What?" She glared at the taller woman. "Are you making fun of me?" Dez shrugged and Jaylynn punched her upper arm. "I can cry all I want right now— I'm not a cop at this moment."

Dez protested. "I didn't say anything!"

"Hmpfh...but you probably wanted to."

"Let's go try out her latest recipe," Dez said as she led the way out of the small room.

She stopped abruptly in the hall and Jaylynn nearly ran into her. "Wait. You go on," Dez said. "I'll run down and bring the laundry up. There are a couple of items I'm sure you'll eventually need."

"Like underwear?"

"Yup."

"Good deal. I was wondering where they'd gone."

Chapter
12

Dez steered past the well-lit River Centre convention hall. It was ablaze with light because of a Self-Esteem Psychology Conference taking place there. She and Jaylynn were assigned away from their regular sector due to all the activities in downtown St. Paul, which included the play *Jekyll & Hyde* at The Ordway Theater at night and a dental convention during the day. She didn't know why it was so apparent, but even without white coats and drills, she thought she could recognize the dentists out on the streets. They looked quite different from the rabid-looking pack of people waiting outside the theater for *Jekyll & Hyde*.

Dez slowed and scanned the area past the theater and across Washington Street near the private St. Paul Club. Walking away from her, she saw a tall slender young man dressed in a baseball cap, ratty jeans, and a light tan jacket. *Hmm...that guy is totally out of place. He doesn't look like he belongs with the esteem attendees, the dentists, or the Jekkies.* Her eyes narrowed as she slowed the car and concentrated on him, and she felt Jaylynn do the same. A man dressed in a suit and a woman dolled up in a wool coat and very high heels strolled toward the police car, obviously headed for the theater. A football-sized purse trailed from the woman's shoulder.

Jaylynn shot a glance at Dez and then back to the couple. "You know what—" but before she could finish, the tan-coated man darted forward, snagged the dangling purse, and took off. "I knew it!" she said. She reached for the radio and reported what was happening, calling for backup and giving a block-by-block account of their location.

Dez gunned the car engine and sped ahead to Kellogg Boulevard. The man cast a brief look over his shoulder and saw them. He tucked the purse under one arm, and, like a wide receiver, cut out across the street, dodged around a honking car, and raced to the left.

There was nowhere for him to go on the Boulevard but down the hill. He was penned in on the river side, along the bluff, and if he were to cross back over to the side he had just come from, he had to know the officers would be out of the car and on him. As long as he stayed herded on the wide sidewalk, they would drive parallel on the street, lights flashing. All they had to do was wait for him to reach the freeway overpass ahead. At the overpass, Kellogg Boulevard became a gradual uphill incline. At that point he would surely run out of energy and they could capture him easily, especially since by then another unit would be heading toward them to cut him off. Every so often he craned his head around, desperately looking for a safe exit.

"Where the hell does he think he's gonna go?" Dez asked.

"He could turn and run across the Robert Street Bridge," Jaylynn replied.

"Unless he jumps, which I doubt he'd do unless he's crazy, we'll have no problem grabbing him there."

"Hmm...what about those warehouses up ahead?"

"But he'll have to cross the street—" He chose that moment to cut across the boulevard. "Yippee-ki-yay! Our boy's outta the chute!" Dez slammed on the brakes, and Jaylynn smacked open the door and peeled out of the car after him. Dez hit the siren and sped ahead, intending to cut him off at the next street.

The man had a half block advantage, but he was slowing in fatigue from the eight-plus blocks he'd already run. He huffed and puffed up the side street next to a row of rambling, broken-down warehouses. He slowed to pull on a door handle, but no luck. Jaylynn was within yards of him when he grabbed another door and, much to his obvious surprise, it opened.

"Shit!" Dez said. She grabbed the radio and called in the address for backup.

Before the heavy metal door shut, Jaylynn had disappeared through it. Dez drove up on the sidewalk, threw the car into park, and got out of the car. She pulled out her gun, raced to grab the door handle, then went in low. Pausing for a heartbeat, she heard the clatter of footsteps on stairs and holstered her weapon, grabbing her flashlight in its place. She ran ahead, passing piles of trash and heaps of unrecognizable junk. The warehouse smelled foul and musty, like there were dead things present. She found the stairs and started up them two at a time.

"Jay!" She no longer heard footsteps and focused on powering her way up. After seven flights of stairs, her thighs burned. She rounded another flight and saw the steps ran out. Another door was just closing at the top. Hitting it with her shoulder before it clicked shut, she burst into a large cavernous room illuminated only by the streetlamps outside. Shafts of light shone in through tall casement windows, which stretched from Dez's waist to near the top of the high vaulted ceiling.

Thirty yards across the warehouse floor, the man stood leaning against the far wall, doubled over and trying to catch his breath. Dead end. Jaylynn held her gun, braced on her left arm.

"Police," Jaylynn panted. "Put...your hands up...turn around...face the wall. Don't move, and...I won't shoot." She gasped the words out, but the man understood because he dropped the purse and followed her directions. She advanced slowly, stepping cautiously across the old wooden floor. Dez kept her flashlight down and drew her weapon.

When Jaylynn reached the middle of the floor, the big cop felt an odd vibration, and then heard a cracking and a roar. Jaylynn disappeared. One second she was standing, crouched, her back to her partner; the next moment she vanished.

Dez's vision was obscured by a plume of dust shooting up from the floor. Their suspect let out a shriek and fell to the floor, cowering against the far wall. The tall cop holstered her gun, dropped to her knees, and scrambled forward. "Jay!" she shouted. She breathed in powdery dirt and choked back a cough.

She heard a sound, muffled and wheezing, but she recognized Jaylynn's voice. "Dez!"

"I'm coming! Keep talking so I can find you."

"I'm afraid to move."

"Stay still then," was the gruff reply.

Dez crawled to the middle of the floor and pulled back just in time to avoid sliding into a gaping seam in the floor.

From below Jaylynn said, "I could almost jump up and grab the edge—but I'm not so sure how secure this is."

Dez lay on her stomach and pulled herself to the edge to look over. "Definitely stay still. It doesn't look secure at all."

The fourth floor supports had rotted away and the brittle planking resting on them had broken, creating a crease in the floor six feet wide that ran from one wall of the warehouse to the other. Jaylynn was perched at the point where some of the cracked boards met but hadn't quite given way. Any minute, the entire jumble of timbers looked like they would go crashing to the floor below.

Dez was aware of the creaking sound of stressed wood separating. "Jaylynn," she said in a low, level voice. "Can you see me clearly?"

"Your head, I can see that."

"See my hand? I'm gonna reach down as far as I can. I want

you to stand very slowly and grab on." With her right hand, Dez gripped the edge of the hole, and with her left she reached as far as she could, angling her body a little to the side. Out of the corner of her eye she saw Jay's hand, then felt it on her wrist. With strong fingers she clenched the smaller woman's arm, felt cloth and skin, and then heard a crunching, crashing sound. The planks under Jaylynn crumbled. A shock of cold air and dust blew into Dez's face, blinding her. She bore the weight of the smaller woman, feeling for a brief instant as though she'd dislocated her shoulder. But she held on and didn't lose her grip. With a growl of exertion, she rolled away to leverage the dangling woman upward. She grabbed Jaylynn's belt with her right hand and practically threw the rookie across her body and away from the hole.

The two women scrambled away from the center of the room. Breathless and wheezing, they sat against the wall near the door by which they'd entered. Dez ran her hand over the back of her neck, feeling grit under her palm. *That was close,* she thought, *too damn close.* She heaved a sigh and rubbed her eyes to clear the dirt from them. She drew her legs up and put her elbows on her knees, letting her hands relax out in front of her. "What happened to our runner?"

A voice sounded from across the room. "I'm still here. I'm not moving until I know the floor's safe."

In a menacing voice Dez said, "Don't move a muscle. The whole floor is unsafe. It could fall in at any minute. I will instruct you when it's safe." Dez shook with silent laughter.

Jaylynn elbowed her and hissed, "I don't think it's very professional of you to laugh when I almost got my ass crushed."

In a low rumble, Dez said, "I'm not laughing at *you.* It's that idiot. He had all this time to split, and he's sitting over there waiting for help." She giggled helplessly, relief flooding through her.

"It is kind of funny," Jaylynn said grudgingly.

"Are you hurt?"

"Not that I can tell. I landed on my butt, plenty of padding there."

"Oh, yeah, your butt is so huge, right." She craned her head to the side to find Jaylynn looking up at her, the hazel eyes serious and penetrating. It was like a jolt of electricity hitting the big cop in the stomach. She looked away, glad of the dim light, and wondered why the rookie kept having this effect on her. *Get a grip,* she thought to herself as she cleared her throat and tried to steady her breathing.

The quality of the light shining through the windows changed from a steady yellow glimmer to periodic red flashes. Backup had arrived. In seconds they could hear footsteps beating their way up the stairs. Dez stood and opened the stairway door. "Fourth floor, guys. Come on up!" she hollered. To Jaylynn she said, "Here comes the cavalry." Jaylynn rose and attempted to brush off some of the dust and crud adorning her uniform.

"Don't bother," Dez said as she stifled a sneeze. "We're both too filthy to worry about it."

The backup cops, three of them, blasted around the corner and came huffing up the last set of stairs.

The tall woman said, "It's Reilly and Savage here, guys. Be careful. The floor up here isn't safe. Hey, Harnish," she said as the first officer's face became recognizable. "How ya doing?"

"No, the question is: how are *you* doing?"

"A little worse for wear, but otherwise okay."

"You look like you fell into a bowl of dirty flour."

"Yeah, well, at least we've got our suspect cornered."

The five officers stood inside the doorway and Dez called out, "All right, buddy, you gonna give us any trouble?"

"No, ma'am."

Dez and the other officers shone their flashlights in his direction. She said, "Stand up and face me. Now put your hands on your head. Wait! Pick up that purse and bring it with you, but keep your hands up. Good. Move to your right and ease your way along the wall until you reach the corner, then walk this way. Just hug the wall and you'll be okay."

In a deep authoritative voice Harnish said, "We've got enough fire power here to blow you away, so don't even think of trying anything tricky."

"No, sir," the man said in a resigned voice as he shuffled along the wall toward them.

Though her breathing had steadied, Jaylynn's heart was still beating wildly. *That was close, too close. I wonder how far I'd have fallen?* She swatted at her pants legs again, raising dust that made her cough.

The runner materialized in front of the phalanx of officers.

"Savage, it's your collar," Dez said. "You cuff him, pat him down. Oh, and read him his rights."

After they'd stowed the runner in the car and backup departed, Dez started to get in the vehicle. Jaylynn stood on the sidewalk, uncertain.

One leg in the cruiser, Dez stared over the top of the car and said, "What? What's wrong?"

"My hat. I lost it."

"So what? I'll give you another one."

In a voice too quiet for Dez to hear across the car, Jaylynn said, "And my weapon."

"What? I didn't hear that—"

Jaylynn frowned and shook her head. She hated to admit losing her gun. She knew that was rule number one: never lose your weapon under any circumstances. "I'll be right back."

"You don't want to go back in—oh damn." Dez leaned in and told the suspect to stay put, knowing full well he couldn't get out of the locked back seat of the squad car. She slammed the driver's door and stomped over to the warehouse door. Out came the flashlight again, and she went back up the flights of stairs to the third floor, through the doorway and around the corner into the main cavern. She found Jaylynn standing in the shadows against the wall. In the middle of the floor, the pile of planks that had fallen from above were strewn haphazardly, the wood broken and twisted. A gaping hole let a faint light shine down from above.

"Jaylynn?"

The smaller woman didn't move.

Dez moved over into the shadows next to the rookie. "What's the matter?

Jaylynn turned to her. "That's a good 16 or 18 feet."

"Yeah? So what?"

"I might have survived the fall, but maybe not. I might have been impaled on something. I could have broken my back, my neck..." She reached out and clutched her partner's biceps. "If you hadn't—"

"Don't go there." Dez took hold of both of Jaylynn's forearms and squeezed gently. "Don't think about that. Let's just find your hat and get the hell out of here before *this* floor falls in."

"That's twice now." Jaylynn's voice quivered.

"Oh geez, Jay! Cut it out. It's not that big a deal."

"It is to me."

"Look," Dez said. She bent down, her hand on the rookie's shoulder, and pulled Jaylynn closer so each woman could clearly see the other's eyes. "Partners watch each other's back. You'd have done the same for me."

"As if I could have pulled you out of that."

"You'd be surprised at what you can do if you have to. Ever hear the one about the woman lifting the Volkswagen off some kid who was trapped?"

"Now you're probably going to tell me that was you."

Dez gave a muffled laugh. "No, you lunatic." She slipped an arm around Jaylynn's shoulders and steered her over toward the heap of over-sized pick-up sticks. "You got about 30 seconds. Find your hat and let's get outta here."

"I don't care about the hat. I want my gun."

"Oh." Dez rolled her eyes and sighed. "That's different. When did you drop it—right at first or after you fell?"

"After I fell."

Dez moved to the jumble of boards and started shifting them away. "It'll be just our luck—it'll be at the very bottom in the middle. Yuck. This is so filthy."

"Here, let me help."

"Be careful. There's nails and splinters—shit!"

"What?" Jaylynn asked with alarm in her voice. She stood up and started toward Dez.

"Never mind. I'm fine. Just one of those splinters I was warning *you* about. I'll get it out later."

Together they shifted through the wood until they found the black .38 covered in dust.

"Guess that'll need a good cleaning," Jaylynn said. She stood, holstered her gun, and turned to leave. Out of the corner of her eye she saw something round several feet away from the pile. She went over and picked up her hat and swatted at it to dust it off. "Hey, what do you know—at least this isn't as dirty."

"Too bad. Then it won't match the rest of your uniform," was the dry reply as her partner led the way to the stairwell.

****

Tim picked up Jaylynn after her shift ended and they came home to the well-lit house. As they went up the back walk, Jaylynn heard the tinkle of the piano keys and both of them stopped on the back porch and listened. Sara hadn't played the piano for months, and Jaylynn didn't want to interrupt. They stood, wordlessly, and listened to the waves and crescendos of a moody classical piece that she thought was Mozart.

They stayed on the porch for several minutes until they were both shaking from the cold. When she finally nodded her head, Tim turned and put the key in the lock. He flicked the kitchen light on and off and hollered out. The music stopped abruptly and Sara appeared in the doorway.

"Hi, guys," she said. She smiled, her large brown eyes shining.

"Nice tunes," Jaylynn said as she shucked off her coat and mittens to hang them on the hook inside the door. Tim draped his coat over the top of hers and rubbed his hands together, blowing on them to warm up.

"Um hmm..." Sara said. "You guys look good and cold. Time for some hot tea, huh?"

The red-haired man said, "I think we should go straight for the brandy, for medicinal purposes, of course."

Jaylynn laughed, and the three bustled around the kitchen getting tea bags and mugs and hot water assembled.

As they all settled at the wooden kitchen table Sara said, "Jay, you never said what happened to those kids in the car wreck."

Jaylynn's face fell, and she set down the sugar bowl with less grace than she should have, wiggling the table and causing her tea to slosh over the side of her over-full mug. She rose and got a rag from the sink, saying, "The two kids in the front seat—they died. I guess they were dead when we got there. Dez and I went to see the other girl who we pulled out and she's a mess." She sat back in her chair and mopped up the spilled tea. She remembered the anguish in the face of the girl's mother, a nondescript woman who looked no older than Dez. The rookie had hardly been able to contain her own tears when she saw the frightened faces of the two little brothers and sister in the waiting room. "I called the hospital again today and she's out of intensive care, but she's going to be hospitalized a while."

Tim reached over and patted her arm. He held up the brandy bottle. "You want a shot of this, Jay-o?"

She shook her head. "Nah. I'll just have bad dreams."

"From a little shot of brandy?" he asked.

She nodded. "Lately I've had some weird nightmares—they're out in full force."

In a soft voice Sara said, "Tell me about it—me, too."

Jaylynn sprang on the opening. "It's still troubling you a lot, isn't it?"

Sara nodded and took a sip from her tea. "It's okay when you guys are here, but when you're not, well, I guess I have The Man In The Closet syndrome."

Jaylynn raised an eyebrow and waited, and Sara went on. "It's like I never really feel safe because they're always bound to be hiding somewhere I didn't look. Even with the doors locked and the windows all shut, it's still scary." She shivered, then wrapped her hands around her mug. "Sometimes I wish I had a gun like you do, Jay."

"Aw, Sara, a gun isn't the answer. And don't forget, I can't bring mine home yet, not until I'm off probation anyway. It's sitting in my locker at work right now." She reached over and covered Sara's forearm with her hand. "Have you had any luck with that technique I told you about?"

"Not really. The only thing that seems to work is just not sleeping."

"Oh, Sara," she said, "that's not good. Just come sleep with one of us."

Tim nodded and closed the top of the brandy, then got up and took it over to the cupboard to put it away. "You can always crawl into my bed." He grinned devilishly. "And Bill can rest assured you won't be ravished by the likes of me."

Both women laughed, then Sara's face turned serious. "I made an appointment at the college counseling center. I'm going to see someone. I know I have to deal with this."

"Good for you," Jaylynn said. She reached over and took Sara's hand and gave it a big squeeze. "You just have to keep talking about it. We're here to listen. Over time it'll get better."

"I hope so," the brown-eyed woman replied.

****

The next day Jaylynn gathered up her courage again. They were patrolling the western sector in a residential area and nothing was happening; a dull day for both weather and criminal activity. The sky overhead was battleship gray, and the wind out of the north cut through her every time she had to leave the car.

"So how about Sunday night after shift?" she asked.

Dez knew exactly what she meant and had been hoping the topic would not come up again. "I don't think I could watch that particular video right now." She didn't elaborate.

"Well, how about *Shadowlands* or *The Evening Star*?"

"Do you know what those are about?"

"Not really."

"Maybe we could go with something a little lighter."

Jaylynn sprang at her chance. "Oh, there are scads there I haven't seen. Pick any of them, whichever you like. You got any you haven't seen yet?"

"No, I don't think so."

"Well, we could rent something. Tell you what, I'll skip bringing the box of hankies and bring the video instead—something not too heavy at all. How's that?"

"All right," Dez said in a low, resigned voice. How could she tell Jaylynn no when she sounded so happy and hopeful? She frowned. *Now I suppose I have to be perky and cheerful when she's there.*

But she wasn't perky or cheerful on Sunday night. Not when Jaylynn showed up at eight p.m. with an older video, gushing about how Debra Winger was one of her all-time favorite actresses. She'd rented *Black Widow*. Dez lied and said she hadn't seen the movie, when in fact she'd watched it in the theater and liked it immensely. But did Jaylynn know about the lesbian undertones in the film? *Geez, she's young,* thought Dez. *Maybe she won't even have a clue. Maybe the subtext will pass her by.*

Dez nuked two packages of Orville Redenbacher popcorn and poured them into a big bowl, and they settled onto the couch to watch the show. Scooting near the middle of the sofa, Jaylynn slipped off her shoes and curled up close to the popcorn bowl. Dez slouched down, stretching her long legs out onto the coffee table and crossing them at the ankles. She crossed her arms, too.

Jaylynn had also seen *Black Widow,* and she'd picked it on purpose hoping she could get some sort of reaction out of Dez. *Is she or isn't she?* The guys at the station treated her with respect to her face, but did she know they made comments about her sexuality behind her back? It seemed everyone assumed Dez was gay—just as they assumed Jaylynn was straight. Wouldn't it be an ironic about-face if it were the other way around? But no, Jaylynn was pretty sure about the tall woman. It was that connection she kept experiencing, something about the way Dez looked at her. They hadn't talked about it yet, but she was sure Dez had to feel it, too.

An hour into the movie Jaylynn glanced over at Dez to find her fast asleep. She looked so tired that Jaylynn sat quietly and watched the remainder of the show alone. *So much for gauging her reaction.* After the movie ended, Dez gave no indication of wakening, so Jaylynn picked up the remote and flipped to an oldies station to watch an old black and white movie, *The Thin Man Returns.*

When the show ended at eleven o'clock, Jaylynn decided to call it a night. She turned the sound down a little with the remote and rose to leave. She took the popcorn bowl into the kitchen and collected up Tim's car keys, then could not resist going back into the living room. Dez slept with a scowl on her face, chin tight to her chest, arms and legs crossed, folded up into herself. Jaylynn crept across the floor and brushed a tendril of hair away from Dez's forehead, then leaned over and touched the lightest of kisses there. The sleeping woman didn't stir.

Dez awoke with a start when she heard Jaylynn let herself out. The clock on the VCR read 11:05. *Oh, crap. I slept for two hours? Geez!* She reached up and rubbed her forehead. *Was Jaylynn kissing me a dream? Live or Memorex?* She wasn't sure. *Probably wishful thinking. Wishful thinking?* She took a deep breath and tried to put the smiling blonde woman's face out of her mind. She got up and undressed, dropped her clothes on the valet chair next to the bed and crawled under the comforter. But she didn't sleep well for the rest of the night after all, and her dreams were frightening. What she remembered when she awoke was fire and blood, gleaming fangs and pain, and screaming—sometimes her own, sometimes not.

****

Jaylynn went home to a house aglow with light from every window. *Oh good,* she thought. *Sara's still up.* She unlocked the front door and called out, "It's me," so that Sara would hear her loud and clear. The first thing that assailed her senses was the smell of cinnamon. She dropped her backpack by the front door and hustled down the hall to the kitchen.

Sara was putting a sheet of cookies in the oven. "Hiya, Jay," she said over her shoulder. She shut the oven door and turned to face her friend. "Uh oh. You're glowing again."

Jaylynn blushed and put her hands in her jeans pockets, then leaned against the kitchen counter.

Sara said, "You're glowing *and* blushing, my friend. Any salient details to share with your best bud?"

"Nah, nothing like that." Jaylynn walked over to the kitchen table and dropped into a chair. "Whatcha making? Smells great."

"Snickerdoodles."

Jaylynn's glance swept the room. "Well? Where are they? They smell so great—you couldn't have already eaten a whole batch!"

"Of course not. I just made one to make sure the dough was right."

"You are the *only* person I know who would do that. I'd just go ahead and ruin 12 or 15 cookies." Jaylynn leaned back in the chair with a smile on her face. "So where is it?"

Sara pushed her brown hair behind her ear. "I guess you could say I *did* eat the whole first batch...even if it was only one cookie. You'll have to wait about 12 more minutes." She put her elbows on the table and rested her face in her hands. "So, tell me what happened tonight with Desirable Dez."

Jaylynn blushed. "Really, truly—nothing. Nada. Zip."

Sara's face took on a sly look. "Ah, but you're wishing."

"Oh yeah. Guess I have to admit that."

"What is it about her? The couple times I've had a glimpse of her, she's just so—so—gee, how do I explain it?"

"Fascinating?"

"Actually, the word I think I had in mind would be cranky."

"Oh, Sara," Jaylynn said earnestly. "She's really not cranky at all. Fascinating, yes. Mysterious, yes. Sexy, oh my God! But not cranky. She's just shy until you get to know her."

"So what did you and Miss Fascinating do this evening to set the night on fire?"

"It wasn't like that. We watched a video. Ate popcorn. She fell asleep. I came home."

Sara stifled a laugh. "Some date that turned out to be! Unless something more intimate happened between the popcorn and the sleep, then I'd have to say BOR-ring!" The timer went off, and Sara took the cookies out. "Mm-mmm. These are just perfect, Jay." By then Jaylynn was looking over her friend's shoulder hungrily. "But you'll have to wait a minute or two 'til they set up a bit." She waved her friend away, and Jaylynn made a big show of sighing and rolling her eyes before she sat again at the table. Sara crossed her arms over her U of M sweatshirt and leaned back against the counter.

Thoughtfully, Jaylynn said, "She's not a very trusting person, Sara. The fact that she fell asleep, well, that means she let her guard down around me. She hasn't done that before. I take that as a good sign."

Sara shook her head and smiled. "You got it bad, girlie. I am *sure* I would never stick with a guy I dated who fell asleep on me right in the middle of the damn date." She turned and picked up the spatula, then scraped the cookies off the sheet and placed them carefully on a brown paper bag already laid out on the cutting board.

"But, Sara," she protested, "it wasn't a date. Actually, it was more of a get-together between two friends. I'm not exactly sure how she feels." Jaylynn frowned. "I know she likes me. She doesn't let anyone else joke around with her, and when we're alone on patrol, she loosens up a lot. But she *is* a tough nut to crack. I'll admit that. I think she's coming out of an awful time. When her old partner died, that really cut her deep."

"I don't want you to get hurt."

"That's not gonna happen! You worry too much."

Sara scooped up the last cookie and walked to the table to drop it into Jaylynn's hands. Jaylynn promptly broke it and devoured half in one bite. "Yum yum," she said with a full mouth. "You do make the *best* cookies." She popped the other half into her mouth and mumbled, "As Seven of Nine would say, 'I require more sustenance immediately.'"

"You and your fantasy women!"

Jaylynn swallowed, then paused. "I'd rather have a real one."

Chapter
13

Wednesday afternoon they met in roll call, and Dez gave Jaylynn a sheepish smile. Jaylynn chuckled and found a chair nearby. One by one other cops shuffled into the room and sat down until the duty sergeant gave out assignments. All the way to the lot Jaylynn kept looking at Dez through narrowed eyes and making tsk-tsk noises.

Once the two women got settled in the police car, Dez blushed and said, "I know, I know, I owe ya for the other night."

Jaylynn laughed and punched her in the arm. "No, you don't."

"Yeah, I do. I'm sorry."

"Maybe I should feel complimented that you felt comfortable enough to zonk out and snore like crazy."

"Oh pulleeze! I didn't snore."

Jaylynn punched her again. "No, actually you didn't. I'm just kidding. You are fun to tease, girl. You take everything so seriously."

Dez hit the gas and pulled out of the parking lot. "No, I don't."

"Oh, yes you do. Just look at your movie collection. Do you have a single comedy?"

"What's your point?"

"That's my point. You're an awfully serious person."

"Not always."

"Most of the time," Jaylynn said.

"What? And you're not a serious person?" She looked over at the warm, smiling hazel eyes, and it occurred to her that she was definitely going to lose this argument. "Okay then, fine. Let's try it again. This time you bring over something funny to watch. Something that'll keep me awake."

"When?"

"Whenever...after shift on Sunday if you want."

Jaylynn paused thoughtfully. "Won't work. I can't borrow Tim's car."

"I'll take you home later—how's that?"

Jaylynn nodded. "Okay, then you can come to the video store and help me pick out something funny."

"All right, rookie, you got a deal." Keeping her eyes on the road, Dez held out her hand palm up expecting Jaylynn to give her five. Instead, she was surprised to feel a warm squeeze. She let her hand drop, but Jaylynn didn't relinquish her grip until their hands hit the seat.

****

"I'm not so sure I like Woody Allen," Dez said.

"Oh, shut up," said a smiling Jaylynn as she inserted the video into the VCR. "This is a thinking person's funny movie. I don't think you're the slapstick type, are you?" She put her hands on her hips. "Did you want to get *Police Academy* or one of those *Airplane* shows?"

"Not really."

"You'll like this one. It's quite entertaining."

"But you've already seen it."

"It's worth a second watch."

"OK, but if you fall asleep, don't blame it on me."

Jaylynn laughed heartily. "*I* won't fall asleep, don't worry." She plopped down on the couch next to Dez and the popcorn bowl and waited for the credits to roll.

Dez groused, "Do you have any idea why movie makers these days feel the need to include 12 or 13 minutes of previews before the movie starts?"

"Sells more videos that way."

"It's irritating."

Jaylyn plucked the remote out of Dez's hand. "I'll fast forward through them then." She got to the beginning of the movie and leaned forward to set the remote on the coffee table, then settled back next to Dez, their shoulders just barely touching. The tall woman picked at the popcorn bowl, which she held in her lap, while Jaylynn munched away on handfuls regularly.

Dez discovered that Jaylynn was right about *Manhattan Murder Mystery.* It was very funny and entertaining and never once did she feel like going to sleep. She sat cross-legged on the couch and laughed her head off during a couple of scenes. By the time the movie ended at 2:30, however, Jaylynn was obviously fatigued.

"Looks like you're running out of gas." Dez flicked the power off on the VCR remote.

Jaylynn yawned. "Guess so. I'll perk right up if you give me something with caffeine in it."

"Uh oh. Don't think I have anything."

"Nothing? What's *with* you?" Jaylynn teased as she looked up at her. "No caffeine, you don't eat donuts, I don't think you drink. Don't you have *any* vices at all?"

Dez shrugged.

Jaylynn put her hand on Dez's knee. In a conspiratorial voice, she said, "Surely at least you eat chocolate? I'll bet you have one whole cupboard loaded full of it, right?"

"Nope." Dez cursed her telltale face. She could feel the blush rising, a warmth that began where the hand was touching her leg and generated heat that traveled from her knee all the way up to her face. Nonchalantly she said, "I should probably get you home then, huh? Won't Tim be wondering why you're so late?"

"Tim? Not a chance. He's on a date with some guy he met at the restaurant. I'd be surprised if he even came home tonight."

Now Dez was thoroughly confused and her face showed it. "Tim's gay?"

"Sure. I thought you knew that."

"But—but—he's always hugging you—you kiss him goodbye when he drops you off."

"It's a peck on the lips. That's to keep those oversexed male cops from pawing all over me. If you're not with someone, some won't take no for an answer. Some sort of proprietary thing." She patted Dez's thigh. "If a woman says no, it doesn't mean no, but if she says her *boyfriend* says no, that's a whole 'nother thing." With her hand still on Dez's knee, Jaylynn curled her feet up underneath her and shifted close enough to lean into the bigger woman. "You, on the other hand, aren't the pawing type, are you?"

Dez's face blushed crimson, but their eyes met, and once again the rookie felt the strange rush of energy flowing back and forth between them. She sat riveted, her heart beating in her chest like someone was pounding on her breastbone with a sledgehammer. With great effort, she choked out, "You feel that, too...don't you?"

Dez didn't reply, but she continued to fix her gaze on Jaylynn, her steely blue eyes reaching into the younger woman's soul. Reaching up, Jaylynn gently stroked the pale cheek above her. Dez met her eyes with an open directness that almost caused Jaylynn's heart to stop. *It's now or never*, she thought and lifted her face to meet Dez's lips.

Dez surrendered to the kiss. For a few brief moments she completely lost track of anything but soft lips and the scent of the woman next to her. She took Jaylynn's hands into her own, then the rookie slipped her arms around the bigger woman's neck. Dez pulled back, breathless, Jaylynn's warm breath on her neck. As she shifted away, kind hazel eyes drilled into her.

Dez looked away. "I can't do this, Jay."

Now it was Jaylynn's turn to be confused, and then she felt a moment of fear. *Maybe I've judged totally wrong. Maybe Dez isn't...but hey, what about this response?* Dez burned with desire and Jaylynn could feel it. "What do you mean?"

Dez said, "I don't date cops."

"No problem. We don't have to do any dating at all."

Dez held her own hands in her lap, balled up in fists. The blue eyes sharpened and peered into Jaylynn's eyes. "I'm serious," Dez said. "I mean it. I don't date cops."

"Fine. I'll quit then."

Alarmed, Dez said, "You can't quit the force."

"Why not?"

"Why would you wanna go and do that?"

"It's just a job. There's a million things out there I could do. But there's only one you."

"Look, you don't have to quit the force—"

With a little half-smile on her face, Jaylynn said, "Did I not hear you deliver an ultimatum?"

"That's *not* what I meant."

"Sure it was."

"No," Dez said firmly. She paused as she struggled for her next words. "I'm your FTO, for chrissake. It would cause so many problems, so much talk, too many questions." She looked down into her lap as her face went crimson again.

"Oh, and driving around every night pretending I'm not absolutely smitten with you doesn't cause problems?"

Dez shook her head and hesitated, then said, "Jay, how can you be sure about this?"

Jaylynn smiled and shrugged. "Don't worry one bit. I *never* start anything I don't want to finish."

Dez let herself relax into the next kiss, feeling a hundred different sensations exploding inside her. Without breaking contact, Jaylynn shifted to her knees on the couch and then swung her leg over Dez's lap so that she was straddling the taller woman's legs. She sat back on Dez's thighs and put her hands on broad shoulders. Jaylynn reached up and gently cradled the dark head in her hands until Dez pulled her closer.

Without warning, apprehension arose and Dez caught her breath. How could she explain the sense of endangerment coursing through her, the alarm bells sounding in her head? There was too much to lose here. She hadn't even been romantically involved with

Ryan, yet the pain she felt at his death still bit into her like a poisonous snake. And then there were the two relationships she'd had in college. Both ended badly. Worst of all: Karin. The pain she felt from each woman's departure had made her gun shy and wary. *To be in love again...why,* she realized, *it was absolutely terrifying.* She couldn't even maintain a cordial relationship with her own mother; what made her think she could satisfy Jaylynn?

Dez pulled away, bit her lip, and looked down, giving Jaylynn the opportunity to slide her hand between the buttons of her shirt. She slipped her arm behind Dez's neck and leaned into her, unbuttoning the blouse the rest of the way. She pressed her lips against the pale white skin at Dez's collarbone. "You're frowning, Dez. You don't seem to be enjoying this much."

Breathless, Dez said, "You're wrong."

"No, I'm not. You're awfully tense."

"I can't help it. I'm sorry." She clenched her jaw in frustration.

"Stretch out," Jaylynn said. "Go on, turn over." She moved aside and guided Dez into a face down position on the couch, then pulled Dez's shirt away from her back and slid it down her arms. After unsnapping the hooks on Dez's bra, she ran her hands over the broad back, then straddled the lean hips. Considering how wide and muscular the tall woman was, her shoulders and back were surprisingly soft, the muscles warm and pliable. It was at her neck and along the shoulders where all the tension lay. Jaylynn kneaded and pressed mercilessly until her hands and arms grew tired. She lowered herself and spread out on Dez, her hands reaching around the dark woman's rib cage. Dez rolled to her side, and Jaylynn slid down next to her on the cramped couch, teetering on the edge for a moment until Dez pulled her close.

"Thank you," Dez said. "Felt good." Her hands stroked Jaylynn's back through her shirt. "I can't do this. Not tonight."

Jaylynn nuzzled against her neck. "I know."

"I need time to think about this more."

"I know. It's okay." She lay with her head near Dez's chest, listening to the slow and steady beating of her heart. "Just hold me a little while, okay?"

"Um hmm." In moments Dez was asleep. Jaylynn shifted to get more comfortable, and Dez's arms tightened around her. Suddenly Jaylynn was as tired as she'd ever been. She pulled the quilt down off the back of the sofa and spread it over them, then closed her eyes and fell into deep slumber.

She didn't awaken again until sometime just before dawn when Dez cried out. In a hoarse voice Dez whimpered and shouted, "No!" then turned her head from side to side as she tensed her fists and shook.

Jaylynn sat partway up and brushed the dark hair out of her partner's face. "Shhh," she said. "It's okay Dez. You're safe. It's just a nightmare. Shhh..."

She shivered and rearranged the quilt over the two of them, then stroked the white shoulder and let her hand rest against the pale neck. Dez didn't wake up. Jaylynn watched her settle and relax, then she pulled her closer and wrapped an arm around her middle. She lay back, pulling the quilt up further, and Dez nestled her head into her neck. Jaylynn's left arm was pinned. With her right hand she softly caressed her partner's back through the quilt. By the even breathing, she could tell Dez had slipped into a more comfortable sleep.

A feeble light shone in upon them from the porthole across the room over the bed. Jaylynn wondered for a moment what time it was, then drowsed, content. *I could get used to this. Despite our differences in height, we fit together well.* The last thing she remembered before falling back asleep was the scent of Dez's hair, a citrus smell, like lemonade on a hot summer's day.

****

Dez awoke, startled to find herself shirtless and cradled in the smaller woman's arms. Her head rested on Jaylynn's chest and one leg was thrown across her thighs. She craned her neck to see the VCR clock. Close to ten already. She was completely amazed she'd slept so long, and for once she actually felt rested. Carefully she extricated herself from Jaylynn's grip, slid off the sofa, and padded into the bathroom.

She stood in the shower, her favorite place to think, and let the water run over her. She used to like the metaphor of washing away troubles, but lately no amount of water washed away her worries. *What to do about Jaylynn? A relationship is the last thing I want. She's so young and full of life...she deserves more than me. Why in the world would she even want me? It's that older woman/mentor thing. She's mistaken about her feelings, confused. This could only be a huge mistake.*

She ignored the rising feeling of panic, stopping to stretch her arms under the hot water. *I'm just tense from the heavy chest and triceps workout yesterday.* She turned off the water and resolutely stepped out of the shower to towel off. Her muscles were sore in all sorts of places. Her stomach clenched. She shook her head and tried to ignore the aches and pains.

When Jaylynn awoke, she lay on her side, covered by the quilt, facing the closed bathroom door. She could hear the shower running. She couldn't really explain why, but a feeling of foreboding spread through her. Though she felt rested, she remembered little wisps of dark and troubling dreams. She lay still, snuggled in the warm blue quilt, and waited for her partner to appear, which she did in short order. When Dez emerged, she wore a red terry robe and held a white towel, which she was using to dry her long, jet-black hair.

Jaylynn lay motionless and watched Dez glide slowly past her toward the bed, her head tipped to the side as she toweled dampness out of dark hair that looked so lovely in stark contrast to the red robe. *She has no idea how beautiful she is,* thought Jaylynn. *She spends all her waking hours guarding her emotions, staying tough, and keeping her feelings bottled up far too tightly. Even now she doesn't look relaxed. She's a shuttered and locked house, no admittance.* For confirmation, she watched as Dez's eyes came to rest on her and the look of surprise when the tall woman realized Jaylynn was awake and studying her. She also saw the grim look on Dez's face as she came to stand next to the couch. Jaylynn sat up, still hugging the quilt.

Dez was direct. "This isn't going to work."

Jaylynn didn't speak. She looked Dez in the eye and waited patiently.

"Jay, think about this. I'm the first uniform you've spent any amount of time with."

Jaylynn shook her head slightly. "You're not a *uniform*, Dez."

Dez ignored that comment and went on. "We all tend to fall into—into—well, into all sorts of feelings for cops we partner with. I mean, I loved Ryan like he was a brother...like more than a brother."

"But you didn't want to sleep with him, right?"

Dez ran her hand through her wet hair and brushed it off her shoulder. "I didn't need to sleep with the guy," she said in an angry voice. "I felt closer to him than I have to anyone." She half-turned so Jaylynn could no longer see her face. "Let's forget about this and go back to the way things were. We'll just chalk this up as a...a—we'll forget it happened, okay? It's just a period of adjustment you're going through, you know, admiration for me and all that stuff left over from the attack on Sara."

"Don't patronize me," Jaylynn said. "I know how I feel, and this is not childish hero worship." She stopped abruptly and took a deep breath, closed her eyes, and considered her options. She couldn't think of any. *This is a losing battle.* She marveled at the fact that somehow she knew it before she awoke. "Dez, I'm confused. I don't understand. I know how you feel. You may think you're impervious to others, but I can see—hell, I can *feel* your emotions. I'm not getting the whole story here, am I?"

Dez looked away, then tossed the towel a few feet through the air onto the valet chair. She pulled the robe tighter and fidgeted with the belt. "I think I told you last night that I just can't date cops. It never works out. It's a rule I don't want to break."

"You don't date *cops*? Or you mean you won't date *me*?"

"C'mon, Jaylynn. Don't make this so hard."

"I just want to know the truth."

"That is the truth. I don't date cops."

"In 24 hours I can be an ex-cop. Would that change your point of view?"

Dez shuddered, then moved away from the couch, her back to Jaylynn. "You can't give up your career."

"But theoretically speaking, if I did, we wouldn't be breaking your rule. So then, what would you say?"

Dez pulled the belt even tighter and turned to Jaylynn, her face a blaze of anger. "No," she said. "I would say no."

Jaylynn felt all the blood run out of her face, and she went cold all over. "So it's not about me being a cop—"

"Yes, it is."

"No. It's not," Jaylynn said firmly. She slipped out from under the quilt and retrieved her running shoes from next to the coffee table. As she sat on the couch and tied her shoes, she said, "You're lying to yourself and you're lying to me. This isn't about us being cops. Why don't you tell me the truth? You think I'm too young to take it?"

Dez's face was grimmer and whiter than Jaylynn had ever seen it. She crossed her arms over the blood red robe and in a calm voice said, "All right. Maybe there is more. My job is too important to jeopardize. I won't risk it by having others find out I'm in a relationship with another officer—and a woman at that."

Jaylynn brushed her hair out of her eyes and in a weary voice said, "Nobody cares. They already think you're gay anyway."

"The hell they do!"

"Wake up, Dez. Believe me when I say it's a subject your fellow officers have discussed at length." She let out a bark of laughter. "There's even money on it."

"Oh shit! That's—that's—don't listen to that station house gossip. It's all bullshit." Now her face flamed red, and fine veins in her forehead showed through. "Those jerks know nothing for sure, and I'm keeping it that way. I've worked too hard building a reputation, creating alliances. I'm not going to blow that now."

Jaylynn's anger surged in response. "You'd rather ride around alone in a patrol car, holding out your sterling reputation and keeping everyone at arm's length than take a chance with me? Is that what you're saying?"

Dez glared at her and crossed her arms around the red robe as though she were cold. "Yes."

"You'd rather ride all night alone than in a two-man car with a partner?"

"Yeah, that's right. What do you wanna do about it?"

"Nothing, Dez. That's your choice." Jaylynn rose and tucked her plaid shirt into her jeans. In a spiritless voice she said, "I'm just sorry you feel that way, that it's more important for you to keep up appearances than to care about other people." She strode through the door and into the kitchen and grabbed her jacket.

Dez came to stand in the doorway. She looked uncertain. "Hey, let me get some clothes on and I'll run you home."

"Nope. That's all right. I can walk."

"Geez, Jay, it's over a mile. I'll take you. It's cold out."

In a voice as cold as ice, she said, "Thanks. But I'd much rather walk." She opened the kitchen door, not looking back, and pulled it shut behind her, leaving Dez light-headed.

The tall woman stumbled back into the living area and onto the couch. *God, that went badly. I didn't mean to hurt her. I didn't mean for it to be so—so goddamn awful.* She couldn't control it anymore. Her eyes welled up with tears and she sat on the couch, her head in her hands, and cried bitter tears until she could cry no more.

****

Jaylynn pulled her hood up and adjusted the snaps as tightly as she could. Despite the weak late morning sun, it was cold. She tucked her hands deep into the pockets of her jacket and closed her eyes a moment, shaking her head. *That went so badly. That was a dose of stubborn Irish womanhood I never expected to see. But hey, I'm a realist, right? I should have realized she wouldn't be able to handle it. I should have known. I blew it. God, I messed that up big time.*

She took a deep breath and closed her eyes for a brief moment. *But does Dez really feel that way? That her career is more important than exploring a relationship with someone else? I can't believe it. I don't want to believe it.*

She kicked every rock she came across, and as she walked, she became increasingly angry. *What a chicken shit!* A little voice in the back of her head tried to argue that Dez was probably still dealing with Ryan's death, that perhaps she needed more time, but Jaylynn pushed the thought out of her mind. No sympathy allowed. Not until she forced Dez to work this out with her. *Dammit, she'll listen to reason or else.*

Jaylynn was chilled, but fuming when she reached the house. She was grateful that neither Sara nor Tim were home as she stomped up the stairs to her room.   She undressed, got into the shower, and kept turning Dez's words over and over in her head. *How could she be so callous, so hard-hearted? I know for a fact that there is a heart in there somewhere. How can she deny herself love and pleasure and happiness? I don't understand.* Steaming hot water coursed over her and she fought back the tears. No tears, Dez had told her. Cops don't cry. *No need to cry about this now. It's not over.*

****

The days off on Monday and Tuesday dragged by for Jaylynn. A tiny fraction of her hoped Dez might perhaps call, but the phone never rang for anyone in the household but Tim. She tried to focus on a book, a video, tidying up her room, all the while trying to dissolve the awful feeling of doom that had sat on her chest since Sunday.

Finally, by Wednesday afternoon, she could take it no longer. Still upset, she'd picked over her lunch, not able to eat much. After the meal, she borrowed Tim's beater and drove over to Dez's place. She went around to the backyard and was surprised to find Luella out sweeping the light dusting of snow off the cement walk.

"Well, hello, dear. How are you?" the older woman said.

"Hi, Luella. I'm fine. Whatcha up to?"

Luella leaned on the broom.   "Nothing much at all. I've got some excellent pork loin leftover if you—"

Jaylynn shook her head. "Thanks, Luella, but I ate a big lunch, and I just couldn't. But thank you so much for offering. I still haven't gotten over how wonderful those ribs were that you made the last time I was here!"

"Secret family recipe," Luella said in a conspiratorial voice. "Someday I'll share it with you."

"Sounds good. So is Dez around? I need to talk with her."

"You go on up, honey. She's been in hermit mode all day. Hope you can get her to come out, enjoy a few of the sun's rays before it's pitch black out. I swear she's turning into a vampire— only comes out at night." The old woman laughed at that and followed Jaylynn up the stairs into the house. "Go on. See if you can liven her up some."

Jaylynn took the stairs two at a time and stood in front of the door a moment trying to compose herself. She rapped on the door and waited until Dez whipped it open and looked at her as though startled. "Uh, hi. What're you doing here?"

"I was hoping we could talk before our shift."

Dez was barefoot and wore an oversized faded blue t-shirt and baggy black sweatpants. She looked like she'd just awakened. She opened the door wider and stepped back to let Jaylynn into the tiny kitchen, then backed up to the counter and put her hands on the edge. She leaned her hips against it, legs crossed at the ankle. Jaylynn came in and shut the door behind her. She turned to face the taller woman. There was a tension about Dez, an edginess directed her way that Jaylynn wasn't used to getting. *How could Dez be so cold,* she wondered, *so distant?*

Dez said, "I wish you'd called and told me you were coming."

Jaylynn shook her head and laughed humorlessly. "I would have if I had known your phone number. I suppose you know you're unlisted, right?"

Dez gave a slight nod.

"So could we talk about Sunday night?" Jaylynn shifted from one foot to the other.

Dez glared over her shoulder, not meeting the rookie's eyes, her face going from pale and tight to pink and impassive in the space of only a few seconds. "There's really not much to talk about."

Jaylynn tucked her hands into her jacket pockets and tilted her head a bit to the side, looking at Dez quizzically. "How can you say that?"

"I think we said it all already. Maybe this is one of those things where we have to agree to disagree."

"And where does that leave you and me?"

Dez shrugged. She looked around the room, everywhere but at Jaylynn.

Jaylynn was glad she'd eaten so little because suddenly her stomach clenched and she felt like she couldn't quite breathe. This was worse than she'd expected.

She made one last stab. "I don't know if it helps to say this, but I'm sorry. I didn't mean to push you or offend you or—"

"No, no, no." Dez made a motion with her hand to cut her off. She straightened up and put one hand back on the counter, the other on her hip. "Forget about it," she said sharply.

Jaylynn stepped back as though slapped. "Okay." She took a deep breath. "All right then." She grabbed hold of the knob and pulled the door open. This time she looked back. Dez had leaned against the counter again, her arms crossed over the blue t-shirt. She looked down at the floor. Jaylynn didn't bother to pull the door shut. She made it to the stairs in four quick steps and hurtled down in a rush, grateful to hit the cold, clear air outside.

Chapter
14

Jaylynn arrived early for her shift only to learn that Dez had called in sick. "First time in a couple of years," the duty sergeant said, "other than that broken arm thing last summer, but that doesn't really count as a sick day."

The rookie was assigned to ride with Officer Cheryl Pilcher, a seasoned veteran in her early forties. Jaylynn only knew her well enough to smile and say hi, but she did know Pilcher had recently had her twenty-year anniversary because some of the other cops razzed her about it. Pilcher was known to be quite a cut-up around the station, playing practical jokes and hamming it up. The rookie looked her over surreptitiously during roll call. A curvaceous woman at least three inches shorter than Jaylynn, Pilcher had sandy brown hair and brown eyes. She moved with confidence, a kind of strutting sureness that Jaylynn wished she herself had.

Jaylynn was nervous at first because Pilcher didn't seem too crazy about the pairing, but once they headed toward the car, her temporary partner said, "It'll be nice to ride with you tonight, Savage. I started out as Vell's FTO, but then he got transferred to Tour I because they were so short. I've been on my own since my partner left for an extended paternity leave, and it gets kinda lonely out here alone. You wanna drive or should I?"

Jaylynn hesitated. "I don't usually drive."

"Oh yeah, that's right. You've been riding with Reilly, and she hogs the wheel all the time. Here. Why don't you take the keys and drive the first half of the shift. I'll catch the second half after meal break. And don't call me Pilcher. My name's Cheryl."

"And you can call me Jaylynn—or Jay." She took the keys and got into the cruiser.

Jaylynn found Cheryl to be an entertaining partner. It wasn't long before they were sharing stories of what had happened to each of them in their first few months on the job. After a particularly amusing story about one of the grumpier old guys in the division refusing to let Cheryl drive because of her "height impairment," Jaylynn said, "Hey, it's good to hear somebody else's old war stories. This is a tough job at first, but I'm getting better at it."

"How many other cops have you ridden with?"

"In training, I had two weeks each with Alvarez, Culpepper, and then Reilly. Since then, just Reilly. I've only been on the force for three months, you know."

"You should ask around, talk to the other women. Some of them can tell you real horror stories. You won't get any out of Dez Reilly though. She tell you anything about *her* first months?"

Jaylynn shook her head.

"Yeah, figures. She must have been born a cop. She's like the golden girl of all the bosses. Never makes a mistake. Well, not until Michaelson anyway."

Jaylynn eyed Cheryl with a puzzled look on her face. "What do you mean?"

"You heard about Ryan Michaelson, right?"

"Yeah, her partner who died."

"He might be alive today if she had stood by him, gave him first aid."

"I don't understand," Jaylynn whispered. "I thought he was shot by some low-life."

"He was. She called for backup and the paramedics, and then went off to chase the shooter—she got him, too—but Michaelson bled to death. I hear she's doing real good at training in rookies, but I wouldn't want to ride with her on a regular basis. Guess I'm just superstitious. Besides that, she acts like she's too good for all of us veteran female cops. I hope she treated you well."

"For the most part, yes, she did."

"Wasn't too hard on you, was she?"

Jaylynn hesitated.

"You know you can report anything to the Lieutenant."

"No, no, there weren't any problems."

Jaylynn felt Cheryl's eyes bore into her, and then the older woman said, "You know her nickname, don't ya?"

"No."

"The Ice Queen. Seems fitting, don't you think? Personally, I think of her as Dez the Lez. She didn't make a pass at you or anything, did she?"

Jaylynn snorted and shook her head. "No. That for sure never happened."

"Well, an awful lot of us wonder if she's gay, but hey, she's the Ice Queen. What's the chance of that when she's so damn cold-hearted? You'll probably ride with her again, and just remember, if she's ever hard on you, you should report it."

Cheryl rattled on about procedures for complaints, but Jaylynn wasn't listening. Things clicked into place about Dez. The way she held herself apart from the other women, her reticence to get involved, the sadness around her so much of the time. *No wonder she didn't want to get close to me. She was probably planning on getting rid of the new rookie as soon as she could anyway. But what were those couple of kisses all about?* Jaylynn felt a flush rise from her neck to forehead and was glad for the veil of twilight that obscured her features from the chattering passenger. *Those kisses were for real.* Jaylynn stopped to reflect. *Well, maybe not. Maybe I just got so carried away feeling what I wanted to feel that I thought it was mutual. Still—she let me hold her all night...wasn't that something? But that could be explained, too. Dez had been so tired, exhausted really. Perhaps she just put up with it because she was overtired. She humored me. She was going to pass me on to someone else when her Field Training Officer assignment ended and she was just being polite. That's why she said she'd rather ride alone. I didn't think it was true, but now I know it must be.*

A call came over the radio, and Cheryl picked it up to respond. Off they went to a domestic call, and thoughts of Dez left Jaylynn for a short while.

****

Dez arrived at work an hour early on Thursday and apologized to the duty sergeant, Belton, for her absence the day before.

"Gee, Reilly, you're never sick. Don't worry about it. Actually," he said as he peered into her face, "you still look like shit. Sure you're feeling okay today?"

Dez felt herself blush. She smiled. "Nah, I feel fine today, even if I don't look so good. Is the Lieutenant in?"

"Yeah, and he's in a good mood, so don't piss him off."

"Never. Would I do that to you?" She smiled grimly and he winked back at her as she stepped past him. She passed the battered metal desk and tapped on the scarred wood trim outside Lt. Malcolm's open office door.

He looked up. "Well, Reilly. How ya doing?" The Lieutenant was elbow deep in paperwork, his suit jacket off with his dingy white shirt sleeves rolled up.

"I'm fine, sir. But I have a request to make about trainee assignments."

"Yeah?" He sat back. "You wanna come in and sit down?"

"No thanks, this will only take a minute of your time. I think

I'm ready to pass Savage on to one of the other FTO's."

"Too late for that."

"What?" Dez frowned, thoroughly taken aback.

"She and Pilcher already asked for reassignment yesterday, and I approved it. Now don't tell me you girls went and had a big fight last tour?"

Dez sputtered. "No sir, we most certainly didn't. I was out sick. I don't know anything about..."

He laughed. "Calm down, Reilly. There's no problem. I was just jerkin' your chain a little. She said she was ready for a change, wanted the chance to ride with a variety of officers. She complimented you. Said you had taught her a lot." He shuffled the pages in his hands. "Sure doesn't happen very often that vets and rookies have the same sense of timing. Good job. You're on your own for a while until the duty sergeant sets you up with someone else."

"Thank you, sir." She turned to go.

"Reilly?" he said. "I really do appreciate you taking the rookies out and showing them the ropes. You've done a good job, and I mean that."

"Thank you, sir."

"Won't be long though, and you'll have to hook up with a regular partner any time you work the East Side."

She nodded.

"Otherwise," he said, clearing his voice, "How ya doing?"

She knew what he referred to, but she wasn't about to speak of Ryan or her feelings or anything else the department shrink had encouraged her to discuss with her superiors and peers. Instead she said, "I'm hanging in there, Lieutenant. Some days better than others, but I'm fine."

"Good to hear," he said heartily. "Nice job then. Go out and get 'em, Reilly. Have a good shift."

"Yes, sir," she said, but she'd only half heard him. Her head was busy trying to figure out why Jaylynn had jumped ship. Beat her to the punch was maybe the better metaphor, for she decided she felt like she'd been socked upside the head. She walked toward the women's locker room in a daze, and sat on the bench outside her locker for several minutes before standing up and unlocking it. Unlike her neat apartment, her locker was stuffed full of gear and clothes. In a fit of frustration, she hauled everything out and piled it on the floor in front of her, then sat back on the bench with her head in her hands. Tears threatened to fall again, and she looked around in alarm only to note that she was alone in the locker room. *Pull it together, Reilly,* she thought as a feeling of panic ran through her. *Don't be foolish. You can't expect her to want to keep riding with someone who just rejected her. Can't go back to holding hands.* She gave a cynical laugh and began sorting through all her belongings and putting them in good order in the locker.

****

Jaylynn arrived in the meeting room seconds before the sergeant called roll. Dez sat on the side, near the back in her regular spot, drinking water from a quart bottle. Jaylynn glanced at her and noted the impassive face, the cold eyes, the alabaster skin. Dez's eyes flicked toward her, not meeting the rookie's gaze. Though the tall cop did give an almost imperceptible nod, she looked away and didn't turn back. Jaylynn felt her knees shake and, instead of sitting in the back near her ex-partner, she took a spot in the middle of the room a few chairs ahead of her.

As the sergeant started calling everyone to order, Cheryl came rushing in to join her. "Didn't miss anything, did I?" she whispered loudly.

"No. He's just starting."

Jaylynn tried to concentrate on what the duty sergeant was saying. It was all she could do to keep from getting up and dragging Dez outside to talk. All she wanted to do was explain the switch, make her understand. But what good would it do? *We can't talk about it anymore, and as she said, we just disagree. What would be the use of forcing the issue again? It didn't work earlier. What could I say now? She's made her decision, and I'll respect it. I don't have to like it, but I'll respect it.*

With a heavy heart, Jaylynn left after roll call ended, followed by Cheryl who laughed and talked with everyone on the way out the door to the parking lot. Jaylynn didn't look back, but she swore she could feel those chips of blue ice burning into her back.

****

It was several days before Jaylynn felt like she'd regained her equilibrium. It was a trial each day to go to roll call, but she did it, hoping each time that it would get easier. It never did. She considered switching from Tour III, but she didn't have enough seniority to bid onto Tour II days, and she sure didn't want to work the Dog Watch graveyard shift. Besides, as much as it hurt, as much as it disconcerted her, she felt compelled to see the taciturn FTO. Sara told Jaylynn she was a sucker for sucker punches, but she couldn't help herself.

Cheryl worked Saturday through Wednesday, so Jaylynn rode with her part of the time, but on Cheryl's days off, she rode with a variety of cops. On Thursday and Friday, Jaylynn went to roll call and tried to pretend to herself that she wasn't hoping she'd get assigned to Dez. But as a few more days went by, it appeared it might not happen. One night she rode with a gray-haired black cop, Reed, who very kindly quizzed her on procedures and helped her to learn the radio codes more thoroughly. Another night she had a miserable time with a handsome officer named Barstow who thought he was God's gift to the world. She chalked it up to experience. After a week, she was assigned to ride with Crystal Lopez on Cheryl's nights off.

Every afternoon, she found Dez in the back of the roll call room calmly sipping water, her face impassive. Was it her imagination or did the quiet cop's face look more hollow and gaunt each day? Usually the blue eyes bored past her like cold icicles, not really connecting at all. *Just one warm look—just one,* thought Jaylynn. *If just one time Dez would look even the slightest bit welcoming...* But it didn't happen. The words to a Stevie Nicks song, "I Still Miss Someone (Blue Eyes)," kept running through her head at inopportune moments. She tried to put the song out of her mind, but it kept coming back to haunt her.

One night after she'd worked with Crystal off and on for a week, they got onto the subject of Dez Reilly. Jaylynn drove slowly through the Selby-Dale area, keeping an eye out for anything unusual. It was a quiet night, with lots of dead time for chatting, and she and Crystal had touched on the lives of many of their fellow officers.

"Can I ask you something?" Crystal asked.

"Sure."

"What's up with you and Dez?"

"What do you mean?" Jaylynn asked, holding her breath.

Crystal reached across the car and punched her playfully in the arm. "Come on, *mi amiga*, I know her well enough, and I'm getting to know you. She's giving you that tough *macha* mean chick routine. She doesn't do that unless you got under her skin. What'd you do to her?"

Jaylynn kept her hands on the wheel, but gripped it tightly. She stumbled on her words, not knowing how to explain. "I don't know...I mean, I can't say. It's not that I did anything to her. It's more that she doesn't want to be around me."

"That's hard for me to believe. She likes you a lot. I can tell. She only said good things about you when she was training you. And believe me, once she's your friend, then it's for always. She's very loyal. We had a big screaming fight one time—" Crystal laughed heartily. "Let me rephrase that—*she* didn't say much. We had a disagreement, and I bitched at her big time. We were really

pissed at each other. The next night I found out my partner's
mother was deathly sick. I lived in a really rough neighborhood
back then, so Dez came to housesit and take care of the dogs so we
could go to Louisiana. I didn't even know she was allergic to dogs
'til we got back. It was winter, and she basically slept on the three-
season porch in a sleeping bag, but hey, she looked out for our
house. She's reliable, that one is. Even if she's pissed at you, she'll
treat you fair."

"What happened to your partner?"

"Nothin'. Why?"

"I mean where is he or she now?"

Crystal gave her a blank look. "She's at home, where else?"

Jaylynn paused a moment. "So she doesn't ride with you
anymore?"

Crystal let out a snort of laughter. "Shayna wouldn't be caught
dead in light blue. Says she only looks good in orange and olive
and autumn colors. Colors like that make me look sallow and
dead." She laughed again. "No, she's not on the force. She never
wanted to be a cop. Ever. She works at a craft store framing stuff,
selling thread and needles and shit like that. And she's my partner.
My sweetie. Know what I mean?"

Jaylynn felt embarrassed for being so dense, but she grinned
and made light of her misunderstanding. "Oh! Partner—like a
wife," she said. "I gotta get me one of them."

"*Si, senorita.* Real good idea. You sure you're the type?"

"Uh huh, though my mother will probably be disappointed."

"No wonder you and I get along so fine," said Crystal. "I
should have known. But hey, I don't assume. Bad idea, you know.
So now you can tell me all about your life and loves. You with
anyone now?"

"Nah, not since the first couple of years of college. Didn't
work out."

"I know quite a few nice girls—single, I mean—I should
introduce you to."

"Oh, I don't know—"

"What?" Crystal reached across the car and punched Jaylynn
playfully in the arm. "You're young, you're sweet, you got those
nice hazel eyes. I bet you look great in street clothes. I could set
you up with a ton of good-looking *chicas*. You just say the word."

"Sure. I'll let you know."

Crystal gave a sigh. "All right, why you holding back, Jay?"

Jaylynn grimaced. "My heart's not in it right yet. Kind of a
rebound thing."

"You let me know then. We can go out to the club, meet some
nice women. I'll show you around. When you're ready."

Jaylynn nodded and smiled over at her, then turned left and headed north over the freeway overpass.

Crystal put her hand out and grasped Jaylynn's forearm. "Let me give you a piece of advice about Dez. Don't let her mean ass routine get to you. She just looks like that on the outside. On the inside she's mush."

When Jaylynn didn't answer and only nodded slightly, Crystal watched her surreptitiously out of the corner of her eye, then shook her head and smiled a knowing smile. She nodded and leaned back, taking a few minutes to think before starting up another conversation about an entirely different subject.

****

Crystal continued to badger Jaylynn about going out and about meeting new friends. Finally one afternoon toward the middle of March, the younger woman agreed to go out after their shift was over.

"All right!" said Crystal as she peeked around the corner in the locker room. "Lemme just call Shayna, and we'll see who we can round up. I know Merilee will come, and maybe Marshall, that other new rookie. I don't know her first name yet, but hey," she said suggestively, "she's *pretty cute*." Crystal flashed her a wide smile and then disappeared through the locker room door.

Jaylynn shook her head. *Pretty cute. Ha. That's the last thing I need.* Paula Marshall was just fine in Police Academy and the rookie had liked her a lot, but not to date. There was no spark between the two of them. Paula might eventually turn into a good friend, though. She finished buttoning up her blue shirt, tucked it in, and fastened her belt. She checked her watch and decided she had better get a move on. She hastened around the corner to the bathrooms and ran smack into 175 pounds of glowering Desiree Reilly.

"Uh, sorry," she said as she rebounded off the solid form.

In response, the scowling woman inclined her head, giving the rookie the slightest of nods, then looked away and hastened past. It occurred to Jaylynn that she must have heard the conversation with Crystal, and she wondered if that was why the tall cop was so abrupt. *No, actually, she was rude.* She went into the bathroom stall and found herself fuming. *She doesn't own me. She can't pick my friends. If I want to go out and whoop it up, then dammit, I will.* She emerged from the restroom and took the stairs two at a time.

As she passed down the hall toward the roll call room, a clerk on the telephone gestured to her, and she stopped, puzzled. "Me?"

she asked, pointing to her own chest.

He nodded. "Yeah. Phone call here."

She walked across the Comm Center and took the phone from him.

"Hello, sweetie," said a kindly voice.

"Luella?"

"That's me. Say, I was wondering if you'd like to come over for dinner again. I haven't seen you for so long, I'm missing you."

"Well, that's so nice of you! Sure I'll come. When?"

They arranged to have supper the following Tuesday night and then Jaylynn hung up the phone and hustled over to the roll call room. She was glad to hear from Luella. She had missed the old woman a lot.

****

Jaylynn arrived at Luella's house and parked her new Camry out front. She got out of the car and slammed the door, looking down with pride at her most expensive acquisition ever. She had gotten quite tired of relying on the bus and the vagaries of Tim's schedule in order to get around, and had been saving for three months. The previous day she had bought the modest gray Camry from a neighbor who'd upgraded to an Avalon. The bank loaned her the money without a problem, and now she was the proud possessor of a neat and tidy Toyota with less than 38,000 miles on it.

When she got into Luella's house she proudly pointed it out, and the older woman surprised her by saying, "Well, hey! Let's take it for a spin."

"You wanna drive?"

"No, but you can be the chauffeur."

"What about your dinner?"

"That's the nice thing about casseroles. I'll just turn it down a bit and we'll come back in fifteen minutes to a nice hot dinner." After a quick visit to the kitchen, Luella returned to the porch and shrugged on her black quilted jacket. Today she wore a scarlet wool skirt and a long-sleeved ivory blouse. She slipped out of the ubiquitous pink slippers and into a clunky pair of Nikes. "Wish I could still wear heels," she said, "but these old feet just won't allow it."

Jaylynn pointed to her Nikes. "I'll take tennis shoes any day. I don't care if I ever wear fancy shoes again." She took the older woman's arm and they made their way down the stairs.

Luella said, "I always liked elegant shoes. Had a whole closet full when I was a young thing like you." She sighed. "But times change. I'm just thankful to God that I can still get around at my advanced age."

Jaylynn laughed. "I can only hope I am in half as good a shape when I get to be your age, Luella." She opened the passenger door, helped the silver-haired woman in, and shut the door.

Dez watched from the upstairs bathroom window. She saw the laughing woman tuck the old lady into the car and then hurry around to the driver's side and get in. As they drove off, Dez wondered where the car came from. She knew it wasn't Tim's. Maybe Sara's? She backed away from the window and wandered into the living room and stood uncertainly for a moment. Luella hadn't told her she'd invited the rookie over, and she wondered whether the old woman knew she and Jaylynn weren't speaking. Sometimes she thought her landlady was psychic.

She cracked her knuckles and then shook her hands out before reaching down to snag her acoustic guitar. She went over and slouched down on the couch, one foot up on the coffee table. Checking the strings, she adjusted the tuning and started picking a pattern and playing various chords with it. Her mind wandered as she played.

She thought about the friendship that had started to develop with the rookie and how it had been ruined. She wasn't sure how she could have done things differently, but she knew she should have. It occurred to her that things never made sense to her until she had thought about them for a long while. It took her so long to figure out what she was feeling that it was no wonder that she didn't have any close friends anymore...not that she'd ever had many.

Stop feeling sorry for yourself, she scolded. *What's the point?* She focused on playing the guitar and found herself moving through a series of minor chords and throwing in some C-majors and F-majors. A little smile came to her. This chord progression and melody was going to stick. Lately, every time she picked up the guitar it flowed out of her fingers, and every time it happened she thought of Jaylynn. *Guess I'll have to call this "Jaylynn's Song." Maybe someday I'll think of some words to go with it.* She leaned the guitar against the couch cushion and got up and moved over to the roll top desk. Sliding the top open, she avoided looking at the pair of photographs on the inside desk surface and instead grabbed a pencil and a stack of lined paper, then shut the top.

She took the paper and pencil over to the coffee table and spent some time writing out the chord progression and the melody line for the song. In the middle of it, she heard the downstairs door slam, so she rose and looked out the bathroom window again. The gray Camry was once more parked out front.

A part of her wanted very much to go down the back stairs and drop in, but she couldn't bring herself to do it. Up until the last few days, her pride would not have let her even think of such a thing, but it wasn't her pride preventing her from doing it now. She didn't think Jaylynn would appreciate the intrusion. It was obvious Friday afternoon in the locker room that she had moved on to other "cuter" friends. Besides, the rookie had made it perfectly clear that she wanted nothing to do with her, so Dez had no intention of upsetting her any more than she already had. She sighed and moved back into the living room, now feeling unexpectedly claustrophobic. Shuddering, she returned to the couch where she picked up the guitar and quietly played the chord progression that she couldn't get out of her head.

Chapter
15

St. Patrick's Day dawned clear and cold, but sunny. Jaylynn rolled out of bed in response to the clock radio blaring. She wasn't happy to be going to work early, by eleven a.m., and working until at least midnight. For one thing, that meant that she wouldn't get a run in at all today. But it was also going to be an awfully long day. The old timers on the force had told her that St. Paddy's Day was always fun because of the parades and festive spirits, but St. Paddy's Night was hell with all the drunk driving and bar brawls. The pleasant March weather was likely to bring out a raft of people, though her colleagues had said it wouldn't be as bad on a Tuesday night as it was when the holiday fell on a weekend.

The rookie showered, dressed, ate a big breakfast, and packed a variety of snacks to take with her to the station. She wasn't used to arriving in the roll call room so early and, obviously, neither were her fellow shift members. Oster looked like he had rolled out of bed and forgotten to brush his short hair. Pilcher and Lopez sat in the folding chairs yawning and complaining. The rest sat in silence, waiting to jumpstart their day. Even the duty sergeant was crabby. Jaylynn sat down in a chair near Lopez, but not before noticing haunted blue eyes in the rear of the room. The big cop leaned back in her chair, arms crossed over her chest and feet up on a chair in front of her. If she didn't know better, Jaylynn would have wondered if the Irish cop had already tied one on the night before. Instead, she suspected that she simply hadn't slept enough.

The rookie listened carefully as the duty sergeant outlined their assignments. At 11:30, all of them were to be out in full force in downtown St. Paul to line the streets during the parade. The sergeant went through a long list of "do's and don'ts," then quickly shouted out which corners each would be assigned for the duration of the parade and its aftermath. Jaylynn knew she would be in front of the parking lot on the corner of Fifth and Wabasha with Crystal down the block near the towering Landmark Center. Then they would go on patrol, have an early meal break, and be ready for events to start rolling as it grew dark out.

Crystal Lopez, still complaining, tossed her the keys and hiked out to the car with her. "I hate this holiday."

Jaylynn gave her a big grin. "Sounds like exactly the same thing happens on Cinco de Mayo."

"Yeah, but at least I get a little respect from the kids."

"Hey, we could get you some nice leprechaun ears or something."

"Thanks, but no thanks. I like my own ears just fine."

In short order, they arrived in downtown and parked in a tow away zone. One of the few benefits of police work was never having to worry about finding a parking spot or about getting ticketed or tagged. They headed down the block on foot, Crystal moving toward the castle-like Landmark Center which was across from Rice Park and the library, and Jaylynn further down the street by the bank. The parade route was blockaded so there was no traffic, but as every moment passed, more and more people appeared and lined the parade route.

A tiny old lady, face full of pink wrinkles and dressed in a light green elf hat, green polyester pants, a bright green jacket, and olive green tennis shoes stopped the rookie to ask what time the parade began and where the best place would be to watch. The rookie explained that the marchers would come up the street and head toward the River Centre. She suggested that the woman cross the street and watch from a vantage point by the St. Paul Hotel because she could get up on the steps and see better. The old lady tipped her hat and moved jauntily across the street in the busy crosswalk. Jaylynn watched her until she made it safely to the other side, and then her roaming eye caught sight of her fellow officer standing on the far opposite corner in front of the new Pazzaluna restaurant.

Dez Reilly stood calmly, her reflective sunglasses glinting in the sunlight. Her head was turned slightly away, but Jaylynn had the distinct feeling that the tall woman was watching her. She let her hazel eyes focus on the mirrored lenses, as though she could see right through them, and with a start Dez turned away. Jaylynn couldn't help but smile.

After a while the rookie glanced at her watch. It was after noon now, and when she listened carefully over the talking and laughing of the crowd, she could hear the faraway boom-boom of a bass drum, which gradually grew noisier until she could also discern the tinny sound of horns. Before long, the band could be heard loud and clear and she saw a bright green banner so wide that it went from one curb across to the other and required six people to hold it. Hundreds of people followed, some as part of civic groups, some as parts of the various clans. The mayor and his entourage crawled along in a convertible, which said on the side "Provided by Chuck O'Leary Chevrolet." There were shamrocks, and green hats, and curly-toed shoes, and green, green, green everywhere.

As the mayor's car neared the intersection of fifth and Wabasha, Jaylynn caught sight of a quick movement. A young man on Dez's side of the street suddenly drew his arm back to throw something light tan in color. His arm came forward. Jaylynn opened her mouth to shout, but before a sound escaped, the light tan object vanished and the man stumbled forward a step off the curb and into the street. A blue arm grabbed him from behind. He jerked back and disappeared from sight as the place where he had been standing filled in with the eager onlookers.

The mayor's car passed. Jaylynn saluted, then in the vehicle's wake, cut across the street toward the hotel. The next band coming down the street was playing "When Irish Eyes Are Smilin'" and she stepped to the beat of the song. She squeezed through the crowd lining the curb and peered over by Pazzaluna. From the St. Paul Hotel corner she could see Dez's dark hair. She was no longer wearing the sunglasses. Her right hand held the tan object and her left grasped the material at the front of the young man's coat.

Jaylynn weaved her way through the people on the sidewalk and hustled across Wabasha. As she drew near the altercation, she saw Dez strong-arm the young man up against the plate glass window of the restaurant, her fist under his chin and still holding his bunched up jacket. The brown-haired man was a good six inches shorter than the big cop, but it was clear he wasn't afraid of her. Jaylynn heard him say, "You can't prove it. You don't know."

A low voice growled, "You're under arrest."

"For what?" he asked, his voice rising to a whining sound

"You were going to throw this at the mayor's car." She held up the object. As Jaylynn drew nearer, she could see it was a paper bag wrapped around a bottle.

Jaylynn reached over and said, "Here. Let me have that." With barely a glance, Dez let go of the bottle. The rookie hefted it in her hand. It was at least half full, heavy enough to have done some damage to the car or to a person, if it hit right. Dez cuffed the man and read him his rights.

The tail end of the parade passed by, and as it moved away, the people lined up along the street began to break up, too, looking curiously at the two cops standing with the suspect. Even though his hands were cuffed behind him, he pressed forward at Dez, snarling and swearing. When he kicked out at the tall officer, Dez sprang back easily and moved into a ready stance.

Jaylynn watched as a predatory look swept across the big cop's face, her eyes alight with excitement.

In the crowd someone muttered, "Police brutality again." Jaylynn looked up, startled, but she couldn't see who had made the comment.

The cuffed man called out, "Look at this, people. Asshole cops, arresting innocent people as usual." Dez grabbed his arm. He jerked away.

Jaylynn reached out with her free hand and gripped the man's ear. He winced and let out a squawk. "Listen up, mister," she said. She raised her voice for the benefit of the milling crowd. "I saw you try to throw this at the mayor's car." She held up the bottle in the bag. "Quit whining and come along."

She pulled his ear and, with his head turned to the side, he shuffled beside her, protesting, but docile, like a small child in trouble with his mom. "You should be ashamed of yourself," she scolded. "There was no reason to be so unpleasant. Come on now." The crowd lost interest and dispersed. When she and the man reached the corner, Jaylynn glanced over her shoulder. "Reilly, where you parked?"

The big cop gave the rookie a quizzical look and tossed her head toward Kellogg Blvd. "'Round the corner there." She trailed a few steps behind, watching the younger woman dragging the sputtering man, and suddenly it seemed very comical. Minutes ago, she had wanted to beat the hell out of this half-drunk moron, and now—well, now it just didn't matter. She watched as the rookie continued to berate the man, her hair shining like white gold in the cold March sun. Dez was struck with a sense of familiarity, as though she had done this before, had followed the blonde woman down scores of other streets hundreds of times. It brought a smile to her lips, though, upon reflection, she had no idea why she felt so happy.

Chapter
16

Jaylynn was happy to see the end of March and the beginning of April, though in her household, April Fool's Day was always a chore. Last year Tim had put green rubber garter snakes in Sara's and her beds and had duct-taped the refrigerator door shut. This year, Jaylynn decided to get back at him, so she had soaked his toothbrush overnight in white vinegar. She also hid his car keys and emptied out the coffee can of all the grounds. She knew she would be home when he woke up, so she figured after he groused for a while, she would confess and have a good laugh.

The funny thing was that Kevin, who had apparently spent the night, was the recipient of two of the three jokes. He went to use the toothbrush, and from her room, Jaylynn heard the response to that quite plainly. He was also the one to discover there were no coffee grounds. That kind of took the fun out of it since Tim was the real target. Jaylynn gave Kevin a clean toothbrush and got out the coffee for the poor guy. She put the car keys back out in plain sight. She was amused to discover that Tim had completely forgotten about April Fool's Day, which was just fine with her.

She went back to her room and turned on her CD player, selecting Gloria Estefan's "Destiny" for background music, then flopped down on the couch. She picked up a letter she was writing to her Auntie Lynn in Seattle, but after rereading a bit of it, she put it down. Arranging the couch pillow behind her head, she kicked her feet out on the cushions and slumped down. She picked up the book of stories she had been reading and tried to focus, but she couldn't. She let the book fall next to her and closed her eyes.

The face that came to mind, as usual, was one she did not want to think about. She couldn't avoid it. Dark hair, arched eyebrows, high cheekbones, liquid blue eyes, and an occasional smile. Jaylynn hadn't seen that crooked half-smile for weeks. She was tired of riding with a variety of officers. She wanted her old FTO back—under any circumstances. She missed the tall woman desperately, and it occurred to her that police work was all drudgery lately. *Face it,* she thought to herself, *I joined the force because of her. I couldn't admit that to anyone, but if anyone asked, I'd have to be honest. Maybe it's ridiculous, but it's the truth. Am I an idiot or what?*

Suddenly full of nervous energy, she stood and went over to make the bed. Looking around the room she decided it was time for a good spring cleaning. In three days her mother and sisters were due for a visit, so she figured she had better get things organized. It was going to be close quarters for five days with her mom sharing the double bed and the girls on the hide-a-bed couch in sleeping bags. She couldn't wait to see them.

****

"Is this it? Is this it?" Two perky little girl voices warbled away excitedly from the back seat as Jaylynn pulled into a parking space. The two sisters opened the back doors and prepared to tumble out of the car.

"Wait, girls," Jaylynn said. "Leave the toys there in the car. You can't bring those Barbies in with you."

After carefully setting their dolls down on the seat, two compact little girls emerged from the gray Camry. They looked a great deal like Jaylynn: hazel eyes, long legs, twitchy with nervous energy. Only their hair was different from their older sister's. Both little girls had a shock of straight sandy brown hair like their father's, while Jaylynn's short hair was white-blonde like her mother's.

Their mother, a slender woman in her mid-forties, picked up her purse and got out. Jaylynn waited for the girls to slam their doors shut, then pushed the auto-lock. She looked admiringly at her new car, of which her mother had eagerly approved. It was so nice to travel in a clean vehicle, unlike Tim's, which was always packed full of newspapers and candy wrappers and crumpled McDonald's bags. She was glad she'd been able to buy the car before the girls' spring break. It made it much easier to show them around town.

"Amanda," their mother said, "tie your shoe. And you there, quit acting so squirrelly." In excitement, Jaylynn's youngest sister, Erin, bounced up and down on the balls of her feet. She paused. When her mother looked away, she resumed her determined bouncing.

"This way, Mom," Jaylynn said, and she led the three of them to the front entrance. The mid-afternoon sun slanted down upon them, but it shed no warmth on this breezy April day.

Erin pushed past Amanda and took Jaylynn's hand. "Will we get to see your gun?" she asked.

"No, sweetie, my gun is locked up in my locker. Police work isn't about guns, Erin. It's about helping people."

"Not on TV," chimed in the worldly-wise Amanda.

"This is definitely not TV," Jaylynn said. She pushed through the front door and led them into the police station.

With a whine in her voice, Erin said, "Do we at least get to meet our hero?"

Jaylynn and her mother looked at one another over the top of the girls' heads and rolled their eyes.

Their mother said, "I don't know why you two insist on this 'Our Hero' business."

"She *is* our hero, Mother," Amanda said in the patient voice of a 9-year-old who knows adults are not always aware of what is important. "She saved Jay and Sara and everything. We can't wait to see her."

Jaylynn interrupted, "There's always a chance she won't be here, so don't get your hopes up." In fact, Jaylynn didn't expect Dez to be around for another half-hour, saving her the discomfort of being in the harsh woman's presence. In a way, she did want her family to meet Dez, but she was also acutely aware of the awkwardness she'd feel.

Amanda and Erin skipped through the halls. They both wore white tennis shoes and blue corduroy pants, but Amanda's jacket was pink with purple trim while Erin's was a solid forest green. They giggled their way along, asking questions, and stopping to greet every police officer they saw. Once, when they saw a dark-haired female cop, they asked, "Are you Desiree? We're looking for our hero." Erin pronounced her name oddly: Desert-RAY with the emphasis on the last syllable. Jaylynn's mother shook her head as she tried to herd the rambunctious girls down another hall while Jaylynn apologized to the perplexed officer who was definitely not Dez. As they moved through the building, she pointed out the Complaint Desk, the Comm Center, and the Property Room.

After telling the girls not to bother anyone, especially if they were changing clothes, Jaylynn led them down the stairs and pushed open the door to the women's locker room. The girls skipped through the door and paused at the first row of lockers, followed by their mother and big sister. Jaylynn winced when she heard Amanda say, "Hi there. Are you our hero? We're looking for Desiree."

A low voice answered. "And who's asking?"

In unison the girls said, "We are." They stood at the end of the locker room bench, looking up, waiting.

The tall woman smiled. "And who might you be?" She finished buttoning her shirt and slammed her locker shut as Jaylynn and her mother came around the corner and stepped up behind the girls. *Ah. I should have figured this out,* Dez thought to herself. *The little girls resemble Jaylynn, and all three of them look just like their mother.*

Dez met the eyes of the older woman and stood for a moment, stunned. *Why, she's beautiful. What a great figure. If Jaylynn looks like that in twenty years, she'll be beautiful, too.* Her eyes shifted to take in the rookie, and she was even more amazed to realize that Jaylynn was—already—quite a looker. She had rarely seen the rookie out of the boxy blue uniform or workout sweats, and the few times Jaylynn had worn street clothes, Dez had to admit she hadn't paid much attention. Today the younger woman wore tight black jeans and a form-fitting white scoop-necked sweater that revealed her shapely figure. She had a soft tan leather jacket over one arm, and a gold locket on a chain rested in the hollow of her throat. Dez's eyes traveled upward to a face that looked worried.

Erin looked back over her shoulder at Jaylynn. "Well? Is this her or what?" she asked in exasperation. She turned back to the tall woman.

Jaylynn gently placed her hands on Erin's shoulders. "Yes."

Amanda and Erin both let out a cheer. "Yay! It's about time we found her!" Erin started her bouncing routine until Jaylynn's hands squeezed her shoulders to settle her down. She knew her face was crimson, but Jaylynn took a deep breath and said, "Desiree Reilly, these are my sisters Erin and Amanda. And this is my mother, Janet Lindstrom."

Jaylynn's mother reached out and shook hands with the tall woman. "I am so happy to meet you. I've heard a lot of good things about you from Jaylynn."

In an excited voice, Amanda said, "We think we might want your autograph."

Dez frowned and gazed over at Jaylynn with a quizzical look on her face. She arched one eyebrow, then turned back to Amanda and said, "Why?"

Jaylynn's mother started to answer but before she could get a word out, Erin cut in. "Because you're our hero. You saved our sister from the bad men and now she's a policeman saving other people from the bad men."

Dez nodded slowly. "Actually, she's a police *woman*."

The girls nodded in unison.

Janet sighed and said, "It's a good thing they've finally met you. I swear it's all they've talked about since we left Seattle. They got this notion in their heads about you, and you know how kids are. I think they expect you to be able to fly or astral project or something like that."

The girls protested and Dez laughed.

Jaylynn's mother went on, "But seriously, how's your arm? Jaylynn told me you broke it in the ruckus."

"Oh," Dez said, surprised. "It's just fine." She flexed her right hand. "No problems at all."

Erin said, in a small plaintive voice, "Can we see your gun?"

Dez sat down on the bench so that she was eye-to-eye with the girls. "No, I'm sorry, but it's not a toy. I only take it out of the holster for two reasons. Do you know what they are?"

Amanda said, "To shoot someone?"

"No, I get it out if there is a threat and I *think* I might have to use it. I also have to clean it and make sure it always works right, but other than that, it stays right here snapped shut in the holster." She patted her hip.

Erin said, "How many people have you killed so far?"

Jaylynn, who had been bearing the interrogation with great embarrassment, piped up and said, "Erin! I told you: zero. The police don't go around shooting people."

"Listen to your sister," Dez said. "She's right." Dez's amused eyes met Jaylynn's, and it happened again, that twinge in the pit of her stomach. Hastily she turned and checked the lock on her locker, making sure it was secured. When she turned back, she avoided the rookie's eyes, though she smiled and said, "When you told me you had two younger sisters, it didn't connect that they would be grade-schoolers."

Jaylynn's mother said, "Third and fourth grade—and quite a handful." She smiled, and Dez was struck by how friendly the woman was.

She nodded in understanding, and then turned her attention to the two girls staring up at her. "Well," she said, "why don't you two come up and have a tour with me. Then we'll see the roll call room. I'll introduce you to all the guys and you can hear how we get assigned our night's work."

"You don't have to do that," Jaylynn protested.

"I don't mind. I've got plenty of time," Dez said. "Shift doesn't start for—" she checked her watch, "forty-two minutes."

As if they'd known her forever, Erin and Amanda both reached up and took a hand. Dez smiled at Janet and led the two girls past and out the locker room. The two women followed. In a quiet voice Janet said, "She's seems very nice, Jaylynn. She's not at all what I expected. You never mentioned that she's seven feet tall."

"Oh, Mother."

"She's...well, she's really tall, hon."

****

For the first time since joining the police force, Jaylynn went back to work reluctantly. She hadn't wanted to say goodbye to her mom and the girls when they'd left the day before, but of course she did, trying not to cry at the airport as she watched them walk away from her down the long ramp to the plane. She was filled with such contradictory emotions. On the one hand, after five days of little girl energy, she was ready for a break, but on the other hand, she wished it wouldn't be months and months before she saw them all again.

She was pleased to find Sara at home when she got back from the airport, and they went to see a movie, *Life Is Beautiful*, which she decided might be one of the most wonderful films she'd ever seen, despite the Italian subtitles. Then she spent a quiet evening reading in her room, went to bed before midnight, and slept until nearly ten in the morning. She awoke feeling groggy, remembering violent, scary dreams. By the time she got to work in the middle of the afternoon, she was feeling more chipper, but still, she was out-of-sorts.

Fortunately, the shift with Crystal went by swiftly, and when midnight rolled around, Jaylynn parked the cruiser and the two women strolled toward the station. With a twinkle in her eye, which Jaylynn missed in the dim midnight light, Crystal said, "Hey, how 'bout we stay an hour or so and lift some weights? We've been on our butts so long I feel like I need a bit of a workout."

"Sure. Good idea." Jaylynn took off her hat and tipped her head forward to stretch her neck. "I feel pretty dang stiff from all that sitting."

They went to their lockers and changed into shorts and t-shirts, then reconvened in the gym. The dim overhead lights cast weird shadows on all the equipment, and the reflection of the mirrors ringing the room multiplied the odd light into strange specters. At 12:15 a.m., all was quiet.

Crystal asked, "You wanna work out together or just go at it alone?" She held her arms out to the side and stretched them, rolling her neck in circles.

"Together," Jaylynn said. "I'm still learning stuff, so it'll be good to watch you, okay?"

"*Muy bueno, chiquita.* I'm doing chest and maybe triceps today. That all right?" Jaylynn nodded and followed Crystal to the bench press.

"What weight do you start with?" Crystal asked.

"I'm only up to 65 pounds max. I'll do some light stuff and work up to that."

"Okay, you start then, and I'll add weights when it's my turn."

Jaylynn lay down on the blue bench and situated herself. She said, "Let me warm up a bit with just the bar."

"Yeah, then I'll slap on the weights for you."

Jaylynn lay on her back and gripped the 45-pound bar, lifted it off the rack, and let it drop slowly to her chest, then pressed it up ten times. She racked it, and Crystal slipped tens on each end and stood over to spot for her. After a brief rest, she repeated the ten reps and replaced the bar. Crystal slipped a 25 on each end and changed places with Jaylynn.

"That's real good," Jaylynn said. "I'd die doing 115 pounds."

Crystal gripped the bar. "Have you ever seen Dez do 225?"

Jaylynn shook her head.

"Well, she can. Makes it look easy, too. And you know what? She can leg press six plates on a side over there, you know, like 600 pounds. Spot for me now, okay? I'm trying for eight reps. I might need help at the end." Crystal pressed the bar up and began her set.

Jaylynn watched Crystal closely from where she stood above, ready to help if needed, so she didn't notice Dez enter the gym and then stop abruptly when she saw the two cops. The tall woman wore tight black shorts, black shoes and socks, and a heavy-duty black sports bra with criss-cross straps on the back. She hesitated for a moment, then shrugged and pulled on a pair of soft leather Ocelot workout gloves, cinching them around her wrists. Moving to the lat pull-down bar, she adjusted the weights to warmup settings, then got a wide grip, sat on the seat and tucked her knees under the pad, then pulled the bar. She warmed up slowly, keeping her back arched and pulling the bar down to her chin, letting her back and shoulders get used to the motion. After she did two sets of 15 light reps, she let the bar back up and stretched her arms and neck. Readjusting the weights to a heavier setting, she got situated to pull down the heavier weight.

Crystal racked the weights she was bench pressing and sat up. She looked back at Jaylynn and was amused to see the young woman watching Dez intently. She cleared her throat. "Guess it was lucky I didn't need your help on that last one, huh partner?"

Jaylynn shook herself and blushed. "I'm sorry. I got distracted." She jerked her head toward Dez and in a whisper said, "Crystal, will you look at her? How does she do that?"

As Dez pulled the bar down, the muscles in her broad back and shoulders bulged and rippled smoothly. Each lat pulldown revealed muscle definition Jaylynn had never before noticed on a woman.

Dez set the weights down and let go of the lat bar, and Jaylynn took that moment to stride over and lock eyes with her in the mirror. "How did you do that, Dez?" She came to a stop directly behind her, crossed her arms, and waited demandingly.

"Do what?"

"Get such incredible muscle definition in your shoulders and back? How in the world did that happen?"

The pale skin of Dez's face went from white to pink to crimson in the few seconds it took her to answer. "I—well—I just worked at it hard. Ate right. You know, stayed at it. It just happened."

"How long did it take for that to 'just happen'?"

Dez spun on the seat to face the smaller woman. "I don't know...couple years or so."

Jaylynn continued to stare at her, fascinated, completely oblivious to Crystal who sat on the bench behind them and watched with an amused expression on her face. "How did you learn what to do to build up like that?" Jaylynn said.

"Books. Magazines. And from Ryan. Mostly Ryan. He pretty much coached me."

"Can you teach me?"

Dez shrugged. "I guess," she said, doubt in her voice.

"You don't think I could learn?"

Dez smiled a full smile, her white teeth twinkling in the low light. She shook her head. "No, I don't think that at all. I just didn't think you'd be interested. You've got a lean runner's body. And you're fast. Wouldn't you rather work at wind sprints and cross country type stuff?"

"No, not really."

Crystal sidled up to the two of them. "Are we gonna get a back lesson from the master? 'Cause if we are, then I'm gonna stop working my chest right this minute." Both women stared at her blankly. Crystal observed that the air about her fairly crackled with energy. *Ooh baby,* she thought. *Any fool can see these two got it bad for each other.* She looked at her good friend, then at the rookie and back to Dez again. She wanted to laugh but forced herself not to. "You know, on second thought, my back has been bothering me. I think I'll just do a quick chest routine and be on my way."

Crystal returned to the bench press and sat watching the two women as Dez grabbed the lat bar and began to explain something, a serious look on her face. Crystal couldn't quite hear what was said, but Jaylynn nodded and asked questions, watching closely as Dez demonstrated.

Crystal lay back on the bench and gripped the free weights. She managed to eke out seven reps before racking it again. When she sat up, she noticed that now the rookie was seated at the lat pull down station holding onto the wide bar with Dez standing behind her, hands patting Jaylynn's shoulders as the tall woman explained something intently. Neither woman paid Crystal the slightest bit of attention. She wondered if she should feel hurt, then decided that the two women needed very much to patch things up. She continued with her presses, moved on to dumbbell flyes, did some push-ups, and decided to call it a night. When she exited, she looked back to see Dez squatting next to Jaylynn as the smaller woman worked at the seated row. Neither woman gave any indication that they noticed Crystal leaving.

****

Jaylynn arrived for roll call right on time, and as usual, Dez was already perched on a chair in her regular back corner. They nodded at one another, and Jaylynn sat in a seat in the middle of the room and waited for the flow of cops to settle so the sergeant could start.

Cheryl entered full of vigor and excitement. "Hey, Jaylynn," she hollered across the room. "Guess what? Stevens is back to work. I didn't expect him until next week, but his wife's doing so well, he's back tonight." She helped herself to a doughnut and came over to sit in the chair next to the rookie. She leaned over closer and said quietly, "He also said he's up every night with a crabby wife and baby anyway, so he may as well get back to work."

The duty sergeant stomped into the room and hollered at everyone to listen up. In the daily updates, he brought up the latest rash of burglaries. "You all know about the Bat Boy Burglaries from this morning's paper. There've been six break-ins in six weeks, usually on Saturday or Sunday evenings. Witnesses ID them as kids with baseball bats. They knock—if no answer, they whack in a window and take money, jewelry, and small items of value. Keep an eye out for three white boys dressed urban style. So far all the burglaries have taken place in the Selby-Dale neighborhood."

The sergeant called roll and made assignments. Jaylynn was paired with someone she didn't know at all named Calvin Braswell who didn't often work their sector. After roll call Cheryl gripped her forearm and leaned over to speak in Jaylynn's ear. "Good luck tonight. He's a dinosaur, that one," Cheryl whispered. "You'll have to put up with some bitchin' from him. He despises women cops. I rode with him a couple of times, and he's a disrespectful, foul-mouthed jerk."

"Great," Jaylynn said. "Just what I need."

Cheryl said, "Maybe you'll have better luck charming him than

I did."

Cheryl slid past and headed out the door with Stevens. Jaylynn rose and fell in line behind the rest of the cops. She sauntered up to the front where Braswell, a rotund sandy-haired man with 1970's sideburns, was engaged in a heated conversation with the duty sergeant. She saw Dez pause behind Braswell, and by then Jaylynn was close enough to hear for herself.

Braswell was saying, "I'm not riding with some fresh-faced punk—specially not a female one. What a pain in the ass. Rather ride alone!"

"Why don't you do that, Braswell?" Dez asked in a deep voice over his shoulder.

He jumped and half-turned. "Jesus Christ, Reilly! Whatchu doing sneaking up on a guy like that?"

"Since it offends your masculine sensibilities so much to ride with a woman, I'll take Savage tonight. Okay, Sarge?" she asked as she nodded toward her superior officer.

"No skin off my nose," he replied. "I'll just update it on the roster and let the Lieutenant know."

Dez turned to Braswell. "You oughta buy me lunch or something though."

"Bullshit. You girls should stick together, leave us guys alone."

"Yeah, right." Dez turned with a twinkle in her eye to find Jaylynn behind her wearing a puzzled look on her face. Dez said, "Let's go, Savage. We gotta make sure we don't get the car with the broken heater." Loudly she said over her shoulder, "I hope Braswell snags it and freezes his fat ass off." She took off out the door, her long legs beating a staccato sound on the tile as Jaylynn raced along behind her.

Dez picked up the keys and loped out to the parking lot. She slid into the driver's seat and Jaylynn got in and buckled up. She waited for Dez to say something, but after they'd traveled a good mile she couldn't take the silence anymore. "Why did you do that?"

"Why not?"

Jaylynn pondered for a moment. She wasn't satisfied with that. "I'm serious. Why?"

Dez said, "You would've hated riding with Braswell. He's a sexist, mean-spirited asshole. Not a very good cop either. You can't trust him with your back. I just figured you didn't need the kind of grief he'd put you through."

"And?"

"And what?" Dez asked irritably. She pulled her sunglasses out of her breast pocket, flipped them open, and put them on.

"And what else? What do you care if I have to ride with some old dinosaur?"

Dez hesitated, then shook her head and looked over at Jaylynn. "All right. I've been thinking maybe it's time we put this cold war behind us. Call it a gesture of good will and concern."

Jaylynn frowned, then looked away. She caught sight of something out the window and did a double take. "Dez, you see 'em?"

"Yeah," Dez said. "Do they match the description or what?" Two slender white boys and a fatter tall boy, all in mid-teens, walked away from them down the alley between Selby and Victoria Street. They wore over-sized sweatshirts and huge baggy jeans. One skinny kid carried a cardboard box in his arms, and the tall boy was juggling two awkward-looking grocery bags. The third boy held two shiny aluminum bats. Their baseball caps were pulled down low and they looked around constantly, surreptitiously checking out the houses along the row.

Dez hit the gas and circled the block. "This has gotta be too good to be true." When she arrived at the mouth of the alley, the boys looked up, surprised, then dropped the bags and box and ran.

"Oh great, they made us," Jaylynn said. She wrenched her door open and decided on a hunch to go after the biggest kid, hoping he might not be as fleet of foot. Dez grabbed the radio to report as the two skinny boys split, one going through a yard on the left of the alley, the other through a yard on the right side. The big kid turned and ran down the alley. He cut through a yard, struggled over a waist-high chain-link fence, stumbled, and then fled out onto Ashland Street. Dez saw Jaylynn vault the fence in one fluid motion and start to gain yardage.

Dez hit the siren and lights and followed down the alley issuing descriptions over the radio to dispatch. Once Jaylynn and the kid veered off into the yard, Dez lost sight of them. She gunned the car forward and drove back onto the avenue, hoping to pick them up on Laurel Street. Wrong direction. The rookie and the boy were nowhere to be seen. They must have crossed another street and run through more than one yard.

She wheeled the car back around the block and up to the next street. As she turned the corner she caught sight of Jaylynn bolting away from her and across the pavement, just yards behind her quarry. Dez couldn't help but smile. *Perfect sprinter's form.* The rookie hardly looked fatigued. The fat boy was ready to have a heart attack and, from all appearances, the rookie wasn't even warmed up yet. Dez accelerated and drove up onto the parking strip, then leapt out of the car in time to see Jaylynn grab the back of the kid's sweatshirt and drag him down with a nicely executed tackle. She had his arms behind his back and the cuffs on before he could even get his face out of the grass. Dez leaned against the door and grinned, then radioed in to report to dispatch.

There were sirens close by, and Dez hoped they'd snag the other two boys. But with just this one, they would likely get the names and information they needed. She'd bet money the Bat Boy Burglaries were over. As she stood watching, neighbors peeped out windows or came out on their porches to watch.

Jaylynn hauled the kid up. He staggered, but she kept hold of his arm, dragged him over to the cruiser and stuffed him in the back seat. Then she leaned back against the car's rear panel and put her hands on her knees to catch her breath.

Dez held back a grin. *Wow! Great collar. Look at her—if you don't count her shirt coming partly untucked, then she escaped the chase with only a grass stain on one knee.* She couldn't help but study the rookie with admiration.

After a moment, Jaylynn became aware of Dez's gaze. She looked up to see the older cop smiling, her bright blue eyes merry. Dez stood facing the rear of the car, one foot in the car and one on the ground with her right shoulder draped over the open door. "Couldn't have done that better myself," she said.

"Let's go back and get the goods," Jaylynn answered. With a satisfied look on her face, she added, "That ought to be a good collar for us."

"No," Dez said. "That one's all yours. You spotted them first; you took him down on your own. It's yours. And you know what that means?"

"No, what?" Jaylynn stood up and tucked her shirt in.

"You also get all the paperwork." Dez laughed and got in the car.

****

Processing juveniles always took longer, and it was well over an hour before they got back to the car again. By then it was eight o'clock and Jaylynn was desperately hungry.

"Where do you want to go for meal break?" Dez asked. "Burger King? Mickey D's? Taco Bell? Your choice."

"Let's hit the The Cutting Board and get some of those sandwiches."

"Oh, I can swing by there later. Pick where you want to go."

"That *is* where I'd like to go," Jaylynn said. "I don't eat fast food anymore."

Dez was surprised. "You don't? Why?"

"I hate to admit it, but you were right. I can't sit around on my butt in a squad car night after night and expect to maintain my girlish figure. I could tell I was putting on weight. So I took your advice before I had an ass the size of Mankato."

Dez laughed heartily. "And you've been working out, too."

"Yeah."

"No wonder you were flying earlier. You looked so—so effortless. Just think what would have happened if you'd been paired with Braswell tonight for that." Dez started laughing. "You'd have made Mr. Pot Belly look really bad. I almost wish I could have seen that."

Jaylynn looked at Dez out of the corner of her eye and wondered what the hell had gotten into her. This was hardly the taciturn, distant woman of the last several weeks. Why the change? "Hey, I'm starving here," Jaylynn said. "You gonna drive or do I have to?"

"Should I put on the siren?"

"I hardly think my meal warrants a code red. Just get a move on," she said, hiding her smile of happiness.

Chapter
17

Jaylynn didn't know what to expect when she arrived for work the next day. Riding with Pilcher had been okay, and she liked when she got assigned with Crystal, but some of the other cops were not fun. She couldn't avoid admitting to herself how much she preferred Dez. She had forgotten—no, she'd chosen on purpose not to remember—how enjoyable a shift could be. The evening before had flown by. It took no time at all for the two of them to slip back into an effective work rhythm. Little needed to be said. On calls, a quick nod or hand gesture, maybe a raised eyebrow, and each knew what the other was thinking. Two domestics and three noise complaints kept them busy until midnight, and when shift ended, she'd felt a twinge of longing for the night to go on and on. But she was Cinderella at the ball, and at the stroke of twelve it was all over. She laughed ruefully at herself for comparing Cinderella's tribulations to hers. *At least I don't have to wear high-heeled glass slippers. Or a skirt with a giant hoop.*

She arrived nearly forty-five minutes early to see the Lieutenant, and then went to the locker room to change into her uniform. She dressed hastily. Sitting on the bench in front of her locker, the back of her knees pressed against the rickety wood, she worked at threading her wide belt through the loops on her pants. The locker room door opened. She didn't look around until she realized someone loomed behind her, someone very tall with long black hair.

"Oh, hi," Jaylynn said. She willed herself not to blush, but it didn't work.

Dez didn't seem to notice. She sat down on the other even more rickety bench across from Jaylynn's back. In a low, soft voice she said, "We need to talk."

Jaylynn swung around, lifting her feet over the bench to the other side, and faced the bigger woman. Not looking up, she finished buckling her belt. "What about?"

"Us."

Jaylynn's head came up swiftly and her eyes met shards of smoldering blue. She waited, not trusting her voice to speak.

Dez looked away, her face grim but determined. "I think I've been sort of hard on you lately." She leaned forward, put her elbows on her knees, and looked down. Quietly she said, "I just want you to know that you're developing into a damn good cop, and I'd like to go back to riding with you—whenever you want, that is, if you want to, I mean—"

"I accept."

"What?"

"Your apology. I accept."

Dez looked confused. "I wasn't aware I was apologizing."

"Well, you should've been," Jaylynn said with a great deal more vehemence than she intended.

Her face now a carefully guarded mask, Dez rose to full height, towering over the rookie. She gave Jaylynn her most merciless stare. "Now see here, you're the one who asked out— not me."

Jaylynn stood up, too, and all five and a half feet of her met the tall cop's gaze with unflinching firmness. "You gave me no choice. Besides, can you stand there and tell me you weren't going to pass me off anyway?" Dez made a gesture with her hand, but Jaylynn interrupted, "Don't lie to me to make me feel better. You didn't want to ride with me anymore, did you?"

Dez glared at her. This discussion was not what she'd had in mind when she'd begun it. She had felt better during last night's shift than she had in a very long time. It felt—right. Like all was right with the world. And she had thought of nothing else all day, had debated back and forth whether she should even approach Jaylynn, and now she was sure she should not have. "What do you want from me?"

Abruptly, Jaylynn sat down and put her head in her hands. "Nothing. Really. Forget it."

Dez stepped over the bench and squatted in front of Jaylynn. She tapped the other woman's knee with her fist. "Hey. Let's not be so serious, okay? If you'd rather not ride with me, that's okay."

"No, Dez, that's not it. I like riding with you. A lot." She looked up and saw the guarded look on the other woman's face. "But what about your reputation?"

"Whaddya mean?" Dez rocked back on her heels and stood up again.

"You've got a reputation to uphold. You told me that before. You sure you want to partner with the lesbian rookie? Believe me, enough people know now."

"God! *Why* are you making this so hard?" Dez tightened her fist and smacked it into the palm of her hand, making a growling sound in her throat. What she really wanted to do was pick up the lockers and throw them out the window—but this was the basement and there were no windows. She sat on the bench again and squeezed her eyes shut. "All right then. I apologize."

"For what?"

It was all Dez could do to keep from screaming. She shut her eyes, drew a deep breath and held it, then expelled it forcefully and opened her eyes. She looked into Jaylynn's hazel eyes and saw a trace of amusement. Suddenly, inexplicably, she relaxed. *What did Ryan use to say? In the face of female adversity, either run like hell or throw in the towel.* She'd already run like hell and that hadn't worked. She wondered how good her towel-tossing skills were. She cleared her throat. "What I'm sorry about is that everything I said and did hurt you. I didn't mean to hurt you, Jay. Can you accept that?"

"Okay."

"And I'd like us to go back to riding together again. I'll keep teaching you what I know if you'll forgive me for being such an oaf."

"Okay."

"So, should we go talk to the Lieutenant?"

"No," Jaylynn said.

Exasperated, Dez groaned. "Why the hell not?"

"I went to see him when I first got here and already put in the request. All you have to do is okay it."

Dez got to her feet and loomed over the smaller woman. "You made me go through all of that?"

Jaylynn tipped her head back, and with a smile of satisfaction said, "Yup. And it was worth it."

In mock anger, Dez grabbed Jaylynn's collar and tugged her to her feet. "You are the most pigheaded woman I've ever met."

"You looked in the mirror lately? Maybe you should have someone introduce you to yourself." She shrugged Dez's hand off and straightened her collar.

In a grumpy voice, Dez said, "Very funny."

The locker room door swung open and in came Cheryl. "Hey there, girls." She launched into an account of her fabulous day. Dez took the first opportunity to slip away, leaving Jaylynn listening intently to Cheryl's rambling. What Dez didn't realize was that although on the outside Jaylynn appeared to be listening, on the inside, she was still talking to Dez, still with Dez, totally immersed in happiness.

****

After shift that night Jay was still wired. She'd been full of energy for nine straight hours. They got back to the locker room and she called out over her shoulder, "Are you lifting weights tonight, Dez?"

"Nah, day of rest from lifting."

"Too bad. I feel like I need to work off some of this nervous energy."

"Let's take a run then," Dez said, as she wrestled off the bulletproof vest.

"Very funny. Just jog up and down the halls of administration or what?"

"No. I'm serious. We take off and run down to the river and back. I do it all the time."

Jaylynn started to pull off her t-shirt, then paused. "Do I need to remind you it's after midnight?"

"I strap my weapon on over my jogging clothes, and presto—no problem. Nobody ever bothers me."

"I'm not running with a gun flapping at my side," she said, but she pulled her t-shirt back down and got out a pair of sweat bottoms.

"You don't have to carry. I don't think we need more fire power than what my weapon offers," Dez said dryly. "I'm used to it anyway. So, are you game?"

Jaylynn swung around on the bench and waited as Dez pulled on her socks and shoes. Jaylynn was already dressed in leotards under blue sweats and three layers of shirts: t-shirt, long sleeved jersey, and an orange sweatshirt. Dez pulled on black sweats and a heavy gray sweatshirt with the St. Paul Police Department logo on it. The big cop finished tying her shoes and fished through her locker until she found a neoprene sport holster. She pulled up her sweatshirt and Velcroed it around her waist, secured her gun, and turned it so the gun was at the small of her back.

"Hey, that's cool," Jay said, "but that's not your Glock is it?"

"No, it's a .38 I like to carry when I run or ride my bike."

She reached over and tugged Dez's sweatshirt up to examine the holster. "It's like scuba dive material."

"Yeah, so it keeps my middle warm, that's for sure." She tucked some money and her license in her sock and faced Jay.

They went out the building into the cool night air. "So what's the route?" Jaylynn asked.

"You want, say, a mile down and back, or the long route?"

"How long is long?"

"Maybe four miles."

Jaylynn stopped to think for a moment. "Let's go long then."

By now they were out on the empty avenue, the street lamps shining down on Jaylynn's hair and making her look as though a halo reflected around her head. Dez's face was shrouded in shadow. Jay walked next to her and looked up, trying to see her eyes, but it was dark enough that they were obscured in the gloom.

"Okay," Dez said, "let's go down Jackson, under the train overpass, across Warner to the river, and then run on that path for a mile or so. Then let's come back up and go through Rice Park. It'll be a nice loop."

Jaylynn nodded and they took off into a slow jog, gradually stretching their legs further, speeding up, until they found a steady rhythm that suited them both. For the first mile they heard only the rasp of one another's breath and an occasional far-off siren. They reached the river and ran side by side on the path. Jay said, "I like...those lights...on the water."

Dez looked out across the Mississippi. Reflections from the buildings on the other side cast wavy golden light on the surface of the water. "It's pretty." The path was well-lit by lamps placed every thirty feet or so, and a waist-high bright blue metal fence ran beside the path between them and the drop down to the river. When the weather improved, there would be flowers and plants galore alongside the footpath.

Soon they reached the end of the river path and turned around. With a sly grin, Jaylynn said, "I'll beat you to the boat mooring sign," and she took off. Dez accelerated after her, long legs beating staccato on the cement. She gained slowly on her companion and drew next to her. Now it was a battle of wills since their legs were fatigued and tiring. Jaylynn fell into a familiar rhythm: knees up, hands loose, breath even. Her peripheral vision slowly narrowed until she was focused only on the sign 70 yards, 60 yards, 50 yards ahead...

With her longer, stronger legs, Dez pushed herself, tenaciously remaining alongside the fleet-footed woman. She was determined to stay with Jaylynn, maybe not beat her, but at least reach the sign simultaneously. Her breath was ragged, and she could feel her lungs burning. 40 yards, 30 yards, so close, so close.

They blew past the sign, abreast, and slowed gradually until they both came to a stop next to the fence along the path. Panting, they bent over and tried to catch their breath.

"Good speed there," Jaylynn gasped, "for an old lady."

Dez reached out and whacked the winded woman's shoulder lightly with the back of her hand. "Easy for you to say," she choked out. "You aren't...packing a...heavy gun."

Jay squealed with laughter. "Oh right...that's a good

one...want me to take it...and we'll try another...400 yards or so?"

"Nah, that's okay...I concede to the...superior sprinter."

Jay looked up at her in mock horror. "Oh my God...what a day. Apologies...and concessions...all in one night!"

Dez could finally breathe better and started walking along the path, still taking deep breaths of the cool night air. "That's where you're wrong. It's after midnight—a whole new day. Yesterday was apologies. Today is concessions."

Jaylynn fell in beside her walking swiftly. "What will tomorrow bring?"

"Who knows, confessions? Maybe I'll divulge a few long-lost secrets."

In a droll voice Jay said, "Ooh, can't wait to hear that!"

"That's enough racing, but let's pick it up now that I can finally breathe again."

They shifted into a slow jog and struggled up the hill to Kellogg toward Rice Park. The ornamental street lamps shone brightly all around the one block circumference of the park. Two cement paths formed an X from corner to corner of the block, and in one quarter of the X was a beautiful fountain, ringed by a wide, waist-high marble retaining wall which enclosed a pool of dark water. The fountain was not operating, and all was quiet in the park. The two women jogged up to the wall and stopped. Jaylynn put her heel up on the wall and proceeded to stretch out her hamstrings on it. At the center of the pool of water was a 10-foot-high iron statue of a woman. She looked downward, her head cocked slightly to the side. She had powerful arms and legs, a narrow waist, and long hair. Her face was mysteriously passive and hard to make out in the murky night light.

Dez leaned back against the wall, pulled herself up, and balanced on the wide edge. The cement was cold against her legs, but she disregarded it.

Jaylynn stopped stretching and shook her legs out. She could keep running. She wasn't yet tired, though she thought she should be. Instead, nervous energy coursed through her limbs. She glanced up at Dez and found thoughtful blue eyes already on her. In two steps, she could put her arms around the bigger woman's waist, her head against her middle. She willed herself not to think about that. She'd be damned if she'd make a fool of herself again. The mischievous side of her was even tempted to push Dez into the pool, and she gave a strained laugh and leaned her elbows on the wall a safe two feet away from the dark form perched nearby.

"What's so funny?" she asked in a low throaty voice.

"You're in a mighty vulnerable position. If I wasn't such a nice person, you could be doing the backstroke right now."

"And you'd have joined me, count on it."

"Hmm, I'm not going to see if you're right. Especially since I see a squad car coming our way now."

Dez turned and looked over her shoulder. Sure enough, a car was slowing on the street. The cruiser's spotlight illuminated them and a streak of light shone their way. Dez jumped off the wall and faced the cops, raising her hands out and above shoulder level. "Hey," she shouted. "Who is that? Patterson? Bentley?"

The spotlight went out and the driver's door opened. "Reilly? Is that you?"

"Yeah," she shouted. "Bentley?"

"No, Patterson." A tall skinny form moved toward them, stepped over a low brick wall, and came around the side of the fountain. "What the hell are you doing out here this time of night? And who's this?"

"Savage and I went for a run."

"Jesus, Reilly, it's almost two-fucking-o'clock in the morning." He was close enough now for them to see his tired face.

Dez said, "Best time to run. There's no roller bladers competing for the jogging path."

"You gals might not be safe, you know. I wouldn't be out this time of night."

"Patterson, you *are* out this time of night," the tall cop said.

"But I'm working. What if somebody came along, hassled you, attacked you?"

"You worry too much. I'm packing." She turned a bit so he could see her holster. "Nobody messes with me. But if it makes you feel any better, we're on the way back up to the station."

"Okay. Whatever." He peered at the rookie. "I haven't met you, Savage. Heard your name. I'm Gus Patterson." He stuck his hand out and she told him her first name. He let go and turned toward the tall woman. "Hey, Reilly," he said. "I hear you're competing in a couple months. Is that right?"

There was a long pause. "Yeah, I am."

"Well, I'll come and root you on. It's for a nice cause. So good luck."

"Thanks, Patterson," was the quiet answer.

"See you two girls around. Just be careful." He spun on his heel and moved away from them.

"Don't worry, Patterson," Dez called out confidently. "Anybody messes with us, I'll shoot 'em. And if I miss, Savage here can just run away."

His voice came back faintly, "Yeah, yeah. Don't call me to take the report." He got back in the car and drove off.

Jaylynn looked at Dez quizzically. "What competition was he

talking about?"

"Nothing. Never mind." She moved away from the wall. "Let's head back up—"

"Wait." Jaylynn grabbed her forearm. "Tell me. What was he talking about?"

Dez shook her head. She spat out the next words. "I didn't want everyone and their brother to know about this, but apparently they must."

"I'm not everyone and their brother, Dez." Jaylynn was getting mad and trying to keep it cool. She still gripped the taller woman's arm and felt warmth and moisture through the cotton sweatshirt.

Dez gave a sigh. "I'm in a bodybuilding competition in four months, and I pledged the proceeds to Ryan's memorial fund, for the kids' college. If I place, that is. It might not be a lot of money, but it's something. Come on. Let's walk."

Jaylynn let go of her arm, and they silently moved out of the park. "You weren't going to tell me?"

"Oh, I don't know. Maybe tomorrow. It's a day early for confessions you know."

Jaylynn looked over at her, startled, then realized she was kidding. "I think that's a really wonderful thing to do. I hope you win."

Dez shrugged. "I guess there's a pool going with some of the officers, too. Some betting for, some against me. They'll probably raise a couple thousand dollars that way." Dez lengthened her stride, and Jaylynn picked up her pace to keep up.

"Where is it? I want to come."

Dez stopped. "This is going to be hard."

"Don't worry. I'll give you moral support."

"It's not that. Geez, I don't know! Ryan's wife will be there. His kids—it's going to be—I don't know why in the hell I agreed to do it." She shuddered. "Except that I'd give every dollar I'll make for the rest of my life to have him back." Her shoulders slumped and she shook her head. In a soft, bitter voice she said, "But I know that'll never happen, so the best I can do is help out Julie and his kids."

It was all Jaylynn could do to keep from throwing her arms around the other woman. She reached out hesitantly to pat her on the back, but Dez was already swinging into action, loping along the street in a slow jog.

Chapter
18

The first half of May blew by and Jaylynn hardly knew where it went. She spent one entire week doing in-service training with the twelve other rookies and a number of the officers hired in the previous 24 months. They focused further on records and forms, report writing, court testimony, note taking, elements of proof, and ethics. She was careful to avoid Dwayne Neilsen, though every once in a while she caught him glowering at her. When she stared back, he would return to his own paperwork.

Dez was gone for a whole week at an in-service training for Field Training Officers, so Jaylynn only saw her once in passing. She rode with Crystal every day that week.

On Monday, the first of a three-days-off cycle, the rookie rose early, ate a light breakfast, and got ready for a run. She wore a lightweight t-shirt with a gray U of M sweatshirt over it, her favorite Nikes, and a light blue pair of nylon shorts over a pair of soft running leotards. Strapping on a waist pack containing her wallet and house keys, she stepped out into a crisp sunny morning, 50 degrees and rising. She stretched her limbs a little and then set out at a leisurely pace to warm up.

She was so glad winter was finally over. All along the roadway she saw buds blooming and little shoots of plants inching up out of the dark Minnesota soil. Children were out in full force, milling around on corners waiting for their school buses. A few brave souls were even wearing shorts and Jaylynn saw one coatless boy standing dismally, his bare legs quivering in the cool air while he clutched a backpack to his t-shirt-clad chest. *Bet his mother didn't see him out the door,* Jaylynn thought. She waved as she ran by and called out to him, "Jump up and down. Move around. You'll stay warmer that way."

She continued down Lexington Parkway and decided on a long

run all the way to Minnehaha Falls Park, a twelve mile round trip. She didn't *love* to run, but after a couple of miles she always fell into a smooth pace and her legs carried her forward, nearly effortlessly. It felt good and gave her mind time to wander. She thought about how she used to write in her journal a lot, but lately she hadn't been able to. Of course she never rode the bus anymore, so some of her journal writing time had disappeared. She was lucky if she even got a letter off to her folks or Auntie Lynn once a month any more. *I really need to make some time to journal—I totally lose track of things when I don't record things occasionally.*

She had no idea lately what was happening with her life. Where once she felt self-directed and certain about her goals, now she found herself drifting along in a holding pattern. Since she and Dez had patched up their differences, work had been much steadier—and less stressful—but she still found herself often on edge. For one thing, she didn't really know where she stood with the taciturn cop. Nothing had changed for the rookie. Every time Dez fixed a razor-sharp gaze on her, Jaylynn felt the same exact butterflies in her stomach that she always had. Fortunately, they spent most of their time staring out the windshield of a squad car or dealing with squabbling people. When their eyes met outside the car or while on the street, it was usually to communicate about the altercation they were involved in and nothing else.

Jaylynn cut through a grassy schoolyard, feeling the springy soil beneath her feet. She felt strong today, like she could run forever. She wished she could run more often with Dez. Until lately, they had been lifting weights every night after work, but since the middle of May, the big cop hadn't wanted to run any distances anymore, saying she wouldn't be able to until after the August competition. She said it was too hard on the muscle she was trying to preserve. Soon, Dez had told the rookie, she was going to have to go on an even stricter diet. *I don't know how her food intake could get any more severe than it already* is. *I'll have to ask about that later.*

They'd both been on their best behavior for weeks and if she was honest with herself, Jaylynn had to admit she felt a little stressed because of it. *How much longer can I continue to be so cautious?* And they had never talked about what had happened when she had spent the night on the couch in Dez's arms. She never would have thought she could kiss someone like that and then turn around and pretend it never happened—but apparently that was what was expected of her. Nothing was resolved. With a passion, Jaylynn hated things left hanging.

She arrived at the entrance of Minnehaha Falls Park and jogged over to the waterfall. A cascade of fresh water poured off a small rock shelf, fell thirty feet, and splashed with a roar in a wide pool. Many of the trees were still bare, but some were starting to bud out, and three immense evergreens provided plenty of green to enjoy. She watched the water churn until she caught her breath, then put a leg up on the back of a park bench overlooking the pool and stretched out each of her hamstrings. The park was silent and peaceful, and she liked the fresh smell of water and leaves as she stood alone on the dirt path surrounding the waterfall. She stretched some more, still feeling plenty limber, and then let her eyes scan the area until she found a water fountain and strolled over to it. She turned the knob and a burst of water sprayed up, catching her in the face. *Brrr! That is cold!* Wiping her face on the sleeve of her sweatshirt, she tried the knob again, this time not leaning in until she had the stream of water under control. She drank her fill, then went to sit on the bench.

Her thoughts went back to Dez Reilly, and she asked herself a series of questions she hadn't yet dared to ask. *Can I go on like this, indefinitely, feeling the way I do? Is it enough to be with her every night, maybe occasionally at Luella's or with others? If it's not enough, what do I do?*

She slouched on the bench, her arms spread wide across the top of the bench, and tipped her head back, looking up to the peak of the evergreen tree overhead. She had never been much for ultimatums, but part of her wanted to confront Dez and deliver a big one. She decided that was why she felt like she was walking on eggshells so much of the time. She was deathly afraid she would just blurt out her feelings and challenge the tall cop to deal with them.

Fat lot of good that would do. In her heart, she knew confrontation was not only unwise, but unfair to Dez. Just because she didn't return the rookie's feelings in the same way didn't mean Dez needed to be hit over the head with it. *This is my problem,* thought Jaylynn. *Even though she may be attracted to me, it doesn't mean she can love me, and she's got enough class not to act on purely physical feelings. I'd rather she actually fall in love with someone and be happy than just "love 'em and leave 'em."*

Maybe over time our friendship will deepen and strengthen. So—I guess we can never be lovers. I have to accept that. I must. I'll be the best friend I can, and I will be satisfied with that and only that.

She stood up and shook her legs out, stretched her arms and shoulders, and jogged away from the falls, looking back once to see the cold, clear water splashing persistently, ceaselessly, over the rock rim and falling to the bottom. *I'll be as steady as that waterfall. I'll just keep on, and no matter what, I won't think of her anymore as anything but a friend.* She picked up the pace as she exited the park and continued the long run back to her house, still feeling strong.

****

Dez woke up the morning of June 7th knowing immediately that it would not be a day just like any other. She got out of bed and padded over to her desk and rolled the top back. She sat in the desk chair in her t-shirt and boxer pajama shorts and made herself look at the two 4" x 6" framed photos sitting on the wood surface. They contained pictures of the two most influential men in her life.

The one on the left was a photo of her tall father in full dress blues. The laughing little black-haired girl wrapped around the policeman's leg was gazing up at him, a look of adoration on her smiling white face. She wore a red corduroy jumper over a white turtleneck. White leotards and brown and white saddle shoes completed her outfit. They stood in the front yard with a low-slung rambler-style home visible in the background. His black hair was cropped short and blue eyes stared directly at the camera with only the slightest trace of a smile on his smooth face. Circa 1975, her father peered back at her as if to ask why she had locked him away for so long.

The photo on the right was of a grinning blond man, obviously on a sunny day at a picnic. He wore light blue shorts and no shirt. His bare chest was golden tan, his abdomen tight and rippled with muscle. He looked like he had just arisen from a picnic table, and in one hand he held a cob of corn, which he appeared to be ready to use as a club on the picture taker. Dez picked up the photo and peered closely at it. She had avoided looking at it every time she got into her desk, but today...today was the one-year anniversary of Ryan's death. This morning she should look at his face, remember him, honor his memory. She set the picture down and turned away. Tears sprang to her eyes, but she did not want to cry, didn't want to start feeling something that would escalate and get out of control.

After she took a shower and ate breakfast, she called Julie and spoke to her for a while. Ryan's wife hadn't adjusted well to her husband's death at first, but today Dez could tell the woman was trying very hard to make peace with it. They managed to make it through the conversation without breaking down and crying, so Dez considered it a success. *Now if I can just get out of the house before Luella gets hold of me.*

She looked out the window and saw it was beautiful outside: sunny, breezy, no clouds. A day suitable for a picnic, just like the day had been in the photograph. It was a day, she decided, when she needed to keep busy. She didn't want to slip into sadness, didn't want to think of Ryan while being sullen and blue.

On an impulse Dez dialed Jaylynn's house and was surprised when the rookie answered the phone. In a low voice, she said, "Hey, it's early. What are you doing up?"

Jaylynn said, "You expected me to be some sort of lazybones lounging around? I've got things to do, places to go, people to see."

"Oh."

"Why? What's happening?"

"Nothing. I'll let you go."

"Wait a minute! To tell the truth, I was just getting ready to take a walk around the lake. Want to join me?"

"Is this really a walk or some kind of a puking sprint?"

"A nice brisk walk—that's all! I'll meet you at the east end in what? Fifteen minutes?"

Dez thought for a long moment. She liked the lake on weekdays. There were usually few people there compared to Saturdays and Sundays. "Okay. I'll see you by the stone arch." She rang off and changed into running shoes, lightweight shorts, and a tank top. She paused long enough to apply some sunscreen to her neck, shoulders, and arms, then grabbed a Twins cap and headed downstairs. Sure enough, her landlady lay in wait with the back door open.

"Desiree Reilly, what are you up to today?" She came to stand in the back doorway, a smile on her face.

"I'm meeting Jaylynn at the stone arch for a walk around the lake."

"Well, that's a good idea. How you getting there?"

"Why, Luella, I'm walking. It's only half a mile."

"So it is. Bring her over for lemonade later if you want."

"I'll see what she wants to do. See ya." She jammed the Twins cap over her dark hair and scooted out the back door.

She was surprised that she beat Jaylynn to the meeting place. It was only about two blocks for the other woman. When the rookie finally appeared, she came running up in very sky blue nylon shorts and a white t-shirt. Dez quickly stifled her admiring glance and said, "Hi, slowpoke."

"Hey," Jaylynn said as she slowed to a walk. "I had to have a snack, and then I had to change from my jammies."

"Ah ha! So you *were* lazing around in bed." Dez fell into step next to her.

"But of course. But I'll have you know I was awake—just remember that." Neither woman made a move to walk briskly. They ambled away from the stone arch on the path in the bright sunlight for a couple minutes before Jaylynn said, "I know today is an important day, Dez."

"Yeah. Unbelievably, it's been a whole year. Seems like less though. Seems like just yesterday." She looked away and out across the lake. An entire flotilla of ducks floated along one side in the shade.

"I can't imagine what it'd be like. The only thing I have to compare it to is when my dad died."

"What? When did that happen?"

"He died when I was nine."

"But—but you always talk about your *parents*."

"My mom remarried when I was 13, and my stepdad has been just like a father to me. I don't call him Dave—I call him Dad. He's a real good guy. I've been lucky to have three good parents."

"What happened to your father?"

"He was killed in an accident with another semi. He was an over-the-road trucker."

"My father was a cop. He died on duty—heart attack. I was thirteen."

"Well that's a strange thing we have in common, both losing our dads that young."

"Yeah. That's true." They continued along the cement path under the canopy of elms and oaks, but after another minute, Jaylynn said, "I wish I'd known Ryan. He must've been quite a guy."

"That he was."

Gradually they increased their walking pace, Jaylynn taking three steps to Dez's two, until both were sweating freely. As the sun shone down upon them and glared off the water, they circled the lake with the rookie chattering about various subjects.

During a quiet moment, Dez abruptly asked, "Do you have any hobbies?"

Jaylynn looked up at her. "You mean like collecting tea cups and saucers?"

"Not really. Like fishing or boating or wood carving—you know, hobbies."

"Can't afford a boat, never liked to hurt the poor fish, and wood carving? Do I look like an artistic person?"

"Sure. Why not?"

"I can't draw worth beans. Haven't you noticed what horrible crime scene sketches I do?"

"You're not *that* bad."

Jaylynn scoffed at her. "Stick men are embarrassed to have been drawn by me."

"That doesn't answer my question."

"About hobbies? Okay." She tucked her short hair behind her

ears and thought a moment. "School has been my hobby, I think. I mean, it took me so long, and I was so busy with it that I didn't have time for much else. I like to run, so I guess you could count that. I love music and to read and write in my journal. I'd like to get into photography but haven't been able to afford a decent camera until recently. I'd also love to travel. I like going to the movies, the theater, to concerts. But I guess I don't really have any actual hobbies. Do you?"

"Weight lifting. Playing guitar. Guess that's about it."

They continued walking in silence and soon they were back at the stone arch for a second time. Jaylynn said, "That's about three miles."

"Wanna quit?"

"Yeah, I suppose."

They slowed from the swift walk to a saunter. Dez said, "Luella asked if you wanted to come by after we're done and have lemonade."

"At your house?"

Dez arched an eyebrow and said, "Well, that *is* where she lives."

Jaylynn socked her in the shoulder and made a face. "I'm all sweaty."

"She doesn't care."

They headed over to the house, strolling along in companionable silence in the sunlight as the sidewalk heated up beneath them. Luella was glad to see Jaylynn and insisted on giving her a hug, ignoring her protests about sweat. They sat in the coolness of the dining room swigging lemonade while Luella stood over them with the pitcher.

"So what have you girls got planned for today?" the silver-haired woman asked.

Jaylynn shrugged as Dez said, "I'm getting out all the gear and painting the back hall finally."

Luella said, "That sounds like a lot of work. Why don't you two go do something *fun* today?"

Dez said, "It needs doing. I've been meaning to work on it for a long time."

"You want some help?" Jaylynn asked.

"Nah, it's a lot of work."

The older woman sputtered, "Isn't that what *I* just said?" She smacked the pitcher down on the table, crossed her arms over her purple housedress, and proceeded to give Dez the evil eye.

Dez turned and gazed at her landlady, her face expressionless. "It's work for her, pleasure for me."

Jaylynn rose and moved to stand next to Luella. She put an

arm on the older woman's shoulder and with a challenging look on her face said, "How do you know it's not pleasure for me?"

"Yeah," Luella said. "She's gonna get a real good lunch out of it, aren't you, honey?" She wrapped an arm around the small woman's waist.

Dez sighed and shook her head. "I give up. I bow to the greater powers." She rolled her eyes. "If you really want to stay, Jay, you'd better take my truck home for painting clothes."

Jaylynn eagerly accepted the keys to the Ford. She'd never driven such a big truck. Once she got the seat moved forward about a foot, she found that it was easy to maneuver and even easier to see out of, which she liked a lot. She returned a short time later with a change of clean clothes and wearing a pair of very short but shabby gray shorts, a baggy Minnesota Twins t-shirt—stolen from Tim— and her oldest pair of tennis shoes. She found Dez, wearing much the same outfit, setting up a ladder in the back hall. She had already spread newspaper over the floor and hung drop cloths on the hardwood at the foot of the stairs. Luella stood in the back doorway, an apron over her housedress. When the rookie opened the screen door and stepped inside, the old lady said, "You got your choice, Jaylynn. Chicken or roast beast?"

She thought for a minute. "Chicken, I think."

"Baked or fried?"

Jaylynn glanced over at Dez. As if reading the tall woman's mind she said, "Baked."

"What else strikes your fancy?"

The young woman stood thinking for a minute. "Everything you make is great. Surprise me."

"Okay. A bevy of surprises coming right up." The silver-haired woman disappeared into the house and soon the two women could hear the clatter of pans.

Dez bent to open one of the cans of paint, and Jaylynn saw it was a creamy yellow. "That's a nice color, Dez. It'll look good in here."

"Luella picked it out. She didn't like this pale gray. It does look pretty miserable, doesn't it?" Jaylynn nodded. "Roll or trim?" the taller woman asked, holding a roller rack in one hand and an angled paintbrush in the other.

"Trim."

"Good. I hate trimming." Dez handed the brush over.

"That's lucky because I never liked rolling. I'm not good at it, and it always seems to turn my hair into a sticky mess."

"Ah. You gotta know the trick of always keeping the roller in front of you." The tall woman screwed an extender onto the end of the rack and picked up the can and poured paint into the metal pan.

As Dez finished pouring, Jaylynn bent automatically with the brush
to wipe away the drips on the can.

Jaylynn said, "I'll stick with the detail work, thank you. That
way my hair will survive the ordeal." She picked up the paint can
and poured a shot into a plastic butter container, then asked,
"Where do you want me to start?"

"Wherever. On crews we found that if the trimmers follow
behind the rollers, we tend to stay out of each other's way. I'm
starting here over the door and working toward the kitchen." She
stepped up on the ladder and began to roll the first stripe across the
high ceiling.

"Okay." Jaylynn moved to the left of the door and began to
paint along the edge of the door molding. "What crews were you
talking about?"

"Oh, in college I did a lot of painting. That's basically how I
supported myself. I worked for a couple of companies."

Jaylynn finished the edge as Dez came down the ladder, loaded
up her roller again, and slid the ladder further down the wall. She
watched the taller woman step back up the ladder and
systematically apply the paint, very quickly settling into a rhythm.
"Can I borrow the ladder for a minute to do above the doors?" she
asked.

Dez stopped rolling and pointed over at the hall closet. "Open
that door. There's a step stool in there that'll do."

Jaylynn followed her instructions and pulled out an aluminum
mini-stepladder. "You know what we need, Dez?" The tall woman
stopped rolling and gazed at her, no expression on her face.
"Tunes. We need some good tunes."

"Fine, go up and move the little CD player off the kitchen
table. The cord'll stretch into the hall up there. Then just pick out
whatever you want, crank it up, and we'll deafen Luella." She
stepped down off the ladder and refilled the roller with more pale
yellow paint.

Jaylynn put her paint container on the stair and carefully set
the paintbrush over the top of it. She checked her hands for stray
paint and wiped them on her shorts, then jogged up to Dez's
apartment.

It had been a long time since she had been up these stairs. The
door to the kitchen was open, and everything looked the same as
before. She stepped inside and headed into the living room toward
the entertainment center. Scanning through the CD titles, she
grabbed four, then turned to leave the room, but the open roll top
desk caught her eye. She hesitated, then couldn't resist.

Striding quickly to the foot of the bed, she stood in front of the
desk. The pigeonholes were neatly filled with pads of paper,

envelopes, a stack of small notebooks, a stapler, and various folded papers. On the desk surface an electric bill sat on top of some sheets of paper, and holding it down was a flat clay paperweight, about six inches across and olive green in color, with a small child's handprint in the middle of it. Embedded in the clay, someone had scratched DEZ. Squinting to look closer, Jaylynn noticed that before the pottery pancake had been fired, someone had written "Jeremy, age 4" at the bottom.

Flanking the clay creation were two photos. Recognizing Ryan immediately, she took note of the man's clean-cut good looks. She'd seen pictures of him at the station, but not with his shirt off. He had really been built—no wonder he won bodybuilding competitions. The other picture struck her so strongly that she set the CD's down and picked it up. She was amazed by how much Dez resembled the black-haired man, and she could see where the tall cop got her height and build. He was a nice looking man. But what struck her most was the leggy little girl in red hugging her father's leg. Her black hair was shoulder length and wavy, and her upturned face displayed rosy cheeks and an irrepressible smile.

Jaylynn was filled with a strange longing. She wanted to go back in time and know this little girl, reach out to her, protect her from the impending loss she was soon to experience. She didn't want the elfin smile on the girl's face to be marred by sorrow. The feeling was so intense that she abruptly set the photo down and backed away. Confused, she turned to leave, but then caught sight of the stack of CD's and reached over to pick them up. She heard the scrape of the ladder on the floor downstairs and, with a guilty start, hustled over to the doorway and back to the kitchen.

Dez situated the ladder and climbed up to the third rung. She rolled the paint right up to the last corner to finish the ceiling. She wasn't used to working overhead, and already it had tightened up her neck muscles. Since her shoulders and trapezoids were already tight from the workout the day before, she was glad to be done with that. She heard Jaylynn out on the landing up above and then a percussion and synthesizer beat started up. The rookie clonked down the stairs as a smooth voice began singing.

Dez frowned. The voice was familiar, but she didn't know why. She listened to more of the song as she started rolling the far wall. After a minute of puzzling, she said, "Who is this?"

"Lisa Stansfield. Isn't she great?"

Oh, the tall woman thought, *it's that CD she gave me for Christmas*. "Yeah. She's got a really nice voice."

The next song started and Dez listened to the words as the woman with the sexy voice sang about finding love, finding the real thing. She got down off the ladder another time for more paint. It occurred to her that she should have listened to this CD again since Jaylynn had given it to her, but in truth, she had forgotten about it. She couldn't recall why she hadn't liked it before, and she puzzled for a moment about that, but couldn't remember. Now she listened to the soulful voice and decided she liked her very much.

Jaylynn asked, "Are we going to paint up the stairs and around the landing above there, too?"

Dez paused on the ladder and fixed her with cool blue eyes. "No, we stop at the foot of the stairs right there. And I'll get done rolling way before you ever finish trimming, so I'll get another brush and help." She paused and fixed her gaze on the younger woman. "You don't have to do this, you know."

"I wasn't complaining. Just wanted to get an idea of the flow here. I've got the doors done and I'll do along the baseboards next, okay?"

"Sounds good. On to the walls for me."

They worked away in companionable silence for several more minutes, listening to Lisa Stansfield's expressive voice. Then "The Very Thought of You," Jaylynn's favorite song on the CD began, the singer's voice full of longing and hope. She had played this song over and over in her room until Sara had asked if there was something wrong with her CD player. She hadn't listened to it for several weeks though, and now she realized why.

Turning away from Dez's line of vision, she sat cross-legged on the hardwood floor and tried to focus on the paint strokes, but the song evoked too many feelings. She was faced with two contradictory sets of emotions. With one set of emotions she just enjoyed being with Dez, talking to her, getting occasional unexpected responses about things from her. She liked riding with her, feeling protected by her tough partner, continually haggling over any number of subjects throughout the course of each shift. In the last two weeks, ever since her resolution at Minnehaha Falls, she had relaxed—and so had Dez.

But despite the resolution, the other set of emotions proved harder to repress than she had hoped. She went home alone every night burning so bright with attraction for Dez that she was surprised no one else noticed. She purposely tried to keep a safe distance from the other woman because when she got too physically close, she was overwhelmed with a longing that she truly couldn't explain as merely sexual.

The rookie had never felt so miserable in her life while feeling good at the same time. But she knew full well that unrequited love was a huge downer. She'd had her fill of it with Sandi in high school. She didn't know how much longer she could go on repressing her feelings. Even though things were definitely going better, it got harder and harder every day to ignore the emotions. It was driving her crazy.

Jaylynn was grateful when that particular song ended. The next tune, which was fluffy and mindless, made her feel a little less desperate. Leaving the paint container on the floor, she set the brush on it, rose, and stretched her lower back.

Dez asked, "You having trouble with your back lately?"

Jaylynn was surprised at the question. "Why?"

"You've seemed uncomfortable. You stretch it a lot like you're in pain."

"It's not so much pain, but my lower back is tight. It loosens up when I'm off duty, then I'm back cooped up in the car with all that gear on. It's just bugging me."

"It's the belt."

"What?"

"The duty belt. They're designed for men. Mine fits me fine because I have no hips, but you do."

Jaylynn grinned up at her. "So, what you're saying is that as long as I have a big fat butt my back is going to bother me?"

"No! That's not what I meant. And you do not have a fat butt." She shook the paint roller in the air for emphasis, then descended and pushed the ladder to the side. She set the roller in the paint pan and rubbed her hands on her shorts, then came to stand in front of Jaylynn, her hands on her own slim hips. "Where does the duty belt hit you?"

"What do you mean?"

"Where does it rest?" She gestured at Jaylynn's middle. "Up here closer to your waist, more over your hips? Where?"

Jaylynn put her hands on her waist. "It kind of sits about here."

"Yeah, that's the problem. It's not balanced for your build, Jay. You need one that's molded and cut to fit around a woman's hips instead of sit on them like men's belts do. You want it to sit here." She bent slightly and brought her hands to Jaylynn's hips where she firmly pressed on either side. "That'd be about right."

Jaylynn blushed. "Or I could just lose some weight."

"What? Are you kidding? That's your natural shape—totally normal. Even if you did lose weight—which you don't need to do— you'd still have the same problem because your waist is slim here." She moved her hands up and made a karate chop motion on either side of the rookie's waist, then stepped back. "You can get a much better belt at the uniform store. They'll measure you and even special order for ya. They're kind of spendy, but you won't have your back bugging you."

"Okay, I'll do that sooner or later. Thanks."

"Let's take a break and get some more lemonade," Dez said. "Haven't heard anything from Luella for a while. Probably fallen asleep. Let's go wake her up." She arched an eyebrow and started tiptoeing into the house. Jaylynn followed quietly, relieved that Dez's back was now to her so that she could take a minute to recover from the tall woman's touch.

Later, after an excellent meal courtesy of Luella, they worked on the finishing touches of the paint job. The sun was high in the sky, and it was humid in the back hall. Wet paint didn't make it any better. Jaylynn felt the sweat dripping off her back. She wiped her forehead with the back of her arm and resumed trimming. A minute later when Dez caught sight of her, she laughed out loud, pointing at the rookie.

"What?" Jaylynn asked.

"You got the biggest smudge on your forehead. It's practically as big as a playing card."

"Yeah, right."

"No, really." She set down her paint and brush, picked up a damp rag and came to stand in front of Jaylynn. Palming the back of the smaller woman's head with her left hand, she scrubbed away at the paint with her right hand until it came off.

Jaylynn looked to the left of Dez's shoulder, holding her breath. She felt the blush start and was grateful when Dez said, "There. Now you don't look like you've been branded." She stepped away and tossed the rag to the side.

The rookie let her breath out in a rush and turned aside. She squatted down and slapped some paint in the corner near the floorboards, then cursed silently when it dripped. Setting the plastic container down, she licked her thumb and wiped the drip off the hardwood, then ran her thumb and fingers across the chest of her shirt until they were dry.

From behind her she heard, "Now I see why you look like this wet rag here while I continue on in pristine splendor."

Jaylynn stood up and turned, and it occurred to Dez that the smaller woman could effect a wicked look quite well. Jaylynn advanced upon her, her eyes narrowed and lips pursed, and Dez backed up, a grin spreading across her face. "Wait a minute..." She stuck her arm out only to have the younger woman grab her wrist and push her back against the closed closet door. "I could wear this shirt again. I—"

Jaylynn smacked Dez's midsection with the flat side of the brush, then grinned devilishly as the big woman extended her hands wide, looked down, and said, "Hey, do I deserve—"

The rookie drew a line diagonally from one broad shoulder down to the other hip, managing to smear a dab of paint on Dez's shorts before the tall woman decided enough was enough. She gave the smirking woman her most fiendish look, and then suddenly snatched the paintbrush from her hand.

Weaponless, Jaylynn backed up toward the screen door. In a mock serious voice, she said, "Careful. That thing's loaded." Dez didn't stop advancing upon her. "Hey! Hey! We just painted all these walls. Don't be messing—" She turned the handle to the screen door and darted out, followed by a laughing maniac who chased her around the backyard. In a flat out run, Jaylynn might have been able to outdistance Dez, but in the backyard the taller woman proved to be quite agile. Before Jaylynn could reach the fence, Dez had a hold of the back of her shirt. One-handed, she pulled the shrieking rookie around in a half hug and lifted her in the air, holding her there while she applied a pale splotch of paint to the hip of the already smudged gray shorts.

"I was going to wear these again," Jaylynn said in a sorrowful voice as Dez set her down. The rookie looked down as she gripped the edge of her shorts. She tried to give the big woman a recriminating pout but ended up laughing instead. "Gimme that paintbrush. I have to go finish that final corner, you big lug."

Dez sheepishly handed her the paintbrush. Big mistake. Jaylynn used it immediately to swipe another line from the opposite shoulder to hip, leaving Dez with a giant X across her shirt. The rookie burst out laughing and dashed away. "You've been marked with the yellow X," she shouted as her feet hit the stairs and she scrambled inside through the screen door.

The big cop stood grinning in the hot sun. She looked down at her paint-stained t-shirt and suddenly experienced an easing of worries she hadn't even known she was carrying. This was the old Jaylynn: the lighthearted, hopeful, confident, sometimes comical, and occasionally irreverent young woman she had first met. It had been some time since the "real" Jaylynn had shown herself, but sure as she herself was now marked, Dez knew that she had just seen the relaxed and happy version of her friend. *I missed that. I missed the "real" Jay a lot.* She strode toward the house, up the stairs, and through the screen door. Jaylynn was down on one knee finishing the last of the trim.

"Thank God we're almost done," the rookie said. "This stuff is drying and getting tacky." She stood up and smiled Dez's way. "Lovely outfit by the way. I hear it's all the rage in Paris."

Dez grinned back. "That's me—Designer Dez."

Luella chose that moment to clear her throat. "If you two are done horsing around, I'd like to know if you need a snack."

The two women exchanged glances. Dez said, "I'm still stuffed from lunch. What about you, Jay?"

"I couldn't eat another thing for at least two hours."

Dez shook her head and rolled her eyes. "How 'bout we all go to the movies then?"

"What?" Luella and Jaylynn asked simultaneously.

"Yeah, I'll even buy," she said.

"Nonsense," Luella said. "You girls just worked like dogs. *I'll* buy. But what would we see?"

Dez said, "That's easy. You've been wanting to see that *Entrapment* flick at the cheap theater." She pointed over at the silver-haired woman, but looked at the rookie as she said, "*She's* got the hots for Sean Connery and they're doing a whole weekend of his films."

Luella pointed at Dez, but looked at Jaylynn and said, "*She's* got the hots for that Zeta-Jones woman."

Dez blushed. "Luella!"

"Excuse me," the rookie said, "but I'm just vain enough to be concerned about my attire, and you," she pointed at Dez, "I'm sure Luella would be embarrassed to be seen with you in that outfit. I know I would."

"Even though you created it?" Dez asked dryly.

"Especially."

The rookie gazed up at Dez and they both smiled warmly. For the first time in a long while, Jaylynn could meet the big cop's eyes without reservation.

Luella asked, "Well? What are we all waiting for?" She slapped Dez on the behind and said, "Get your skinny butt upstairs and make yourself presentable. And you," she gestured to Jaylynn, "come with me and get into those clean clothes you brought."

Dez took the stairs up to her apartment two at a time, pulling her t-shirt off as she reached the top. The apartment was warm and muggy, the air almost moist against her damp skin. She ducked into the bathroom and stripped off all her clothes and stepped into the shower for a quick rinse. After toweling dry, she moved back into the living room and dressed. Seated on the couch, she slipped on her Adidas and double-knotted the long laces. She rose and her eyes came to rest upon the two photos on her desk. She walked over and stood for a long moment studying the picture of Ryan, then closed the roll top desk and headed downstairs.

Chapter
19

Dez hovered in the roll call room, sipping from her ever-present water bottle and awaiting Jaylynn's entrance. The rookie had arrived extra early, at the Lieutenant's request, and was currently talking to him behind closed doors. It had been more than six months since the young woman had started her official probation period, so today she was getting her second quarterly progress report. Dez had already put in her two cents about Savage, Oster, and Mahoney, the three recruits she'd had experience with. She'd also made a few informal comments about Dwayne Neilsen.

She was proud of Jaylynn's development, but secretly, she was just as pleased with how Oster had advanced. The young man had gone from bumbling, underconfident, and pudgy to smooth and thoughtful, with an evolving competence that earmarked him as the kind of officer who would be steady and effective. He'd been lifting weights, watching his diet, and studying like crazy. She knew that things did not come to him easily as they did for Mahoney or even for Jaylynn, but his hard work and concentration were paying off. She had gone out of her way to encourage him and offer advice whenever possible. It gave her a good feeling to take on a mentoring project some of the other FTO's had deemed a lost cause. There was a side of her that greatly enjoyed being able to say, "I told ya so." When Oster passed probation at the end of the year, she looked forward to saying that to a couple of people, especially Lieutenant Andres.

She grinned when she heard a clatter on the stairs. *No mistaking those footsteps.* The rookie exploded into the room full of energy and excitement.

"Hey, guess what! I'm doing better than I thought." Jaylynn

slid into the chair next to Dez. "The Lieutenant says I'm exceeding standards in some areas and making excellent progress. Wow, isn't that great?" She fixed her hazel eyes on Dez, smiling at her warmly.

Dez couldn't help but grin back. She nodded at the rookie. "Congratulations. Six months down, six more to go."

Jaylynn chattered on about the details of the performance review, all of which Dez already knew since she had written most of the data the Lieutenant had used to score her. As she half-listened, Dez thought about the training she had gotten when she became an officer nine years earlier. Everything was hit-and-miss back then, and not nearly as organized as it had become. She was lucky to have ridden along periodically with her father when she was small, and then regularly with her father's best friend, Mac MacArthur, when she was in her teens. She had attended every Police Officers' Father/Daughter Banquet with her father, and then, after his death, with Mac until she was age 22.

Dez had always had the good fortune of being in the company of cops who told her stories and cautionary tales. Before she ever donned the uniform, she already had a wealth of anecdotes and information to draw upon. By the time she joined the force, she'd seen the results of people's poor choices: dead bodies, homeless children, bleeding victims, vandalized schools, a bombed business, and the aftermath of so many brawls that she couldn't have possibly counted them. Most new recruits were not so lucky as she, and they didn't know what they were getting into.

She turned her full attention to Jaylynn who was now saying, "So are you ready for this shadow phase?" Dez nodded. "It's going to be hard for you though, isn't it?" the rookie said with a smirk on her face. "Hanging back, mostly watching, not taking the lead—"

"I'll manage," Dez said in a low voice. For the next three months they would no longer work so much as a team. Instead, she was to focus on Jaylynn's handling of everything while the rookie went through the motions as though she were out entirely on her own. The veteran cop's role was to take notes, evaluate performance, give the rookie feedback, and discuss, discuss, discuss. After every shift Dez would have to give a verbal summary of the evening's events to the sergeant and then a weekly written report to Lt. Malcolm. As far as she could tell, it would be maddening. But she wasn't going to admit that to Jaylynn.

Once roll call began, it seemed to go on forever and ever, with a great many more reports and updates than usual. *Here it is, the second of July, and everybody and their brother is reporting their car stolen.* There had also been a rash of break-ins and street thefts. Despite the improving economy, they still had the same drug dealers and burglars and con artists to deal with. *The only good thing is that homicides are down.* In fact, now that she thought about it, she didn't think Jaylynn had even been to a homicide crime scene yet. That rosy situation couldn't continue forever, she was sure of that.

****

The Fourth of July dawned cloudy and cool. Dez awoke later than usual feeling cranky and hungry. It was only six weeks until the bodybuilding competition, and she had to admit that even she was tired of herself. Trying to sluice off all possible fat cells and get down to lean muscle entailed eating lots of protein and scarcely any carbohydrates other than romaine lettuce, a few fibrous vegetables, and small amounts of brown rice or sweet potatoes. The lack of carbs made her irritable, and she wasn't sure how she could make it through the next few weeks.

She was glad she no longer had to lift so heavy, but her weight routine still included a full array of exercises—only with lighter weights and higher repetitions. No challenge and very boring. *Forty-one days,* she thought. *I can make it forty-one more days, and then I never have to do this again if I don't want to.*

By the time she reported for duty in mid-afternoon, it was drizzling out. On account of the weather, the first part of their shift was quiet, but as the evening went on, it stopped raining and the loonies came out in full force. Firecracker complaints, loud parties, drunk drivers, and the never-ending domestic assaults kept them occupied nonstop. It wasn't until nearly ten p.m. that the veteran and the rookie decided to sign out for a meal break. Dez had already eaten two cold chicken breasts and a protein bar in the car, and now all she needed was a fresh quart of water. Jaylynn, as usual, had her sights set on something Dez could not eat.

"Even though you're eating healthier stuff," Dez groused, "I still can't believe how much you can pack away." She got out of the passenger's side and headed toward the 7-11.

Over the top of the car Jaylynn replied, "Hey! It's a hard job doing all the work out here with you just tagging along to take notes. I've gotta keep up my strength, don't I?" She slammed her door shut, straightened her collar, and stepped up on the sidewalk. "I don't think an ice cream snack will kill me."

"Yeah, but I gotta sit and watch you eat it and hear all those happy noises you make."

Jaylynn grinned. "You could join me, you know."

The tall cop pushed open the 7-11 door as she glanced back, exasperated. "Jay! You know I can't. Don't torture me."

Dez took two steps into the convenience store, her eyes scanning for the dairy case, before she noticed the clerk and saw his frightened face. Standing with him at the checkout counter, profile to them, was a perilously thin black man clad in a pink t-shirt and baggy black shorts. The big cop stopped abruptly and Jaylynn bumped into her as the man turned. Dez saw the gun swing her way and she reached for her Glock. Her ears filled with a roar as her chest absorbed a blow like nothing she'd ever felt before. She stumbled back. Sliding sideways against Jaylynn, she desperately tried to stay on her feet. Before she even hit the ground, she heard another roar, and the man in pink clutched his chest, then crumpled to the ground. She felt a blow to the back of her head, and then everything went white.

Dez couldn't breathe. Her lungs ached. A buzzing in her ears wouldn't stop, and a light-headed floating feeling came over her causing the world to tilt sideways and out of focus. She tried to keep her eyes open, but the tears streaming from them burned and blurred her vision. She pinched her eyes shut.

Dez opened her eyes. Lying flat in the open air, she was as cold and bone weary as she had ever felt. She lay on her back, staring into the night sky, waiting for her vision to clear. Placing her palms down, near her sides, she let her fingers move about until she realized that the crunchy things below her were leaves, and she lay in a flowerbed.

She tried to sit up, but a stab of pain shot through her rib cage. She raised her hands, crossed them over her chest and closed her eyes. Barely breathing, she squeezed her eyes shut tight and lay still until the wave of pain passed.

Once she could choke in air again, she began to relax and listen. Above her, sounds wafted down. It took a moment for her to realize that she was hearing a persistent, high-pitched call for help punctuated with screaming and slapping sounds.

I have no idea where I am or why I'm here, but someone is in trouble. *She turned her head to the side and moved as if to sit up, and once again, the explosion of pain blasted through her, leaving her weak and with tears in her eyes. To her right was a wall. She reached out to touch the uneven stucco surface. Angling her neck around, she saw that she rested right next to a light-colored house. With great effort, she rolled onto her side. Keeping her hand on the rugged wall, she forced herself to her knees. She ignored the pain as she got one foot up and flat on the ground, then rose unsteadily to stand swaying next to the house.*

Far away, she heard a woman calling her name. "Dez!" *The hauntingly familiar voice was suddenly cut short by slapping sounds. She staggered out of the flowerbed and onto the cement walk next to the house. From an open window above her head, she saw the flapping of a ripped screen, and again, a shriek rang out, which was muffled, and suddenly it was silent in the night air.*

"Hang on! Hold it together, Jay," she tried to shout, but only a hoarse croak came out. She stopped and took a deep breath, then reached upwards with her right arm, feeling a nearly unbearable pain shoot through her chest. With a strong hand, she grabbed the windowsill, but there was no way she could pull herself up, no way to get up and through the window. Panting, she limped down the walk and to the front stairs. She didn't know how she did it, but she managed to drag herself up the steps to the door, only to find it locked. Wheezing and barely able to keep her eyes open, she made her way around the house, trying every door and checking each window.

No luck. She stood on the side of the house where she'd started and felt tears of frustration leak out. "Help me! Somebody help," she whispered in a panic. "Something bad has happened to her...help me!"

She could no longer stay on her feet. As she hit the ground, she felt the breath knocked out of her, and her vision grew fuzzy again. Gasping in short breaths, everything spun around her, and in a moment, she was out.

Ears ringing from the report of her gun, Jaylynn scrambled out from under the deadened weight that had fallen partly against her. Her heart screamed out to Dez, but she forced herself not to look, to focus instead on what had been drilled into her over and over: halt the imminent risk, then render first aid.

Crouching, her gun held level, she moved quickly to stand over the shooter. He lay on the floor panting and twitching, the .45 near his hand. She put her foot on the barrel of the gun and eased it away from him, kicking it behind her and under the candy bar display case.

"Oh my God," the clerk yelled repeatedly. He stood behind the cash register, clutching the counter with shaky hands. Jaylynn nodded toward him in a daze, then bent over to fasten a handcuff to the shooter's hand. She rolled him to his side. He cried out in pain, but she clicked the cuff on his other hand anyway. Touching her shoulder mic, she put out the call for help. "Officer down." In a mechanical voice she answered the questions dispatch asked and listened to their assurances that help was on the way.

Only then did she holster her gun. She paused for the briefest second, afraid to turn, her heart pounding so hard she thought she was having a heart attack. She spun shakily, and in two steps landed on her knees next to the wheezing woman.

"Dez!" she shouted. Frantically she ripped open the pierced blue shirt, popping buttons every which way. She saw the exploded hole in the vest and felt the flat lump of hot metal imbedded there. Struggling to loosen the gray vest was awkward, but with a grim look of determination, she undid the Velcro and tugged up the white t-shirt underneath to reveal the smooth alabaster skin and the terrible mark on the right rib just below the pale breast.

She smoothed the t-shirt down. "You're going to be okay, Dez. It's okay." Jaylynn swung her legs around in front of her, sat back, and leaned against the checkout counter. She splayed her legs out and leaned forward to drag Dez's upper body, face up, into her lap. The big cop stared at her, eyes glazed. "Dez, can you hear me? Your vest caught it. The bullet didn't penetrate."

"Help...me. Somebody help..." the injured cop whispered. "Something...bad has happened...help...me..."

"Shhh," Jaylynn said. "Lie still. You'll be okay." She brushed the hair out of Dez's face and held her gently, trying not to squeeze too tight.

"Unnnnhh...it hurts." She closed her eyes and let out a groan.

"I know, I know." Jaylynn leaned over her and made soothing noises. "Don't worry. Help is on the way."

Dez's eyes popped open. Without blinking, she focused in on her partner's face. "Jay...Jay...the shooter. What about..."

"He's down."

Dez sighed and squeezed her eyes shut, then opened them again. "Are...you...sure?"

"Yeah. I shot him. He's down and cuffed. Stop worrying. You're safe now."

A flash of light exploded in Jaylynn's face. She blinked and squinted. The clerk stood over her ready to take another photo with an orange disposable camera.

"Stop!" she shouted. Click-flash. Click-flash. "You are dead meat, mister," she said in her sternest voice. He paid no attention, instead moving down the aisle to capture another angle. When it was clear he wasn't listening, she turned her face away from him and held her partner closer to her. He then moved over to take shots of the man in the pink shirt who lay bleeding on the floor. Jaylynn was grateful for the sound of the sirens approaching.

A low moan escaped and in a strangled voice Dez said, "Ow. Shit, this hurts."

"It's all right," Jaylynn soothed. "You're gonna be okay. I gotcha."

Dez looked up into the worried face, so close to hers, and the words tumbled out in a choked whisper, "I...love you...Jay."

"I know. Shhh—don't talk now. Just save your strength." Jay cradled her gently, oblivious to the clerk's continued photographic antics. She pressed her face in the dark hair, feeling tears rising and not being able to control them.

"Hey." Dez's voice was raspy as she reached an unsteady hand up. "Cops...don't...cry. Remember?" She tried to wipe away the tears, but Jay turned her head aside and swept her face clean with her own sleeve. Dez's large hand slid down the front of her partner's uniform shirt, and the rookie grasped it, pulling it close to her heart, watching as her partner's eyes squeezed shut in pain.

"I'm so sorry, Dez."

Through gritted teeth, she said, "Thought you said I'm okay."

"Yeah, you are—"

Cop cars screeched into the parking lot. One. Two. Three. Jay could now see four through the front glass door. Her brothers in blue, armed and dangerous, descended upon her and calmly took charge. She was mildly amused to see Cooper and Braswell in the door first. Pudgy Braswell, red-faced and sweating, went down on one knee before them.

Jaylynn said, "Her vest caught it."

He nodded. "Good. Reilly, honey, you're gonna be all right. We'll get you outta here."

"Don't...call me...honey...Braswell," Dez choked out, "or I'll...rip your...testicles off."

"Atta girl, Reilly." He reached down and patted Jaylynn's knee. "She's gonna be fine, Savage. The EMT's will be here any second. Just hang on." He grunted as he struggled to his feet, then pulled his belt up over his prodigious gut. By then a string of eight more cops had come into the store, stopping to check on Dez.

Braswell stood over the two women and in his gravelly voice kept saying, "Vest took it. She's okay." The clerk was off to one side gesturing and talking loudly, trying to explain what had happened.

Jaylynn closed her eyes and leaned her head back against the counter. She continued to hold Dez, the taller woman's head cradled in her left arm and her body lying face up in the V of her legs. She opened her eyes and watched her fellow officers as they secured the scene and then escorted two sets of paramedics in the door, one set for each injured party. It was with reluctance that she relinquished her hold on her partner and then, embarrassed, she stood and joined her fellow officers. She jumped when she unexpectedly felt a warm hand grab hold of her fingers, and she looked to the side to find Oster, his eyes brimming with held-back tears. He wouldn't look at her, but he didn't let go of her hand as they watched the EMT's prepare to load Dez on the stretcher.

After the big cop was wheeled through the 7-11 door, she took a deep breath. "Who's the responding officer? You, Braswell?"

"Yeah, me and Cooper. Let's get your statement now while it's fresh in your mind, and then you can take the squad car over to the hospital to check on her." He cleared his throat. "One more thing: department policy. You need to give me your weapon."

She nodded in understanding and unholstered the .38 to hand it to him. Cooper opened a plastic bag and Braswell placed it inside. They waited while Cooper labeled the bag.

None of the cops noticed the young clerk tucking an orange box into his shirt pocket.

****

Dez spent the better part of the night in the ER, which meant Jaylynn spent it in the waiting room. Cops came and went as the night went on. The Police Chief appeared, stomping through the waiting area in jeans and a lightweight t-shirt, her face a pale mask. Jaylynn met her eyes, but the grim-faced woman merely nodded and swept by. Four medical personnel in blue scrubs appeared, took the Chief off into a side room and shut the door.

Cowboy came tumbling in, sleep in his eyes and without his customary off-duty cowboy boots. "I came as quick as I could. Oster called me. Is she okay?" He stood awkwardly until Jaylynn rose, nodding, and then he engulfed her in a hug. "Thank God," he said. "I just couldn't go through that again." Wordlessly she let him hold her, feeling the solidness of his back and torso, and then she led him to the too-soft waiting room chairs and told him what had happened. She never even noticed when the Chief departed through the automatic glass doors.

When they were finally allowed to see Dez, she'd been moved to a regular room. She lay at an incline in the bed because her ribs and torso, under her hospital gown, had been taped. A blanket covered the wounded cop up to her midsection, and Jaylynn thought she looked overly warm. Even in the semi-darkened room, her face was unnaturally white and she looked like she had two half-moon bruises under her eyes.

"They gave me something for the pain, so I'm feeling pretty fine now," Dez said.

"I'll bet," Jaylynn said. She went shyly to one side of the bed while Cowboy went to the other. Each of them took a hand.

Cowboy asked, "Cracked rib, huh, little lady?"

Dez's pale face relaxed into a crooked half-smile. "I'm not little."

"Yeah, yeah, whatever. Next to me you'll always be little, you know. Now you just sit back and take it easy, okay? When they letting you out?"

"Probably tomorrow. Wanna keep an eye on my head. Got a big bump on the back."

"Well, I'll come back if they keep you longer. Otherwise, you take good care of yourself, okay?"

"Sure, Cowboy." He leaned over and placed a soft kiss on her forehead, and a slight blush washed over her face.

"Good night," he said as he sashayed out of the room leaving the two women alone.

Dez shifted and winced in pain. "Gosh, that stuff they gave me sure made me tired."

"Have you considered that it's four o'clock in the morning and you've been shot? I'd be tired, too!"

Dez looked at her seriously and said, "Only good thing about getting shot was you holding me." Jaylynn caught her breath and nearly let go of Dez's hand, but the injured woman held tight. Dez said, "Don't get the wrong idea. It's okay." She twisted her hand around and entwined her fingers with the rookie's.

Jaylynn said quietly, "We're going to have to talk about what happened."

"I know, but it's part of the job." She looked away, across the room, then back at Jaylynn.

"That's not what I mean."

"Look at the bright side—odds of me ever getting shot again are slim." She gave a little laugh, then groaned in pain.

"That's not what I mean," Jaylynn repeated, then decided it was the wrong time to broach the subject. "We'll talk tomorrow," she said. "You should try to get some sleep."

Dez looked alarmed. "You'll stay a few more minutes, won't you?"

"Sure." Jaylynn reached behind her and pulled a chair up close to the bed and sat, never letting go of the warm hand. *I'll do one better than that,* she thought. *I've got nowhere I need to go. I'll be here when you wake up in the morning.* Dez closed her eyes and slipped off to sleep. Jaylynn sat in the darkened room, her fingers threaded with the sleeping woman's, and puzzled over things. She had a lot to think about. After a few minutes, waves of fatigue washed over her and she let her head rest against the edge of the hospital bed. Before she knew it, she was asleep.

Chapter
20

Jay woke abruptly just a few minutes later when she heard a gasp. Through bleary eyes she saw a tall, silver-haired man in the doorway. He was dressed in tan slacks and a brown bomber jacket, and his arm was around a regal silver-haired woman in her late fifties. She wore navy blue slacks and a beautiful powder blue top. Over one arm she had a purse and a raincoat. The gasp had come from her and she now stood with a hand over her mouth and tears welling up in her eyes.

"Oh, Desiree," she whispered, and she crossed the room to stand on the opposite side of the bed. The man followed her and put a protective arm around her waist, his hand caressing the side of her stomach. He leaned down and whispered something in her ear, which Jaylynn could not hear. She thought it must have been soothing because the woman nodded and took a deep breath, composing herself in an instant.

The rookie stood awkwardly, not knowing what to say, and was relieved when a nurse bustled into the room. "Dr. Reilly," the nurse said brightly. "She'll probably sleep for several more hours."

Jaylynn's head snapped up and she squinted to get a good clear look at the woman. She didn't think she looked at all like Dez until her eyes rose and met the rookie's, and then the rookie saw the same piercing blue eyes.

The blue-eyed woman turned back to the nurse. "Prognosis?"

"Excellent. She's going to be sore for a week or so, but she'll be fine. We're keeping her now to make sure there are no internal injuries, but that's unlikely."

"Thank you," the woman said dismissing the nurse. She turned back toward Jaylynn. "Who are you?" she asked. "Her partner?" Jaylynn nodded. "Who did this?"

"A guy in a 7-11. He was robbing the place."

Dez's mother looked her up and down and then the man spoke up. "What happened to the suspect?"

"I shot him. He's either dead or in intensive care." Unexpectedly Jay's knees went weak, and she suddenly found herself sitting in the chair, her hands shaking. *I shot a man,* she thought. *I may have killed someone.* She looked up at the two people standing over Dez and tried to get control of herself.

The piercing blue eyes had softened, and the woman said, "I'm very sorry. I'm sure you did what you had to do. What's your name?"

"Savage," Jay choked out.

The woman grimaced and looked up at the silver-haired man. She said to him, "You cops are all the same." Shaking her head, she took hold of his hand and turned back to Jaylynn. "Don't you have a first name?" Embarrassed, Jaylynn told her. "I'm Colette Reilly, and this is Mac MacArthur. I'm Dez's mother, and Mac has known Dez since she was a little girl."

"It's nice to meet you," Jaylynn said. She stopped there, leaving off the next cliché: *Dez has told me so much about you*—because she'd never heard one word about either of these people. She wished Dez had prepared her just a little.

A hoarse whisper sounded from the figure lying on the bed. "Mac. Whaddya doin' here?" Dez squinted open her eyes, but didn't seem to be able to focus.

"Hello, Dez. Just came by to check on you. Sounds like you'll get to go home later in the day."

"Ummm...Mom." She swallowed and tried to keep her eyes open. "Why are you here?"

"Luella called me." She reached a hand out and nervously smoothed the covers over her daughter's abdomen. Jaylynn watched as Dez's mother stroked Dez's arm, sliding down the forearm to grip the long fingers.

Dez closed her eyes and in a slurred voice said, "Thought you didn't like me anymore."

Her mother's face went visibly pale and she bit her upper lip. She glanced up at the silver-haired man uncertainly. Just when it seemed she was going to answer her daughter, she looked down to see that Dez was fast asleep.

Tear-filled blue chips lifted and met the rookie's hazel eyes. They were filled with such pain and anguish that Jaylynn looked away, feeling she was intruding. Mac, standing slightly behind Dez's mother, slipped his hand from Colette Reilly's shoulder and let it run down her side until it came to rest protectively against the silver-haired woman's abdomen. Jaylynn thought she should leave, but when she rose and cleared her throat, Colette Reilly seemed to come out of her sorrowful state. Suddenly she was all business. She peered intently at Jaylynn, then shook her head. With a half smile lighting her features, she asked, "Are you staying here or did you need to go home?"

"No, ma'am. I didn't intend to go home, but if you want—"

"Stop. I was just going to say that if you would keep an eye on her, I'd appreciate it." She fished in the purse hanging over her arm and pulled out a piece of paper and a pen. She scribbled for a moment and then handed the piece of paper to Jaylynn. "Please call me if I'm needed."

Once again she smoothed the covers, then stepped back reluctantly. With one last look over her shoulder, she headed for the door. Mac slipped an arm around Dez's mother's waist and held open the door, then glanced back in the room with a hopeful look on his face and winked at Jaylynn before they left.

Jaylynn continued to sit in the chair, feeling the fatigue wash over her. She supposed she should go home. She stood up and moved to collect her jacket, but then Dez whimpered. She leaned over her and saw that in her sleep, Dez was crying. Jaylynn didn't have the heart to leave. Before she could turn around and sit, the hospital room door opened and Luella shuffled in.

"How's she doing?" the older woman asked. She shucked off her windbreaker, tossed it over the visitor's chair by the door, and came to stand by Jaylynn. "You poor child. You look done in." She wrapped her arms around Jaylynn and held her while she cried. "Sorry it took so long to get here. Had to wait for a cab, and they don't send 'em fast in the middle of the night!"

"I'm just glad you're here," Jaylynn sniffled. "It's been an awful night."

"Sounds like it, hon."

Jaylynn pulled back a little, leaning her face to her shoulder to blot her eyes with her sleeve. "I'm probably messing up your nice dress."

Luella sputtered, "Who cares! You're more important than a dress." The older woman glanced over her shoulder and caught sight of the chair Jaylynn had been sitting in. She took the young woman's hand and led her over, then sat herself down and pulled the rookie toward her lap.

Jaylynn resisted. "I'll squash you, Luella."

"No, you won't. Just relax. I've had bigger kids than you on my lap before." She gestured with a toss of her head toward the bed where Dez lay sleeping. "Her, for instance." She pulled the young woman into her lap and enfolded her in a tight hug. "Tell me everything that happened, beginning to end."

And Jaylynn did that, feeling that she was confessing terrible sins. Luella listened and comforted her, and after a while, the silver-haired woman talked her into going home, sleeping a while, and coming back later in the morning.

Jaylynn stood, feeling numb, as the landlady picked up her lightweight jacket and kissed Dez on the forehead. Even though she was still a little shaky, Jaylynn led Luella out to the parking lot and dropped the older woman off at her house, then drove herself home where she changed clothes and got back in the squad car. She stopped by the precinct and dropped the car off. All was quiet on First Watch, and she was happy not to run into anyone she knew. She dropped off the car and checked out, then returned to the hospital.

****

When Dez awoke, she was in a foul mood. Half her torso ached and throbbed, and she had a headache that wouldn't quit. When she forced her eyes open and examined the room, she realized there was a blonde head lying on the bed to her left. She carefully lifted her hand and flicked her wrist that direction. When she connected with the crown of the head, she heard a groan, and then the head rose. Dull, sleepy hazel eyes met hers in a face full of worry and fatigue.

Dez sighed and softened her cranky attitude. "How you feeling?"

Jaylynn said, "Isn't that supposed to be my line to *you*?"

"I feel like shit. Get me outta here, okay? I'm sure Luella can take better care of me than these yahoos."

Jaylynn stood and stretched, looking like she was in pain. "I can see that you're going to be fine."

"Yeah," she snapped. "What was your first clue?"

Just then a heavy-set nurse hustled into the room. "Good morning," she said brightly. "And how's our hero today?"

Before Dez could snarl a response, Jaylynn squeezed her arm and said, "She's fine, just fine."

The nurse looked the rumpled woman up and down. "Actually," she said, "you're the one we should be calling the hero."

"What?" Jaylynn asked.

The nurse spun on her heel and headed for the door. "Be right back," she called over her shoulder. When she returned a minute later, she was toting a section of the newspaper, which she folded open and spread out on the hospital bed facing Dez.

Both women gasped.

The Metro section of the Twin Cities Courier carried the bold headline *Saint Paul Cop Shot,* and splashed below it was a one-foot square color photo. Under the photo the caption read: "Nine year veteran officer Desiree Reilly, shot on duty in an Eastside 7-11, is comforted by rookie partner Jaylynn Savage."

The color photograph was clear. Jaylynn sat on the floor, a red counter at her back, with her legs splayed out in a V. Dez lay in the V, her eyes squeezed shut and a look of obvious pain on her face. Her legs were sprawled over Jaylynn's right thigh and her upper body was cradled in the rookie's arms. But what made the picture most remarkable was the proud, defiant look on the young officer's face as she faced the camera, one solitary tear etching a distinct line down her cheek.

The nurse said, "They say a picture's worth a thousand words, and this one definitely is. We need to get the guns *off* the streets, that's for sure." She looked at the shocked faces of the two women. "Ah...well, ah, why don't you two go ahead and keep this?"

Jaylynn looked up at her, worry evident on her pale face. "What happened to the man I shot last night?"

The nurse hesitated and then with a sigh said, "You'll see it in the article, so I may as well tell you. He died on the way to the hospital."

"Oh, God," the rookie said. She sat down hard in the visitor's chair and burst into tears.

Dez tried to sit up. A jolt of pain shot through her ribs, and she lay back on the bed sweating. Feeling totally helpless, she grimaced and said, "Jaylynn. Hey. Come on. It wasn't your fault."

Jaylynn stared at her blankly through the tears. In a quiet voice, almost a whisper, she said, "I've killed a man. Someone's dead because of me."

The nurse came around the side of the bed and patted the young woman awkwardly. "There, there," she said. "Go on and get it all out. It's awful, isn't it?"

Dez wanted to leap from the bed and throttle the nurse. She gritted her teeth to keep from screaming at the woman. She took a deep breath to speak, but just then there was a tap on the door, and it opened. A gray-haired man in a business suit entered. He carried a clipboard and introduced himself as the hospital administrator. "Good morning, ladies, nurse," he said. "Ms. Reilly, we have a number of reporters asking for interviews. Do you wish to grant anyone an audience?"

"Hell, no," she snarled.

With a trace of a smile, he said, "Well, that was perfectly clear. Now then, we also have several officers here. Do you wish to see any of them?"

"Who?"

He consulted the clipboard. "Lopez, Culpepper, Oster,

Coombs, Mahoney, Milton, Swenson, and last but not least, a Lieutenant Malcolm."

Grudgingly she said, "Yeah, they can all come in." He turned and exited the room.

She cast a worried glance over at Jaylynn who was now sitting silently. She was no longer crying but looked as though she was in another world. Dez was relieved when the horde of cops, led by Lt. Malcolm, filed in respectfully, one after another. She caught the Lieutenant's eye immediately and tossed her head toward Jaylynn, but before he could make a move, Crystal was already at the rookie's side.

The Latina went down on one knee before the rookie. "Hey, Jay. It's me—Crystal. Time to head home. Come with me." She pulled the teary-eyed young woman up out of the chair, pausing long enough to grab Dez's hand for a split second and say, "Sorry it's a short visit, but you look fine. Catch ya later, okay?"

In a low voice Dez responded, "Just take good care of *her*," and then Crystal led a very tired Jaylynn out the door.

The Lieutenant said, "I'll get someone from Departmental Assistance for her, Reilly. Don't worry. She'll be okay. We'll take care of her."

Dez cast one last look toward the two cops as they disappeared out into the hall. She took a deep breath and winced when the pain in her rib coursed through her again.

****

The hospital released Dez late in the afternoon. Cowboy came down to pick her up and take her back to her place. He also agreed to go by the station and get someone to help him deliver her truck. She knew she wouldn't be driving for a little while, and she didn't want her pickup sitting in the lot for days on end.

It was a struggle, but she changed out of her uniform and into jeans and a sweatshirt, no bra. Then she turned her attention to her biggest worry: Jaylynn. She hadn't seen or heard from the rookie since Crystal dragged her off earlier in the day. She'd tried to call her house from the hospital, but no one, not even Tim or Sara, had answered the phone. She tried now to reach Shayna and Crystal, but their answering machine was the only response she got. She didn't leave a message.

She limped into the kitchen and got a glass of water so that she could take a pain pill and then walked slowly down the stairs and knocked on Luella's door. It took a minute, but when the old woman finally opened the door, she looked like she had just awakened.

"Thank goodness you're home. Come in. Come in." She held the door open wide and Dez hobbled along behind her into the living room and then sank down on the couch.

The old woman asked, "Can I get you something?"

"No, no. I'm fine. Have you by any chance talked to Jaylynn this morning?"

Luella came to sit right next to her and laid a soft hand on her thigh to pat the denim there. "Yes, she called a little bit ago. She wanted me to let you know she's okay, but she's off work for a while."

Dez nodded. "I figured that."

"She flew home to Seattle late this morning. I don't know when she'll be back."

"What!"

"Dez, honey, that poor kid needs her mom right now, that's what. I don't blame her. She was a wreck last night, and I can only imagine how she felt when she found out she killed that fellow."

Tears rose and spilled over, and Dez couldn't stop them. Luella put her hand over Dez's left arm and squeezed it gently as the tall woman hung her head in shame. The landlady chuckled. "You know you don't have to be that way around here. I don't expect you to be Miss Big Shot Cop in this house. I'd rather have you human and hurting than tough and hard. You could learn a lesson from Jaylynn, you know."

"Yeah," the tall woman choked out. "I know."

****

Jaylynn knew enough about post-traumatic stress disorder to realize she could have a full-blown case of it if she didn't deal with the events of the last few hours. It was all she could think of on the plane and in the taxi on the way to her parents' house as she fidgeted and fought back tears. Late Monday afternoon, she arrived at long last on her parents' doorstep, unannounced, and Erin and Amanda nearly flipped with excitement. The girls had just been home from summer school daycare for a short while, and Dave and Janet Lindstrom were in the kitchen getting ready to prepare dinner.

It took Jaylynn's mother only seconds to discern that something was wrong, and after the girls finished jumping all over their big sister, Janet led her daughter upstairs to the master bedroom. As soon as the door was shut, Jaylynn collapsed on her parents' unmade bed and burst into tears.

"What's the matter?" her mother asked in a voice tinged with desperation.

"I can't believe this. I—I—Mom, oh my God...I killed a man."

"What!" Janet sat next to her daughter and wrapped her in her arms. There was a tap on the door, and Dave stepped inside, shutting the door behind him.

"Janet?" he asked, glancing between the two women. They looked at one another helplessly as Jaylynn, doubled over with grief, sobbed.

Dave sat down on the other side of his stepdaughter. "Jaylynn—Lynnie, honey...Jay! Stop! Stop right now. Look at me." In response, Jaylynn slowly sat up and turned tear-filled eyes toward him. "What *happened?*" he asked. "Start at the beginning and tell your mother and me."

And so she did. They sat on either side of her, shocked, and listened and held her as she cried. And so began the process of grieving.

****

Dez sat at Luella's dining room table and watched the older woman putter around and water the plants on the windowsills. The three large windows facing the front yard contained a total of ten plants, five of which were violets. Dez wasn't sure what the other leafy ones were. She leaned back in the squeaky chair cautiously. Her ribs still hurt when she moved, but it was a dull ache and nothing like the sharp pain she had gotten for the first 48 hours.

"You're gloomy today, Dez." Luella took a tiny trowel, no bigger than a fork, and tilled up a bit of the dirt around the African violet in one pot, then filled in some potting soil from a green beans can.

Dez started to cross her arms, as she had a hundred times since the shooting, and was reminded most painfully that it hurt too much to do that. She let her hands drop into her lap.

Luella paused and the injured woman felt her gaze. She met the brown eyes and listened as Luella said, "You ever notice how plants like to sit right next to each other? They don't like to be alone any more than most people do." She waved a wrinkled hand toward two potted violets next to one another. One was a deep, rich purple—the color of royalty. The other was pale lavender with dark purple trim. Despite the gray weather outdoors, it was clear that both plants were thriving inside. "Look at how these two are all over each other."

Dez craned her neck. "Whaddya mean?"

"Just look. They're reaching out to touch each other."

"Looks to me like they're growing toward the light the window lets in."

"They are. But they're also inclining toward each other. See?"

Dez heaved herself up out of the chair and moved to stand over the plants and next to her landlady. She felt old today, old and defeated. The late afternoon sun tried to fight through the clouds, but was failing miserably, so the day was dark and dreary with little chance of change before nightfall. Dez examined the two plants as a tentative hand reached around her middle and a silver head leaned against her upper arm.

"What's the matter, Squirt?"

"Don't know. I just feel like shit."

"Want me to make you something to eat?"

"No thanks, Luella." She sighed. "You really shouldn't have to take care of me. I'm a grown woman."

"I like taking care of you."

"You're a generous person, but you shouldn't always have to give, give, give. Makes me feel selfish."

"You do a lot for this old woman, Dez."

"Not *half* what you do for me," she said in a cranky tone. "It's not really fair to you."

Luella bubbled with laughter. "Oh, girl, you may be a grown woman, but you're still a babe in the woods."

"No, I'm not," she said in an icy tone.

"Yes, you are. You don't fool me." Luella looked up at her, kind eyes appraising the pale face. "And you still don't get it. Sometimes accepting help from others is actually a gift to *them*— not to you. I don't do one thing for you that I don't want to. What I do makes *me* feel good." Shifting around to face the tall woman she put one hand on each of the tenant's hips. Looking up and into Dez's eyes, she said, "I love you like you were my own kid. I don't want you in pain. I want you to be *happy*. That's all. It makes me feel good any time I can contribute to that."

Tears sprang to Dez's eyes, and she started to pull away. Luella's eyes narrowed and she tightened her grip on the tall woman's hips. "Don't you go shutting me out. We've come through too much now for that." She reached around Dez, pulled out a chair, and pressed her into it, then slid another chair over and lowered herself until she was knee to knee with the younger woman. She took Dez's hands into her own. "I'm not going anywhere until you 'fess up and tell me what's troubling you."

Dez looked out the window, her teeth clamped together so hard that her jaw began to hurt. She felt the soft hands squeezing her fingers and turned stubborn eyes toward her landlady. "I'm worried about Jaylynn."

Luella leaned forward, put her elbows on her knees, and kept hold of Dez's hands. "She's a resourceful girl. She knows how to take care of herself. She'll be okay."

"What if she's not?"

"Why wouldn't she be?" Luella asked softly.

"I don't know," Dez said, her voice bitter and ragged. She turned away to stare out the window.

"I've got a hunch here. Let me tell you what I think." Luella paused a moment, then reached up to turn Dez's face toward her. "Look at me, Desiree Reilly. It's not your fault some loony-tune decided to rob and shoot up the 7-11. There's nothing you could have done. It's *not* your fault."

"But it shouldn't have happened that way!" Dez said emphatically which caused her side to rip with pain.

"Why? What could you have done?"

"I should have seen it coming faster. I wasn't...I didn't pay close enough attention." The words came out in a rush. "He should never have got a shot off. I should have reacted quicker, taken control—"

"And then you wouldn't have been wounded, huh?" The old woman had a sly look on her face. She peered intently into Dez's eyes, and suddenly the big cop wanted to get up and run.

"It wasn't that so much...I don't care about that."

"Ah, I see then. You think *you* should have shot that idiot. The fact that Jaylynn did it, that she's upset, that she's gone—it's all *your* fault, right? You're afraid she's blaming you. Is that it?"

Dez refused to answer and just stared daggers at Luella. She felt a swell of anger rise in her and said the first thing that came to her mind. "Why in the hell did you call my mother?"

Luella let go of Dez's hands and pursed her lips into a tiny smile. "She's your mother, Dez. She needed to know her child was hurt."

"I have *you* on the call list because I don't want her to know things about me. And then you go and call her and don't even come to the hospital yourself."

"What?" Luella looked startled for a moment, then she shook her head. "You must've been out of your mind on the drugs, girl, because I was there. I got there fast as I could."

Now it was Dez's turn to be surprised. "I don't remember that," she said indignantly.

"Well, I'm telling you the truth. I was there and I know exactly how Jaylynn was feeling. She wasn't a bit concerned about herself. She was worried half to death about *you*!"

"If she was so worried about me, why didn't she say goodbye?" Dez struggled unsuccessfully to keep the bitter tone out of her voice.

Luella shook her head slowly, then patted Dez's knee with one hand. With a groan she rose. Picking up the tiny trowel she moved back over to the windowsill. "You two are *both* exactly like these plants here. Both of you pretend to be straining toward the sun while you're really leaning toward each other and spying out of the corners of your eyes. But you just watch—those plants sit there long enough and they'll be entwined, just like you two. I know you can't see it right now, but wait and see. You mark my words."

Dez sat silently for a moment, fighting with herself. She thought about her source of strength, which she had always thought was her ability to stay cool and keep down any troublesome emotions. But now every single thing she did, everything that happened, served to unblock carefully constructed walls and fences. Her feelings ran amok, and there was nothing she could do to stop it. It occurred to her that perhaps she shouldn't have dammed things off so effectively—perhaps she had denied herself the opportunity to learn to control the maelstrom of emotions that threatened to unnerve her now.

She listened to a tuneless song Luella was humming under her breath as she pinched an old leaf off one of the nonflowering plants. Without any further consideration, Dez rose and wrapped her arms around the silver-haired woman from behind, surprising her. Luella twisted in her arms and returned the hug, causing Dez to groan.

"Oh, sweetie, I'm sorry. Didn't mean to squeeze."

"That's okay. I deserved it for being rotten."

"Oh yeah, you're rotten. Rotten through and through." She chuckled. "That's why I keep you around, 'cause you're such a rotten kid."

Chapter
21

Jaylynn borrowed her mother's Bonneville and took the short drive around Green Lake to the apartments where her aunt lived. After 48 hours with two inquisitive girls and a pair of sympathetic parents, she was feeling less out of control. But she recognized that she still slipped in and out of periods of numbness.

At least she was better rested now. When she had first arrived, she was so exhausted she hadn't been able to think clearly, and it wasn't like anyone in that household ever went to bed very early. Besides, her body was on Minnesota time, which was two hours later than West Coast time. It took her a whole day to get reacquainted with the noises in the old house and with the racket her sisters put up. A night in her old double bed with two little girls, warm as twin toaster ovens, had done a lot to revive her. Last night the girls had each snuck into bed with her again, but once they went to sleep, she crept away and slept in the twin bed in Erin's room. She hadn't slept well, but she'd stayed in bed from ten p.m. until nearly nine a.m., so she figured that in between waking from the bad dreams, she probably slept six or seven hours, and she didn't feel too terribly tired. She hoped tonight would be better.

In the five years that she had been living in Minnesota, it seemed the traffic in Seattle had gone from terrible to disastrous. The six-mile trip from the Ballard area to the far side of Green Lake used to take fifteen minutes at most. Today it took so long that her bare legs were stuck to the seat with sweat by the time she drove into Auntie Lynn's neighborhood. It had also given her time to remember wisps of a dream she had in which she and Dez, running hand in hand, were being chased by phantom aliens. Suddenly, the ground dropped from beneath the veteran cop. Her hand was wrenched from Jaylynn's, and she disappeared into a gaping hole. Frantically, Jaylynn tried reaching into the hole for the taller woman, but all she could hear was screaming and gnashing of teeth. And then the monster appeared again with gleaming jaws dripping blood and emitting deafening shrieks. The dream had made her scream until her mother came in to awaken her.

Great. A new version of the horrible dreams. Just what I needed. She shuddered and decided to try very hard not to think of it anymore.

Jaylynn stepped on the gas, maneuvered up her aunt's street, and arrived at the complex a few minutes after noon. The nightmare came to mind again while she waited for her aunt to buzz her in to the security apartments, and she resolved not to think of it again. Walking down the long hallway to unit 108, she concentrated on her surroundings. She felt the same thick carpet underfoot, smelled the same air-conditioned eucalyptus scent that she'd always noticed. *Some things might change, but Auntie Lynn isn't one of them*, of that she was sure. It gave her a feeling of security knowing her aunt was always there.

Jaylynn's father's younger sister, Lynn Savage, opened the apartment door and engulfed her niece in a bone-crushing hug. Though very nearly Jaylynn's height, she seemed shorter, and she was totally the opposite in looks. Long curly dark hair framed a mischievous face often lit up with a smile. While Jaylynn was shapely, her aunt was rail thin. Her gray eyes didn't miss much, and when she asked a person how she was doing, Jaylynn knew she really wanted to know the answer. So did her students. She was an extremely popular psychology professor and counselor at the University of Washington.

Auntie Lynn had come over to see her niece the day after Jaylynn's tumultuous arrival, but this was their first time to talk privately without the distractions of Erin and Amanda.

"Are you hungry for lunch yet?" Lynn asked. She led the other woman over to the sofa and each curled up on one end facing the other.

"I haven't been hungry since I got here," Jaylynn confessed.

"That's unusual for you, Ye Old Bottomless Pit."

Jaylynn nodded. "I know—it's not good, but nothing tastes appetizing at all."

"I'll get hungry pretty soon and I'll make some lunch, but in the meantime, you want something to drink? Juice? Pop? Tea? Lemonade?"

"Orange juice?"

"Sure. Back in a flash."

The petite brunette disappeared down the hall into the kitchen, and Jaylynn looked around the apartment living room and dining area. She had always liked this apartment because it was old-fashioned and roomy. The wide molding was dark mahogany wood and gleamed in the sunlight streaming through the windows. The walls were pale yellow—pretty much the same color Luella had selected for her back hall. She thought for a moment about that day with Dez, how playful the big cop had been, how much fun the three of them had had at the movies. Though it was only a short time earlier, it seemed like forever.

She gazed up at a painting hanging over the wing chairs across the room. It hadn't been in the apartment when she'd last been to visit. The only way to describe it would be to say that it was a four-by-five foot explosion of colors. At first glance the colorful brush and palette marks gave the impression of great chaotic energy, but upon further inspection, Jaylynn began to notice something strange. The whirls and dips of the paint on the canvas contained intricate outlines of faces. After studying the painting for another minute, she was sure that she could pick out at least twelve faces, all overlapping and shading into one another.

When her aunt returned to the room with the juice for her and Pepsi for herself, Jaylynn pointed at the artwork. "Where did that come from?"

"A very talented psychology student painted that for me."

"What's it called?"

"*Psych 5000*, believe it or not. Notice anything interesting about it?"

"The faces?"

"Good, Lynnie! Almost no one ever picks them out. Everybody gets stuck on the color and overlooks the details. How many faces do you see?"

Jaylynn tilted her head to the side and counted. "I for sure see twelve, but somehow I bet there are more."

"Not bad. The young man, Michael is his name, painted it to represent the liveliness of the 14 students in the class. There are actually 15 faces there, me included. Michael's very talented, very troubled, and brilliant to complicate matters."

"It must be nice to teach somebody like that—someone so fascinating."

"He can be very difficult at times, but I have a soft place in my heart for him." She set her glass of soda on a blue coaster on the coffee table. "But that's enough about me. I want to hear about you. I want to know about your partner."

Startled, Jaylynn looked at her aunt. "Dez?"

"Yes."

"She'll recover just fine, Auntie."

"I know that. But you and she are not fine."

Jaylynn smiled at her aunt, a bemused expression on her face.

If she didn't know better, she would have to say her aunt and Sara went to the same mind reader's school. "We're better now, thank you." She hesitated a moment, then went ahead and asked the question that came to mind. With a quizzical look, she asked, "Why would you ask me that particular question first?"

"Because I sensed it was the most important—because of the arc of your letters."

Jaylynn blushed and looked down. "I wrote about her a lot, didn't I?"

"Yes. And then she disappeared from the narrative a while back, and I've wanted to know what happened to her ever since."

Jaylynn sat quietly for a moment, her eyes resting on the vivid painting across the room. She hadn't come out to her family, hadn't ever even mentioned a single person she'd dated. It occurred to her that it didn't really matter who knew anything anymore. She didn't care one iota. She lifted her eyes to meet the level gray ones across from her, eyes looking at her with a love and affection she could never doubt.

Her aunt said, "Tell me about her."

Jaylynn held her breath. She had never been able to resist her aunt's openness and honesty. Since she had been a little girl, she could tell her anything. When her father died, it was Auntie Lynn she confessed to, saying with inimitable nine-year-old logic that his death had been her fault because she hadn't kissed him goodbye that morning, preferring instead to sleep in. In short order her aunt had set her thinking straight and helped her to mourn. For every step of the young woman's life, her father's sister had been there, like a guardian angel, hovering in the background just in case.

And here she was again, ready to listen and understand.

Jaylynn exhaled and burst into tears.

Scooting down the couch, Auntie Lynn moved over next to her niece and put her arm around her. "It's okay, Lynnie." She grabbed up the box of tissues from the shelf under the coffee table and set them next to her niece.

"It's really not okay," Jaylynn said. "I love her."

"There's nothing wrong with that."

"No, I mean I *really* love her." She reached for a tissue and wiped her eyes, then let her hands drop into her lap.

Lynn squeezed her shoulder. "Like I said, there's nothing wrong with that."

"She doesn't return the feelings."

"Oh, I see. Well, that's a tough one." They sat for a moment, Jaylynn letting silent tears run down her face and Lynn rubbing circles on her upper back. "Lynnie, there's something else. What is it?"

Through the tears, Jaylynn let out a chortle. "What is it about me—do I have something written on my forehead? Some sort of display that says 'Keep Probing'?"

Lynn laughed. "No. I just know you, that's all. Nothing is ever simple with you, punkin." She reached up and smoothed a lock of hair out of Jaylynn's eyes. "There's always been way more than one layer. So I just thought I'd ask."

"Well, as usual, you're right." She pulled out another tissue and blew her nose. Once she felt more composed she said, "I keep having the same kind of recurring dreams, and they're scaring the hell out of me."

"You used to have bad dreams when you were little, after your dad died."

"I *still* have those dreams."

"What? I thought they went away."

"Oh no. You just taught me a way to control the fear. Remember My Hero?"

"Who could forget! I've never had a kid get so excited about an imaginary friend."

"She's not imaginary anymore. It's Dez." She shifted uncomfortably on the couch. She met her aunt's eyes, then looked away.

"You mean you *dream* about Dez now."

"No. I mean My Hero was—is—Dez, always has been Dez." Again, she held her aunt's eyes, nodding, hoping Auntie Lynn would be able to understand.

"She resembles her?"

Jaylynn placed her hands palms down on her knees and squeezed, the cords of her hands standing out. "I know it sounds crazy, but she *is* her."

"Okay. So go on."

"The first time I saw her, something clicked." She turned to face her aunt, and in an excited voice, she said, "I can't explain it, Auntie Lynn, but I knew—I just *knew* Desiree Reilly was somehow the one. I feel it here." She patted her breastbone with her fist then returned her hands to her knees. "It's like a—like a connection, a strange linking of souls. Every time I look her in the eye, it's like looking at the other half of my heart. I get this jolt of familiarity—of déjà vu—that doesn't quit. And even though she tries to pretend otherwise, the same thing happens to her, too—I can tell."

"You're saying she's your soulmate."

"Yes! That's exactly it."

"So what's the problem between you then?"

Jaylynn sat back, doubt clouding her face. "I don't know. I...I just don't understand at all."

"Have you tried talking to her about this?"

The younger woman's face reddened. Avoiding her aunt's eyes she said, "Let's just say I messed that up real good and haven't been able to broach the subject since."

"Hmmm, okay. I'll say it again. What else is there, Lynnie? I can tell there's more."

Jaylynn didn't want to recall any of the dreams, but she forced herself to explain anyway. "Remember how My Hero used to come to me in my nightmares and help me escape or rescue me?"

"Um hmm."

"That's not happening anymore. Now the monsters and aliens—or criminals or whoever they are—they get her and they beat her senseless. They torture her, break her bones, shoot at her, try to devour her, and there's nothing I can do. It's terrifying. In my dream I can't do anything to save her. I run all around, frantically, but I'm totally helpless. I wake up sweating, screaming—Mom had to come in last night to wake me up and tell me everything was all right."

Lynn reached over and patted one of her niece's hands. "Hey, you're gonna bruise your knees doing that." Jaylynn stopped clenching her kneecaps and relaxed her hands. "So," Lynn said. "When did this new development in your dreams occur?"

"Since I've been here."

"Jaylynn," she said in her kindest voice, "Dez just got *shot.* Your dreams are reflecting reality."

"But I can't help it, Auntie Lynn. I have the most unbearable feeling of foreboding, of anxiety. Every damn time I dream it, it's like it's actually happening, like she's really dying, and there's nothing I can do."

Lynn turned to face the shaken woman and peered into her face until the hazel eyes met understanding gray eyes. "Listen to me, Jaylynn. What you're feeling is normal. This happens a lot when people go through a critical incident like you've just experienced. It's *normal.* You need to talk about it, deal with it. Promise me you won't bury it."

"Ha. Fat chance of that. It's all I think about."

"I see. And you're scared you're going to lose her for good."

"That about sums it up." Tears came to her eyes again.

"Will you promise me that when you get back to St. Paul you'll go see a counselor and talk about these feelings?"

"Yes. The department provides a psychologist."

"Good. Take advantage of it, okay? I'll be checking on you, you know."

Jaylynn nodded. She put her arms around her aunt and squeezed her tight. In a choked voice, she said, "Thanks for listening to me, Auntie Lynn."

"My pleasure, dear. I love you."

"Love you, too."

Chapter
22

After three days of rest, Dez went back to desk duty, where she found she was bored half to death. The days dragged by while Jaylynn was gone. She cleaned up paperwork she had totally forgotten she'd ever neglected and then was more than happy to get the doctor's clearance to go on patrol again. But it felt empty to be out on the mean streets of St. Paul without the rookie along. She had to face it—she missed Jaylynn.

She wanted to call, but she didn't know the number in Seattle. Finally she got up the courage to call over at the house and someone named Kevin answered, but no one else was there and he didn't know Jaylynn's parents' phone number. Exasperated, Dez gave up and resolved to wait more patiently, but it wasn't easy.

It wasn't until Friday, the fifth day after the shooting, that Dez came home from work and found a note on her door from Luella.

Dez,
Jaylynn would like a call at 206-555-3579.
She doesn't have your phone # with her. Don't
forget it's two hours earlier on the West Coast.
Love,
The Chief Cook and Uniform Washer

What time did Jaylynn call? She hurried to open her door and, without pausing to turn on the lights, rushed into the living room area to the phone. She checked the red LED time indicator on the VCR: 12:20. That made it 10:20 in Seattle. *Is it too late to call?*

She didn't care. She grabbed up the phone, still dressed in the uniform she hadn't bothered to change out of when shift ended, and when the touch-tone numbers lit up, she dialed, hoping she wouldn't wake anyone up.

A faraway voice said, "Hello?"

"Jaylynn?"

"Hey you. How are ya?"

"Ahhhh..." Suddenly Dez was tongue-tied. She shuffled over to the couch and sat down, cleared her throat and said, "Did I wake you up?"

"Not in a million years. Seems no one ever goes to bed around here. The girls are like rats scurrying around half the night." Jaylynn laughed, a throaty purr in the phone. "My hours have been so weird—I'll be totally screwed up for time when I get home."

Dez let out a breath she didn't even know she'd been holding. *She* is *coming back,* she thought, and a feeling of relief washed over her, which caused an involuntary shiver.

"Dez? You still there?"

"Yeah."

"How about your ribs? Are they healing?"

"Oh yeah. Still have the bruise, but I'm back on patrol. It's going fine."

"Good. I was hoping you'd mend quickly. You do seem to heal fast, you know."

Dez didn't want to talk about her own healing. All she really wanted to know was when Jaylynn would be returning. She wasn't sure how to put it so she said, "The Lieutenant asked me tonight how you're doing."

"Oh? That was nice. Tell him I'm fine and I'll be back to work on Wednesday. I'll fly home Sunday."

"Sunday, huh? You need a ride from the airport?"

"No, don't worry. Sara's coming. But thanks."

"Okay," Dez said, trying to keep all hint of disappointment out of her voice. "So I'll see you in a few more days?"

"Uh huh. Well, hmm, anything exciting to tell me?"

"Nope, guess not." Her mind felt like it was stuck in neutral and she scrambled around trying to think of something to stay on the line. "Oster stepped on a nail on the street outside the civic center construction site."

"Oh?"

"Yeah, it went right through his boot and into his arch. Had to get a tetanus shot. At least he isn't complaining."

"That's good. But he's really not much of a complainer. He's a good guy."

"He is." She racked her brain for something—anything—that might be interesting. "Oh, hey! Something good did happen. Some cop in a little town in Michigan—Grand Ledge, I think—caught that guy who raped Kristy South."

"You're kidding? How'd they catch him?"

"I don't know, but Lt. Malcolm told me today they're gonna extradite him. So that was good to hear."

"Yeah. I'll have to check on her when I get back." Dez cleared her throat, suddenly tongue-tied again. Jaylynn said, "Hey, this is costing you money."

"That's okay," Dez said in a grumpy voice. "I don't mind."

For some reason, Jaylynn found this funny. Giggling in the phone she said, "Some things never change."

Dez was puzzled. "What's that supposed to mean?"

"I'll see you soon, Dez."

"Do you want my phone number—you know, just in case you need to call or you need a ride or something?"

"Sure."

Dez gave her the number and they said goodbye and hung up. She sat in her darkened apartment, sweating with nervousness, and held the cradled phone in her lap. *Get a grip,* she told herself. *It's gonna be okay.* After a few moments, her heartbeat returned to normal, and she became drowsy. She rose and set the phone back on the top of the entertainment center and got undressed in the dark, tossing her uniform on the valet chair. Wearing only a sleeping shirt, she crawled into bed, exhausted, and fell into an immediate sleep.

The dream began as it often did. She was crazy with pain and grief, pinned into a tight enclosure. Her chest hurt and she could hardly breathe. Dim pinpoints of light illuminated a console in front of her, and as her eyes adjusted, she began to make out twisted metal rods, cracked glass, and sparking wires hanging down around her in what seemed to be a tiny spaceship. The smell of burnt plastic permeated the air, and for a moment she thought she might vomit.

All she could think of was getting out. Fumbling in front of her, she grabbed blindly until she found a metal clasp at her waist, which she pulled, loosening a harness and causing immediate relief to her ribs. With effort she hauled herself up, and as she did so, she rose into the smoky air and up and out a hole in the hull of the craft. Without warning, she fell, and as she did, she felt cool wind against skin and realized that her flight suit was melting away. Her knees stung and ached, and when she rose to her feet and looked down, they were a mass of rawness, warm blood running freely down her shins. She brought her hand up, her fingers brushing her abdomen until they were stopped by something shiny and hard protruding from her breastbone. Her fingers groped at a metal rod so firmly embedded that she could not pull it out. Her hands dropped to her sides, and she took a step, finding herself on a dirt path that led away from the small craft.

The full moon shone down upon the hillside, casting enough light to clearly outline evergreen trees and rocks and bramble bushes. The narrow path was emblazoned with silver, and she shuffled along hesitantly as it angled off to the side and led down to a lake.

Each step was painful and her breath came in short sharp wheezes. Something burned in her eyes, and when she wiped her brow with her forearm, it came away from her head covered in dark, sticky liquid. She was beyond caring and sought only oblivion. Lurching down the path she tripped once on a root and nearly fell, but she recovered her balance and continued down, faltering only once more before she came to stand at the water's edge.

The moonlight shone on the lake, revealing gentle ripples near the shore. She stepped one foot forward and felt the cool water lap at her foot. So close, I am so close. Closing her eyes, she took one last breath, as deep as her wounded lungs would allow, and then she fell face forward into the salty tasting water.

Sinking...sinking...light receding...darkness all around. The water grew colder until she shivered with the shock of its continual plunge in temperature. Instead of oblivion, instead of peace, the pressure intensified. She fought it, twisting and struggling. When she opened her mouth to scream, nothing came out. The brackish taste of bile rose up in her throat and choked her. She opened her eyes in alarm, sinking more, feeling the water crushing her. Suddenly she stopped fighting it. Letting her arms open and fall to either side of her body, she closed her eyes and gave herself to the descent.

It was then that she felt it. She opened her eyes and through the murk watched as capable white hands grasped the metal rod bulging from her chest. Gradually, inch by inch, the arrow was removed until she wept with the cessation of the pain. Strong arms wrapped around her, pulling her upward. She felt the silken pressure of bare skin against her shoulders, legs, and breasts. Each time she made a move or struggled, the ascent ceased, but when she went limp again, the arms tightened around her and they advanced upward until she was aware of moonlight shining bright in her eyes and cool wind brushing her tear-stained face.

She lay in the water, floating face up, all of the ache washed away, her body cleansed of the blood and grime and wounds. Resting, trusting, suspended in warmth, she became aware of that other presence, those other arms which felt so hauntingly familiar. She turned her head, searching for confirmation and fell into iridescent depths, a smiling presence of love.

The phone woke Dez, and she had trouble shaking the sleep out of her eyes. She decided to let it ring and tried to turn over on her side. Her body was still stiff and sore, mostly from holding herself so erect and with such caution. She cursed the day she had ever walked into that 7-11. Suddenly it occurred to her that it could be Jaylynn calling. She swung her legs over the side of the bed to grab up the phone. Leaning to pull the handset toward her sent a sharp pain through her side. She winced and answered the phone with a hoarse, "Hello."

"Desiree?"

"Yes?"

"This is your mother."

Dez's heart sank. In just those few seconds before picking up, her hopes had raised considerably. "Good morning," she said cautiously.

"I'm calling to check on you. How are you feeling?"

The tall woman dragged her legs up on the bed and leaned back against the pillows. "I'm all right."

"How are your ribs?"

"I'm healing okay, Mom."

"You back to work?"

"Yeah. Finally done with boring desk duty."

Dez heard a faint chuckle. "Just like your father. He never liked being cooped up inside, either."

"I've had enough of it this year. I was glad to go back on patrol—couldn't wait."

"How's your partner holding up?"

"Savage?"

"I believe her name is Jaylynn," her mother said dryly.

"Yeah, it is. I think she's doing all right. She's off work for a couple more days."

"Don't count on her doing all that great, dear. She was thoroughly shook up the other night at the hospital. She was frightened very badly."

"Nah, she's tough."

There was a pause for a moment. "Not everyone can shut out bad things like you can, Desiree. Don't expect it to be all that easy for her."

Dez started to get mad. Who was her mother to lecture her about the rookie? She'd spent—what?—five or ten minutes in her presence? "I gotta go, Mom. I need to take a pain pill again."

"All right. Call me if you need anything, okay? You've got my number at the clinic, right?"

"Sure."

Dez hung up, feeling quite irritated, and got out of bed to

stomp toward the bathroom. Every step made her more aware of how out-of-sync her body was. She pulled aside the shower curtain and lowered herself carefully to sit on the edge of the big whirlpool tub so that she could turn on the faucets. After testing the water temperature with her right hand, she plugged the tub and stood up. She moved over to the sink while she waited for the whirlpool to fill. She grabbed up her toothbrush. Looking in the mirror, she thought she looked old. There were bags under her eyes, and her face looked drawn and more pale than usual.

A wisp of a dream rose to the surface of her memory. Water. Thrashing and drowning. Pain. She shivered. She couldn't exactly remember what happened, but she knew it was unpleasant. *But it turned out all right, didn't it?* She had this odd sense that something good happened...but it wouldn't rise up to consciousness. *Oh well.* She brushed her teeth and then turned on the whirlpool jets. She slipped out of her sleeping shirt to step into the steaming, bubbling water. Once she'd lowered herself carefully into the tub, she took a deep breath, closed her eyes, and let her mind float off.

The jets soothed her aching muscles and relaxed her. She sank lower in the over-sized tub until only her face poked up out of the water. Deeper she went, relaxing, drifting. She imagined a forest full of blooming deciduous trees, the branches so thick that the tiny path she followed was almost indiscernible.

She put one leather-booted foot in front of the other, making no noise, and moved along the dirt path. The air was still, not even the sound of birds. She could feel her own heart beat, and a thrill of elation ran through her body. She let her left arm reach back, and it was promptly grasped by a warm hand that sent shivers of delight up her arm. She stopped in her tracks and slowly turned. Bright eyes met her own, a pair of laughing hazel eyes dancing with joy. You, *she thought.* I know you...

The whirlpool stopped and Dez jerked awake. She felt dizzy and overheated, her breath coming quicker than usual. Jaylynn's face. She had been dreaming of Jay. She didn't think she had dreamt of the rookie before, at least, she didn't remember, and yet, somehow, the dream felt very familiar. Dez sat up abruptly and shook the water off her neck and shoulders. She put her hands on either side of her temples and pressed, shaking her head slightly. Her head ached. Her ribs hurt. In fact, she felt like she'd been trampled by an elephant. Maybe she shouldn't have used such hot water in the whirlpool. She definitely felt overheated and faint.

With effort, she rose and stood as the water trickled off her

pink skin. She felt shaky as she took hold of the grab bar on the
side of the tub. Stepping out onto the rug, she leaned on the sink
for balance. Once the room stopped spinning, she wrapped up in a
towel and made her way into the kitchen. She didn't feel a bit
hungry, but she made a fortified protein shake and forced a sip
down. She carried it into the other room and changed into a t-shirt
and shorts.

She had no idea whether this interruption in her training and
lifting would ruin the possibility of competing in August's bodybuilding competition, but she knew she had to eat or her body
would devour muscle from her large frame. She sat on the couch.
Switching on the TV remote, she flipped through the channels until
she came to reruns of *Star Trek: Voyager*, which she knew was one
of Jaylynn's favorite shows. She watched as a strange woman called
the Borg Queen attempted to assimilate the captain of the ship and
a striking blonde woman with a numerical name. When she
finished her shake, she set the glass on the coffee table, then
scooted down on the couch and promptly fell asleep.

Chapter
23

When Dez arrived at the station an hour before roll call, she was surprised to see Jaylynn's gray Camry already in the lot. She angled her truck in a few spaces away and grabbed her gym bag, then hopped out of the Ford. It was blazing hot, the black pavement oozing heat that she could feel burning against her sandals. She didn't think it would be much fun to patrol this afternoon, and she looked forward to the sun going down.

Dark blue Dockers shorts and a tank top revealed her well-muscled legs and arms. Despite the rib injury, she hadn't gained weight—or lost any substantial amount of muscle. She strolled across the lot and to the back entrance shifting her shoulders from side to side and feeling the tension around her rib cage. She wasn't entirely healed, but every day the muscles in her torso felt looser. She just wished she could sleep better.

With a light step, she hustled down the stairs to the locker room, but all was silent there. Puzzled, she wondered where the young woman was. She hadn't seen her anywhere on the way down. She wished she had gathered up the courage to call the rookie the last two days, but she felt she would somehow be intruding. Luella had told her Jaylynn phoned her with a positive update, so she knew from her landlady that all was well.

Dez opened her locker and sorted and arranged her things. She laid out her uniform and dressed, then sat down on the end of the bench with her back against the wall. She checked the magazine in her Glock and ran a long forefinger down the barrel before holstering it. Pulling her handcuffs out, she checked their mechanism and then put them away. She sat for a few moments, letting her breath come and go, trying to relax. Checking her watch, she saw it was forty minutes until roll call.

She rose and rooted around on the top shelf of her locker until she found an ankle knife and sheath. She pulled up her pant leg to affix it over her sock. Rearranging her slacks to conceal it, she fussed with it some more until she got it set just right on her ankle. She sat back on the bench and leaned against the wall, bringing her knee up to her chest and wrapping her arms around her shins.

Every moment that went by made her more and more nervous. She had been looking forward to seeing Jaylynn tonight. After over a week of wondering and worrying, she thought this would be a relief. Instead, she knew she was becoming edgier by the moment. It didn't help that she had gone back on the low carb diet. The doctor had pronounced her healthy, though still bruised, and the minute he had given her the go-ahead, she shifted back into weight training mode. The last two nights she'd surprised herself with how well she'd lifted.

She heard voices, and the locker room door opened and shut a couple times, but no Jaylynn. The nasally sound of Pilcher's voice wafted down the corridor. Dez had never much cared for Pilcher, and she concentrated on ignoring the sound. So she was taken by surprise when Jaylynn rounded the corner abruptly and said, "Oh. Hi, Dez."

Dez hadn't thought at all about what she had expected to feel, but it certainly wasn't this sudden thunderbolt to her heart and the immediate rush of blood to her head. She stammered out, "Jaylynn. You're back," instantly feeling stupid for stating the obvious.

Considering all she had been through in the last ten days, Jaylynn had never looked better. Her blonde hair had been recently cut and shaped close to her head. Hazel eyes shone brightly, and she looked rested. She walked right up to the bench, swung a leg over, and put a hand on Dez's ankle as she sat down. "How *are* you?"

Dez nodded, still feeling dull-witted. "Great."

Jaylynn squeezed the long-legged woman's ankle and then frowned, tilting her head to the side. "What is this...a gun?"

"Knife." Dez shrugged. "Just felt like wearing it tonight."

"In case we wanted to whittle, or what?" The rookie peered up at her, a smile on her face, her hair shining white-gold under the fluorescent lights. She wore a loose gray T-shirt that said "U of M Track & Field" in maroon lettering on the front and a pair of jeans shorts that revealed suntanned legs. Setting her car keys down on the bench, she reached down to untie the laces of her Adidas.

Dez smiled. A series of words came to mind to explain how she was feeling: foolish, silly, bird-brained, idiotic, giddy. Perhaps giddy described it best. She could almost imagine herself wrapping her arms around Jaylynn, but of course she restrained herself. In a low, controlled voice, she asked, "How was Seattle?"

"It was good." The rookie stood and unlocked her locker, pulling out various items. "Ugh. What a mess I've got going here."

"You have some fresh uniforms back from the laundry. Want me to go get 'em for ya?"

"Sure."

Dez was glad to head to the rear of the locker room so that Jaylynn could undress in privacy, but when she came back with two hangers full of clothes, she found the rookie waiting in her bra and briefs. She could honestly say she had never before paid attention to Jaylynn when she dressed, but today she couldn't keep from looking. Her eyes traveled up from the floor taking in the lean runner's legs, the flare of hips, the slender waist with tight abs, and the swell of breasts, topped off by well-rounded shoulders and, of course, those eyes. Eyes that were currently looking at her with amusement.

"Earth to Dez. Hey, you wanna give me those?"

Mechanically she handed Jaylynn the two heavy hangers full of uniforms and turned away to her own locker, attempting to swallow before realizing there was no liquid in her mouth. She pulled a water bottle from her top shelf, sat on the bench with her side to the young woman, and drank three big swigs. "You're here early, Jay," she mumbled.

"Yeah, I came down to see the Lieutenant and then to meet with the department psychologist. Gosh, she's sure nice."

"What's her name?"

"Raina Goldman."

"Goldman! You *liked* her?"

"Oh yes! What's not to like?"

Dez remembered the intense, intrusive woman she had been required to see—six times—after Ryan's death. She had hated every moment. The poking and probing and prying of her psyche was more than she could bear. "Isn't she a nosy twit?"

"Nosy? No...inquisitive, maybe. I thought she was real nice, and I'm going to see her twice a week for a while, at least until things settle down some."

Dez was amazed. *Someone would actually* want *to see the department shrink?* She spun around on the bench and gaped at Jaylynn, but the young woman didn't notice. She was pulling on her black oxfords and tying them.

"Dez, how's the bruise coming along? Is it fading any?"

"Oh yeah." She took another pull from her water bottle and then set it on the bench so she could lock up.

"Oh crap!" Jaylynn said. "I forgot to tell you that Lt. Malcolm wants you to drop by and see him for a minute." She looked at her watch. "You've got lots of time. I'm sorry I forgot." She looked over at Dez with a sheepish look on her face.

"Okay. I'll check with him now. See you up there."

She took the stairs two at a time and appeared in front of Belton. "Evening," she said.

"Go in, Reilly. He's expecting you."

She ducked her head in the door and found the Lieutenant looking the same as he always did, a bit harried and tired, but in good spirits.

"You wanted to see me, sir?"

"Yes. I just wanted to make sure everything's on track. Savage and I talked, and she requested to continue riding with you. You okay with that?"

"Yes, sir."

"Internal Affairs ruled it a good shoot. You don't have any problems with that, right?"

"Heck, no. She did everything by the book."

The Lieutenant smiled. "She did, didn't she? She didn't panic, didn't freeze up. You can take some credit for that. You've taught her well."

"She's got a good head on her shoulders, Lieutenant. She's an excellent student."

"I'm really glad to hear it." He paused. "One more thing, Dez. I've been meaning to say this for a couple days. You've had a lot of stress this year. I'd like you to see the department psychologist again."

She scowled. Glaring at him she said, "That's really not necessary, sir. I'm not suffering any trauma or anything. Believe me, if I was, I'd go."

"Look, you're a valuable member of this team here. I don't want you to be offended, but I'd be remiss if I didn't look after you a little. I just want you to check in with Goldman, okay?"

"But sir, with all due respect, I've been fine for a week and a half. There's no need—"

"Reilly!" he interrupted. "This is not negotiable. I've meant to say something sooner, but I got hung up on other things. This is important, and I should have mentioned it before." She gave him her best stony gaze, but he didn't pay attention. He went on. "One session. Answer her questions, let her give me a report, and you're outta there. Okay?"

Reluctantly, she said, "Yes, sir." She backed up. "Is that it?"

"Yup. Go forth and do good things, hear me?"

"Yes, sir." She turned and strode out of the office, a slow burn starting at her neck and reaching up to the roots of her hair. She felt like hitting someone. She imagined hitting Goldman. Instead she stomped downstairs to the locker room and tossed some water on her face. After drying off with a crinkly brown paper towel, she walked back upstairs, her hands and face now feeling chilled in the station's air conditioning.

Jaylynn took one look at Dez's face when the tall woman entered the room, and she knew something was wrong. When she asked, though, Dez shrugged her off and sat in the next chair, placing her water bottle on the floor. Her face went flat and expressionless, and she wouldn't meet the rookie's gaze. Jaylynn watched her from the corner of her eye. Tight-lipped and angry, Dez seemed to be struggling for control.

No one else was in the room, so the rookie reached over and patted the muscular thigh closest to her. She let her hand rest there for a moment and craned her head around, silently asking her partner to look at her. When those blue eyes finally did turn to meet hers, what she read there was stubbornness. And something more—an angry pride. She couldn't resist; her lips curled up into a tiny ghost of a smile, and as she studied Dez's face, the shock of recognition and desire welled up in her again. Her stomach kicked into performing gymnastic feats while the ability to remember how to breathe departed from her brain.

The anger in the pallid face before Jaylynn drained away to be replaced with something else she couldn't quite identify. The rookie pulled her hand back as casually as she could, relieved when the tall cop bent to pick up her water bottle. *Oh no,* thought Jaylynn. *These feelings of mine just won't quit!* She reminded herself of the commitment she made to focus only on friendship. She had hoped that with a little perseverance and discipline, it would be easy to carry out. She could see now this wasn't the case, and she was disappointed. It was going to be a long shift.

****

The veteran and the rookie fell back into their routine, and the next two weeks passed quickly. On Wednesday and Friday afternoons Jaylynn came to the station early to meet with Raina Goldman. She was surprised to learn that some of the old-timer cops were appalled that she'd go willingly to see the "department shrink," as they called Goldman. At first Braswell tried to sympathize, telling her it was tough luck she had to go "get her head shrunk." When she told him she didn't mind, he looked at her through narrowed eyes as though she'd lost her mind. Dwayne Neilsen cornered her and tried to make sport of the counseling angle. She laughed at him and cut into the women's locker room.

Jaylynn was to the point where she didn't care what anyone

thought. Very few officers seemed to understand that she relished the chance to talk about what happened and how she felt about it. She certainly didn't get to do that with Dez, much as she wished she could. Every afternoon they got in the patrol car and made small talk, casually avoiding any emotionally loaded conversations. In fact, most of the time lately, Dez was distant and cranky. When Jaylynn tried to kid her out of her constant mood, the tall cop just glowered. All in all, it was a tiring couple of weeks.

It was actually a relief to ride with Crystal on a Friday night. Dez had been in court all day testifying about an old homicide case, so she was off work for the evening. For two days it had been extraordinarily humid. They had the air conditioning going full blast in the car, but the late afternoon sun still beat in on them and heated up the dark seats.

Crystal brought up Dez. "Hasn't tall, dark and handsome been tall, dark and *bitchy* lately?"

Surprised, Jaylynn turned from her spot in the passenger's seat. "You noticed, too?"

"Noticed? Everyone on the East Side has noticed. I think the main headquarters must be in the know by now. If you see her heading your way, everyone knows to split. God, she's been unbearable. How can you ride with her?"

Jaylynn shook her head sorrowfully. "It's been tough. I just cut her a lot of slack and don't talk too much. It's tiring, I'll admit. I thought she was gonna clobber this foul-mouthed drunk last night. You should have seen this guy. I thought he was going to wet his pants by the time she got done with him."

"I pity you, you poor thing."

"Oh, Crystal. It's really not that bad. It's just a little too tense. I can't wait 'til this stupid diet is over. It's that more than anything, I think."

"Yeah, maybe," Crystal said thoughtfully. "I figured maybe she was having trouble with getting shot."

"No, that's not it. I don't think she even thinks about it...though, hmmm...we haven't been back to that 7-11, not once. I keep meaning to go there, but I've put it off." Her hazel eyes met Crystal's sympathetic glance. "I don't think I ever told you thank you for taking care of me that day at the hospital."

"No need. You'd have done it for me, too, right?"

"For your sake, I pray I never have to look after you under the same circumstances. It was pretty awful, wasn't it?"

"Nah. You were just upset, Jay. Anyone would have been."

"Not Dez. She would have handled it."

Crystal looked over across the dimly lit car with an incredulous look on her face. "You're kidding, right?"

Jaylynn shifted to her left a little and laid her left arm across the top of the seat so she could look at Crystal better. "Actually, I'm serious."

"*Chica*, let me clue you in on a little secret. Miss Big Bad Cop—the one you've got on a pedestal a thousand feet high?—had her own quiet little breakdown after Ryan was shot. You think you were shook up? You should have seen her."

"What do you mean?" Jaylynn asked, her face puzzled.

"She was on admin leave for two weeks, and when she came back, she retreated into some faraway place, deep inside herself. She only talked when talked to, carried out orders, pretty much didn't look anyone in the eye. She basically started coming out of her shell when she began training you. At least you have the smarts to go to counseling—not her! Well, her body went, but her mind didn't." Crystal sighed. "I was really afraid for her. Didn't you notice how out-of-sorts she was when you first started?"

Feeling guilty Jaylynn said, "No. Maybe I was too preoccupied with training. I didn't—I never had any idea. I probably should have paid closer attention." She thought back to those first days observing with Dez. The big woman had seemed shy, certainly standoffish, but after some initial awkwardness, she remembered Dez being helpful and attentive. As the weeks traveled on, the tall cop had seemed to relax and settle in. She had chalked it up to them getting to know one another.

Crystal said, "You've been good for her, Jaylynn. She needed a friend, somebody who wouldn't let her sit around and brood. I couldn't get through to her at all. I'm really glad you came along when you did."

Impulsively Jaylynn reached across the seat and gave Crystal's shoulder a squeeze. "That's nice of you to say. I've really enjoyed working with you, too. You're the best."

"Hey, hey! Don't go getting all mushy on me now. I have to deal with enough of that from Shayna."

Jaylynn clicked her tongue and shook her head. "You butchy cops are all the same—tough on the outside, marshmallows on the inside."

Crystal smiled across the humid car, her teeth flashing white in the slanting sunlight. "Works for me," she said.

****

Dez had spent the better part of her day cooling her heels in court, and she hadn't testified until mid-afternoon. Despite the book and magazine she brought along, she was bored silly and, now that she was home, she almost wished she were on duty for the night. At least it would give her something to do other than think about all the breads and pastas and potatoes she was missing. *Time for some aerobic work.* Morning, noon, and night she was walking or biking. If she got her heart rate up to about 125 beats a minute for at least 45 minutes, she knew she was burning fat off her tall frame. She'd already gone from 175 pounds down to 154 in the last six weeks, and she hoped to be under 150 for the bodybuilding competition. She was glad she only had to work at it for another week—it would be an incredible relief when it was over.

She changed into biking shorts and a hot pink sports bra over her regular bra. Flexing and stretching her shoulders and chest muscles, she decided the contusion from the shooting wasn't hurting much anymore, though she could still see the faint green bruising.

On her way through the kitchen she snagged a quart bottle of water and headed out to the garage. After getting her bike and helmet, she mashed the helmet on her head, pushing down the neat French braid. She mounted the bike and put her feet in the toe clips. Sticking to residential streets she began what she hoped would be a good ninety minutes of riding. It took little time to get good and warm on the back streets as she passed yards of freshly mown grass and young boys playing basketball at driveway hoops.

After she figured the rush hour traffic had slowed down, she ventured out to a busier street, Larpenteur Avenue. Hunched over and dripping sweat in the eighty degree heat, she pedaled powerfully up a slope toward Rice Street. Glancing to the side, she saw a white vehicle tracking her and realized it was a St. Paul cop car. Darting a glare at the occupants, she found a pair of warm hazel eyes peering out the window at her. She almost fell off the bicycle as her stomach did the funny little leaping trick it had been doing lately every time she looked at Jaylynn.

In fact, she had been spending a considerable amount of energy lately trying *not* to look at Jaylynn and coming to the unavoidable conclusion that she was attracted to the younger woman. She'd been attracted to plenty of people in the past, but she'd never had so much trouble controlling her reactions before. She found that worrisome. Of course, she hadn't had to ride around with the other objects of her interest in a hot squad car for hours on end. She remembered when Jaylynn had told her, last winter, about how much trouble it was to ride around lusting after her—a thought that embarrassed the big cop to no end. But the rookie didn't appear to have any trouble with that at all anymore. Jaylynn could look her straight in the eye—with that infectious little smile—and *she* didn't seem to be having a single issue.

Dez didn't know what she was going to do about the unwelcome feelings, but right now she thought she'd pull into the strip mall up ahead and talk with Jaylynn and whoever was at the wheel. She nodded upon seeing that Crystal was driving. She hadn't seen much of her lately. Frowning, she pulled up to the sidewalk in front of the drugstore and stopped the bike with her foot on the curb. *It's August,* she thought, *and I can't remember the last time I spent any time with Crystal and Shayna.* She felt bad about that and decided she should probably have them over to Luella's or do something with them soon. She caught her breath as she pulled her helmet off and hung it on her handlebar.

Her colleagues got out of the car to find a scowling, sweating Dez swigging half a quart of water. Some of the water escaped as she drank and ran along her chin, dripping down her neck. The big woman wiped her face and forehead on a bare arm glistening with sweat. It didn't help. Jaylynn thought Dez looked overheated and miserable.

"Uh, hi," the rookie said as she met a pair of dark blue eyes which bored right through her and traveled along every nerve ending from her head straight to her groin. She crossed her arms uncertainly and tried not to stare at the bare muscular midsection, the broad shoulders, and the beautifully planed face.

With a grimace Dez nodded. "How's it going?"

"Not bad," Crystal said. While Jaylynn hung back, leaning against the front panel of the car, Crystal strode up to Dez and grabbed hold of her forearm. "So, *mi amiga*, you ready for the show? Let's see a nice biceps."

Dez stared daggers at her, but pulled her arm away from the laughing cop and made a fist, then flexed her biceps.

"Not bad, *chica*. Not bad." Crystal flexed her own arm and said, "Not quite as good as mine, but hey, who's counting?"

In a dry voice Dez asked, "Who could tell with that T-shirt and uniform sleeve covering it up?"

"Trust me, it's there. A mountain of strength."

"Yeah, right." She took another long pull of her water. "Anything exciting going down tonight?"

Jaylynn and Crystal shook their heads simultaneously, and the rookie said, "You're not missing a thing—though maybe it'll pick up when the sun goes down."

Dez looked around. "I better get going before that happens." She tucked her water bottle away and pushed off the curb and past the police car. "See ya."

Jaylynn gazed after her, watching the incredibly long legs and the lean hips. She'd never seen anyone look so luscious in biking shorts, thighs rippling with muscle and sinew. *Nice buns,* she thought. *Really nice everything.* The rookie hoped that if she fainted right now, Crystal wouldn't figure out it was because of excess lust. She let out a soft sigh and gulped in some air as she got back in the stuffy car.

Crystal slammed her own door and started the engine. "See what I mean?" she asked. "She's got no sense of humor at all right now. She looked like she wanted to hit me."

"She would never do that."

"Who knows what goes on in that dense head of hers."

Yes, who knows? thought Jaylynn. *I sure don't.*

****

Saturday night, Crystal and Dez left the locker room for roll call at the same time. Cautiously Crystal asked, "Hey, Dez, what's up?"

"Nothing much."

"We're going bowling tonight after shift. Wanna come?"

"Nah, I'm a terrible bowler."

Crystal snorted out a loud laugh. "Who isn't? Geez, that's the point, Reilly. We have a hilarious time. You really ought to come. I tell ya, my abs usually hurt for three days afterwards from laughing."

"You ought to work 'em a little harder in the gym. You'd have more fortitude that way."

Crystal stopped, put her hands on her hips, and gave Dez her best dirty look. "Very funny. Too bad yours are in such good shape that a little laughter isn't necessary."

"Aw, come on," Dez said. She considered for a moment. *What could it hurt?* "Who's coming?"

"Me and Shayna, Merilee, Jay, and that other new rookie, Marshall—I think her first name is Paula. If you join in, we'll have six and we can use two lanes. That's even more fun."

"Shayna's coming? Hmmph. All right," Dez said reluctantly, "but only if I get to keep score."

"Fine by me! I can never keep it all straight anyway."

****

After shift, they converged on the lanes shortly after midnight. Merilee and Paula, both tall and slender, took to one another right away and were soon discussing vacation hot spots. For the first time, Jaylynn got to meet Shayna, and she was pleased and surprised at the same time. For one thing, Shayna was friendly and gregarious. She gave Dez a hug—which surprised Jaylynn—and patted the rookie on the shoulder. Shayna's warm, brown eyes shone upon her. Taller than Jaylynn by only a couple inches, Shayna's skin was cocoa-brown, and she was plump. She wore a pair of half dollar-sized dangly gold earrings and six or seven gold bracelets on each wrist. Jaylynn liked the tie-dyed shirt Shayna was wearing and told her so. With an arm across her shoulders, Shayna walked her over to the shoe counter, talking nonstop about tie-dye methods. Before she knew it, Jaylynn had committed to taking a tie-dye class with her.

Bo's Bowling Center was crowded, but they were lucky enough to get the last two lanes together. True to Crystal's description, it was amusing. Jaylynn threw a strike on the first ball and followed it up with a gutter ball. Shayna managed to roll one ball across the double gutter and into the next lane, surprising their neighbors with a strike. Dez made up for lack of finesse by rolling powerhouse tosses, fast and furious, which caused the pins to explode noisily, though there were often one or two pins left standing. Everyone teased everybody about everything. After the first game, Dez had won with 120 points.

"Should we do another round?" Crystal asked.

Shayna, who had managed to rack up a mere 56 points, said in a grumpy voice, "No! Now I remember why I hate bowling. The ball's heavy, the shoes hurt your feet, and they play crappy music."

"Oh, come on," Crystal said, laughing as she circled Shayna's waist with a strong arm. "We haven't even been here an hour!"

"You come on," Shayna said. "Admit it. Do you actually like this music?" Blaring over the tinny loudspeaker was Billy Ray Cyrus doing "Achy Breaky Heart." Suddenly Shayna's face lit up. "I know! Let's go dancing."

"Yeah, good idea," Merilee said. "Let's hit the Metro and dance the night away. Whaddya say?"

"I don't know," Dez said doubtfully.

Jaylynn watched the interactions from her seat next to Paula.

Crystal aimed a karate chop at Dez's midsection, which the tall woman blocked handily. "It's not even one o'clock yet," Crystal said. "Listen, *chica*, you need to kick up your heels a little bit."

"Yeah," Shayna said. "Please come. And you, too, Paula. Jaylynn?" She looked around at everyone with a hopeful smile on her mahogany brown face. "Girls?"

Jaylynn shrugged and glanced over at Dez.

Crystal feigned another series of jabs at the brunette. "If you're real nice," she said, "you can dance one with me. I'll even let you lead. Maybe." Her eyes twinkled with glee as she stifled a laugh and took hold of Shayna's arm. "Come on," she said as she looked back toward Dez, "let's get Twinkle Toes out of her uncomfortable shoes and go."

Throughout this discussion Jaylynn felt torn, not sure if she wanted to tag along or not. She was surprised Dez relented so easily, but the tall woman was changing her shoes and didn't appear to have a problem with the idea. Jaylynn sat on the molded blue plastic chair and exchanged the two-tone leather monstrosities for her sneakers. Silently she followed the laughing group of women to the shoe return counter, threw in some cash for the line, and then listened as they all argued about who should ride with whom, who would drink, who would abstain. Jaylynn rode with Crystal, Shayna, and Paula, while Merilee hopped into Dez's truck to follow Crystal's Chevy Impala over to the dance bar.

"It's a hot spot tonight," Merilee said gleefully as she got out of the car. "Looks like fun." The boom of the bass could be heard in the parking lot. "Cool. Must be a live band."

The six women made their way to the door, which Dez grabbed and held open. Jaylynn stepped into a dim room, about sixty feet wide and forty feet deep. The bar, on the far wall from the entrance, was staffed by three bartenders surrounded by thirsty patrons. The left half of the room contained tables and chairs while the right section was a dance floor, currently full of writhing bodies moving to the thump of the band. The stage for the band was set in the wall in the far right corner. Jaylynn saw a drummer, guitarist, bass, keyboard player, two horn players, and two backup vocalists. A scary looking man wearing what appeared to be a black fright wig—but wasn't—was singing a rousing rendition of Rod Stewart's "Do Ya Think I'm Sexy." The crowd danced at a fever pitch.

"Let's go, girls," Shayna shouted. She and Crystal, Paula, and Merilee made a beeline for the floor, leaving Jaylynn standing, uncertain, next to an equally reticent Dez. The four women pressed through the crowd and joined the swirling mass.

The music pounded loud, so Jaylynn jumped when a low voice tickled her ear. "Dance? Or sit?"

Jaylynn shrugged. She shouted, "I hate this song."

Dez nodded in agreement and gestured toward the tables. Jaylynn sat at a rickety brown table. Spilled beer dripped off the side, so Dez wended her way through the crowd and got a rag at the bar. She returned and wiped up the table. She leaned down and said, "You want something to drink?"

Jaylynn shook her head.

Dez took one last swipe at the tabletop and headed back. Jaylynn watched Dez gracefully negotiate between tables and patrons, her broad shoulders dipping and twisting to pass through the throng. She slipped into the crowd and the waiting woman lost sight of her.

Jaylynn looked around the busy nightclub full of happy,

dancing people. Scooting her chair forward, she put her elbows on the table and leaned her chin in her hands. Her eyes combed the crowd until they lit upon a dark form, half a head taller than most everyone around, and Jaylynn watched Dez, carrying two glasses, worm her way through the mob surrounding the bar.

As the tall woman made her way back, women seated nearby stared at her appraisingly, some with obvious interest. Dez didn't seem to notice. She set the drinks down and slipped into the seat next to Jaylynn, facing the dance floor, and slung an arm across the back of the rookie's chair. With her other hand she picked up the tumbler and drained it, then set it back on the table.

Jaylynn shouted, "What did you get there?" as she nodded toward the glasses on the table.

"Ice water," Dez said.

"What?"

Dipping her head down near Jaylynn's ear, she repeated herself and said, "Want some?"

Jaylynn shook her head. Dez picked up the other glass and took a sip. They sat like that through three more songs. Every once in a while Jaylynn caught sight of one of the other cops out on the floor dancing, laughing, caught up in the music.

Next to her Dez sipped her drink, then bent to say, "You like to dance?"

Jaylynn nodded. Dez's face was inches from her own, and the rookie was relieved it was dark enough to disguise the fact that she was blushing. The band was now playing an old Van Morrison song, "Wild Night," and she couldn't resist tapping her feet with the rhythm of the horns and the upbeat tempo.

Dez leaned in again. "Sure you don't want something to drink?"

"Maybe later."

"What?" Dez leaned down very close, tipping her head to the side to hear.

"Later," Jaylynn enunciated.

Dez nodded as she sat back, but she kept her arm on Jaylynn's chair. The band segued into Madonna's "Holiday," complete with the horns playing. Jaylynn smiled. She turned to Dez. "I love this song," she said into the tall woman's ear.

"Me, too," Dez shouted. "Shall we?" She downed the last of her water and inclined her head toward the dance floor. Jaylynn swallowed, her heart pounding mercilessly. Suddenly she didn't want to do this at all, but Dez grabbed hold of her wrist and pulled her up and toward the floor. She let herself be dragged along behind like a skier on a towline. Once they merged into the throng of dancers, once she let herself feel the beat, once she allowed

herself to breathe again, she relaxed.   The singer was doing a
passably good job with the vocals, and the band's sound was lush
and full.   Dez did a little shimmy and then Jaylynn let herself slip
into a rhythm complementing the taller woman.   She was surprised
at how adept Dez was, all sinew and legs.   But why wouldn't
someone as coordinated and physical as Dez be a good dancer?
Jaylynn just didn't expect it for some reason.

A new song began, one that Jaylynn didn't recognize at first,
but it had a nice fast beat, and she slipped right into a groove.   Then
she heard the words and recognized it as a Gloria Estefan song and
broke out in a smile.   She moved closer to Dez and shouted, "I love
Gloria!"   Dez nodded back at her.

She lost herself in the dance, feeling her body purring with the
fun of it.   She closed her eyes and just let the pounding of the music
guide her motion.   Opening her eyes, she watched Dez for a
moment until the tall woman moved closer and bent down, saying
into her ear, "You got moves, woman."   Jaylynn blushed some more
and ripped a quick jab to the dark woman's shoulder.

"Hey!" Dez said as she stopped and grabbed Jaylynn by the
shoulders.   "How come everybody's hitting me tonight?"

Jaylynn twisted away and grinned back.   Then the song was
ending, winding down to a slower beat, and the keyboard cut in,
playing the first few strains of a song Jaylynn couldn't quite identify
at first, but then recognized as Toni Braxton's love ballad, "I Don't
Want To Sing Another Love Song."   Half of the dancers fled the
floor, leaving the rest to move closer to their partners and gear
down into a slower, more sensual dance.

The two women's eyes met.   Jaylynn stepped back.   *I can't do
this tonight.   Definitely not possible.*   She tore her eyes away from
the shiny blue chips burning into her, but before she could turn to
go, she felt hands on her shoulders guiding her into a light embrace.
She let her hands drop to Dez's hips, feeling the leather of a belt
against her palms.   Her cheek would fit so perfectly in the crook of
Dez's neck...but she resisted the urge to press her face there,
holding herself just a little apart.   A brush of lips against her ear
and the low voice asked, "You okay with this?"

"Yes.   No.   I mean...I don't know."   Warm hands against her
back pulled her closer, and she sighed as she dropped her forehead
into the crook between the tall woman's neck and chin, only to hear
a heartbeat that matched her own, beating wildly.   She couldn't stop
herself from moving closer, wrapping arms tight around the slim
waist, her body craving more while her mind told her to resist.   She
felt a gentle stroke from the top of her head, through her blonde
hair, down the back of her neck where the hand stopped, the palm
hot and dry against the skin above her collar.

It was too much.

Jaylynn tore herself away and dashed through the crowd, heading blindly toward the door. She passed a startled Merilee and apologized to Crystal as she cut by her. Then she was at the door, pushing against the heavy wood, and she burst into the humid night air, gasping for breath. The door behind her popped back open and Dez was at her heels, grasping her shoulder, but Jaylynn refused to face her and tried to shrug her off.

In a low, frightened voice, the tall woman asked, "Jay, what is it? What's the matter?"

Jaylynn turned, eyes blazing, and said, "I can't *do* this anymore. I can't. I won't. I can't take it." She closed her eyes and retreated within, backing away from Dez. When she opened her eyes again, Dez stood before her, hunched over, trying to look in her eyes.

"What do you mean?"

Jaylynn drew a deep breath. "I thought I could do this, be with you, pal around, ride with you every night. I thought I could, but I just can't. Not anymore."

Dez stared back at her as though she'd had the wind knocked out of her. "What are you saying? You don't want to ride with me anymore?"

"Look, you made your feelings very clear, and whether you realize it or not, now you're sending an entirely different message to me. I could handle it when it was all business..." She leaned back until her leg bumped against the front grill of a car, then turned slightly and put her foot up on the bumper. She rested her elbow on her knee and her head in her hand. "I just can't ride around with you anymore, pretending I don't feel the way I do. I can't slow dance with you. I'm not sure I can fast dance with you." In a strangled voice, she said, "I just can't," then turned away to hide the tears threatening to come.

"Then don't pretend," the low voice said. The door to the club slapped open and a crowd of laughing men emerged, casting curious glances their way. "Come on," Dez said impatiently, tapping her on the shoulder. "Let's get outta here."

"What about the rest of the crew?"

"They'll manage," Dez growled as she ushered Jaylynn toward the red truck.

Jaylynn was appalled at her lack of control. She had been in far more tense situations with Dez and she hadn't cracked. *What has come over me?* She ran her fingers through her blonde hair and took a deep breath before stepping up into the truck. She had no idea what to expect now—much less what to do.

Dez backed out of the spot and gunned the engine out of the

lot. She found she had been holding her breath and let it out in an audible rush, then glanced over at Jaylynn who slumped silently against the passenger door. *Where should I go?* Dez wondered. *My place? Hers? A restaurant?*

"Where are you taking me?" a soft voice asked.

"I—I guess I don't really know. Any suggestions?"

"I think I need to go home."

Disappointment in the form of a sudden sinking sensation hit Dez's stomach hard, and she decided she had made a monumental mistake. For once she *wanted* to talk, to attempt to express the conflicting emotions boiling up inside, regardless of the awkwardness. *But what would I say? How do I really feel?* With unexpected clarity, it occurred to her. She wanted Jaylynn—it was as simple as that. She wanted her, and she needed to let her know that, even at the risk of rejection. She turned onto the lane that led around to Jaylynn's house. Como Lake, glittery in the moonlight, shone in front of her. She pulled the truck to a stop and cut the engine as Jaylynn popped open the door, which turned on the overhead lamp. Dez blinked in the harsh light. She reached across the truck cab to rest her hand lightly on Jaylynn's knee.

"Please...don't go," she said in a choked voice. "Not just yet. Please?"

Jaylynn clicked the door closed, extinguishing the light, and Dez pulled her hand back reluctantly. By the dim light of the streetlamp Dez thought the quiet woman looked beautiful, her face all sharp planes and large hazel eyes, eyes that now looked haunted and unhappy. *How do I say this? How do I make her understand?* She swallowed nervously and said, "Could we walk by the lake for a while?" She held her breath waiting for Jaylynn to say no.

"Okay," was all the smaller woman said, and with a sigh, she opened the passenger door. The overhead light startled Dez again. She hopped out of the truck, slammed the door, and was glad for the dim light of the streetlamps.

Wordlessly they walked across the street, through the grass, across the bike path. They stopped at the lake's edge. Dez put her hands in her pockets and looked out on the shimmery surface of the lake, smooth as glass. Jaylynn headed toward a bench and sat, pulling her feet up and wrapping her arms around her knees. Hesitantly Dez followed and sat a couple of feet away on Jaylynn's bench.

In a quiet voice the smaller woman said, "I like to come here with my journal some evenings and watch the sun go down."

Dez angled her body to face Jaylynn and leaned her left shoulder against the back of the bench. "If we sit here long enough, we can watch the sun come up."

Jaylynn sighed. "Not tonight. I am way too tired."

The normally talkative woman sat in silence watching the lake. Dez tried to see her face, but it was shrouded in darkness. *Tell her. It's now or never,* thought Dez. *Say something.* She cleared her throat and mentally kicked herself. "Jay," she began.

The smaller woman turned and cocked her head to the side a bit and studied her. Jaylynn waited a moment and when Dez didn't go on, she said, "I'm confused. What do you *want?*"

With an explosive sigh of relief, Dez said, "I want to talk about us."

The crickets chirped in the background. Far away a car could be heard speeding into the distance, gears grinding. Dez held her breath as seconds passed and Jaylynn did not respond.

"Why now?" Jaylynn whispered.

The tall woman was at a loss to respond. *Is Jaylynn saying it is too late?* Dez knew she had been slow to understand, slow to come to the realization that she loved this woman. *Love?* She gulped and gripped the back of the bench hard, glad she was seated. *Yes. That's it: love. How embarrassing.*

The last time she'd thought she loved someone she had been betrayed, laughed at and mocked, and since then, she had purposely made sure no one could get too close to her. She liked it that way. No complications. No risks. She always thought she had reconciled herself to spending her life on her own. But this was different. All of the old rules of the game seemed trivial, totally inapplicable. She stood, put her hands in her pockets, and paced, taking four steps with long legs, then twirling on her heel and pacing back.

"Why does this have to be so hard for you?" Jaylynn asked.

Dez shrugged. She faced Jaylynn and turned her palms up. "I don't know."

"Dez, I am not Karin."

Dez felt like she'd been socked in the stomach. For a moment she couldn't breathe at all, and her legs felt weak. She managed to get her breath and choke out, "How—how in the hell do you know about Karin?"

Jaylynn said simply, "Crystal told me."

"I'm gonna kill her," Dez said. She smacked her fist into her palm. "*Why* did she tell you? Why?"

"Because she cares about you. Because she wanted me to understand you a little better."

"That's a goddamn excuse. How did she even *know*—dammit!" Furiously she paced back and forth in front of the bench. Jaylynn waited silently until Dez slowed down, then the tall woman abruptly sat on the bench and put her head in her hands. "There was no reason for Crystal to run around spilling her guts about *my* life."

"She was very worried about you at the time."

"Oh, what the hell for?"

"For God's sake, Dez, you're starving yourself! Do you hear me? You're starved! You've deprived yourself in every way. Food. Sleep. Love." Jaylynn paused and stared at Dez's passive demeanor. "Aren't you listening?"

Dez looked up defiantly and then looked away. "Yeah, but I don't have to agree."

In a bitter voice Jaylynn said, "Look at you. You're thin as a rail. You don't sleep more than three or four hours a night. You work yourself to exhaustion, and most of the time you shut out all your friends."

"What's your point?"

Jaylynn let out an exasperated growling sound. "My point is— you don't have to do that. Stop the punishment. You're slowly choking the life out of yourself." She scooted down the bench, grabbed Dez's arm and implored, "Don't you want to live? To be happy?"

Dez stared over at the rookie's sincere face and shrugged. "I'm okay with my life."

"You're *okay with your life*?" The sarcasm in Jaylynn's voice was unmistakable. She let go of the arm she was grasping tightly. "You're *miserable*! How can you not see that? How come everybody else on earth can see that so clearly—except you?"

Dez sighed. "What do you want from me, Jay?"

Abruptly Jaylynn started to cry. "Nothing," she said, "and everything." She quickly wiped away a tear and tried to choke back her feelings. "You don't realize what gifts you have, what a gift you *are*. You don't have to be alone. You don't have to feel this way, Dez. Look at you! You don't even defend yourself. I've just told you your life is shit and you don't even fight back."

In a detached voice, Dez said, "Why is your life so great in comparison?"

Jaylynn squeezed her eyes shut, took a deep breath, and composed her thoughts. "I wake up most every morning feeling alive. I feel a pulse of happiness here in my heart that runs through my whole body. I look forward to the new day and wonder what interesting things will happen. Food tastes good. I feel the weather. I have energy. I talk, listen, hug, yell at people. I learn. I follow you around watching, trying new things. I laugh. Sometimes I cry—whether you approve or not. At the end of the day, I'm tired, and when my head hits the pillow, I sleep and wake up ready to go again. That's it. That's my simple little life. It may not be much, but I've been happy with it."

"Maybe compared to your life, mine isn't as great, but I'm content."

"You either need to see a psychologist or raise your expectations!" Dez sighed again and looked away. "You asked for it," Jaylynn said, "you got it. Obviously you aren't going to change, no matter how much concern anyone shows. So I'm not going to bug you anymore. I guess this is another area where we'll just have to agree to disagree." She stood and turned to leave.

"Hey," Dez said, "where ya going?"

"I'm outta here. See you tomorrow."

Jaylynn stomped off leaving Dez sitting on the park bench. The longer she sat thinking, the more upset she became. *That upstart rookie thinks my life is shit. How dare she? Who does she think she is judging whether I'm happy or not?*

Upon reflection though, she wondered if maybe her life was indeed shit. *Am I happy?* she wondered. *Do I enjoy each day?* She sat for a few moments, not really thinking any coherent thoughts. Dez stood and faced the lake. The water was silent, no waves, no noise. All she could hear was the chirping of crickets. Streetlights on the other side of the lake winked and blinked as the warm night wind blew tree limbs back and forth in front of them. *I envy her. Where does she get all that energy? And why is she so upset with me?* A chilling thought rose and with a sick feeling in the pit of her stomach she considered it. What if the rookie asked for a transfer again? What if she changed shifts? Last time they had this kind of disagreement, it had resulted in a time of misery. Would that happen again?

Bone-tired and feeling depressed, she turned and made her way back to her truck. It occurred to her that Jaylynn was likely right about her life—or lack thereof—but she was too tired to explore it further. *Tomorrow. I'll talk to her more tomorrow.*

Chapter
24

With a heavy heart, Dez got ready for her shift. She had had another restless night full of awful nightmares. She dreamed again of Ryan and, though she couldn't remember most of the dream, she awoke at five a.m. remembering a vision of his face, pale and lifeless, his eyes staring blankly up at her. She couldn't get back to sleep after that, and now here she was before roll call, feeling so tired that she almost wanted to go home sick.

"Hey, girl," Crystal said. Dez looked up in surprise to see Crystal leaning against the bright blue locker at the end of the row. The smiling cop said, "You're here early today."

"On the contrary," Dez said in an icy voice as she rooted through her locker. "*You're* the early one. What's up?"

Crystal sat down on the bench and unlaced her street shoes. "Shayna had to go in to work early, so I just moseyed down here myself."

Dez picked up an old belt and hung it up on a hook. She glanced back over her shoulder. "You're always so full of it, Crys. You've never been early on purpose in your life." She returned to sorting items in the locker.

"All right, so maybe I did have an ulterior motive." She pulled her socks off and wiggled her brown toes as she relaxed on the bench. "What happened to you guys last night? Everything okay?"

Dez glowered at her. "Why?"

"You two tore outta there like you were on fire. And—well, Jaylynn didn't look any too happy. We were just—we just wanted to make sure—"

"What? That I didn't beat her or something?"

"Oooh! Groucheee. Must have been a rip-roarin' fight, huh?"

Feeling a sudden surge of energy, Dez got in her face and in a quiet, deadly voice said, "Who the hell do you think you are telling her about Karin? And how the hell did *you* know?"

Crystal rolled her eyes. "Good God! I've only been friends with you for what, eight, nine years? And everyone knew what Karin was all about. Come on, Dez! I could tell. Why do you think I made a point to get to know you? I could see what she'd done to you, and you didn't deserve it."

Dez backed away. She reached up and gripped the top of her locker door and squeezed it so hard her knuckles turned white. "You never said anything."

"You're a private kinda gal, *mi amiga*. I respect that."

Dez turned abruptly and sat down at the other end of the bench. "Why did you have to talk to her about that?"

"Oh, *chica*, you can't even see it, can you? Nothing is so amazing as she who will not see."

"What's *that* supposed to mean?"

Crystal slid down the bench and began to speak, her face near Dez's ear. She whispered, "Listen to me—because I'm only going to tell you this once, and then if you must, you can go back to your self-imposed isolation." She paused as Dez put her elbows on her knees and her chin in her hands. The big woman looked down at the floor, but she appeared to be listening, so Crystal went on. "That girl, she's so much in love with you—it shows in every smile, every glance, every pore of her body. You've got some kind of electricity going. And if you don't feel it, well, you're blind, deaf, and dumb. Shayna—she laughs about this—says she feels we'll all be electrocuted soon if you don't get your head outta your ass."

Dez's head jerked up and she glared at Crystal. "How do you know this?"

Dark eyes snapping, Crystal stood and put her hands on her hips. "Oh, pullease! For once in your pigheaded life could you trust someone else? I'm telling you, it's the truth. Pay attention. *Wake up,* girl!"

In a muffled voice, Dez said, "I feel like I'm in a soap opera."

Crystal let out a deep belly laugh. "Maybe so. Maybe you are." She picked up her shoes and socks and padded over to the other side of the locker room. She didn't say anything when she heard Dez open the door and leave. She just shook her head and mumbled to herself, "Get a clue, Dez, before it's too late."

****

Dez found Jaylynn digging through her locker twenty minutes before roll call. "Hey," she asked. "How are ya?"

Jaylynn turned to face her, misery etched into the worried planes of her face. The rookie stood for a moment studying the taller woman.

"What?" Dez asked. She arched an eyebrow and spread her long arms out, her palms upright as though she expected rain. "All I asked is how you're doing."

"I can't believe you're still speaking to me."

"What do you mean?"

Jaylynn shook her head. "You don't remember last night's conversation?"

Dez took a few steps and slid down onto the flat bench, facing Jaylynn on the rickety bench in front of her locker. She put her elbows on her knees and rubbed her eyes with her knuckles. "Yeah, I remember it clearly. Why?"

"How can you not be upset? You should be pissed at me." Jaylynn dropped down on the other bench across from Dez. "I'm sorry. Okay? I—I said—I said some things I didn't mean, okay? I shouldn't have done it." She looked as though she was about to cry.

In a quiet voice, Dez said, "You don't have to apologize. You were right."

"No, Dez. I was pretty harsh. I didn't mean it that way."

"Yes, you did." Dez met Jaylynn's gaze and held it. "Aren't you the one always telling me to be honest? You were just being honest."

The rookie put her head in her hands and stared down at the floor. She looked so miserable that Dez rose and sat next to her. She nudged the rookie's leg with her knee. "Hey. Stop thinking about it. I took it to mean that you cared, Jay, that you were worried about me. You didn't tell me anything I didn't already sort of know anyway." When the rookie didn't respond, Dez said in a soft voice, "Look, I've been a pain in the ass lately—I know. The competition is this weekend, and I'll be less crabby when I can start eating more carbs. I gotta tell you," she said, as she hung her head, "I haven't been much fun these last few weeks. I'm sorry."

"That doesn't excuse me for how I acted—"

Dez cut her off. "Please," she stood and leaned back against the lockers with her hands behind her, "just quit talking about it. I—I don't want to talk about this—not now." She ran her hand over her head smoothing back already tidy hair. "Can we just make it through tonight? Then I'm off 'til after the show. You won't have to put up with my crankiness, okay?" Abruptly she turned and headed for the locker room door.

Jaylynn hustled to throw her stuff in her locker. Her relief was so great that she actually felt shaky. She had imagined all sorts of terrible things since the night before, and to be honest, she was just exhausted from lack of sleep. She hadn't realized that Dez had taken off work for the next several days, but in a way, that was okay with her. She needed a break from her intense partner, and the big cop needed to get away from the stresses of the street. She locked up and raced up the stairs to roll call.

****

Saturday of the competition dawned clear and beautiful. Jaylynn dressed in lightweight slacks and her favorite green v-necked shirt. She ate a huge breakfast of cereal, toast, juice, and leftover fried potatoes, and she took a few minutes to pack some goodies to eat during the day.

The rookie arrived at Central High School an hour before the competition was scheduled. She figured Dez would be there early, and sure enough, she was. The tall woman, dressed in grey sweats and flips, was seated on the floor next to an oversized black gym bag. She leaned against a brick wall in the hallway, her knees drawn up to her chest, and her arms around her legs. Her face and hands and feet were dyed such a deep brown that for a moment Jaylynn didn't recognize her. Dark hair was woven together from the top of her head and down the back in a tight French braid that tucked under leaving no hair on her neck. She was gazing out the side window and didn't even notice the rookie until she was sliding down next to her.

"Hey," Jaylynn said. "How'd you sleep?"

The dark head swung around and bright blue eyes in a mahogany-colored face surveyed the younger woman. "Hi, Jay. Okay, I guess."

"Which means what? Five? Six hours?"

Dez gave her a slight smile and looked away. In truth, she had probably slept most of the last twelve hours. She actually remembered some pleasant dreams between waking every three hours when her internal clock told her she needed to eat. At this point she was so sick of protein powder, amino acid pills, romaine lettuce, and chicken breasts that she could gag just thinking about them. But she didn't feel tired; she also did not feel very energetic, but she knew she had to get pumped by shortly after eight.

Jaylynn reached over and grasped Dez's forearm. "Wow, you sure are dark. When you said you'd be using a tanning dye, I had no idea it would look like this!"

"Yeah, but ya gotta do it or the bright lights bleach you out and the judges can't see any muscle."

Dez looked so embarrassed that Jaylynn changed the subject. "Any competition to watch out for?"

Dez stretched her legs out and let her hands fall into her lap. "Yeah. Looks like at least two heavyweights. They both look pretty good from what I can tell."

Jaylynn reached over and patted the grey-clad forearm. "I've got a good feeling about this. You're going to do well."

"Thanks for coming so early. I just hope Cowboy gets here soon."

She pulled her gym bag over closer to her and hunted around in it, coming up with a pint of bottled water. "Want a swig?" she asked as she twisted the cap open.

"Nope. I brought my own." She gestured to her own leather bag, which contained plenty of goodies to make it through the day. "So tell me, what happens now?"

Dez closed up the bottle and stuck it back in her bag. "We weigh in at eight and then get pumped up for the 8:30 start. It's all compulsory poses at first, and then we do our one minute programs. They start with women teens, then the boys. I'm pretty sure they do the Masters competitors, then the rest of us novices, women first, followed by men. Somewhere along the way, the pairs get squeezed in. I haven't actually seen the schedule yet, but I know from the one other show I did that they'll give us a timeline to follow."

"Where's the best place to sit?"

"Oh, anywhere. The closer you are, the better though. You can see symmetry from a distance, but muscles and vascularity are best seen up close."

"So you don't care if I sit in the front row?"

Dez chuckled and shrugged. "Whatever."

"How long does this take?"

Dez thought about that for a moment. "Mmm...two, maybe three hours. I like to stay and see the men. When I'm done, I'll come out and sit with you to watch—that is, if you're staying that long?"

"Sure I am." Jaylynn grinned. "I'd like that. Maybe then you can give me enough information so I understand all of this."

Dez nodded. "You also better buy tonight's tickets now or else you'll get crummy seats."

"I told Luella I'd get a pair for her and Vanita. She tried to tell me her tired old eyes needed to be up close. Hey, why didn't Luella come this morning?"

"I talked her out of it. It's just the compulsories, and they go on and on. I thought it would be a lot more fun for her to see the show tonight. You didn't have to come this early either, you know."

"Oh, but I wanted to," Jaylynn said, a twinkle in her eye. "So I should get tickets this morning before the show?"

"Yes, go get them now." Dez looked at her watch. "They'll open up any minute. Go be first in line. They've already sold a lot in advance." When she reached for her bag, Dez said, "You can leave that here. I'll keep an eye on it."

Jaylynn rose and hastened to the table where two men were setting up to sell tickets. Dez watched her walk away, smiling approvingly at the cream-colored Dockers, white tennis shoes, and a form-fitting forest green v-neck shirt. Her hips were shapely and her white-blonde hair shone under the fluorescent lights.

Dez felt a little blush creep into her face as she remembered some of the images of a dream she'd had the night before. In it, they were in a sunny glade near a lake. Jaylynn had been wearing considerably less than now—a maroon bathing suit top and the shortest of jean shorts. Her legs were lean and sinewy, her stomach muscular and tight. Dez frowned and shook her head. She didn't know why she was suddenly dreaming about the rookie all the time. And the part that caused her to blush now occurred when the young woman had slipped out of those clothes and stood nude before her. Dez recalled looking down and realizing that she herself wore no clothes either. In her dream, she didn't feel the slightest bit shy. They waded into the water, and the dream went on, but she couldn't remember any more details, only that she had awakened from it unwillingly, her stomach protesting for food.

She looked at her watch again. *7:55. Time to weigh in.* Jaylynn was walking back toward her, tucking tickets into her back pockets. Dez rose and picked up both of their bags.

"Time to go?" Jaylynn asked.

"Yup. I'll look for ya in the audience."

She stood awkwardly until Dez handed her the leather bag. "Good luck," Jaylynn said. "I'll be rooting for you." It seemed so lame, but it was all she could think to say.

Dez flashed her a smile, and her white teeth were such a contrast to the dark skin that Jaylynn was taken aback. That was the face of her Hero. It was uncanny and gave her the shivers. She watched the grey-clad woman walk away from her, and she was struck by how thin she appeared. In fact, those sweats bagged on the tall woman so much that Jaylynn thought they'd look more shapely on the hanger. As she turned away she heard a clock-clock-clock noise, and in came Cowboy wearing his ever-present leather boots and hauling a bag even bigger than Dez's. He was nearly running as he caught up with the tall, dark-haired woman who stood next to her bag, hands on hips, shaking her head at him.

Jaylynn made her way into the auditorium where the audio techs were making final checks on the sound system. The high school's theater hall was large and seated around two thousand. Right now there were seven judges sitting at a long table right in front of the stage and little knots of early birds scattered throughout

the first fifteen rows. She picked her way down the stairs toward
the front row, passing a huge man eating from a gallon-sized
Tupperware container full of rice and chicken. Picking a spot to the
right in the fourth row where she thought she had the best angle of
vision, she sat and proceeded to think about Dez.

The tired woman hadn't seemed nervous at all. Then again,
she had done this before. If she were Dez, Jaylynn was certain
she'd be throwing up right about now. She looked around the
auditorium. On the stage there were three banners that advertised
other sponsors, including the Sports Nutrition Warehouse, a
chiropractor, and three fitness clubs. On one side wall, two men
were hanging a thirty-foot-long banner with red, white, and blue
lettering that read: *"All Natural Bodybuilding Championship
sponsored in part by the St. Paul Police Department."* The wall on
the other side already contained another gold banner that carried
the seal of the police department and the words *"To Serve and
Protect: In memory of Ryan Michaelson."*

Jaylynn felt the hair on her arms stand on end, and once again
she found herself wishing she had met the man who all of her
colleagues had respected so much. In photos around the
department, he was as blonde as she was. He was stocky, broad-
shouldered, and wearing a mischievous grin in every picture. She
thought she probably would have liked him a lot.

A string of people—many of them cops whom Jaylynn vaguely
recognized—wandered in and found seats. And then the chief
judge up front spoke into a microphone before him. "Let's get
started, ladies and gentlemen." Without any fanfare or intro-
ductions, he went on, "Let's have the teen women—oh, wait a
minute. We've got no teen female competitors. All right. Bring out
the teen males."

Jaylynn watched as the judges took the six boys through a
series of mandatory poses. She was impressed at the muscle and
sinew the young men displayed, not to mention their poise. They
were all clearly nervous, but each held steady throughout the ten
minutes of poses. After the compulsories were completed, each of
the boys was called individually to the stage to perform his sixty-
second program, a succession of poses chosen by the competitor to
highlight his best features. The first teen emerged and stood
waiting motionless at center stage. Suddenly, Jaylynn was startled
to hear acid rock music blaring out of the speakers. She covered her
ears and winced for the full sixty seconds. The accompanying
music for all six boys was variations of painful, screaming guitar,
booming bass beat, indistinguishable words. Jaylynn had to grin. *I
guess I'm old now,* she thought as she protected her ears. She didn't
know how the judges could stand it.

By the time the Masters women and men had done their compulsories and individual programs, Jaylynn was beginning to understand what bodybuilding was all about. She listened to the comments from the crowd, some of whom obviously knew what they were talking about, and she studied the physiques. What she found most appealing were men and women with well-defined muscle, and a lean, symmetrical presentation of it. She thought about how thin Dez had become, and she wondered if that would be detrimental.

In the Novice/Open class, the judges started with the lightweight women and moved on to the middleweights. As each moment passed, Jaylynn found herself becoming more and more nervous until her stomach was a roiling mess. She purposely closed her eyes and made herself breathe twenty deep breaths. Then she re-situated herself in the lumpy auditorium chair and watched the final middleweight finish her routine.

The judges called the heavyweights out. The three women filed out on the stage, their muscles pumped up. Jaylynn's eyes found Dez immediately, and her jaw dropped. In an electric blue suit, Dez's skin was super-shiny with a deep, dark tan, though Jaylynn could see that the lights made her look less brown than she had appeared in the hall. What stunned her the most was how impossibly *huge* the well-sculpted woman looked. The other two women were shapely and muscular, but they were four and six inches shorter respectively. Dez, standing in the middle, towered over them, a veritable mountain of muscle and sinew. The three women stood, "at rest," which meant they were not striking any poses, but every muscle in their bodies was tight and flexed.

The judges took them through the compulsory quarter turns. She saw the tall cop's broad shoulders with the defined delts, the abdominal six-pack, and legs bulging with muscle. Somewhere off in the distance Jaylynn heard cheering, but everything seemed muddied and unintelligible. She only had eyes for Dez. The three contestants turned to face away from the audience to do back lat spreads, and Jaylynn wondered if she could believe her own eyes. The back the tall woman presented was sinewy and so rippled that she looked hard as rock.

Before Jaylynn knew it, the compulsories were over and she realized she hadn't paid the slightest attention to the other two women. She had no idea what their strengths or weaknesses were. She hoped Dez wouldn't ask for any comparisons because she wouldn't be able to give them.

The judges called for the first individual program, and Jaylynn was relieved that Dez was first. The sooner she performed her sixty-second routine, the sooner the rookie could relax. The tall

woman strode out to the middle of the stage and waited for the
music to start.   The first notes of "Sisters Are Doing It For
Themselves" came over the speakers bringing a smile to the rookie's
lips.   Holding her breath, Jaylynn was struck by how much her
dream Hero looked like Dez.   Then again, she had to admit that she
had never envisioned her protector in anything other than tight
leather.   But if she *had* imagined her in next-to-no clothes, she
couldn't think of any figure better than Dez's to visualize.

Near the end of the incredibly quick minute, Jaylynn felt faint,
then realized that she should remember to breathe.   She watched,
spellbound, as Dez went through her series of poses, and it wasn't
until the music ended and the tall cop exited the stage that Jaylynn
was able to take in great gulps of air and settle back in her seat.
Now Jaylynn managed to look around, and she heard and saw the
enthusiasm of the spectators.

The final two heavyweights performed, but it was all a blur to
the young woman.   She couldn't get over how Dez had appeared.   It
wasn't until the judges called the pairs out to perform that she was
able to focus again.   She watched three different routines before
Cowboy and Dez came on the stage.   Next to him, she looked
diminutive.   Both had huge shoulders and biceps, but his
musculature was so much larger and even more defined than Dez's.
They did their routine to "Simply Irresistible" and with a wave, left
the stage.

The judges called for a ten-minute break.   It was then that
Jaylynn realized she was sweating.   Her face was hot, and suddenly
the auditorium seemed to close in on her.   Jaylynn reached into her
bag and pulled out a bottle of water.   In addition to drinking it, she
considered pouring some of it down her shirt, maybe over her head.
With a start, she discovered she was dizzy from hunger, so she
rooted through her bag again until she found a Snickers bar.   She
had just opened it and taken a bite when someone slid over the back
of the chair beside her and settled in next to her.   She looked over
and was amazed that it was Dez, dressed again in her grey sweats.

"So, how'd we do?" Dez asked.

"Good," the rookie said, her mouth full.

Dez shook her head and laughed.   "I should have known you'd
be out here munching away on something."

Jaylynn chewed furiously and swallowed.   "I just got this out
this very moment," she said indignantly.

Before Dez could reply, Jaylynn saw someone standing in the
aisle to her left.   She craned her head back to see a thin, fortyish,
red-haired woman with striking blue eyes.   She wore tailored jeans
and a black blouse with a starched collar.   Boots with stiletto
heels—and Jaylynn's seated position—made the woman look quite

tall and thin.

"So, Dez," the woman purred, "you looked pretty good up there." Her eyes raked over the seated woman. "You've certainly changed since I last saw your—ah, physique."

Jaylynn looked to her right. The body builder's face was grim, but she didn't seem too upset.

Dez said, "Well, hello, Karin. Surprised to see *you* here. You run outta sweet young things at the BCA?"

Karin looked Jaylynn up and down appreciatively. "No, but the sweet young things around *here* aren't too bad."

Comprehension dawned on Jaylynn and she realized who the red-haired woman was. In a fury, she shot up out of her seat so fast that her bag, which had been on her lap, spilled onto the auditorium floor. Without warning the red-haired woman found herself faced with a 130-pound spitfire.

"Who the hell do you think you are discussing me like a piece of meat?" Karin stepped back, obviously surprised. "Get lost," Jaylynn said fiercely. "I'll kick your ass if I see you here again."

Karin looked down at Dez who was still slumped in her seat. "You let your little friend do all the protecting around here, huh?"

"She's a better cop than *you* ever were."

Again, Karin looked surprised. She shook her head as though she didn't quite believe what she'd heard, and then turned on her heel and disappeared up the aisle.

Jaylynn picked up her bag off the floor and sank down into her seat feeling foolish and embarrassed. She sneaked a glance at Dez expecting the worst. Instead the big woman sat with a goofy grin on her face. She turned to Jaylynn and said, "Now *that* was rich. Did you see the look on her face?" She started laughing, stopping abruptly when she caught the look on her companion's face. Dez asked, "What? What's the matter?"

"How could that—that *woman* be so rude? I'm still furious!"

"Jay, Jay. It's just the chocolate."

Jaylynn gave her a blank look. "What?"

"The Snickers. What have I been telling you? Too much sugar is bad for you." The tan woman couldn't hold back anymore and laughed uproariously. "That was great when you told her you'd kick her ass. Ha ha ha..."

"I'm glad you find this so amusing."

"I needed a good laugh." Dez started laughing again, but tried to stifle it. "Be quiet now. It's the guys. We gotta root for Cowboy."

For the next hour they sat in the fourth row, heads together, while Dez told Jaylynn everything she could about proper form, posing, muscularity, and all the myriad details that made up the sport of bodybuilding. When Cowboy came out on stage, Jaylynn was surprised at all the hooting and catcalling from Dez, but it only made Cowboy preen and look all the more confident.

Once the heavyweight men finished and the morning judging concluded, Jaylynn turned to Dez. "Now what?"

Dez, who had been munching on a rice cake, shrugged her shoulders. "I come back in six hours. Until then, I just meander around avoiding anything remotely related to those Snickers bars you've been snacking on."

Jaylynn felt herself blushing. "*One* Snickers bar. It was one. Didn't you pay attention to the sandwich or the banana or the orange or the pretzels?"

Dez interrupted her. "Yes! I paid attention to all that, and believe me, the endless parade's been killing me." Irritably she said, "I can't wait until I can eat something other than rice cakes and chicken, chicken, chicken." She stood and stretched.

Jaylynn rose, too, and put her hand on Dez's arm. "Hey, I didn't know it would bother you—me eating, I mean."

Dez scowled at her. "It didn't *bother* me. You could have been eating dried squid and I would've wanted it. I'll just be glad when this is over." She crumpled up the wrapper from the rice cakes and flung it on the floor.

"Uh oh," Jaylynn said, still gripping Dez's forearm. "I think your blood sugar is low. Let's go get you some salad and chicken." She picked up her bag and slung it over her shoulder and pulled Dez along behind her. "Where's your bag, Dez?"

"I put it in the truck." She let Jaylynn drag her up the aisle. "I can't go out to a restaurant or anything like that," she protested.

"I know. You've got the next three meals all set up in your fridge, right?"

"Yeah. How'd you know?"

"Desiree Reilly, I know you far too well." She rolled her eyes. "Come on. I'll drive. You can just sit and cogitate, okay?"

Chapter
25

Jaylynn and Dez spent a leisurely afternoon hanging around at the tall woman's apartment. After Dez had a meal—cold chicken breast and romaine lettuce—she sat on the couch to watch TV and promptly fell asleep. Jaylynn went out to the kitchen and opened cupboards until she found Dez's toaster, but despite looking high and low, she found no bread.

She cracked open the apartment door and crept downstairs to tap on Luella's door. When Luella opened it, Jaylynn put her finger to her lips, squeezed inside, and pushed the door shut. "Dez is actually sleeping, and I don't want to wake her. Just one little problem—I'm starving."

"Well, you've come to the right place." Luella beamed at her, her silver hair swept back and bobby-pinned stylishly. Jaylynn took a deep breath. Luella's house always smelled like freshly baked bread and fruit—maybe strawberries.

"Really, all I need is two or three slices of bread and I'll be fine."

In her pink slippers and blue green housedress, Luella shuffled down the hall and into her kitchen. "I've got some nutty oat bread. That strike your fancy?"

"Sounds great."

"You want some jam or some roast beast with that?"

"Nah, I was just gonna make an omelette upstairs."

"Bet she has no butter either." When Jaylynn shrugged, the landlady shook her head. "What are we gonna do about that girl?" Luella foraged around in her pantry closet and pulled out a loaf of bread. "She got anything to drink in that godforsaken icebox of hers?"

Jaylynn leaned against the doorway and tried to visualize the contents of the upstairs refrigerator. "I think she has ice tea, but that may be it."

"An omelette's no good without a little milk in it and a little in a glass to down it with. You agree?"

Kind brown eyes twinkled at Jaylynn, and it made the younger woman smile. Impulsively, Jaylynn blurted out, "Luella, I wish I'd met you years ago. You have to be one of the most wonderful people I've ever met." Jaylynn could see the flush of happiness suffuse the chestnut colored skin. "Oh, I didn't mean to embarrass you."

Luella set the loaf of bread down and stepped over to Jaylynn, taking the small woman's chin in both her soft brown hands. "How can she resist you, Jay? That's what I don't understand." The wise old eyes gazed seriously into the now bashful face of her friend. "Don't give up on that fool. She's gonna figure this out sooner or later, you know." With a final stroke, she released Jaylynn's face and turned to the cupboard to get a plate down. Her back to the blushing woman, Luella said, "Guess you didn't think I knew about that, huh? Well, these eyes may be old, but they're not blind."

She moved over to the refrigerator and opened the door. Over her shoulder, Jaylynn could see it was packed more than she had ever seen it. Luella ducked in and pulled out a plastic half-gallon container of milk and a stick of butter. Just before she shut the door, she reached back in and snagged an egg from the indentations in the door.

"Am I so obvious?" Jaylynn choked out.

Luella handed her the milk jug, then arranged the bread and stick of butter on the plate so that the egg wouldn't fall off. "No," Luella said thoughtfully. "I wouldn't say that. But I do know the two of you. That girl is really something else, but she's street savvy and not heart smart. You'll have to be patient with her." She handed Jaylynn the plate. "Careful not to drop the egg. It's no fun cleaning up yolk. Now if you mix it in with one of those little boxes of egg whites she uses, your omelette will have a lot more body. Tastes better, too."

"Thank you, Luella. I'll bring this milk right back."

"You're always welcome, Jay. No hurry on the milk either. I don't need it for hours. And hey, hon, I'm rooting for you."

Momentarily confused, Jaylynn realized Luella was referring to her love life—not to Dez's competition—and she felt her face flushing again. She retreated down the hallway, and Luella followed to open the door for her.

"See you in a bit, Luella."

The older woman gave her a brilliant smile, her teeth flashing bright and her brown eyes sparkling. Once again Jaylynn was struck by how beautiful she was. A little gray hair and a few wrinkles didn't mar the effect.

Jaylynn made her way up the stairs and set everything down on the counter, then peeked around the corner. Dez continued to sleep on the couch, her face frowning slightly even in her sleep. This brought a smile to Jaylynn's face. She got out the egg whites, sliced up a tomato and green pepper, added Luella's egg and milk, and put some chunks of Dez's baked chicken breast in a fry pan to make the omelette. With a glass of milk and three pieces of toast slathered with the rich butter, her stomach was satisfied.

She went into the living room and sat on the couch near the slumbering woman. She didn't want to wake Dez, but she got up and put a video in. *Truly, Madly, Deeply.* She'd wanted to watch it since the first visit to the apartment, and now she had three more hours to kill.

The wind blew in her face and she smelled a musty, verdant odor. As she opened her eyes, Dez thought she was flying in a green tunnel, but as her vision adjusted, she realized she was traveling at high speed through a forest of trees and bushes. Her body was overly warm, and the clothing she wore felt constrictive. Tight leather chafed against her elbows and the inside of her thighs. She looked down and her eyes focused on the gleaming black of a gas tank. Gloved hands held handlebars, and, astride a powerful motorcycle, she sped down a narrow path. Something tightened around her waist and for the first time she noticed a pair of arms, clad in brown leather, around her middle.

"Whoa!" she said, and the motorcycle roared forward even more quickly than before. An inexpressible joy raced through her. Blood coursed in her veins, pumping with excitement. Her legs gripped the cycle tightly, and she knew without a doubt she could outrun every single one of Hell's Angels. She felt the warmth at her back and knew who it was without looking back.

She guided the bike through a slim opening in the brush and burst out onto a vast plain covered with dust and scraggly wild grass. Kicking up the dust behind them, she slowed the bike to a putter and angled along the treeline. Hearing a protest from the body fastened to her back, she turned and looked over her shoulder. Her breathing quickened and the feeling of glee rushing through her body continued.

Without warning, a flurry of movement caught her eye. Looking sideways to the treeline from which they had just ridden, she saw a line of dark figures on smoking cycles erupt shrieking and screaming. The figure behind her tightened her hold and shouted, and with a gasp she revved the engine and peeled out over the uneven ground.

"Uh oh! Let's get out of here!" she growled.

Something wasn't right.   Dez inhaled as she struggled to consciousness. One blue eye squinted open, and she found herself curled up on the couch next to one silently sobbing woman. She jolted up, alarmed, and asked, "What's the matter?"

Jaylynn turned to her, tears running down her face.   She choked out, "That is the saddest movie I've ever seen."

"What in the hell are you watching?"

"*Truly, Madly, Deeply*. It just got over." She picked up the remote and clicked it to rewind.

Dez let out a deep breath and sat back. "I thought I told you it was a three hanky movie."

"But you lied. It was a three *boxes* of hankies movie."

"Yeah, well, at least it had a happy ending," she said grouchily.

"But it's such a *sad* happy ending." Jaylynn wiped the tears away. She stood and took the video out of the VCR and returned it to its place on the shelf.

Dez asked, "What time is it?"

Jaylynn looked at her watch and said, "4:10."

Dez rose to her feet and stretched her arms so high she could touch the ceiling. "Guess we'd better get a move on. I need to stop at the store and buy another can of Pam."

"Pam? Cooking oil Pam? You want to fry something after the show's over?"

"No, that's what we use on stage. I have enough, I think, but just in case, I like to be prepared."

"You use Pam on *stage*?"

"Yeah. Works better than any other oil. Everybody uses it."

"You're kidding, right?"

"Nope."

"I did wonder how you all got so shiny. Pam, huh?" Jaylynn didn't say it, but she had begun to think bodybuilding was a wee bit odd.

****

The evening program began at 6:30, and it was a packed house. Jaylynn sat through the first hour waiting impatiently for Dez's appearances.

There was a short break between the middleweight and heavyweight divisions when something went wrong with the PA system. Jaylynn sat in the audience between Luella and Vanita, and the two older women talked across her to one another. She had already offered to switch seats with one of them so they could talk more conveniently, but they both hushed her and said they each wanted the fun of sitting by her. A soft, warm hand patted her arm, and Luella gazed at her kindly, then went back to giggling with her sister.

Jaylynn was so nervous that she hardly heard what the two sisters were discussing. When Luella finished a statement with, "...and don't you think it's true?" and then looked at her expectantly, all she could do was shrug and say, "I'm sorry Luella. I can't concentrate at all."

"You're not worrying about Dez now, are you?"

She nodded.

"Oh, stop fretting. She's done this before. The girl's a powerhouse. No need to worry. You said she did good this morning."

Jaylynn fidgeted with her program. "I know, but this feels different." Tonight Julie and the kids were there, and pretty much every cop she'd ever met and several dozen she had never seen before. The morning compulsory posing hadn't been nearly as well attended, and she had liked sitting right near the front. Tonight she was stuck 12 rows back, and the place was so full it made her feel claustrophobic. "This is just more nerve-wracking than the morning was."

Vanita said, "You haven't seen nerve-wracking until you hear about what happened to me the time I—"

The announcer interrupted. "Okay folks, we're back and ready for the women's heavyweight routines. We've got three contestants tonight, all three from the Twin Cities. And here's a little about our first contestant."

Jaylynn didn't pay attention to the rest of it. Dez was scheduled to perform third. The rookie sat through the other two women's programs and tried to evaluate each fairly. In her estimation, neither of them was anywhere near as good as Dez. The first woman was well built with incredible biceps. You could see every muscle in her back, and she had washboard abs. But Jaylynn thought her legs looked weak in comparison. The second contestant had great shoulders, muscular legs with good definition, and actual striations in her pec muscles, but her abs and her upper back didn't have the kind of cut her competitors had. The rookie wasn't a judge, but she knew she favored the symmetry Dez displayed—not to mention the fact that she felt weak in the knees every time she saw Dez in the very skimpy electric blue two-piece suit. That didn't happen when she looked at the other two contestants.

When the second routine was over, Jaylynn's stomach went crazy, and for a moment she thought she might be sick. She was so relieved when that feeling passed, but then it was replaced with a general inability to breathe. She found herself holding her breath until the announcer began to introduce Dez. And then the tall woman emerged onto stage walking gracefully, her body impossibly long and lean and muscular. The cops in the audience went wild.

****

Dez stood in the stage wings with her eyes closed, concentrating on keeping her body loose and yet tight at the same time. It was a delicate balancing act, staying pumped up and flexed without cramping. She was past the bout of nerves she'd experienced earlier, and now she only had to get through this sixty seconds, just this short routine. And then, unless she won her weight class— which she dearly wished would happen—she would be done with the hard part.

The sixty seconds ended for the second competitor, and the music stopped. From the wings Dez could hear the appreciative applause. Unlike the morning's quiet attendees, tonight's crowd was a rowdy stomping wild bunch—a lot of them cops. She pushed that out of her mind and focused on breathing and on gathering all her energy inward so that she could direct it outward as needed. Her main competitor was statuesque and a steady poser, she knew she needed to be solid in this routine.

She didn't even hear the brief biographical announcement about herself that preceded her performance. Instead she found herself thinking of Ryan and knowing that he would have been out in the front row watching and cheering for her until it was time for the men's division to start. And suddenly she felt a crack in her legendary control. She looked about in alarm. There was nothing to be done. The stage monitor tapped her on the shoulder and gestured her out to the stage.

The house erupted into applause as she strode uncertainly to the middle of the stage. She knew she did not want to look at Julie or the kids or at Luella or at any of her brothers in blue. Unlike the morning when she concentrated on the judges, tonight she was expected to work the crowd. She didn't know how she could do it.

She stood at ready, every muscle in her body flexed, arms out a few inches from her sides, and one foot in front of her, toe pointed downward. She knew it was cocky, but she had worked up a completely different routine from her morning program using new music. She had chosen Queen's old song, "We Are The Champions" because it was Ryan's bodybuilding theme and she knew that would matter to Julie. The first strains of the song began. And that crack in her control widened.

She didn't have time to think. She knew she had to hit every pose to the best of her ability. But as she moved through the poses—front facing abs, twisting double biceps, side chest—she broke. Not physically, but emotionally. On the outside, she continued through the longest sixty seconds of her life, but on the inside, a tidal wave of raging grief welled up and threatened to spill over. There was a moment of relief as she turned away from the audience and moved into the rear lat spread and rear double biceps, but as she hit the right side triceps and looked out at the audience, tears sprang up. Her vision blurred, and she blinked, horrified at what was happening.

Dez didn't hear the cheering, the loud clapping, the rising crescendo. In her head everything clanged in an indistinct din. In a panic, she jerked into the next pose, a front lat spread, and through the tears she gazed out into the crowd. She blinked again, and when her vision cleared, what she saw was a shock of short blonde hair and warm hazel eyes. Despite the tears running down her cheeks, Dez held eye contact. She saw the younger woman's fist go up in an emphatic movement, and over all the crowd noise, she swore she could hear the rookie say, "It's okay, you're doing fine."

The tall woman breathed in and steadied enough to move into the lunging single bicep twist she liked to end with. As she turned away from those hazel eyes and bowed her head in the final pose, the last strains of music sounded. She held the pose, tightened every muscle until it felt like she would fly apart. Looking down she saw one glistening silver pearl of liquid fall and splat on the floor below her.

The song ended. She exhaled in a huff and stood up straight, and the house went wild. Giving a wave she turned to walk off stage. Once more, her eyes sought out the rookie, but she couldn't find her in the confusion.

Once off stage Dez bent over, hands on knees, and tried to get her breath. Someone handed her a towel, and she daubed at her face. She knew she had to return to the stage right away with the other two heavyweights, and she took the brief moment to steel herself. All she really wanted to do was escape. She felt like she had when she was fourteen, when she used to grab her bike and ride miles and miles just to get away from everyone and everything. *And here I am without a bike,* she thought sarcastically.

Back at the podium the announcer was saying, "I believe the judges have their final decision. It's time now for the presentation of awards. Let's bring out our three heavyweight competitors, Cindy, Nancy, and Desiree. Here they are, ladies and gentlemen!"

He turned and gave them a hand as the three women filed out to center stage and stood in their "relaxed" poses. For the first time this evening, the three women stood next to one another on stage, and it was clear that Dez, on the far right, was much taller and more powerful looking than either of her rivals.

The announcer went on: "Presenting the trophies is last year's champion and three time Ms. Minnesota winner, Sandy Marx!" The crowd applauded with enthusiasm, then grew quiet. "And now ladies and gentlemen, third place in the heavyweight division goes to Nancy Daniels."

The audience clapped and cheered. Through it all, a stony-faced Dez gazed out into the audience at Jaylynn. She didn't break eye contact and the rookie returned the gaze. Then Jaylynn smiled mischievously and blew her a kiss, and for the first time in hours, Dez broke out in a full smile. She almost didn't hear the announcer call the runner-up, Cindy Schmidt, and was startled when Nancy and Cindy smacked her on the back and gave her admiring hugs.

"Dez Reilly," the announcer said, "step into the center there." She moved into the middle position between the two body builders and accepted the gold statuette from the presenter. She looked at it as if amazed and then set it down in front of her like the other two women had. The announcer said, "Okay now, ladies, for the cameras, go ahead and strike a double bicep pose."

****

Jaylynn rose. Frantically she said, "Excuse me, Luella. I'll be right back." She crawled over Luella and into the aisle. It was all she could do to keep from running up the section. She made it out the side exit and back to the "Pump Up Room" before it occurred to her that perhaps she was being too hasty. What if Dez didn't want her there?

Too bad. She couldn't stop herself.

She scooted around pairs of dumbbells left lying throughout the room. As she rounded the corner and headed toward the stage wings, she saw the three heavyweights being interviewed by a man with a video camera, but as she neared, they finished, and Dez turned away. The brunette held a baggy gray sweatshirt in her right hand and was turning it right side out. Jaylynn reached her. She wanted to grab Dez into a hug, but she wasn't sure that was a good idea. Instead she stretched out a hand and gripped the bigger woman's glistening forearm.

Surprised, Dez spun around. Her face softened when she saw who it was. "Hey, you."

Jaylynn broke into a grin. "You did good."

"Right." Embarrassed, Dez looked down. "I choked."

Jaylynn squeezed the taller woman's arm, which was warm and

oily. "Just because it was emotional doesn't mean you choked." She took both of Dez's hands into her own. "I've got news for you, Dez. Cops *do* cry. Half of the police in the audience were, anyway. It was really beautiful. You were wonderful."

Dez gave her hands a squeeze, then let go, and they looked at one another intently. The rookie started to say something, but then the stage director interrupted. "Hey, all of you women pairs...some of you are gonna be called out on the stage now. They're awarding the Pairs Trophy."

"Afterwards, okay?" Dez asked as she moved away, her eyes smiling though her mouth didn't.

Jaylynn nodded, her heart full, her eyes brimming. She didn't wait to hear Dez and Cowboy's names called as one of the top three pairs of couples. She knew they would be. She made her way back to her seat and sat patiently, relaxed, for the rest of the program. And she wasn't one bit surprised when a totally composed Dez Reilly was awarded the Pairs Trophy, hugging and kissing Cowboy on the cheek, or when she won the posedown between the three weight classes to take the Overall Champion Award.

Chapter
26

The *All Natural Bodybuilding Championship* ended, and a large share of the audience departed for a raucous, earsplitting party at Luella's house. Carloads of people started appearing almost as soon as Dez arrived with Luella and Vanita. Cops and kids and friends and neighbors spilled out of the house and into the yard. They all showed up and waited impatiently for Dez to come downstairs after cleaning up. Party food covered the tables: pop and beer, hamburgers and potato salad, cookies and bars, and every kind of snack imaginable. Luella and Vanita worked the crowd like veteran caterers, stuffing everyone full of the tasty food.

Luella had insisted on clearing off the mantel for the trophies, which were constantly admired and fingered by the crowd. The 3-foot tall Overall Champ award was a shiny obsidian black nude, and with its sculpted broad shoulders and graceful muscles, the woman on the trophy actually resembled Dez. The two smaller gold trophies were half the height and bookended the larger one. Scores of people crowded around to look at and admire them.

Jaylynn circulated through the house wiping up spills, clearing away discarded plates, and occasionally chatting with folks. She wanted very much to join Dez upstairs, but she restrained herself, waiting patiently like everyone else.

When Dez finally came clattering down the back stairs and burst into Luella's living room, a great cheer went up. She skidded to a halt, obviously surprised, as happy people circled around her, patting her on the shoulder, shaking her hand, and giving her hugs. She ran a hand through long dark hair, which was loose and still damp from her shower. She wore a pair of cutoff denim shorts and a bright yellow t-shirt. She had not been able to wash away much of the tan, and her skin was still unusually dark. It would be a week or so before the skin dye washed completely away. Even under the tan, it was clear she was blushing. Her eyes raked through the crowd until they came to rest on Jaylynn. The rookie felt a crackle of electricity that made her stomach flip-flop, and then the bigger woman looked away and accepted more congratulations from the horde of well-wishers.

A grumpy voice from the crowd called out and a big, white-haired man pushed his way through. "I just want you to know you cost me five hundred bucks, Reilly."

"Lieutenant Andres," Dez said with a wry smile on her face. "You've been called many things, but cheap has never been one of them." She slapped him on the arm. "By now you should know better than to bet against me, but hey, look at the bright side: it's all going to a good cause."

Just then the "good causes" squeezed through the crowd. "Dez, Dez!" Jeremy said. "That was cool. Me and Jill were *so* happy when you won."

Jill stepped shyly forward and took Dez's hand. The big woman looked down at her and said, "What did *you* think?"

"Well, parts were awful boring, but when you were up there, it was great. And those are neat prizes."

"Yeah? And which one do you like best, the black or the gold trophy?"

Jill thought a moment, but Jeremy burst right in. "The black one is so big—and you can see her chest!"

Everyone laughed hilariously. Julie caught Dez's eye and shook her head. "Just like his dad," she said. "Always looking at the chest." This drew more laughter.

"What do you think, Jill?" Dez asked.

"I like the gold ones a lot. The black one *is* awfully big."

Dez headed across the room, and the crowd parted to let her through. She took the two gold statues from the mantel and headed back to stand before the two kids. She handed one trophy to each. "They're yours," she said.

Julie said, "Wait a minute, Dez."

Dez said, "I won those for Jeremy and Jill. I want them to have them. I don't need 'em."

"Yeah," Luella said. "If you all went up and looked at that bare apartment of hers, you'd see why she's giving them away. She's totally into minimalist art—as in the art is so minimal it isn't even there." Again the group laughed, and Luella went on, "There's a ton more burgers and salad. I don't want a bit of left-overs, so eat up."

Julie made her way over to Dez and pulled her off to a corner to argue. Dez listened for a moment, then just stepped up and enfolded Julie in a hug. Into her friend's ear she said, "I can't give them back their daddy, Julie. The least you could do is let me give them a couple of dumb trophies." She pulled away a bit, still holding Julie's shoulders. "Look at them strutting around showing them off. It makes 'em happy. So let it be, okay?"

Wordlessly Julie nodded. She wrapped Dez in a tight hug. "Thank you. This—all of it—means a lot."

"I'm glad," Dez said gruffly.

****

All through the evening, Jaylynn watched and listened as the partygoers cheered Dez and laughed and sang, and generally acted like teenagers rather than the rode-hard cops most of them were. Crystal and Shayna spent part of the evening going over the "take," and after checking their figures, they reported that over six thousand dollars had been collected. Even Dez was surprised.

Periodically Jaylynn looked up from whatever she was doing and caught sight of those bright blue eyes watching her from over the heads of the many guests. Each time, her heartbeat took off and she got butterflies in her stomach. They both smiled a brief little smile, just for each other, and then turned back to what they had been doing.

As Jaylynn reached down to pick up some stray paper plates, she felt a touch on her arm and straightened up. "Oh, hi," she said.

"Hi, Jaylynn. I'm Julie, and I haven't gotten a chance to introduce myself to you yet." The statuesque brunette reached out and shook the shorter woman's hand.

"I'm glad to meet you," Jaylynn said as she smiled and squeezed the woman's hand and let it drop.

"Luella has told me a lot about you and about how much Dez cares about you."

"Luella?"

Julie leaned in conspiratorially. "Yeah, I get most of my good info about Dez from her. Isn't she great?"

Jaylynn wasn't sure whether she was talking about Dez or Luella, but she opted for Luella. "I've met few people in my life quite as wonderful as Luella. She's a sweetie."

"Yes, she is." The slender brunette beamed at Jaylynn. "And so is Dez." In a quiet voice she said, "And I see the way you look at her." She nodded and smiled. "It's not like Dez would fill me in on anything, so I'm glad Luella rats her out to me. She's told me all about you."

Jaylynn wondered what exactly Luella had said. *And what did Julie mean about the way I look at Dez?* She looked around the room, and again, Dez caught her eye. The tall woman arched an eyebrow and raised her bottle of sparkling water, then turned back to Cowboy. Jaylynn blushed.

"See what I mean?" Julie asked.

"Wha–what?" Jaylynn started to feel sick to her stomach.

"You, young woman, are very nearly transparent. Come here." Julie grabbed the rookie by the wrist and pulled her down the hallway to the spare bedroom. She sat on the edge of the double bed as Jaylynn hovered in the doorway. "Sit down," she said and patted the bed beside her. The rookie shuffled over in a daze and sat next to her. "Look," Julie said, "Dez was very dear to Ryan. He'd want her to be happy. But she hasn't been for a very long time—not since he died."

Jaylynn's head was spinning. She didn't feel prepared to take in this information at all, but she tried to focus on what Julie was saying.

"Ryan and I always hoped she'd find someone special, but he didn't live to see it." Her face clouded over and she got a faraway, wistful look in her eyes. Then she sighed and refocused on Jaylynn. "Do you know there's something between you two—a kind of electricity?" She smiled and gazed quizzically into Jaylynn's face. The younger woman gulped, and Julie went on. "I feel like I know you because of Luella, and this probably feels too weird to you, but I just wanted to say thank you for looking after Dez. She's a tough one to read, but Luella was right. I can see how much she cares about you. Don't give up on her no matter what, okay?"

"Okay," Jaylynn replied, her face red and her heart pounding. Julie rose and Jaylynn popped up, too.

The older woman said, "I'm glad we had this talk. And I'm very glad to finally meet you. I hope you two will come over often, maybe take Jill and Jeremy on an outing."

"I'd like that."

Julie smiled and reached over to squeeze the rookie's hand, then said brightly, "Guess we'd better get back to the party, huh?"

They went out to the living room, and Jaylynn looked over into the next room to find Jeremy and Jill sitting at the dining room table looking tired and bored. She moved toward them and saw Luella open a drawer in the built-in buffet. Over the sound of laughter from the living room the silver-haired woman said to the two kids, "You want to play a game? I've got about ten decks of cards here."

Jeremy nodded, though Jill looked skeptical. The rookie advanced to the table, saying, "Do you two know how to play 'Hand and Foot'? It's a really good card game."

She sat down at the table with the two kids and began to patiently explain the rules of the rummy game. As she dealt the

cards, she glanced out into the living room to find blue eyes
observing her in amusement. The tall woman winked at her and
turned back to Crystal, leaving Jaylynn's heart skipping beats.

The party went on until past midnight. If any neighbors were
upset it was their misfortune because every cop on duty managed to
swing by at one time or another. At one point there were five police
cars double-parked in a row outside the house.

Finally, when the last of the partygoers bid goodnight, Luella,
Vanita, Jaylynn, and Dez plopped down on the couch and chairs
and surveyed the wreckage.

"That's the most fun I've had in ages," declared Luella.

From the rocking chair Dez said, "I had no idea...you must
have spent a fortune!"

"Whew," Jaylynn said. "The evening just blew by. I can't
believe how late it is."

Luella said, "Time flies when you're having fun." Her eyes
came to rest on the lanky brunette rocking slowly across from her.
"Well, sweet pea, was it worth it? All those days and nights of
rabbit food—are you glad you did it?"

Dez looked at her seriously as she continued rocking. "Yeah, I
think it was. It was hard." She paused and thought for a moment.
"But I could do it again if I had to."

Vanita said, "You mean if you were *nuts* enough to!"

Dez smiled. "Are you referring to the food constraints, Van, or
do you mean the actual competition process?"

"The food, of course," Vanita said. "I am surprised to say this,
but I actually liked the show. It was kind of a shock at first to see
all those nearly naked people running around, but once I got used
to it, I did start to understand all that business you've been talking
about—you know, about muscle definition and leanness and such. I
enjoyed it, 'specially when you won."

Jaylynn sat in the recliner and watched the two older women
sitting side by side on the sofa, both so alike and yet so different, as
they rehashed the pomp and pageantry of the evening. She studied
Dez from her spot across the room. She looked tired, but content,
her face relaxed and open. Still listening, Jaylynn rose and
gathered up a few stray paper plates and cups left on the table and
windowsills. She carried it all into the kitchen, pulled the garbage
container out from under the sink, and began tossing in trash and
tidying up the counters. She went back to the dining room table to
clear away the leftover food, and saw Dez nod toward her. The
taller woman stood and said, "Let me give you a hand, Jay."

Luella sighed and started to rise. Dez said, "No, no, not you.
You've done enough work for the night, ladies. Just relax."

"We can help," Vanita said, but she didn't budge from her

comfy spot on the sofa.

Luella continued to struggle up off the couch. Dez shook her finger at her. "You just sit that sorry carcass back down, Luella. Your legs are sore, I can tell."

"No, not at all. I'm ready for a foot race."

"Yeah right." Dez rolled her eyes. "You've done enough for me for the day. Please! Let us clean up. Jay and I won't break a thing."

"Kinda hard to break paper plates, young lady," Luella said in a mock serious voice as she settled back on the couch near her sister.

"That's right," Dez said. "So just let us put things in order for you."

Dez joined Jaylynn in the dining area and started carting dishes and platters into the kitchen. Jaylynn gave a shy smile. "How about you put the leftovers in containers, and I'll wash stuff up?"

"Okay."

Dez whistled softly as they worked wordlessly for several minutes. She went back out to the dining room table with a wet rag to wipe it down, then returned to the kitchen. She tossed the rag in the dishwater and took Jaylynn's arm. With a finger to her lips she said, "Shh." She beckoned with her other arm as she pulled Jaylynn along. They peeked around the corner into the living room.

Luella and Vanita sat on the sofa asleep, their feet up on the coffee table and their heads leaning back against the couch cushions. "Ready for a footrace," whispered Dez. "Ha."

They retreated back to the kitchen and Dez finished wiping down the stove. When she had finished, she stood awkwardly with her hands in her pockets. Jaylynn crossed her arms and leaned back against the counter searching out blue eyes. "Guess I'd better head home."

Dez smiled at her warmly. "You were great today, Jay. Thank you. Thanks for everything, for coming to the show, for being here today and tonight." Suddenly shy, she looked down. "It really mattered to me that you were there." She pulled her hands out of her shorts pockets and stepped closer, spreading her arms wide. "Can I hug you?"

Jaylynn uncrossed her arms and welcomed Dez into an embrace, first tentative, and then secure and tight. Wrapping her arms around the thin waist, she could feel the taller woman's palms flat on her back, a belt buckle at her stomach, hips pressed close. Flustered, she released her hold and stepped back, saying, "Dez, you really are just skin and bones! How in the world did you manage to look so gargantuan on stage?"

"Ah, smoke and mirrors. You know, a little grease, a lot of tanning dye." She winked and then shrugged.

Jaylynn said, "What happens now?" As the words came out of her mouth, she hoped Dez would take the question in the way she meant it. She hastened to add, "I mean, do you stay on that severe diet or what?"

Dez stepped back, leaning against the counter again. "Nah. Some guys start packing away tons of food and ice cream and crap, but I won't do that. I'll increase my carbs, eat a bit more of the so-called forbidden foods, and try not to gain too many pounds. I think I feel best weighing in about 165, maybe 170." She looked out the darkened kitchen window. "I guess I'll be glad to get back to a normal routine. It was hard to do that."

She looked so tired that Jaylynn was reminded of the hour. "I'd better go now."

Dez nodded. "Sneak out the back, okay? Let's not wake up the oldsters if we don't have to."

Jaylynn pulled her car keys out of her pocket as she moved toward the back door. "See you Wednesday?" she asked over her shoulder as she reached the door and turned the knob.

Dez looked startled for a minute. "Yeah, sure. Call me if you want to do anything before then though."

Now it was Jaylynn's turn to look surprised. "Like what? What do you mean?"

"You know, like go see a movie or something."

Jaylynn moved lightning quick across the hall and put her hand to Dez's forehead. Then she grinned and said, "No fever, but who are you and where is the *real* Dez?"

Dez blushed and stuttered out, "I–I–I just thought..."

Jaylynn laughed at her and retreated to grab the doorknob again. "Listen, you goofball, sounds like a good idea to me. Don't take me too seriously. I'm just teasing. Go ahead and give me a call if you like. I'm around all day tomorrow. That is, after I get about 12 hours of sleep." She opened the door and looked back smiling.

In an offhand manner, Dez said. "I'll watch to see that you get to your car safely."

"Hey, I'm a cop. Nobody messes with us, right?" Jaylynn pulled the door shut and walked around the side of the house to the front in the warm August night. She could hear a mosquito buzzing nearby and smell Luella's overgrown lilac bush. As she turned onto the front walk, she glanced back at the house to see the outline of a dark head in the window. She raised one hand in a quick wave, then reached her car, got in, and headed home.

On the way to her house, the evening's events went round and round in her head. She thought about Dez, about her performance, about her physique. And she thought of the years and years of dreams and nightmares she'd always had. There was no longer any doubt in her mind that her Hero and Desiree Reilly were, somehow, by some strange destiny or coincidence, one and the same. It was amazing how different the black-haired, alabaster-skinned woman looked with a tan and most of her clothes off. Jaylynn felt a lecherous grin tweak her lips. The tall woman looked positively delicious, fit to eat. A shiver ran down her neck, and she smiled sheepishly and told herself to stop being so naughty.

Back at the house, she saw that Sara was still up. As usual, nearly every light in the house was on. Suddenly she couldn't wait to talk to her best friend. She parked next to Tim's old beater and skipped up the walk. She found Tim and Sara huddled on the couch watching a *Mary Tyler Moore* rerun. When she burst around the corner, they both looked up and asked simultaneously, "Did she win?"

"Yup. She won everything—her weight class, the pairs trophy, and all-around. And she really *was* the best. You guys should have been there. It was just incredible. Wish I'd had a camera." She plopped down on the end of the couch and tucked her legs under her, then turned to face them.

Tim clicked the TV off with the remote as he said, "It sure ran late. It's like almost two now."

"I went back to Dez and Luella's place and there was a great party with about a million people at it." Jaylynn grinned as she hugged her knees to her chest. "It was just a blast."

Sara said, "Hmmm. Do tell. You look way too happy to be real."

"I *am* happy. I've never seen Dez quite like this, so open, so relaxed. I mean, she even cried on stage."

"What?" Tim and Sara exclaimed at the same time.

"You guys sound like a Greek Chorus," Jaylynn said, and she went on to tell them about all of the events of the evening. As she finished her narration, she stretched her legs out over Tim's lap and pressed her feet against Sara's, sole to sole.

Tim said, "Girls, girls! You're squishing me." He shifted and pushed their legs aside, and both women ended up putting their legs on the coffee table. "So, she gave you a great goodbye hug. She should have given you money for how patient you were all day."

"Oh, Tim," Sara said. She turned to Jaylynn and rolled her eyes. "Don't mind him. He and Kevin had a lover's quarrel."

"We did not," Tim protested.

"What do you call screaming at him on the front porch and

then slamming the door in his face?"

Disgruntled, he said, "Whatever. He'll probably apologize tomorrow." He crossed his arms over his chest and stared forlornly at the wall.

Jaylynn poked him in the arm. "Quit being so stubborn. Go call him now. You know he'll be over here in minutes. Why does *he* have to be the one to apologize?"

"Geez, Jay," Tim said, "you don't even know what the argument was about!"

She smiled at him. "I'm telling you, life's too short to be sitting here stewing over some dumb disagreement. You love the guy. Go call him."

"I'll call him when I'm good and ready." He continued to sit there seething.

"Back to you, Jay," Sara said, rolling her eyes. "What else happened? Tell me more about this hug."

Tim stood and stepped over Jaylynn's outstretched legs. She pinched him on the thigh. "Gonna go call lover boy? I tell ya, you'll be thanking me for the encouragement."

In a grumpy voice, he said, "Like *your* love life is going so well."

"I'm hopeful," she said, and she slapped him on the butt as he passed her by.

Sara stretched her legs out on the couch. "Okay, tell me all the nitty-gritty details. What about this hug?"

"It was a great hug! You know how there are three types of hugs?"

Sara tipped her head to the side and gave Jaylynn a quizzical look. "What do you mean?"

"Well, think about it. There's the quick shoulders-only kind of hug between people who are sort of doing the obligatory thing. Sometimes one person is even turned a bit to the side. Know what I mean?"

Sara nodded.

"Then there's that upper body one where maybe the front of you presses a bit, but it's brief, friendly, respectful?"

"Yeah."

"And then there's the last kind." Jaylynn smiled.

"And that would be?"

"The one where you're enfolded in an embrace that goes from shoulders to chest to hips to thighs. Whew! It's intense."

With a twinkle in her eye, Sara said, "Am I to assume that the latter was the variation you experienced?"

Jaylynn was nodding before the question even ended. "But maybe I'm giving it too much credence. I really don't know. But I am going to call her to go to a movie tomorrow."

"Why don't you have her over for dinner? In fact, why don't I make you guys dinner one day next week? Do you realize that in just nine days it's the one year anniversary of you meeting her for the first time?"

Jaylynn stopped and thought for a moment. "That's just amazing. I can hardly believe a whole year has passed." From the kitchen she could hear the murmur of Tim's voice as he spoke on the phone. She lowered her voice and said, "I don't know how much longer Tim is going to live here, Sara. Either he's gonna move out, or else Kevin is going to have to move in. He practically lives here now. What do you think of that?"

"I've thought about that lately, too. Kevin can move in. I don't mind. The more the merrier." With a wicked smile on her face she said, "You can have Dez move in, too, for all I care."

"I think you're jumping the gun a bit."

"Maybe. Will you ask her over for a thank you dinner from me? I'll make you those barbecue chicken wings you like so much."

"Okay. I'll ask."

Just then, Tim returned to the room. He ran his hands through his red hair and did a cannonball jump over the back of the couch and slid down between them.

Sara rolled her eyes. "Guess who's on the way over?"

He smiled. "Yup."

With menace in her voice the rookie said, "And *who* gets thanks for the suggestion?" He stared at her with a blank look on his face.

Jaylynn rose up to kneel on the couch and looked at Sara, raising her eyebrows. Both women attacked at once, tickling him mercilessly until he begged for mercy and forgiveness.

****

On Sunday, Dez and Jaylynn went to see the latest *Star Wars* movie, and then the two women walked around Como Lake in the bright sunshine. Though humid, the temperature was surprisingly mild.

"I didn't like that one as well as the other three," Jaylynn said.

"Me neither. I figured out too fast about the queen."

"Yeah, I kept wondering why they'd have all these short little brown-haired attendants who looked just like the queen. I thought maybe it was bad casting at first. But the kid was cute."

Dez said, "Too bad he's gonna grow up to be the evil Darth Vader."

They kept the conversation light as they made two loops

around the lake. Jaylynn could tell Dez was tired. She said, "Did you sleep well after yesterday's hoopla?"

Dez shook her head. "Nah. Maybe tonight."

"You should go see Dr. Goldman. She does great visualization exercises. Helps me with my nightmares."

Dez glanced down at the rookie affectionately. "It was bad enough that the lieutenant made me go see her after I got shot. I'd prefer not having to go again."

Jaylynn stopped on the path and put her hands on her hips. "What is it with all you tough-ass cops? How come none of you ever want to talk about your feelings?" She tapped her foot on the ground. "And I want a serious answer."

With an amused expression on her face, Dez said, "I dunno. She's a stranger." She bent over and picked up a round rock from beside the path, then pitched it into the lake. She turned back to Jaylynn who was still waiting, patiently. "If I wanted to talk about stuff, I'd tell Luella. Or maybe you. Not some nosy shrink."

Jaylynn sighed and shook her head. "You are incorrigible." She dropped her hands from her sides and started walking again.

In three long strides Dez caught up with her. "Hey, not everyone can process things the way you can."

"Sure they can. Just takes practice."

"Geez, Jay, there are a lot of other much more pleasant things to practice than that sort of junk!"

"Now, why do you say that?"

Dez shrugged, though Jaylynn didn't see it.

In an irritated voice, the rookie said, "There's processing—and then there's *not* processing. How come everyone thinks I'm crazy for wanting to avoid the latter?"

Dez frowned. "Maybe they're just jealous."

"Why? That makes no sense to me."

"There's a lot of shit in this job, Jay. Not everyone can deal with it head-on like you do. Sometimes it's easier to just not think about things."

"But it's self-preservation for me. If I don't deal with this stuff, I have *terrible* dreams. Why is that so weird?"

"Hmm...never thought of it that way." She smacked at a mosquito that came to rest on her forearm. "Well, the damn bugs are coming out. I better head home before I'm eaten alive." They stopped on the path near the stone arch. "See you at work Wednesday?"

Jaylynn nodded. "Sure. Hope you sleep better tonight."

"Yeah, me, too. See ya, Jay."

They parted. Dez crossed the street without looking back and set out toward home. Jaylynn headed on around the lake. She decided to put in a few running laps and started off at a slow jog. She was puzzled as to why she seemed to be one of the only cops she knew who was willing to discuss how the job—and other things—made her feel. At least Oster talked to her a bit. But no one else did. Didn't the rest of them feel like they would explode otherwise? She picked up her pace and fell into a good rhythm. She decided that she wasn't going to change for the rest of them, not even for Dez. If she wanted to see Goldman every single day, she would.

It wasn't until she was on her third lap that she recalled Sara's dinner invitation. *Oh well. I'll ask Dez at work.*

Chapter
27

On patrol Wednesday night, Jaylynn told Dez about Sara's dinner request and asked her if she wanted to come over. For some reason she did not understand, she expected Dez to beg off. So she was taken aback when the other woman said, "Sure. When?"

Surprised, she said, "Gosh, I don't know exactly when, but she said one day next week. I'll check with Sara. What works for you?"

Dez shrugged. "Whenever. I guess Monday or Tuesday since that's when we're off."

Jaylynn nodded. "I told her you're a picky eater—"

"No, I'm not!" Dez said with a little more vehemence than she expected. In a softer voice, she said, "Not so much anymore."

"Give me a break. So you're eating a few carbs now—big woo! You still don't eat things normal people eat." She paused and pointed out through the windshield. "Hey! Check out that Volvo. Is that the one on the hot sheet?" She grabbed the sheaf of pages they kept on the seat between them and turned on the center light.

Dez hit the gas and pulled closer to an orange station wagon. "Nah, the other one had 024 in the license number and I think it was blue."

Jaylynn, by then, was perusing the hot sheet. "How do you *do* that?" she asked, exasperated.

"Do what?"

"Remember the details like that?"

"I don't know. It doesn't change that much from night to night. You drop a couple cars from your memory and add a couple." She passed the Volvo and turned right onto University. "And I'll have you know I've gained eight pounds already, so don't be telling me I eat weird."

Jaylynn had indeed noticed that her partner's face had taken on a less gaunt appearance since the weekend bodybuilding competition. She reached across the seat and gripped the tall cop's upper arm. Dez gave her a startled sideways glance.

Jaylynn said, "Yes, I *did* notice. You look much healthier now. You had started to look haunted before." She let go of the short-sleeved arm, but not before she squeezed the tight muscle there. "You're still solid as a rock."

Dez made a squinty face at her and flexed her right arm. "Damn right."

****

Tuesday night found Dez parking in front of the stucco house and making her way up a cracked front walk bordered with freshly mowed lawn. The day had again been humid, and the evening promised more of the same, with the unfortunate addition of mosquitoes. She slapped at one and juggled the items she carried, a bottle of Chablis and a six-pack of Twinkies. She was happy she had worn shorts, a tank top, and sandals because, if she remembered correctly, the old house didn't have air conditioning.

Before she could reach the top of the cement stairs, the screen door was thrown open and a familiar white-blonde head poked out into the late afternoon light. "Whatcha got there?"

She stepped up to the top stair. "I didn't know what we were having, but I brought some wine, and then I thought a special dessert was in order." She waved the package in Jaylynn's face.

"Twinkies? You wouldn't—"

Dez silenced her by running a big hand through the rookie's hair and messing it up, smirking as she sidled past. Out of the corner of her eye she took in the golden tan displayed quite nicely by cut-off jeans and a sleeveless white shirt. The shirt tightened against Jaylynn's body as she ducked and shifted away with a smile on her face. Dez said, "I may surprise you yet."

Jaylynn took hold of Dez's arm. "Believe me when I say you already keep me in constant amazement." She led the tall woman into the living room where Tim was lounging bare-chested in crazy-colored boxer shorts. He sat in front of the oscillating fan looking miserably hot.

Jaylynn said, "He just finished mowing the lawn."

Tim replied, "Yeah, and I don't think I'll ever recover. Hi, Dez." She nodded and smiled as he fanned himself with a *Cosmopolitan* magazine. Dez resisted the urge to ask if it was his or Sara's. She was pretty sure it wouldn't be Jaylynn's.

"You *are* full of surprises," Jaylynn said. "I'm surprised enough for one night that you showed up with alcohol. I didn't think you ever drank."

"Oh, I've been known to tip a few upon occasion."

She handed the bottle to Jaylynn who accepted it and then pointed the bottle at her red-haired friend. "Tim, go take a cool shower. Go on. You'll feel much better." He grumbled, but rose with a groan and padded off to the staircase. Jaylynn said, "Sara's in the kitchen. Come on. Let's get some wine glasses and drink it with dinner."

A short time later, the four of them sat down at the picnic table in the backyard near the grill, which was emitting considerable heat. The sun no longer burned so hot and was rapidly falling behind the stand of evergreens across the alley, though rays of bright light still streamed through. Sara placed four citronella candles at the corners of the picnic table and lit them to ward off the bugs. On the menu were teriyaki chicken wings, brown and white rice, corn on the cob, and a green salad laced with chunks of cucumber, tomato, and broccoli florets.

Sara and Jaylynn settled in on one side of the table. Dez sat across from the rookie with Tim beside her. As she dug into a generous helping of salad, Tim popped up from the table and stepped over the picnic bench. "Forgot the salad dressing," he said. "Anyone want thousand island?"

"Sure," Sara and Jaylynn said in unison. He ambled off toward the back door.

Dez asked, "He works at a restaurant, right?"

Both women nodded and looked at one another. Jaylynn's mouth was full, so Sara said, "He wants to be a chef someday. Right now he's in charge of salad prep and is trying to get into a culinary school."

The kitchen screen banged open and Tim emerged juggling several bottles of dressing. He stood at the head of the picnic table and set out seven bottles.

With a smile on her face, Jaylynn said, "That's a lot of thousand island."

He replied, "It's not just thousand island. We've got bottles and bottles of this stuff. What do you girls do—buy another jar every time you make a salad?"

Jaylynn picked up the tongs and rose as she said, "Yup. And every time we make a steak we buy another bottle of steak sauce."

Sara said, "And every time we get a hair cut we buy a new brush. It's a girl thing."

Jaylynn laughed out loud and moved over toward the grill. As she passed Tim she poked him in the butt with the tongs and giggled some more. She lifted the lid off the grill and busied herself turning the chicken wings.

Tim moved around the side of the table and startled Dez by putting his hands on her shoulders. He leaned his face down close to her ear and quickly whispered, "Jay's birthday is next week. Will you help us with the surprise party?" When she nodded, he glanced up to ensure Jaylynn's back was still to them, then squeezed Dez's shoulders and stepped back over the bench to settle in next to her. He cast a conspiratorial glance at Sara and back at Dez and waited until she choked down the bite she was chewing.

"Details?" Dez asked.

He whispered back, "Later."

Sara jumped right in then and said, "Tim, we were just telling Dez about your salad work at the restaurant. I think she'd be interested to hear about your new job."

"Yeah," Dez said. "Which restaurant do you work at?" She spoke to Tim but her eyes followed Jaylynn as the small woman bent to pick up the grill cover, replaced it, and then came back over to the table. Jaylynn's eyes flicked to the tall cop and caught her looking. She smiled and blushed ever so slightly, regarding Dez with amusement and then giving her the tiniest little wink.

Tim was saying, "The new one that just opened in downtown St. Paul called Pazzaluna. It's a really nice Italian place."

Dez turned her attention to him. "I haven't been there yet."

"We should all go," Sara said. "I haven't tried it yet either."

"Excellent food and good service," Tim said. "Of course how could they go wrong with Kevin as the maitre d'?"

Dez said, "I'll have to meet this Kevin sometime. You and he met at the restaurant?"

Tim nodded, his mouth full of chicken wing.

Dez pushed her plate away, put her elbows on the plastic tablecloth and said, "How did the three of you meet?"

Jaylynn and Sara smiled at one another, and Jaylynn said, "My sophomore year Sara moved to my dorm. I didn't have a roommate at the time—"

"And I had a real jerk for a roommate," Sara said. "I was only a freshman, but Jaylynn let me move into her room, and we've been roommates ever since—"

Jaylynn finished, "In two more dorms and then this house."

Tim said, "I advertised in the school paper for housemates, and these two applied. I liked 'em right away."

"And the rent was reasonable," Sara said. "So we've been living here for almost two years. I'm still working my way through classes part-time."

Tim said, "And I quit halfway through so I could get restaurant experience and get accepted into the Culinary School instead."

Dez nodded as she listened to the information. She thought

about the fact that this was pretty much the same way she'd met Luella—by answering an ad for an apartment. Sometimes people got lucky and turned strangers into better family than family was.

Later in the evening, when the paper plates were tossed and the glasses and utensils cleared away, they all agreed to watch a video. Sara had brought a stack home from the video store, and they had their choice of adventure, thriller, drama, or two comedies. *The Wedding Singer* won by a vote of three to one, though Jaylynn had held out for a drama. She accepted the loss with grace.

Dez sat in an overstuffed chair in the warm living room and regarded the three roommates who sat across from her on the couch. *Huggiest damn group of people I've ever been around. If they aren't poking or tickling or hugging or pinching each other, then they're patting or touching me!* It was a bit disconcerting. She couldn't recall when the last time was that anyone invaded her personal space so repeatedly, well, unless you counted Jaylynn. *Come to think of it, the rookie has always been in my personal space, practically since day one.* She glanced at Jaylynn, a frown on her face, and wondered why she hadn't noticed that sooner. Instead, she realized she somehow had been comfortable with the younger woman, and perhaps that was one reason it was so painful to have been separated from her those many awful weeks during the winter.

She thought about the fact that, with the exception of Luella, people usually didn't come near her. She didn't want people to touch her, to get inside her bubble. Not friends, not relatives, not other cops, not suspects. There was safety in distance. Her eyes came to rest on the three laughing roommates across from her, and she watched as Sara made a smart retort to something Jaylynn said. The giggling brown-haired woman launched herself practically into the rookie's lap to tickle her. Tim rolled his eyes and looked over at Dez, who smiled politely and shrugged.

Tim said, "If you two are done mauling one another, I think Dez and I would like a little dessert before we start the video."

Dez eyed Jaylynn, silently daring her to put out the Twinkies. Somehow she knew that the hazel-eyed woman understood. Jaylynn popped up off the couch and took Sara's hand. "Come on," she said. "It's ice cream time." She dragged Sara off toward the kitchen.

Tim watched them go, then gestured to Dez. "Spsss...come over." He patted the couch next to him. She rose and moved around the coffee table to sit in the middle of the sofa.

He said, "The nice thing about our house is you can put your feet up on anything." He slipped out of his Birkenstocks and stretched freckled, tan legs out on the coffee table, nodding an invitation to her to join him, which she did.

Once they got settled, she looked over her shoulder at him and he said, "As soon as the kitchen door opens, launch into a description of a bad meal you've had, okay?" She frowned and then assented. "Okay," he said, "it's a surprise party next Saturday at noon. We're planning it for before she goes to work, but if you could, can you help us fix it so her lieutenant secretly gives her Saturday off?" When Dez nodded, he went on, "Even if he doesn't, we're covered. But if he will do that, then she'll never expect a party at all, especially since her birthday isn't until next Tuesday. Her mom, dad, and the girls are flying in Saturday morning. Will you pick them up at the airport at ten?"

She nodded and he glanced nervously over his shoulder at the kitchen door. They could hear the two women talking and laughing so he went on. "I've got to figure out a way to get her out of the house."

Dez whispered, "Call Luella. She's very inventive."

"Sara already asked Luella to come to the party, and she's coming over to make something—I don't know what. She and Sara are doing the food. My job is to get the surprise part worked out."

"How 'bout I keep Jay busy until just before noon and we have someone else pick up her folks?"

"Yeah! That could work. Let's do that. If you can get her out of the house for the morning, then Sara and Luella can set up, and I can run out to the airport. Works for me."

Just then the kitchen door whacked open, and Dez stammered, "It was the worst meal I ever had."

Tim looked at her blankly and then started to laugh. Dez gazed shyly over Tim's shoulder at the two women and saw Jaylynn's eyes upon her. The smaller woman gave a surprised look to see Dez cozied up to the red-haired man, but she didn't say anything. She waved at them to move their feet, and Sara set a tray down on the coffee table bearing four stacked bowls, four spoons, a dish of peanuts, a brown plastic container of chocolate sauce, and a pile of Twinkies on a Melmac Cookie Monster plate. Jaylynn carried a tub of vanilla ice cream and a scoop.

"Everybody help yourself," Sara said. She sat down next to Dez.

"I'll scoop the ice cream," Jaylynn said. "It gets so messy." She proceeded to dole out generous globs for everyone and then went back in the kitchen to put the ice cream away.

Sara took the brief opportunity to whisper, "Are we all set?"

Tim nodded. "Details later, but yes. Dez is in."

Sara smiled at Dez, her brown eyes full of warmth and caring. "Thank you. It'll mean a lot to her if you come." She reached a hand over and patted the bigger woman's thigh. "By the way," she said, "nice quads you got there."

The tall cop was still blushing when Jaylynn came back into the living room and squeezed between Sara and Dez to settle in for the video, totally oblivious to the clandestine planning that had. gone on. The rookie grabbed up the TV remote and pressed the button. As she set the remote down, Dez juggled her bowl of ice cream, leaned forward, and snagged a Twinkie with her free hand. With a smirk directed at the rookie, she took a generous bite and offered the remainder to Jaylynn who accepted it with a roll of her eyes. "Don't blame me, Dez, if you get fat overnight," the rookie said, as she bit down on the remaining half.

****

All week Dez racked her brain to think of something she could do with Jaylynn from nine a.m. 'til noon on Saturday. Nothing seemed compelling enough to warrant a nine o'clock start. Finally she talked to Crystal, learning that she and her partner had also been invited to the party.

Crystal said, "Why don't you bring her to our house for brunch?"

Dez thought about it. "That could work...but then you'd miss the surprise."

Crystal considered that for a moment. "What if we got totally ready so that the minute you pulled away around noon, Shayna and I would jump in our car and race over there. Then all you'd have to do is stop to fill up with gas or pick up a coke at the drive-thru or something. Then we could be there on time."

"Okay. What do you want me to bring on Saturday morning?"

"Let Shayna worry about that. You just bring Jay over about nine and we'll keep you both occupied. At roll call tomorrow night, I'll invite you guys over. For once, I'll actually show up early."

The next night, true to her word, Crystal was there ahead of time and corralled the two of them. She said, "Dez, Jay, I got a favor to ask. Would you be willing to come over on Saturday morning for brunch? Shayna has a couple new recipes she wants to try—and Dez, don't worry. They're not too high cal."

Dez said, "Sure. What time?"

"Oh, about nine, how's that?" She looked from one woman to the other.

Skeptically, Jaylynn said, "I won't be very awake, but okay. What's your address?"

Dez interjected smoothly, "I know how to get there. How

about I pick you up at 8:45?"

"Okay," Jaylynn said, "but I'm not promising to be a very entertaining brunch companion."

Crystal squeezed Jaylynn's arm and said, "Nonsense. You're always entertaining, right, Dez?"

Gruffly Dez said, "Yeah, right. C'mon. The sarge is on the way." They all found seats as the sergeant entered the room and began his announcements.

****

The day of the party dawned clear and bright, only a few fuzzy clouds blowing around in the bright blue sky. A shaft of rich gold light glowed through the small window above Dez's double bed. On her back, she lay with the sheet over her warm body and watched dust motes floating in the beam of light. She only remembered waking once during the night after another bad dream. She vaguely recalled struggling, like she was drowning, and she woke up with a pain in her chest as though she had been shot again. Reaching her arms out to either side of her, she stretched, twisting her torso, tensing her chest muscles. She sat up and swung her legs over the side of the bed, and her eyes fell upon the two presents on the coffee table. They were wrapped in plain red paper, no bows, and the tape more than apparent. *Pathetic wrapping job.* She figured she should have had them professionally wrapped. *Oh well, it's the thought that counts, right?* She had a hunch Jaylynn would like both gifts.

She ate her regular breakfast of oatmeal and a protein shake and then got ready for the day. By the time she left the apartment, she was actually feeling perky.

Just as she had said, Jaylynn wasn't very lively when Dez picked her up, but as they drew closer to Crystal and Shayna's house in south Minneapolis, she seemed to wake up. "Nice t-shirt," the rookie said.

Dez looked down at her WNBA shirt for the Minnesota basketball team, the Lynx. "Didn't you know? I tried out for the team, but they don't allow cops. So they gave me this free t-shirt."

Jaylynn rolled her eyes. "You're certainly full of it today."

Dez raised her eyebrows and gave an innocent look. She slowed the truck in front of a cyclone-fenced yard. "We're here," she said.

The couple lived in a side by side duplex. Their dog had been put in the backyard, and all the windows were open so that the early morning breeze could blow through. Since there was so much fresh air circulating through the duplex, Dez didn't think her dog allergies would act up at all. She hadn't been to her friends' house for a long time, and she commented about the new couch, a giant tan L-shaped monstrosity of a thing piled up with various sized pillows. Six or eight people could easily sit there—if some of the pillows were removed. Otherwise the room looked the same: wild-colored African paintings on the living room walls; a six-foot-long tapestry of green, gold, black, and red hanging next to the doorway to the dining room; knickknacks and figurines all around the room on shelves and tables. Dez always found their place to be very "busy" and she liked to tease Shayna about how much dusting she must have to do.

The four women sat around the living room for a while, chatting, until Shayna got up to work in the kitchen. They all followed her in and kept talking. The three cops stood around, mostly in the way, until Shayna shooed them into the dining room where she could still hear but not have them underfoot.

Jaylynn sat in one of four majestic wooden chairs at the table and watched Dez out of the corner of her eye. Her partner was in good spirits this morning. In fact, she had been in good spirits— almost happy—for days now. *Give that girl a carbohydrate*, Jaylynn thought as she smiled to herself. She decided she herself would be horribly mean if she wasn't able to eat the variety of goodies she liked so well. *No wonder Dez has been so grumpy.* She was just glad the weird diet was finally over.

Crystal said something and the rookie turned her attention to her. The smiling Latina asked, "Did you read that latest article this morning about Dolly the Sheep?"

Jaylynn raised her eyebrows and looked at Crystal skeptically. She realized she hadn't been following the thread of the conversation, so she asked, "What? Some kind of interview with her?"

Dez barked out a laugh, surprising Jaylynn. "I think it was *about* the sheep, not with her."

Jaylynn purposely ignored her. "What are you talking about, Crystal?"

"You know...that sheep they cloned—Dolly they named her."

"What about her?"

"I read something about how when they clone the clones, it shortens their lifespan, and I was just going to comment that the department now has to end their experiment."

Jaylynn looked at Crystal, confused. She could see the smirking woman was about to say something humorous, but she wasn't able to track with it. "All right," she said. "I'll bite. What experiment?"

Crystal grinned and said, "The one where they clone Reilly

here. They're not gonna do it now that they'd end up with a bunch of mutant lesbians with tiny little lifespans."

From the kitchen Shayna laughed. Dez gave her friend a level stare which caused Jaylynn to laugh out loud and say, "She can dish it out, Crystal, but she can't take it."

Dez said, "I don't get mad. I get even."

With a smirk on her face, Crystal nodded toward Jaylynn with a knowing look. "Truer words were never said. You should have been around the time she and Ryan put flour in Lieutenant Andres' coffee sweetener."

Jaylynn watched the flash of emotions move across Dez's face, first uncertainty, then a slight wince of pain, settling into a tiny smile. It occurred to her that Dez very rarely talked about Ryan, and she hoped she would right now.

In a low voice, Dez said, "It was Ryan's idea."

"But you got blamed." Crystal sat forward in her seat and put her elbows on the table. Her face was lit up with pleasure, her brown eyes twinkling.

"He paid for that later. I made him buy me supper," Dez said, an eyebrow arched. "Andres would never believe that his darling protégé would pull any tricks on him, but Ryan thought up more sneaky stuff...you wouldn't believe it. Guess I didn't mind being blamed. It was worth it to hear that Andres spit his coffee halfway across the room in Commander Paar's office."

Dez grinned, and Jaylynn saw the tip of a pink tongue run between the tall woman's teeth. The rookie couldn't keep herself from staring. She didn't often see Dez smile like that, her face totally relaxed and her eyes glinting with humor.

The women spent the next hour talking and laughing, with Shayna contributing occasional comments from the kitchen. It was well after ten when brunch was finally served. Jaylynn munched on scrambled eggs and blueberry pancakes. She said to Shayna, "So, what's new about this pancake recipe?"

Shayna looked at her blankly.

Comprehension dawned on Crystal and Dez's faces about the same time. They both started to speak at once, but Dez shut up right away as Crystal said, "Shayna was going to make a new thing, but it didn't work out. Hope you don't mind."

Shayna's brow was furrowed, and she looked back and forth between her partner and Dez, but she was wise enough not to say anything.

"Hey," Dez said. "How 'bout the Lynx? You guys go to any of their games?"

After eating, they continued to laugh and chat. Nearly another hour passed, and finally near noon, Dez rose. "Guess we'd better get going. We've got roll call at three, and I have errands I gotta run."

They said their goodbyes, and Dez led the rookie out to the truck. Jaylynn was quiet as they drove out of Minneapolis. "Looks like it's gonna be hot again tonight," she said.

Dez sighed. "Yeah, but we're sure to get a nice thunderstorm. You can feel it building, can't you?"

"Maybe. I'm looking forward to cooler weather—not snow, mind you. But I like fall a lot."

"Me, too. You mind if I stop for gas?"

"No, I'm not in any big hurry."

Dez got off the freeway and pulled in to an Amoco gas station on Lexington Parkway. She took her time filling the truck. Jaylynn got out to try to wash the windows, and Dez thought it was lucky the rookie's back was to the street when the smoking Chevy Impala containing Crystal and Shayna went peeling by. Dez bit back a smile and turned her attention to the rookie, who was doing a fine job washing the side windows, but when it came to the windshield, it was a lost cause.

"Need a step stool?" Dez asked.

"Very funny." The rookie obstinately opened the passenger door and levered herself up to stand on the edge of the doorframe so she could reach the windshield with the squeegee scrubber. She finished the driver's side at the same time that Dez topped off the tank and removed the nozzle from the gas tank.

"Be right back," Dez said. She ambled into the store, wondering how much time it would take Crystal to park the car around the block and hustle up to Jaylynn's house. She waited in line while the harried clerk counted change for the customer ahead of her. Picking up a pack of Big Red cinnamon gum, she tossed it on the counter to be rung up, too.

When she got back to the truck and pulled out of the lot, she offered Jaylynn a stick of gum.

"Uh, no thanks. That kind always burns my tongue."

"You can eat salsa straight from the jar and spicy barbecue stuff, but you can't chew gum?"

"Not *that* gum." She frowned and cast a puzzled look Dez's way. "I just have to say you're certainly feisty today."

Dez smiled at her and wouldn't meet her eyes. She couldn't believe it, but she thought she'd actually pulled off this little diversion. She parked in front of the stucco house, busily congratulating herself, before it suddenly occurred to her that she was dropping Jaylynn off. But how was she herself going to get in there without arousing suspicion? She wanted to clonk herself on the head for not even thinking of that until now.

Hands on top of the steering wheel she sunk down a bit and said, "Uh, Jay?" The younger woman glanced over at her with a questioning look on her face, her eyebrows raised as she waited. Dez asked, "Do you think I could come in, ah, to ah, use your bathroom?"

The rookie shrugged. "Sure. Come on." For a moment Dez thought Jaylynn was going to ask why she couldn't make it one measly mile and use the facilities at her own house, but she didn't. Instead, Jaylynn opened the door and hopped out, smacking the door shut. Dez followed with what she was sure was the reddest face on the planet, partly from having to make the embarrassing request and partly because there were a dozen or more people waiting behind the shuttered windows of the stucco house, all of whom would be looking at her and Jaylynn as they entered. She didn't want to face the crowd, but at the same time she didn't want to miss the expression on the rookie's face.

Jaylynn made her way up the front walk, inserted her key in the door and stepped inside with Dez hot on her heels. There was a split second pause as the young woman obviously realized something was amiss, and then a resounding "SURPRISE!" rang through the front hall. Jaylynn jerked back so fast that, without thinking, Dez automatically brought her hands up and grasped the rookie's shoulders to steady her.

"Oh, my God," Jaylynn said. She turned and looked at Dez over her shoulder with her mouth open and the most stunned look on her face that Dez had ever seen. "You—you—you *sneak!*"

She turned back to the group standing in front of her: her mom and stepdad, Amanda and Erin, Crystal and Shayna, Tim and Kevin, Sara, Luella and Vanita, and Mitch Oster and his fiancée, Donna. Jaylynn rushed forward and began hugging people right and left while Dez hovered in the foyer, her hands in her shorts pockets.

A big banner hung over the entertainment center, obviously penned by her little sisters. It read *Happy Birthday Jaylynn!* Pink and purple, green and blue crepe paper was strung from one corner of the room to the other and tacked indiscriminately all over the furniture in the living room, again appearing to be the work of either the girls or an adult with no sense whatsoever of balance or design. A large sheet cake sat on the coffee table. *Happy Big 25* it said in multi-colored frosting. On one half, a running woman was drawn in blue shorts and top. On the other half was a picture of a lake and trees.

After being hugged by her big sister, Erin sidled over and looked up at the big cop. "Hi, Desiree," she said shyly.

"Hi, Erin. How ya been?"

"Fine."

Dez didn't know what in the world possessed her, but she opened her arms wide, and the little girl wriggled with delight. The tall woman bent and picked Erin up under the arms, lifted her high in the air, and twirled the giggling girl around.

Like a shot, Amanda was at her side. "Me, too! Me, too!"

Dez put Erin down and lifted Amanda up in the air and spun her energetically. As she set her down, she peeked up to find everyone in the room looking her way.

The room had felt warm before, but now she suddenly found it stifling. She knew she was blushing and cleared her throat. Before she could get more embarrassed, a sandy-haired man with broad shoulders stepped forward. His twinkling brown eyes met hers and he stuck out his hand. "Hi," he said. "You haven't met me yet. I'm Dave Lindstrom, Lynnie—Jaylynn's—stepdad."

She shook his warm hand and sized him up. He was handsome, about six feet tall, with a dark blonde mustache. "Glad to meet you," she said.

"Thanks for keeping the birthday girl occupied," he said. "Gave us time to get here and settled."

Sara chose that moment to hasten over to the piano and open the lid covering the keys. She sat down and played a familiar intro and then, in a clear, true voice, launched into the happy birthday song. Everyone else joined in and clapped at the end as Sara added some final piano grandstanding.

"A quarter century, Jaylynn—how's it feel?" Mitch teased.

"Hey, watch it, buddy," the rookie retorted. "You're next, you know."

"Ah, but you'll always be older than me," he said as she advanced upon him and grabbed his arm to give him a mock slug.

Jaylynn said, "How do you put up with his teasing, Donna?"

The shy woman said, "I just threaten not to feed him."

Everyone laughed, and then both of Jaylynn's sisters were standing in front of her. "Presents first," begged Erin. "Please?"

"Yeah," Amanda said. "We got you something real good, Lynnie." She scurried over to the coffee table and hauled out a square package. With a goofy smile on her face, she waved it in the air.

"Oh no," her mother said. "Vanita and Luella went to a lot of trouble with the lunch so we should eat first."

Jaylynn turned accusingly to Shayna and Crystal. "How could you two let me eat so much brunch?"

"We had to keep you busy some way," said Shayna.

"Yeah," Crystal said, "and everyone who knows you is aware that food'll always do that."

Luella said, "What all did you have?"

Jaylynn squinched up her nose. "About a hundred blueberry pancakes—and I'm still stuffed," she wailed.

Luella said, "Well, let's open presents first then," a statement that was met by cheers from the two little girls.

Dez took that moment to duck outside to the truck so she could retrieve her gifts from where they were hidden behind her seat. She was glad to have a few moments to compose herself and she took her time walking back to the house. When she came back in, she found the whole crew crowded in the living room around the cake and presents with Luella, Vanita, and Jaylynn's parents on the couch, and everyone else on the chairs or sitting cross-legged on the floor. Erin and Amanda knelt next to the table near their big sister and jabbered at her excitedly.

From the doorway, Dez looked at the kneeling woman and her sisters. The rookie was laughing, her face alight with pleasure and her hazel eyes sparkling. She reached over and encircled Amanda's waist with one hand and pulled the girl close for a hug. Her mother said something to her daughters, which Dez didn't catch, and Jaylynn nodded and then reached over and patted her mother's knee. The tall cop stood uncertainly as a feeling of bittersweet regret washed over her. She knew what her life had been like before Jaylynn had come into it, and she could imagine the emptiness she'd feel once the young woman moved on. She realized she didn't feel complete without the rookie, but that Jaylynn was already whole without her.

The thought hit like a hammer blow to her heart, and she was filled with an odd wistfulness she couldn't explain. Before she could slip further into remorse, a pair of shiny hazel eyes met hers and beckoned her forward. Shyly she handed the two packages over the top of the couch to Erin and slipped around to the side to sit on the floor between Mitch and Crystal. She knew that Jaylynn's friends had all gone in together to buy her a simple 35 mm camera starter kit, and Luella and Vanita bought film to go with it.

"This is great!" Jaylynn said. "I've been wanting to learn more about photography for *ages*." She opened the camera bag and pulled out the various boxes. "Let's put it together now so I can take pictures this very moment."

"Dontcha need film?" Amanda asked.

Jaylynn said, "Oh yeah."

Luella leaned forward from her perch on the couch. She said, "I think you'll want to open that one next." She pointed at a classy package wrapped in gold paper and expertly wound with colorful string and topped with a tangle of curled ribbon. Dez decided she should have had Luella wrap her gifts. Jaylynn gave the silver-haired woman a mischievous look, then tore into the gift, revealing four rolls of 24-exposure film.

"Thank you, Vanita and Luella!"

Mitch said, "Hey, rookie, you want me to assemble that thing for you?"

Dez said, "You actually know anything about cameras, Oster?"

"I'll have you know I was the lead audio-visual aide for my high school," he said in a huffy voice. "You're not the only one with many skills." He gave her a devilish grin and reached over to snag the camera bag that Jaylynn slid toward him. He opened one of the boxes.

The rookie picked up the bigger package from Dez, and the big cop felt herself start to blush. She watched as Jaylynn opened it and pulled the cardboard flap open on the plain box. Out slid a leather duty belt, and Jaylynn looked over, surprise etched on her face. "Dez! Is this that kind you were telling me about—made especially for women?" When Dez nodded, Jaylynn said, "But these things are expensive!"

Dez shrugged. "It'll help your lower back a lot."

Jaylynn turned to her parents. "My regular work belt doesn't fit exactly right and hurts my back."

Dez said, "I got the size I thought would fit ya, but if it doesn't feel right, you can exchange it."

Jaylynn wrapped it around her middle. "I think it's just right." She set it down on the floor next to her, and picked up the smaller present, obviously a CD. "Is this from you, too?"

Oster chose that opportunity to say, "You can tell it is by the incredibly masterful wrap job."

Dez, embarrassed that the eyes of everyone in the room were on her, gave him the evil eye and said, "Watch it, Oster, you're still on probation." But she couldn't help but smile at the young man's enthusiasm. She looked over at Luella to find the silver-haired woman gazing at her with love in her eyes. Then she made a face at Dez who made a mental note to give the landlady a really big hug later—and a pinch for sticking her tongue out at her.

Jaylynn unwrapped the CD. "Gloria Estefan. I *love* Gloria!" She beamed over at Dez, and the big cop decided it was worth all the soul-searching and worry she'd been through trying to decide what to give the rookie for a birthday present. Now that the two presents were open, she could sit back and relax.

Jaylynn moved on to the present Erin had been patiently holding on her lap. She removed the gold bow and tore off blue and green paper to uncover a journal. It had a gold spine and gold trim with trees and forest scenes all over the back and front. "Wow!" she said. "This is really beautiful."

"We bought it at the museum," Erin said. "Look! See, we got your initials put in." Turning it over, she practically wrenched it out of Jaylynn's hands to flip the front cover open. Sure enough, Jaylynn's initials, J M S, were on the first page in two-inch tall gold lettering.

"This is really neat," Jaylynn said. "I'll have fun writing in it." She picked up the gold bow and stuck it to Erin's head. "You should have just put bows on your heads 'cause you guys are all the present I would ever need."

Her mother said, "That's sweet, Jaylynn. We're glad you feel that way since we *are* your major present."

"Mom, how long are you here?" she said with excitement in her voice.

"We fly out Tuesday. Have to get the girls ready for school to start the next week."

Jaylynn looked at her watch, then looked up in disappointment. "Darn, it's already after one, and I have to be at work at three."

Dez cleared her throat. "Actually, you don't. I hope you don't mind, but I cleared today and tomorrow off for you with Lt. Malcolm. You don't have to go back until Wednesday."

If she didn't know better, Dez would swear that the rookie would have liked to launch herself across the room and hug her. She'd never seen Jaylynn look so thrilled. "Thank you! Oh, Dez, thanks so much for doing that!"

Crystal said, "I, on the other hand, have to show up."

"Me, too," said Mitch. He snapped the back of the camera shut, and handed it to Jaylynn. "Here you go. It's all set."

Jaylynn put the camera strap around her neck and stood up. "Everybody, this has been the best—and most surprising—birthday party I've ever had. Thanks! You all get on the couch and let me take a picture."

After Jaylynn took the picture of the group piled on and around the sofa, Mitch insisted on taking several other pictures so Jaylynn could be in them. Once they'd shot nearly a whole roll, Luella hoisted herself up. "Come on, Vanita," she said. "Time for the goodies. We better get eatin' so these working fools can have cake before they go." She and her sister, plus Tim and Kevin, made a beeline for the kitchen.

One by one, the pile of people on the couch extricated themselves and headed out to the kitchen. Jaylynn peered down at Dez who was sitting cross-legged on the floor jammed between the coffee table and the front of the couch. She said, "Do you go in at three?"

Solemnly, Dez shook her head. "Day off."

A wisp of a smile planted itself on Jaylynn's lips, and she turned away to take a picture of Crystal and Shayna as they stood by the kitchen door and Shayna complained about how warm it was getting to be in the house.

Jaylynn's sisters came and each took one of her hands and led her out to the backyard where there were streamers and balloons decorating the trees and fence and table. Luella and Vanita supervised the laying out of the food, which Dez was amused to see was mostly done by Kevin and Tim. In quick order, barbecued chicken, three kinds of salad, bowls of fruit, corn chips and potato chips, and a platter of cheese and crackers, pickles and olives were set out. Dez loaded up on the chicken and green salad. She took her plate over to sit under the canopy of the black walnut in the middle of the yard.

She watched Jaylynn talking and laughing as she helped load up a paper plate Amanda was holding. A plump strawberry slid from one side of the plate to the other, and Dez observed its descent over the side almost as though it were in slow motion. In a smooth movement, Jaylynn swept her hand under Amanda's arm and plucked the berry out of mid-air. She looked at the red fruit and then bit into it as Amanda watched.

Dez's view was obstructed as Sara walked the few steps over to where the big cop sat. She lowered herself next to her.

"You don't mind if I sit here, do you?" Sara asked.

"Nope. Make yourself comfy."

They sat eating in companionable silence, both watching the antics of the rest of the party. Tim and Kevin were telling some complicated story complete with exaggerated gestures, while Dave and Janet, Luella and Vanita listened intently. The little girls sat at the picnic table near Shayna, Crystal, Mitch, and Donna. And Jaylynn flitted around, always laughing, hugging, teasing.

Sara said, "We're surrounded by flaming extroverts."

"You can say that again."

"They'll all run out of energy in the hot sun."

"Meanwhile we're keeping so cool in the 85 degree shade," Dez said, in a dry voice.

Sara gave her a sidelong glance. "It is a bit too warm, isn't it? I'm glad we kept the cake in the house."

"Hey, Sara," Dez said. "I didn't realize you played piano."

"Actually, I'm a music major. I play piano, violin, clarinet, even a little guitar. I hear you're a guitarist. What do you like to play?"

Dez set her empty paper plate in front of her and cleared her throat. "Pop, folk, some bluesy stuff, a little country. Nothing too complicated."

Sara finished chewing a bite of chicken. "I like to hear stuff on the radio and then see if I can duplicate it on the piano."

"Me, too," Dez said.

"Have you heard that good song, "Baby Don't You Break My Heart Slow" by Vonda Sheppard and Emily from the Indigo Girls?"

"I think so. You figure it out already?"

Sara looked down at her near-empty plate. With a toss of her head she gestured toward the back stairs. "Come on, I'll show you."

They went into the house, leaving the rest of the crew out in the yard, and both settled in on the piano bench, backs to the living room. "You play?" the brown-eyed woman asked.

"No, not really."

"What do you mean—not really?"

"I can pick some things out, you know, play chords and such, but I don't sight read well or anything."

Sara nodded. She put her hands on the keys and began an introduction, and in an instant, Dez recognized it. "Oh yeah, I like this song a lot."

"Know the words to it?"

Dez winced and shook her head. "Some, but not well enough to sing."

Sara stopped playing and fished around in the papers and books stacked on top of the console piano until she found what she was looking for. "Here it is. I wrote the words down. I think you can read my writing—yeah, for once it's pretty legible. Let's run through it. Which part do you want?"

Dez was taken aback, but Sara was already playing the intro again. "You lead off," the tall cop said, "and I'll try that second verse and sing choruses with ya." She glanced around, but no one was in the house, so she relaxed and closed her eyes.

Sara started to sing and immediately her voice soothed Dez. It was clear and rich, a strong voice well suited to a variety of musical styles. She had a hunch Sara could sing jazz or blues or rock. Her touch on the piano was deft and true, the rhythm reliable. After the first verse, Dez hummed a background harmony to the chorus. She let her voice curl around Sara's. In her mind, she could feel the tones she sang surrounding and supporting Sara's, helping to keep the song aloft. When she lost track of the words, she opened her eyes and checked the lyrics, then closed them again to let the reverberation of the piano thrum through her.

She started the second verse and Sara's strong voice joined in. Dez felt elation flow through her. She loved music. It had such power over her, the power to relax, excite, or soothe—or to make her cry. It was a refuge, a home, a path to her soul. When she sang or played her guitar, she felt whole in a way she didn't usually in the rest of her day-to-day life. And then when a song ended, she felt bereft, as though she'd lost something she desperately needed. They finished the verses, and then sang the final repeated chorus three times. Dez reveled in the fact that they were hitting all the harmonies together with no planning, without a word or a glance.

When the song came to an end and the piano faded to silence, Dez opened her eyes. "Nice piano work," she said.

"Thanks. I've been working on that. You sounded good, Dez. It's nice to sing with someone who stays on key and on their line. Lots of people can't do that." Sara picked up a book. "Here I've got one for you. See if you can sing this one—if you remember it—but I bet you will."

"Oh, a real oldie but goodie. Christopher Cross, huh. I know this." The piano intro began and Dez let it wash over her. She marveled at how much tone Sara could coax out of the old piano. And then they started to sing "Arthur's Theme."

Jaylynn stood in the kitchen and listened as the two women finished that song and moved into another and another. She was so thrilled, she hardly breathed. Right now they were singing Mary Chapin Carpenter's raucous romp, "Down at the Twist and Shout." Jaylynn felt like a voyeur, but she knew if she went in the living room, they'd stop. She didn't want that. Sara had sung so little all year, and when she did, she tended toward mournful tunes. She was pleased to hear her friend belting out a song like she was thoroughly enjoying it.

The screen door creaked open, and Luella entered carrying an empty chicken platter. Jaylynn smiled at her and put her finger to her lips. The silver-haired woman set the plate down carefully and moved to stand next to her. Propped up against the counter, side by side, Jaylynn leaned into the older woman and let her head drop to rest on her friend's shoulder.

Luella whispered, "I love it when she sings. She doesn't do it enough."

"Same with Sara. And listen to how great they sound together." They finished "Down at the Twist and Shout" and, without stopping, Sara segued into "Fast Car." Dez was singing now by herself, her voice deep and expressive. Jaylynn felt the hairs on her arms stand on end, and even in the heat of the kitchen, she shivered. *Oh my,* she thought. *Oh my. What I wouldn't give to hear that voice singing quietly in my ear, even just whispering a song.*

Soon, she knew, she was going to have to have a heart-to-heart talk with Dez. She couldn't go on like this much longer, her feelings constantly boiling to the surface. Any time soon she could lose her head and say or do something to really freak out the tall cop. She couldn't afford for that to happen, but it scared her to think of all the risks involved in revealing her feelings. Still, she knew something had to change.

She felt an odd sense of hope though. The entire atmosphere between the two women had changed since the bodybuilding show. Though not a single word had been exchanged, her intuition was running on high, and what it was telling her was that something profound was going on with Dez—and between the two of them. She didn't know what had prompted it, but she wasn't going to argue.

The screen door clattered opened and in came Erin. As soon as the girl heard the piano, she was out of the kitchen like a shot. Jaylynn peeked around the corner and watched the bundle of squirmy energy insinuate herself between the piano and Dez. The big woman shifted back on the bench so that Erin could sit on the edge of the bench between her legs and lean into her. Long arms circled around the little body. Jaylynn couldn't hear the conversation that went on for a minute as Sara hunted through the various books and papers on the piano. She looked over at Luella.

The silver-haired woman whispered, "Just go in there. They won't stop now without disappointing the little pipsqueak."

Jaylynn rounded the corner just as the piano started up again. It took a moment of puzzling before she recognized the old Beatles song. She heard her little sister's quavery voice, displaying the family penchant for singing slightly off key, as she warbled the Beatles' "I Wanna Hold Your Hand." Dez sang quietly behind Erin, keeping her on track, and turning the pages of the music for Sara.

They were so into the song that neither of the women nor Erin seemed to notice as, one by one, all the guests made their way into the hot living room and camped out behind them. At the end of the song Vanita clapped and said, "Let's hear it for the latest new star, Erin Lindstrom." Erin peeked back, her little face squeezed between Sara and Dez.

Sara leaned over and whispered something into Dez's ear, and Jaylynn saw the two women nod at one another and break into conspiratorial grins before they turned away again. Sara got her hands set on the piano and started a bass rhythm that Jaylynn immediately recognized. The two women hollered out the opening words to Steppenwolf's "Born To Be Wild."

Jaylynn looked around the room. Everybody, even Luella, was singing the chorus, bellowing it out so loud that the neighbors must be able to hear it. The rookie couldn't seem to get the silly grin off her face, and she hoped no one was paying attention to her. She felt this bubble of joy gurgle up from deep inside her, and she wanted to run through the room screaming with delight. Instead, she lowered herself onto the arm of the couch near Vanita and joined in, shrieking at the top of her lungs with the rest of them.

Sara ended the song by playing the same rock chords she had started with, to the cheers of everyone assembled. She hit the final crashing chord and let up, then spun around on the bench a sheepish grin on her face.

"You got talent, girl," Vanita said.

Sara smiled. "It's an inspiring group, that's all."

Jaylynn saw that Dez still had her arms around Erin, with her back to the room. She was whispering something in the nine-year-old's ear. The two of them nodded and Erin rose. She took Dez's hand and they moved away from the piano.

Luella said, "We've gotta cut that cake now or these two," she pointed at Mitch and Crystal, "aren't going to get any. Come on, Jaylynn." She picked up a large kitchen knife and handed it to the rookie.

"I'm terrible at cutting cake," Jaylynn confessed. "Really, I am."

In a droll voice, her mother said, "She's not lying. If you want a mangled piece of cake mashed up in a pile on your plate, then go ahead and let her cut."

Tim, in his best prissy voice, said, "C'mon, Kevin." He reached over and took the knife from Luella. "What *would* you people do without us?"

Jaylynn was laughing so hard that she didn't notice the big cop and Erin heading out the front door.

****

"You're sure you know which room is Jaylynn's?" Dez had squatted down next to her truck, and was looking up at Erin who held an envelope in her hand.

The little girl nodded emphatically. "Oh, yeah. Me and Amanda put our stuff in there on her couch. We're hoping she lets us sleep over with her."

You're not the only one, thought Dez, then caught herself. *What am I thinking?* She shook her head from side to side as though that would cause the idea to fall out of her head and stop plaguing her. She said, "Will you sneak upstairs and hide this on her pillow so she won't find it 'til tonight?"

Erin nodded, a serious look on her face. "What is it?"

"Just a birthday card."

The little girl's forehead wrinkled as Dez stood. "Why don't you give it to her now?"

"I want it to be a surprise. Now hide it under your shirt, okay?"

Erin tucked it in the waistband of her pink shorts and pulled her shirt over it and then reached up for Dez's hand. "Okay, I'm ready."

They strolled back in the house, and when they got inside, Dez gave the girl a look and nodded toward the stairs. Erin took off like a firecracker, making such a racket on the way up the steps that Jaylynn looked up from the cake plate she was holding for Tim. "What's got into her?" she asked Dez.

Dez shrugged and gave her a bashful smile. Inquisitive hazel eyes rested upon her for a moment longer before turning back to the cake serving, and Dez breathed a sigh of relief. She had debated long and hard about whether she would actually give the card to Jaylynn, and now it was too late to take it back. Well—she could ask Erin to retrieve it, but she wasn't going to. She heard the pounding of little feet and Erin was back, breathless and triumphant. She tipped her head up and put her hands around her mouth. Dez bent over so the child could whisper in her ear. "Mission accomp—accomp—"

"Accomplished?"

"Yup. Under the covers on top of the pillow." She looked up with a very proud smile.

Dez bent to her ear and said, "Good job. I owe you one."

Erin wrinkled up her nose. "Okay, you can take me to the zoo or something."

This caused Dez to laugh out loud, and again, Jaylynn looked over at her quizzically. "What are you two in cahoots about?"

Erin straightened up, put her hands behind her back, and assumed an innocent look. "Nothing," she said.

"Yeah, I'll just bet," her big sister said. "You having any cake?"

Dez said, "I think Erin should get a piece with lots of frosting, don't you, Erin?" The girl leaned back into the tall cop's legs and hooked her right arm around a strong thigh.

"Oh, yeah," the little girl said as she gazed up at Dez, a look of gleeful adoration plastered across her face.

Jaylynn's mother watched her youngest daughter with amusement, then caught Dez's eye. The tall woman smiled at her and winked.

Chapter
28

After midnight, Jaylynn's sisters finally fell asleep on the downstairs couch while watching "Balto," a kid-vid Sara had brought home. Her parents had gone to their hotel before dinner, Tim and Kevin were out, and Sara had hit the hay much earlier. Tired but satisfied, Jaylynn headed up the stairs to her warm and stuffy room. She got ready for bed, stripping down to a t-shirt and briefs, and brushed her teeth with a goofy smile on her face. She peered in the mirror in the bathroom, stared herself in the eye, and thought that she looked like a real dolt with the dumb, lovesick expression on her face. But she couldn't help it. With a sigh she turned out the bathroom light and padded over to her room.

She sat on the couch and examined the new camera. She had taken an entire roll of film at the Minnesota Zoo and couldn't wait to get it developed. She still couldn't believe Dez had consented to go along with her sisters to the zoo late in the afternoon after the party, but then again, who could resist Erin or Amanda when they begged? *She* couldn't—which was why, against her better judgment, they'd had hotdogs and popsicles for a late dinner. The zoo had been fun, and taking the girls there gave her parents a chance to get away for a while by themselves.

The two women and two girls had walked miles, eaten cotton candy, and looked at mammals and fish and birds and reptiles. Amanda and Erin screamed with delight on the kiddie rides, and they all petted scores of animals at the petting zoo—except for Dez, who was allergic to them. Jaylynn had had to explain to the girls what that meant. For a few moments, they were disappointed that the black-haired woman had kept her distance, but she was soon forgotten in the rush from one animal to the next.

Jaylynn picked up the new CD and painstakingly unwrapped the cellophane. She put the disk in her CD player next to the bed.

Closing her eyes, she listened to the mellow tones of piano and Gloria's sultry voice, letting the song roll over her and soothe her. And then the song's tempo picked up and she wanted to be dancing. *Nice beat.* She curled her feet under her and read the words in the libretto. With excitement she realized it looked like an entire CD of salsa love songs. *Wow. I can't wait to hear this whole thing.*

Jaylynn reached over and adjusted the volume to a low level, clicked off the bedside lamp, and stood. She pulled back the covers and something pointy flew at her, poking her in the thigh as it fell. She clicked on the bedside lamp and stretched a hand down, half under the bed, to find a plain white envelope. With a frown on her face she picked it up and ripped open the flap. The picture on the card inside was a black and white photo of the back of two small girls, hand-in-hand and barelegged. They wore old-fashioned jumpers that she imagined were probably corduroy. One was a curly-haired blonde, the other had short black hair and sported a beret. She opened the card and read:

> *Jay,*
> *Thanks for sticking by me through thick and thin (literally!) This last year has been hard for both of us in a lot of ways. You've been a good friend and have come to mean a lot to me. Hope you have a great birthday on Tuesday and that everything today was memorable. I'm glad I was a part of it.*
>
> *Love,*
> *Dez*

Her heart was beating so fast she almost couldn't breathe. She read the card through once more. *How...when?* She narrowed her eyes and remembered back to the early afternoon when she had seen Erin and Dez conspiring, and now she knew what that was about. *Well, well, Miss Big Shot Cop, you got the drop on me repeatedly today. Hmm...we'll see about this.*

She got up, still carrying the card, and slipped out to the hall, hunting around for the phone cord. She found it trailing along the wall near the attic where it disappeared under the door that led upstairs. She opened the door to Tim's nest and grabbed the cord, pulling it toward her as she climbed the stairs. She heard the telephone sliding along the floor, and before she reached the top of the steps, it appeared, teetering on the edge. She grabbed it up and skipped back down the stairs, hauling the heavy, old-fashioned phone into her room and shutting the door behind her before setting it on the bed with the card. She crawled up on the bed, cross-

legged, and leaned back against the pillows. Gloria's voice, in
Spanish, sang to a peppy salsa number, and Jaylynn couldn't keep
still. She rocked from side to side, happiness pulsing through her.

Jaylynn dialed the number she now knew by heart but rarely
called, and when a familiar husky voice answered, she said, "Hey,
you."

There was a pause. "Uh, hi."

Grinning from ear to ear the rookie said, "So you think you're
pretty clever, huh?"

"Some days."

"Today is definitely a day I'd have to agree with you."

"Oh?"

"Oh, yeah. Thanks for this card, and I'm listening to Gloria
right now."

"So you didn't have that CD? I thought you might have gotten
it already."

"Nope. I've wanted it, but I didn't get around to it yet. It's just
fabulous."

In a low voice, Dez said, "I'm glad you like it."

Jaylynn imagined the tall woman's face, knowing that she'd be
blushing a bit right now. "You were great today with my sisters.
They like you a lot."

"They're a lot like you," said the gruff voice.

"You mean energy-wise?"

"That—and they don't listen to anything anyone tells 'em to do
if they don't want to."

"What? I don't do that!"

"Yeah, right."

Jaylynn heard a low chuckle in the phone. "I believe I'm
getting a bad rep here."

"Well-deserved is what I say."

Jaylynn laughed, a warm, throaty sound that traveled through
the phone line like a shot of adrenaline, and suddenly, with great
intensity, Dez wished she were there with the laughing woman. She
swallowed and asked, "Where are you?"

"In my room, sitting on my bed. Where are you?"

"Standing in the middle of the apartment. Where are the little
squirts?"

"They fell asleep on the couch downstairs, so—unless they
wake in the middle of the night and search me out—I get a peaceful
night of sleep."

Dez nodded to herself. She picked up the phone and carried it
over to her bed then, tucking the receiver against her chin, lay
down, crossed her legs at the ankles, and put her hands behind her
head. "What are you gonna do with 'em tomorrow?"

"I don't know. My stepdad has only been here once before, so we'll probably do some sightseeing. They won't be here that long. Dez, I still can't believe they're here!"

Dez smiled. "That was a pretty good surprise party. You really *were* surprised, weren't you?"

Jaylynn made a snorting sound into the phone, "Are you kidding—blown away! I was totally clueless, though I did think you and Crystal were acting kind of odd. Then again, as far as I knew, it could've just been you two being your same weird selves."

"Who you calling weird? You're the one who thinks a reporter can talk to Dolly the Sheep."

"Ha! That's rich," Jaylynn said in a taunting voice, "from someone who breaks out in a sweat when a little petting zoo sheep strolls by."

"Can I help it if I'm allergic?"

They talked on, joking and teasing, until Dez glanced over at her bedside clock to see that it was almost one a.m. They'd been on the phone almost half an hour. "What time are the midgets gonna get up tomorrow?"

"Why?"

"'Cause it's getting late, and before you know it, they'll be jumping on your bed. You better get some sleep."

"Good point." Jaylynn let a wave of fatigue wash over her. Much as she wished she could keep talking, she was feeling as tired as she ever had. She yawned. "If we go to the movies tomorrow, you wanna come?"

"Not if it's to *Pokeman* or one of those Disney movies."

A bark of laughter burst out of the younger woman. "At least I know where *you* stand."

"Probably couldn't go anyway, Jay. I have to work, remember?"

"Oh. Well, that sucks."

"Enjoy your family. Call me after they leave Tuesday—if you feel like it, that is."

"Okay." She yawned again. "Good night, Dez."

"'Night, rookie."

Jaylynn put the receiver back on the cradle and set the phone on the floor. Fluffing up the spread, she pulled it over her legs and lay on her side, her arms clasped against her chest and the card still next to her on the bed. With a sigh of contentment she closed her eyes, listening to the full, lilting voice on the stereo. She felt herself drifting, and *"...don't make me wait much longer..."* were the last lyrics she heard before she fell asleep.

****

Sunday and Monday flew by. Jaylynn's family constantly kept busy hiking, shopping, going to the movies, eating meals with various combinations of Sara, Tim, and Kevin, and even riding on a paddlewheel boat from St. Paul down to Hastings. All too soon, it was Tuesday and time to say goodbye.

At the airport, Jaylynn parked the totally overloaded Camry, and the five occupants extricated themselves, pulling out suitcases and bags and backpacks. They had so much stuff that Jaylynn finally set off to find a cart. As she strode away, leaving her folks with the girls by the car, her mother caught up with her. "Lynnie," she said. "Wait up." They walked side by side through the parking ramp and over to the cart rack by the elevators.

Jaylynn pulled some quarters out of her shorts pockets. "Darn. It takes six, Mom. You got any quarters? I only have three."

Her mother rooted through her purse and came up with a handful of change. "Here you go." Jaylynn bent to insert the money and when she stood up, her mother was eyeing her uncertainly.

"What?" The younger woman gave her mother a slight smile. "What's on your mind, Mom? You look like you want to say something."

Her mother cleared her throat and looked at her daughter. She raised a hand up and swept a stray lock of Jaylynn's blonde hair away from her forehead. "I don't mean to be presumptuous or anything, Lynnie, but I have to say this."

Jaylynn stood, puzzled, her brow knit in concentration, as she waited for the rest.

Janet paused as if searching for the right words "Anyone can see how much you care about Dez, honey, and—and—well, we've never had a conversation about this, and maybe now's not the time, but I just need you to know it's okay. Dave and I just want you to be happy. Do you understand?"

Jaylynn stood mutely, her hands in the pockets of her shorts. She felt her face flaming and had no idea what to say.

Her mother stepped closer and slipped an arm around her daughter's waist. "What? Have I rendered my gabby child completely speechless?"

"No. I—I just didn't realize..."

"That I knew about you and Dez? Or that I simply knew about you?"

"Either—or both," she stuttered. "But Mom, there's nothing between us."

Janet erupted in laughter, squeezing her daughter around the waist. When she stopped chortling, she said, "Believe me, there will be."

Jaylynn felt the blush rising up her neck, across her ears and face, all the way to the top of her head. "Could you please tell me why everyone else sees this when I don't?" She slipped away from her mother's embrace and grabbed the cart, jerking it from the rack, then raised her eyes shyly to meet her mom's amused gaze.

"It's plain as the nose on your face. Her face, too." She reached over and ruffled her daughter's short hair, then cupped her eldest child's chin in her hand. "Your father would be proud of how you've grown up, Lynnie. He'd be *very* proud."

Tears filled Jaylynn's eyes, and she turned to the side, stepping out of the way when another family bustled up to the rack. When she turned back, her mom looked at her in alarm, "Hey, sweetie, you're not supposed to cry on your birthday." She put her arm around her again and said, "Come on. Let's go get those antsy girls before they drive Dave crazy."

****

Jaylynn drove home from the airport feeling teary-eyed and slightly stunned in the wake of the brief conversation with her mom. How many years had she worried about telling her folks? How much had she strategized, role-played in her mind...and the whole subject was suddenly moot. It would take her some time to get adjusted to it. Now she wished she had had time to ask a few questions—like, *how long have you known about this, Mom? What is it you see when you look at Dez and me?*

She thought back to high school and how confusing it had been for her. Small and "cute," she'd never lacked for guys to date, but by her junior year it seemed a useless expenditure of energy. She focused her time and attention on her studies, on running, and on her friend Sandi. Her schoolmate was safe to hang around. She could be in love with her, and no one, not even Sandi, need ever know.

It wasn't until the freedom of college, far away from home, that she allowed herself to get involved with anyone. She had never brought Dana home to Seattle or mentioned her to her parents. They'd only been together for about eight months, and they were eight of the most confusing and painful months she had ever experienced. By the time they had broken up, Jaylynn was a lot more jaded about love than she had thought she could be. After the fiasco of her second lover, Theresa, she had all but given up, deciding that she would devote her time and energies to causes that mattered to her: children's issues, human rights, poverty problems. Issues were reliable; people weren't.

Now she wondered if her other relationships hadn't worked out because there was someone else floating around out in the world, someone meant to be her soulmate. She felt that it was true. She didn't think dreams lied, and nearly a decade and a half of dreams couldn't be that far off, right? She pulled off Lexington and made her way to the back of the house, got out, and headed into the house.

*Maybe I should go for a walk around the lake...*instantly her body rebelled. She wanted to see Dez so badly that just thinking about *not* seeing her actually made a hollow spot behind her rib cage hurt. *Guess that solves that question.* She smiled and shook her head. *Oh, girl, you've got it bad.* She checked her watch: 2:10. *Well, let's go call Miss Tall, Dark and Dangerous and see what's happening.*

Dez picked up the phone on the first ring.

Jaylynn teased, "You sitting on the phone or what?"

The big woman blushed. "It rang. I picked up."

"Ah, I see. So, whatcha doing today?"

Dez wanted to say that she'd been sitting by the phone, trying to make herself play her guitar, but really waiting for Jaylynn's phone call. Instead she said, "Just practicing a little guitar. You got a better offer?"

"Not really." Jaylynn racked her brain for something to suggest, but she drew a total blank.

"So you got 'em off on the plane safe and sound."

"They're on their way."

"You ever play any basketball?"

"Sure. In high school. I didn't play in college."

"There's a pick-up game over at Central later this afternoon. Wanna go play?"

"Who's this with?"

"Buncha female cops, mostly from the St. Paul and Minneapolis precincts, get together to play on Tuesdays and Thursdays from four to six. It's usually fun."

"Are we talking regular athletes or superhuman ones like you?"

"Oh, come on. Basketball was never my big forte. Besides, it's been months since I've played. Been too busy bodybuilding. You're in way better shape than me."

"Okay. I'll dig out my hightops and give it the old college try."

"I'll come by and pick you up at 3:30, okay?"

"Sounds good."

But Jaylynn found out Dez had exaggerated the extent of her rustiness. She was quick, powerful, and a decent ball handler. Blessed with long arms and great jumping ability, the tall woman could even dunk it. Jaylynn watched from the sidelines as the first crew of rough and tumble cops went at it on the floor. She didn't

know any of these policewomen, and most were good ball players.
They were rowdy, but not flagrant foulers, and there was a lot of
good-natured ribbing between the players.

The game was fast and physical. And watching the black-clad
Dez weave and scramble through the jungle of limbs was pure joy.
She wasn't the tallest player on the floor, but she could outleap any
of the others. The rookie watched her fake out the woman guarding
her, thread the needle, and lay one up left-handed. She admired the
way the brunette could rocket a pass up the floor with unerring
accuracy and then follow so quickly that if the fast break shooter
missed, Dez often got the rebound and put it back up.

Jaylynn watched how Dez, the blonde-haired post, and the two
wings moved about the floor, and she took note of the point guard
on both teams. Dez's team had a point guard who wasn't
particularly fast, but was able to make some incredible 3-pointers,
so the other team guarded her closely. Jaylynn knew shooting was
not her strong suit. But if she was guarded closely, she figured she
could penetrate and pass off.

They didn't keep score. It was not a game of numbers but of
endurance. After the first twenty minutes, the guards ground down
and needed a rest, so Jaylynn went in, accepting the ball on the
sideline and passing it in to one of the forwards. She cut through
the key and popped back up on top, received the pass, and put the
ball to the floor. She surveyed the defense. Feinting right, she cut
left around her defender, penetrating the top of the key. The
defense collapsed on her, but she had already located three of her
four fellow team members. Looking left, she flipped a bounce pass
right, and the blonde-haired post snagged the pass and shot it for an
easy 8-foot jumper.

With a little smile, she retreated to the other end of the floor.
"Good one," a husky, panting voice said in her ear. As Dez passed
her, she whacked the rookie on the butt, then kept moving to her
position at the base of the key.

Later, thinking back to the game, Jaylynn remembered
scrambling for the ball, dribbling furiously up and down the floor,
fast breaking right and left, and passing, passing, passing. The two
opportunities she got for shots didn't result in baskets. But her
favorite play of the day occurred late in the afternoon when
everyone was sucking air and worn down. She flitted around the
point guard, stayed in her face, and just generally dogged her until
the scrappy woman bobbled the ball. As the rookie snapped it up,
Dez and two players from the other team were on their way past
her. Jaylynn got control of the ball, dribbled fiercely up the court,
and streaked past the two defenders. She felt one breathing down
her neck two steps before the key. So instead of going for the layup,

she alley-ooped it up toward the backboard. Two long arms plucked the ball from midair and dropped it in the basket.

"Perfect!" Dez shouted as her feet hit the ground. She spun and grabbed Jaylynn around the waist, swinging her up off her feet, a look of complete joy on her face. "That *never* happens. Nobody ever feeds me like that!"

"Hey!" Jaylynn said, a happy grin on her face. "Put me down."

Dez complied. "On that note, I think that's enough for one day." To the protests of the other ballplayers, she shook her head and said, "It's almost six anyway, so we're outta here." They moved off the court where Dez picked up a towel and daubed at her forehead. "Wanna go get something to eat?"

In disbelief, Jaylynn looked down at her sweat soaked t-shirt.

"Oh, geez, I'm even sweatier than you," the tall woman. said "Pizza? Or how 'bout Mexican?"

Jaylynn narrowed her eyes. "Are you sure you're not a Stepford Dez?"

The big cop laughed. "Why—because of the dinner offer or the sweat?"

"Oh, definitely the food. I've worked with you for what, eight months? And I've *never* seen you eat pizza or tacos."

"Join me at the local cantina, and I will display my great burrito eating talents. I'll even buy on account of it being your birthday and everything."

"Okay, it's a deal."

Later that night, as she lay in bed, Jaylynn thought back to the day and how much fun it had been. She had enjoyed the basketball game, though she was definitely going to be sore tomorrow. Eating chili rellenos with lots of hot sauce and talking with Dez had been exhilarating. Two and a half hours had passed in what felt like thirty minutes. She liked how Dez listened to her, giving her full attention and asking astute questions. She found herself talking way more than half the time, but Dez held up her side of the conversation—she just had a more economical way of stating her points.

There was no doubt at all that the big cop had changed, and Jaylynn didn't know what had brought it on. She wasn't one to question it though. It would be interesting to see how work would go from Wednesday through Sunday. She rolled over and went to sleep to the salsa tones of Gloria Estefan on the CD player.

Chapter
29

Labor Day passed without anything of note occurring at work. The following week, the rookie worked two extra days, covering the worst beat in their sector in a two-man car with Cooper. Cooper's regular partner covered for Crystal who had gone with Shayna to Cancun. Jaylynn only had Tuesday off and was really tired, though she was relieved to say that the low back pain she had been getting from the old duty belt had instantly gone away once she started wearing the belt Dez had bought her. She couldn't believe what a difference it made.

Fatigued, Jaylynn lay around the house reading and taking it easy, knowing she had to go back to work on Wednesday. The only bright side was that she'd spend the next several nights riding with Dez again.

From Wednesday until Sunday night, the week's worth of work was rather routine. In the station, Dez was her same cool and distant self, but in the squad car she loosened up, though not as much as she had around Jaylynn's birthday. By Sunday night, Jaylynn found herself wondering if she'd see Dez at all over the next three days. Not a word had been mentioned about doing anything together, and she was too nervous to bring it up. A gust of cool air breezed in from the open window on Dez's side of the car. The hot and humid days of summer seemed to be over, which was fine with Jaylynn. One of her favorite times of the year had always been the cooler days at the beginning of autumn, and she loved the changing colors on the trees and the crisp night air. Right now it actually seemed chilly.

She checked her watch, glad that it was after midnight. The shift was finally over. As if she had read the rookie's mind, Dez did a U-turn on University and headed west. In less than a minute they were parked in the station lot.

"You know," Dez said, "after a shitty night like that, I feel like beating the crap out of someone." She pulled on the door handle and kicked the car door open, slamming it behind her.

"I think that's what the last guy we arrested said, wasn't it?"

"You know what I mean. Was there something in the air tonight or what?"

They had spent the evening going from one domestic assault to another, and Jaylynn had to admit that it had been frustrating. On the last call, they had had to physically restrain the drunken apartment dweller who had beaten up his girlfriend. Paramedics took the bruised young woman off to the hospital with what the rookie suspected could be a broken jaw.

Dez stomped from the car toward the station house and Jay-lynn hustled to keep up with her.

The tall cop asked, "Why do people have to be so damn mean and stupid?" Worst of all, Dez knew that it'd be hours before she got to sleep. In a mood like this, she'd be lucky to catch any sleep at all. "I may as well just take a trip," she said as she grabbed the stationhouse door and wrenched it open. She stood aside for Jaylynn to enter.

"Thank you, Gallant Knight," Jaylynn said with a laugh. "I don't know how I would have gotten that door open, much less handled the night's lively activities without you."

Dez glared at her. She followed Jaylynn down the long hall-way. "I'm just gonna get in my truck and drive until I reach water."

"That'll be what? Two miles? I think you'll hit Como Lake in about three minutes. What then?"

Dez just made a growling sound and kept on moving. They both signed out, then started down the stairs to the locker room. Dez smacked open the door and went to her locker. She pulled out her wallet and checked it. "I've got sixty-seven bucks. Wanna go to Duluth?"

Jaylynn had her shirt unbuttoned and her vest half off. Over her shoulder, in a voice of disbelief, she said, "What? Are ya nuts?"

"Yeah. Certifiable." Dez quickly stripped off her uniform and changed into blue jeans and a baggy bright green "Luck of the Irish" sweatshirt. She sat down on the bench and pulled off her shoes, reached for a pair of sneakers, and jammed a foot into each shoe. As she tied them, she said, "I'm getting in my truck and driving to Duluth. You can come if you want—or not. Whatever."

Jaylynn hung her vest up on a hook in her locker. In her t-shirt she turned to face her partner. "You're serious? It's after midnight."

The only response she got was a grunt as Dez finished tying her laces, stood up, and grabbed her wallet and keys. "See you on Wednesday then." She moved as if to go, but Jaylynn reached out and grabbed her arm to stop her.

"Wait a minute, Miss Speedy Dresser. Give a girl a minute to get her act together."

Dez frowned. "You're not saying you wanna come?"

"Sure. Just let me get organized here. Not everyone is as lightning fast as you, at least not us *normal* people."

Dez crossed the floor and stood by the sink. She looked in the mirror and noticed that her braid was in disarray. She went back to her locker for a brush, then returned to the mirror and undid her hair and brushed it out. She hadn't expected Jaylynn to accept her offer. She had been imagining herself driving silently up the darkened Highway 35, good tunes on the stereo, reaching the shores of Lake Superior before the sun rose. With a sigh of impatience, she decided she'd rather have company, even though she felt apprehensive about it. She started to braid her hair, then gazed in the mirror. *The hell with it. I'll leave it loose. I'm going to get this damn mane cut one of these days.*

She wheeled around and marched back to her locker, dumped off the hairbrush, and rooted through her stuff until she found a black Twins baseball cap, which she mashed down on her head. Then she leaned back against the locker, crossed her arms over her chest, and let out another big sigh.

Jaylynn said, "Okay, okay. I think I'm ready." She cocked her head to the side as she watched Dez slowly straighten up. "Are you sure you want to do this?"

Dez nodded her head. "Let's hit the road, Jack. But we'll come back." Full of nervous energy, she took off toward the door.

Jaylynn shook her head. She thought, *what am I gonna do with you? You* are *certifiable.* She allowed herself a quick chuckle, then jogged after the bigger woman who was already halfway up the stairs at the end of the hall.

As they walked through the parking lot, Jaylynn reached out and touched Dez's arm. "I have one confession to make right here, right now, before we take off."

Dez glanced at her but kept walking. "And that would be?"

"Within fifteen minutes of departure, I'm likely to fall asleep. But I only need a short nap," she hastened to add, "and then I'll be totally perky when we get up there."

"Ohhhhh, *I* see," Dez said in a droll voice. "I've just invited a snoring companion. Well, don't worry about it. I'll keep the stereo up good and loud to drown it out. And just for the record, it's way over two hours up there. That'll be quite the *nap.*"

"Just letting you know." Jaylynn paused as Dez walked on. "You can always un-invite me."

Dez hit the button on the keyless entry, and the interior lights blinked on. She waved her partner forward. "Oh, come on," she said in a grumpy voice. "Get in." Jaylynn opened the door and climbed up into the shiny cranberry-colored truck. She settled into the comfortable seat as Dez started the engine and then ejected a CD saying, "Any musical requests?"

Jaylynn said, "Oh, no. You pick what you want. The driver should always get to choose."

"Don't you mean the person who's *awake* chooses?"

Jay smirked at her. "Very funny. I'm not asleep *yet*." She adjusted her seat to lean back slightly and put on her seat belt.

From the small crate on the floor, Dez picked up a CD she had recently bought and unwrapped the plastic around it. Peering closely, she picked away at the clear adhesive tape on the top. "Don't you just hate these damn CD wrappers? I've got no clue why they feel they have to weld them shut." She painstakingly peeled the tape off, pulled out the disk and inserted it, then stuck the cellophane and tape in the garbage holder.

Dez looked at the dashboard clock: 12:37. She put the truck in gear and pulled out of the parking lot as the strains of her new Ann Reed CD started. When the chorus came, she was intrigued to hear words that closely echoed her own feelings:

I've spent some time being somebody else,
surprised to find I can still be myself.
Oh, love's a long road home...

She turned onto the freeway and accelerated into the empty road, then set the cruise control and let out a deep breath.

What a ride, what a trip it's been,
looking back I'd hardly change it a bit,
Oh, love's a long road home...

When the song ended, she hit the replay and listened to it all over again.

She glanced over at Jaylynn and couldn't help but smile when she saw the younger woman slumped against the window, already crashed, her face relaxed and soft. Her short blonde hair shone white in the moonlight slanting in the window. Dez looked at the clock on the dash: 12:44. Seven minutes. She shook her head. *Geez, if I could go to sleep that quick and sleep as soundly—well, I'm jealous, that's for sure.* Tossing the black baseball cap behind the seat, she ran a hand through her hair and brushed it out of her eyes, remembering exactly why she tied it back or braided it most of the time. She turned down the music a notch, but she could still hear it clearly:

Everyday
This road don't stay the same
It's smooth, it buckles, it's firm, it falls apart
It's just the road of the heart.

The dark road was calming to her nerves, and she soon found herself thinking about the last several months. She felt like she had been on a long forced march, short of energy, short of faith, bereft of all hope. Since Ryan died...she didn't like to think about it, but to be honest, it had been a year of hell. She wasn't sure why the world seemed to have returned to a reasonable equilibrium, why she suddenly, without any warning or explanation, had regained some sort of inner balance. All she knew for sure was that she had a wild yearning to feel alive again, to feel energy and excitement. It didn't seem true to Ryan's memory, but then again, it didn't seem true to his memory to mourn indefinitely. She thought of the goofy smirk his face so often held and how much like a little brother he always seemed, even though he was older. Remembering his constant teasing and good spirits brought a bittersweet smile to her face. Many days he was the only good thing about her heart-wrenching job. He was, anyway, until Jaylynn came along.

She heard a sigh from her companion and looked across the cab. Jaylynn shivered and groaned in her sleep. Dez reached over and turned the heater up one notch, which, since she was perfectly comfortable, was all she thought she could bear. She flipped up the seat's center arm console and grasped the steering wheel with her left hand. Using her right she fished around behind the seats until her fingers found the soft material of an old baby blue car blanket. She pulled it up and over, onto the top of the bench seat, then stretched across the truck cab and gripped the sleeve of Jaylynn's jacket. The sleeping woman shifted and let out a quiet whimper.

Dez tugged on her sleeve a bit more and pulled her companion toward her. Jaylynn turned to the left and leaned. Softly Dez said, "You can lie down, Jay."

With a sigh, Jaylynn shifted the seat belt off her shoulder, and slid down onto the seat until her head came to rest using the bigger woman's thigh as a pillow.

That's not quite what I had in mind, Dez thought. But she awkwardly unfolded the blanket one-handed and tucked it around the sleeping rookie. She had to smile when Jaylynn's response was to snuggle into the blanket and nestle up closer. The smaller woman curled her legs up on the seat and fell back into a deep sleep.

The CD continued on to another song, and Dez listened to the words again. With a long arm she reached over her companion and grabbed up the jewel case and checked the song name: "Second Chance."

> *Made mistakes, I know it's true,*
> *I know what I put you through*
> *And I'm sorry I'm just beginning to see*
> *You're the one with most to lose*
> *I'm the one who's got to prove*
> *That I'm tryin', I'm beggin' you please*
> *For a second chance*
> *One more try*
> *Oh I don't wanna live without that*
> *One romance*
> *A second chance with you...*

Tentatively she placed her hand on the rookie's shoulder and was surprised when Jaylynn shifted and pulled the bigger woman's hand to her chest so that Dez cradled her protectively, her fingers laced with the smaller woman's.

Tears came to her eyes and spilled over. She wiped them awkwardly on her left shoulder, but they wouldn't stop. Through brimming eyes, she looked out on the dark road snaking through the night. *This woman doesn't lie, not even in her sleep. She trusts me. She really does care about me.* A sense of wonderment came over her. Looking down, she checked to see that Jaylynn was still out and was relieved to feel the sleeping woman's even breathing. She didn't know how she would explain to Jaylynn what she was feeling, but she knew she had to try sometime soon. She looked at the clock: 1:20. She figured she had another two hours or so to consider.

****

I am so cold, so cold. *Jaylynn lay on her side, and through sleepy eyes, she saw the crackling fire. But the small blaze didn't give off enough heat to warm her. She crossed her arms over her chest and curled into a ball.*

I am so numb, so very cold. *She couldn't wake up though, couldn't rouse herself enough to sit up and find a way to warm herself.*

Cool night air blew against her face and the smell of freshly cut pasture tickled her nose. Over the sound of crickets she heard a shuffle and then a toasty warm arm encircled her chest. A blanket covered her over and hot flesh pressed against the entire length of

the back of her, radiating heat. Warm breath against her neck, a
hand pressed flat against her chest. She laced her fingers with the
toasty hand and slipped deeper into the dreams that beckoned her.

Oh, thank you, *she thought as she went under.* Thank you so
very much.

"Hey, sleepyhead. Wake up."

Jaylynn opened her eyes and took a deep breath. "Don't
wanna," she said grumpily.

"We're on the hill going down into Duluth. If you wake up
now, you *may* be able to catch sight of the lake before we hit the
industrial park."

Jaylynn let out a groan and snuggled deeper under the blanket.
"It's pitch black out," she groused. "Unless there's a million lights
shining on the lake, I won't be able to see a thing." Suddenly she
moved her right hand and realized it was touching warm skin, a
hand definitely not her own. She let go and sat up with a start,
gaping at Dez out of the corner of her eye as she settled herself on
the other side of the seat.

"Ah, *now* you're awake."

"Yeah, yeah, I am." She ran both hands nervously through her
short hair and smoothed it down. "Sorry about that. Didn't mean
to use you as a pillow."

"Oh, yes you did," Dez said, holding back a smile.

"No, really. I apologize. Won't happen again."

Dez couldn't hold it in any longer. She laughed out loud.
"You mean it won't happen again until at least the trip home."

Jaylynn relaxed. "Can I help it if you're like a forest fire over
there?" She reached out and playfully punched Dez in the arm.

"Can I help it if you're some sort of heat seeking *miss*?"

"Ha ha. Very funny. For someone who got off shift in the
crabbiest mood on earth, you sure are in a good mood now." She
looked at the dashboard clock. "Is it my imagination or have we
been listening to this same CD for hours?"

"Yes, we have."

"You could have switched—it wouldn't have woke me up."

"A car crash wouldn't wake you up." Dez grinned. "It's a CD
I just got. I like it." She turned it up. "I decided she's my new
favorite artist."

Jaylynn closed her eyes for a moment and took a deep breath.
She felt nervous, her stomach skipping and churning. She sneaked
a glance at her companion from the corner of her eye and was
surprised to see the happy, content look on her face. "Hey," she
said. "I like your hair loose like that. You should wear it that way
more often."

Even though she couldn't actually see her in the darkened cab, she knew Dez was blushing as she said, "Thanks. But it's like a horse's tail. Drives me crazy, so I usually tie it back." She steered the truck through one of the many Duluth tunnels and emerged onto a darkened main street.

Jaylynn reached over to stroke the brunette hair and then entangled her fingers for a moment before reluctantly pulling her hand away. "Yup, it is thick, isn't it? It's nice. My hair doesn't have near the body."

Before she knew it, a big hand shot over and palmed the back of her head, then tweaked her hair. "I can imagine you with long hair."

"Oh, it *was* long. I wore it long most of my life and only got it cut a couple of years ago, much to my mother's chagrin. This is much easier though."

"Maybe I have seen you before when you had long hair," Dez said thoughtfully. "From the first time I saw you, I thought you looked familiar." She turned right on Canal Park Drive, and when they crested the hill, she knew Lake Superior was just beyond.

"It's funny you should say that," Jaylynn said. "I sort of thought I knew you from somewhere, but I always wondered if maybe I imagined it. Maybe you saw me on campus my freshman year when my hair was long."

Dez shrugged. "Who knows?" She looked across the cab and grinned, then wheeled into the parking area and nosed the truck into a spot facing east. She shut the engine off and looked at the clock. "Sun'll be up before too long."

"Dez?" The bigger woman turned to look at her. "It's three o'clock in the morning."

"3:10."

"Whatever. Unless I miss my guess, it's two or three hours before sunrise."

"What's your point?"

"It's dark, nothing's open, we have to wait hours for this wondrous event, and it's getting cold in here."

Dez shook her head and gave a big sigh. "You are *such* a wuss."

Jaylynn gave her a happy smile. "I didn't sign on to be frozen to death. You wanna keep the heater on low?"

"What a waste of gas. Just come over here."

Jaylynn squinted at her partner in the darkness. Dez reclined her seat a couple notches, tilted the steering wheel up, then lifted the blanket from the middle of the seat and pulled it up. Hesitantly Jaylynn unhooked her seatbelt. She cast an anxious glance as she slid over. Dez fluffed the blanket and gathered the smaller woman up against her. With long arms, she tucked the blanket around Jaylynn's legs and shifted her own hips so that she faced her slightly and her back was angled partly against the driver's door.

Jaylynn found herself in the bigger woman's embrace, her ear against a wildly beating heart. She hugged her left arm to her own chest and tentatively reached her right arm around her partner's middle. In response Dez encircled her with both arms and pulled her closer, her chin resting on the top of the blonde head.

They cuddled together, wordlessly, for some time, and after a few minutes, their hearts calmed. The last thing Dez remembered before slipping off to sleep was a feeling of comfort and relaxation, a feeling that had not come to her for many months.

****

Jaylynn sleepily opened her eyes. She sat on a rocky promontory high above the sea. The ground was chilly despite the blanket she sat on, but she was mostly warm due to the morning sun streaming down upon her and the heating pad enveloping her back. She smelled the fresh sea air, and before her she watched a roiling ocean of water. Cozy and content, she sighed. Wow, that's an amazing heating pad—and it's outside, too. Wonder where the cord is? *She turned her head, only to realize she was nestled into the arms of one scorchingly heated woman.*

Tilting her head up and back, Jaylynn studied her. The slumbering woman leaned back against the wall of a cliff, her eyes closed. Worry lines creased her forehead, and there was a tiny V-shaped scar above her right brow, but otherwise, her face was unmarked. Without warning bright blue eyes popped open and focused on her, and a feeling of glee rose in the young woman. I know you! You are...you are... *Confused and perplexed, she frowned. She felt strong arms tighten around her middle, and lips, soft and moist, tickled the skin on the side of her neck.*

Her thoughts were in a jumble. Disjointed images rose in her mind, images of burning buildings and the sensation of falling, of bloodthirsty monsters with huge gaping teeth giving chase, of space ships crashing, and of pain coursing through her body. Wait, she thought in a panic as she looked about her. She saw only the jagged rocks, felt only the warmth of the sun on her legs. Are they coming? Are we safe? *She struggled and the arms tightened around her middle.* This doesn't happen in my dreams. You're supposed to save me. I'll do my part, but I don't recall how we got here, to this place...

She heard a voice whispering in her ear. Shhh. It's okay. Everything is going to be fine...trust me...it'll be fine...

****

Dez awoke with a start as a seagull swept low making a high-pitched "kwee-kwee" noise. It didn't get a stir from the slumbering bundle nestled up against her. She hugged Jaylynn tighter and looked out across the parking lot and toward the horizon. The sun would soon emerge, but at the moment all she could see of the lake was a solid dark gray mass and the faintest line where the sea met sky.

She took a deep breath and thought about the rookie and their relationship and how it was changing. She felt as though a deep chasm had been bridged, and the chasm had all been due to her own failure to understand the first thing about Jaylynn—not to mention herself.

What had Luella said about the two of them? Something about them being drawn to one another like those violets on her windowsill. Dez thought she was right. She couldn't explain it at all, but the pull she felt from the sleeping woman in her arms was more than she could resist. And she knew somehow that the feeling was mutual, though the idea of that scared the hell out of her. She'd faced down robbers and police chiefs, street thugs and drug runners, but none of them made her blood run cold with fear the way the idea of revealing her feelings to Jaylynn did. At the same time, there was a certainty about the rightness of doing it that made her resolve to figure out how to broach the subject.

One moment the world seemed dusky gray, and the next Dez saw fluorescent pink begin to appear before her. The lake shifted from an inky black mass to a choppy gray sea right before her eyes. Gradually, rays of sun peeked over the edge of the horizon, and Canal Park became more visible. Over her shoulder was the bronze statue of the old man and the sea. To her left and stretching around in front of them was a rocky beach full of stones and riprap. A leaning metal anchor, taller than Dez's head, was planted in the middle of a raised platform. All around it seagulls landed and walked, bobbing along in the wind like bits of Styrofoam.

Jaylynn shifted. "Dez?"

"Yes?"

She sat up and stretched her neck, then turned to gaze into serious blue eyes. "Do you know your heart beats only 54 times in a minute?"

"That's the last thing I expected to hear," Dez said, laughing. "How do you know that?"

"Because I've been counting all night."

"No, you've been *sleeping* all night."

Jaylynn sat up a little and reached for Dez's hand. "I've been awake for the last few minutes. I thought you were asleep still."

"Nah, just watching the sun come up." It was now peeping up over the horizon, and the light was bright. "It's going to be a nice day. Windy, but really pretty."

Jaylynn leaned her head against the bigger woman's shoulder and squeezed her hand. "What are we going to do once the sun's up?"

"I can guess what your vote is." As Dez said that, they both heard the rumble from Jaylynn's stomach.

"Yeah, yeah, I'm hungry. As usual."

Dez let go of Jaylynn's hand and reached to start the engine, but the other woman grabbed her arm to stop her. "Wait. Let's stay 'til the sun's all the way up. Then we can find a place to eat." If the truth were told, she'd have to say that she couldn't care less about the sun at that moment, but she didn't want to break the spell they both seemed to be under.

"All right." Dez opened her hand and looked at her palm. Jaylynn shyly placed her smaller hand against it and intertwined their fingers. She looked up into Dez's eyes, unsure if this was okay. The warm twinkle of the blue eyes that greeted her set her mind at ease.

Dez asked, "Do you sometimes wish we could start over, maybe meet all over again for the first time? Like at a coffeeshop or—or a basketball game, or maybe at a party?"

Jaylynn thought about that. "I really don't know. This has seemed so fated, so, hmmm, I'm not sure how to explain this, but it seems almost—"

"Like some sort of strange destiny?"

"Yeah. Do you believe in that?"

"I didn't use to." She paused. "But maybe I do now."

****

They stopped at a bakery on Superior Street. "Mmm, it smells *so* good in here," Jaylynn said. "Don't you love the smell of baking and cinnamon?" Dez nodded as she studied the huge variety of donuts in the long glass display case.

They bought donuts, coffee for Jaylynn, and bottles of water. As Dez stood at the register, insisting on paying for the treats, her companion asked, "Do you mean to tell me you're actually going to eat *two* apple fritters?"

The low voice said, "By that, are you insinuating that two is too many?"

Jaylynn gave a snort of laughter. "No! I just can't believe

you're actually going to place that much fat and sugar in the temple
of your body. You gotta admit—they are enormous."

The lady behind the counter, who was herself a rather substantial woman, laughed merrily. "She could use a little meat on
them bones," she said. "I'll throw in an extra for you."

So they departed with their drinks and five donuts. They
stopped at a gas station to use the restrooms. While Dez filled up
the truck with gas, Jaylynn called her house and left a message for
Tim and Sara so they wouldn't worry, and then they continued up
the road.

With her mouth full of a delectable chocolate Long John,
Jaylynn said, "Where to, Magoo?"

Dez suddenly realized she hadn't even asked Jaylynn what she
wanted to do. *What if she wants to head home?* But she was
already on the coast highway heading north, so she simply said, "I
was heading toward Gooseberry Falls. You been there?"

"No. I've passed by a few times, but never stopped."

"Feel like hiking?"

"At six a.m.?"

"Hey, it'll be seven or so when we get there."

"Sounds like that gives me just enough time for another nap,"
she said as she took a last swig of her coffee.

"Wait a minute. I thought coffee was supposed to keep a
person awake."

"Nah, never affects me." She slung the blanket over her
shoulders and looked at Dez as if for permission.

Dez let out a sigh. She patted the seat next to her. "Go ahead.
I'll wake you up when we get there."

Jaylynn stretched out on her left side and returned to the
snuggly position with her head on Dez's right thigh. Dez gripped
the wheel with her left hand and rested her other hand on Jaylynn's
shoulder. A small hand promptly reached up, grabbed her hand,
and pulled it to her chest.

****

Later, at Gooseberry Falls, Dez parked the truck. As Jaylynn
got out, she could hear the rush of water and smell the fresh scent it
carried. The big waterfalls were close to the bridge, and she could
see the water as she hiked excitedly down a series of stone stairs.

"Wow, this is great," Jaylynn said. She stood gazing out over
rocks carved out of the hillside from many eons of erosion. Aspen,
birch, and evergreen trees lined the sides of the deep chasm, the
leaves of the deciduous trees starting to change from green to gold.
She squeezed past an older couple who stood looking at the

crashing water and stepped carefully across the dark brown rock as if spellbound. She stood close to the first large pool of water. Dez followed a few paces behind, her hands in her jeans pockets. Turning around, eyes shining, Jaylynn said, "Oh, I wish I had my camera. I never knew this was so beautiful." She spun around and knelt on one knee, thrusting her fingers in the water only to jerk them out just as abruptly. "Eeek! That's *cold*!" She stood and shook her hand out, drying it on the leg of her pants.

Dez smiled and said, "There are five waterfalls all together. These two here," she pointed to the left, "are the biggest, but there's usually a lot of people here." She looked around at the kids throwing rocks and other sightseers taking photos. In a grouchy voice she said, "What are all these people doing here on a Monday anyway?"

"They're here because it's so gorgeous." She let her eyes scan the area yet another time and decided it was one of the loveliest spots she'd ever been to.

"We can take that path—it's called the Gitchi Gummi Trail," Dez said, pointing alongside the water. "It comes out at Agate Beach where this runs into Lake Superior. Let's walk out there, okay?"

She had such a hopeful look on her face that Jaylynn found she couldn't refuse. She looked down at the lightweight jacket she was wearing. "But I bet I'll get cold."

"I'll run up to the truck and get that blanket, and I'm pretty sure I have a sweatshirt behind the seat."

"You don't have to do that."

"I don't mind," and with that, she was off like a shot. Jaylynn watched as her long legs ate up the flights of stone stairs, and then she disappeared around a corner at the top. In moments she was back, skipping down the stairs like a kid. She arrived, breathless, carrying the light blue blanket, her black baseball cap, and a gray U of M sweatshirt.

Jaylynn took the sweatshirt and said, "Hey! I think this is mine. I was *wondering* where it was."

Dez mumbled, "Yeah, guess you left it in the truck a while ago." She jammed her black cap on over windblown hair and started off down the path, carrying the blanket and not letting the rookie see the embarrassed look on her face. She had been toting the sweatshirt around for months. She knew she should have returned it long ago, but it was the only thing she had of Jaylynn's, and she couldn't bring herself to give it back. She'd even worn it a couple of times. She looked over her shoulder to see Jaylynn pulling the thick sweatshirt on over her polo shirt and then zipping up her jacket over it. The younger woman hastened to catch up with her.

"My sweatshirt smells like you, Dez."

The taller woman blanched. She stopped and faced the rookie. Stuttering she said, "Gosh, I hope it's not sweaty or anything. I–I–I think I did wear it. Yeah, I guess I must have."

Jaylynn pulled at the neckband a bit and ducked her head down to sniff it. "No, it doesn't smell bad at all. It smells good—like you."

Dez wheeled around and began walking faster, her face flaming. Jaylynn hustled behind her and continued to talk. "Ever notice how people all smell so different? And did you ever read about pheromones and all that stuff in biology?" They stepped up on a wooden bridge. It was only five feet across and carried them over a muddy wash of water. "Smells are so interesting. Like have you noticed that some people who really like each other a lot seem to smell the same, and if you're around someone whose smell doesn't appeal to you, you just don't seem to like them at all?"

Dez didn't answer, so Jaylynn kept on. "For instance, Tim and Kevin. You probably didn't get close enough to notice this, but I'll just tell you anyway. They smell the same. If I hug either of them, they carry the same scent."

Over her shoulder Dez asked, "Like they use the same cologne, or what?"

"No, not that. They just have the same smell—I'm sorry. I think I'm explaining this badly." She stepped over a twisted tree root and ducked under a low-hanging branch. "Whatever they eat, they both carry the same exact scent. Their breath is even the same. They probably sweat identically or something. And you know, they're perfect for each other, can't resist each other. It's that pheromone thing, I'm just sure of it. This guy is the one for Tim. I can tell. Nobody else has ever affected him this way. But they're not the only ones like this. So are Sara and Bill. And my mom and stepdad. And have you ever noticed that about Crystal and Shayna? Those two always smell like a vanilla candle."

In a low gruff voice, Dez said, "I'm not sure I ever get close enough to people to test your theory." She didn't know where the rookie was going with this idea, but she was relieved she seemed to have forgotten about the sweatshirt.

Jaylynn thought about that as she strode along right behind the taller woman. "Guess you'll have to take my word for it 'cause I think it's true."

The path twisted to the right and wandered around a bit. Just when Jaylynn thought they were deep in the forest, they suddenly emerged from the trees and found a pebbly beach spread out before them. She stopped and stared. Two hundred yards away were huge cracked glacial rocks, tossed haphazardly in what looked like an enormous pile at the water's edge. The water was blue, the color of Dez's eyes, and it lapped gently at the shore.

The sun shone bright but cold. Dez had kept walking and now stood forty yards away near the water, the blanket over her shoulder. She had her hands in jeans pockets, her long hair whipping to the side in the brisk breeze. Dez glanced over her shoulder, then wheeled around and found Jaylynn with her eyes. She raised her arms parallel to the ground, then tipped her head to the side slightly and shrugged as if to ask why her companion wasn't keeping up.

Jaylynn smiled and slogged through the pebbles to join her. The air was crisp and smelled fresh, like clean laundry, and she breathed it in, letting the familiarity of the place soothe her. She came to stand right next to the taller woman and reached up to grasp her upper arm. "It's really beautiful here, Dez. What a great place."

Dez nodded. She hadn't been to Gooseberry Falls for several years—not since Karin. She'd always loved it and had hiked it high and low. She'd climbed the rocks and cliffs with her dad when she was younger, but she had thought Karin had spoiled it for her. She was surprised that the association of the place with Karin no longer had an effect on her at all. She realized, unexpectedly, that she could reclaim a favorite spot, and it made her feel relieved and warm all over.

On impulse she grabbed Jaylynn's hand and pulled her toward the rocks. "Come on, let me show you something." She hauled Jaylynn up on one gigantic rock.

The younger woman perched on the large flat rock, squatting with both palms flat on its surface. "Do I need to remind you that I'm kind of afraid of heights?"

"We won't be very high. Don't worry." Dez pulled herself up another level and reached back to help her companion. They crawled up the pile of massive rocks. Dez picked her way along an edge and squeezed through a narrow space between two boulders, reaching back to help Jaylynn when necessary. Beyond the boulders there was a wide flat spot, and then a cliff, and from it they could see the craggy shoreline and the lake, which stretched out for miles.

Jaylynn inched over to stand behind Dez as the bigger woman gazed out from the precipice. In a worried voice she said, "Don't get too close."

Dez turned to face her anxious friend and gave her a brilliant smile. "I thought *I* was the worry wart around here."

"We'll trade off. It can be my turn today." She reached for Dez's hand and pulled her away from the edge.

Dez looked around and then pointed to a smooth depression in the rock against a tall outcropping. "There's a great place to sit." She realized she was nervous, but she moved over and arranged the partly folded blanket in the hollow, then sat on it and scooted back. She gestured to Jaylynn. "It's a good spot here—out of the wind. Come join me?" She patted the blanket in front of her and drew her knees up. Jaylynn gingerly stepped over and lowered herself to sit, her back against Dez's shins. The bigger woman leaned back against the cool rock. "Is that okay?"

"Um hmm." Jaylynn shivered.

"Are you cold again?"

The rookie nodded. "A teeny bit hungry, too."

Dez laughed. She reached into her jacket pocket and pulled out a pack of Hostess Chocolate Cupcakes, which she set beside her. She unzipped her coat and moved her knees apart and made a V with her legs, then surprised Jaylynn by wrapping her arms around the shivering woman and pulling her closer. Once she got the smaller woman settled comfortably against her midsection, she put her hands on her own knees. Dez hoped this was okay. It was all she could do to keep her hands off Jaylynn. But she had resolved not to be pushy, to let whatever happened happen. *If we are only destined to be friends, I will live with that—maybe.* She grinned and picked up the cellophane-wrapped treat next to her and thrust it in the rookie's face.

Jaylynn twisted around. "Hey! Where'd you get that?"

"Bought it in the food mart when we stopped for gas."

"Well, aren't you the clever one." She ripped into the package and nestled back into the warmth. Dez pulled her open jacket around the smaller woman as far as it would go.

As she munched, Jaylynn suddenly remembered fragments of a dream. She swallowed a bite of cupcake and said, "You won't believe this, but earlier today in the truck, I dreamed of us in this place, this cliff, sitting here. Weird, that is *so* weird...hmm..."

"What?"

Jaylynn squeezed her eyes shut and willed the dream to come to the forefront but it would not. "I *hate* when that happens!"

"What? What do you mean?"

"When a scrap of a dream comes into your mind but before you can really remember it fully, it slips away. I *hate* that. But it was a good dream, I think." She closed her eyes again and waited, but it was too late. She opened her eyes and looked out on the broad expanse of the lake. A movement caught her eye. Along the shore was a stand of poplar trees, and a bird rose from high up in the branches and took flight. She watched the hawk ascend, then circle above the treeline, floating and dipping in the morning wind.

Dez's hand rose from her knee, and Jaylynn saw her pointing toward the hawk. "Yes, I see. Isn't she beautiful?" She reached up and took the big hand in her own and pulled it down and around her.

A husky voice said, "How do you know it's a she?"

She shrugged. "I don't know. It just seems right. I imagine she's circling above her nest, keeping an eye on it." She squeezed the hand she held. Tentative arms encircled her waist, and Jaylynn drew her own knees up and leaned back with a peaceful sigh. When Dez shifted, Jaylynn twitched and asked, "Am I squishing you?"

"Oh, no. I'm just settling in," she said in a husky voice. "Hold still. You're fine."

Jaylynn sat peacefully. She couldn't help but smile and was glad Dez couldn't see her face because she didn't want to be asked any questions right now. She wanted to sit with this woman on the rocks gazing at Lake Superior forever and ever. *But I'd get awfully hungry,* she thought and then stifled a giggle.

A deep voice near her ear murmured, "What's so funny?"

"Just thinking about my stomach again." She picked up the cupcake package and held it up. "Do you want this second cup-cake?"

"No, I'm fine. Go ahead."

"I'm not used to eating something so sweet anymore."

"Wanna save it for later?"

When she nodded, Dez took the cellophane package and tucked it into her jacket pocket. Quickly she returned her arm to its place around Jaylynn's middle, feeling the smooth surface of the windbreaker beneath her palms. When the rookie contentedly wrapped arms over the top of her forearms, Dez felt a warmth rise from her midsection and spread through her body. Jaylynn's blonde head nestled under her chin on Dez's chest and she could have kissed the white-blonde hair without stretching a bit. She took a deep breath and savored the smell. It occurred to her that maybe Jaylynn was right: maybe it was the scent of a person that attracted you to them. And she certainly felt attracted now. She hoped the woman snuggling comfortably between her legs didn't realize what was happening. She didn't want to scare her away or overwhelm her—but suddenly, Dez was flooded with heat. She tried to still her breath, to pace her thumping heart, but the sensations racing through her body seemed to short-circuit her will. With one slight shift her lips could be at the smaller woman's ear, her neck. With every ounce of will, she fought against what her body urged her to do.

Dez cleared her throat and said, "Should we head back home?"

"Are you in a hurry to get back today?"

"No."

"We could look around some more if you want." There was a question in her voice.

"Is anyone expecting you—I mean, do you have to be anywhere today?"

"Nope. If Sara or Tim come home and wonder where I am, they'll get my phone message. You're stuck with me for as long as you want."

Dez tipped her head to the side and thought to herself, *what if it's forever? What if I want to be stuck with you forever?* She could no longer avoid this conclusion. She felt complete when she was with Jaylynn, as though all was right with the world—even if that did sound trite and corny. At the same time, the intensity of her feelings scared the hell out of her. *What if this woman here in my arms doesn't feel the same way?* She had spoken once of lust, but lust was not enough. *I want love. Passion. Commitment. Forever. What likelihood is there of that?* And Dez had felt the price of unrequited love—how could she live through that again?

They sat for some time, long enough for a ship to appear on the horizon and steam south until they could no longer see it over the rocks.

"Dez?"

"Hmmm?"

"Do you ever think about the man who killed Ryan? Aren't you glad you didn't have to shoot him?"

All thoughts of love and sex and commitment vanished from the tall woman's mind. She shifted uncomfortably. "I try not to think about any of that. Why?"

"'Cause I can't stop thinking about the guy I shot..." She paused, fumbling for words. "He was so young. He could've had a life." In a whisper Dez could hardly hear, she said, "It's my fault he doesn't. I still can't believe someone's dead because of me."

In a firm voice, Dez said, "He's dead because of his own choices. It's not your fault. If you hadn't shot him, he'd have shot you and probably the clerk, too."

"We don't know that," she said in a strangled voice.

"It's likely though. He was high. It wasn't your fault, Jay. You have to believe that." Now she leaned forward and nuzzled the smaller woman's neck with the side of her cheek. She tightened her grip and made a soothing sound in the back of her throat.

"I wish I could go back and do it all over again," Jaylynn said, and Dez realized the younger woman was crying.

In a choked voice Dez said, "You did the right thing. You probably saved my life—and yours. What else could you have done?"

"I could have shot to wound," she choked out.

"It happened too fast, Jay. You just reacted out of instinct."

"No. I made a choice." The events played out in Jaylynn's mind as they had hundreds of times already. The startled face of the gunman as he swung toward them. Her arm going back automatically and unsnapping her holster. The explosion and Dez falling back against her. Instinctively using her partner as a shield as she pulled her weapon. Aiming. Firing. And then a split second feeling of a weight descending upon her chest and choking all the air out. "I shot to kill, not to wound."

Dez leaned forward and inclined her head around to see Jaylynn's face, but the smaller woman turned the other way. "Don't look at me, Dez. I probably look terrible."

Dez shook her head. "No, you don't. You look fine, Jay. Listen to me. I think what you're feeling is totally normal. I would feel all the same things. Jay, when we became cops, we knew this kind of thing could happen. We're trained to respond a certain way, and you acted exactly the way you were taught. You did the right thing. If it happened again, I would want you to react the very same way."

"It—it really bothers me, Dez. I think about it far too much."

"I know what you mean," the tall woman said bitterly.

"Will you tell me what happened that night, the night Ryan got shot?"

Dez stiffened, her breath stopping in her chest. *Not today. I can't.* She forced herself to take a breath and then relaxed her hands, which she found she was gripping in tight fists. "Yes," she said. "I will someday. Just not now, okay?"

Jaylynn's head nodded in front of her. "Another thing keeps bothering me. I couldn't take it if it happened again. I—I don't know if I can—I'm not sure if...oh geez! How were you able to stay on the job?" She wiped her eyes on the sleeve of her jacket and shifted to the left so that she could look back at the concerned woman behind her.

Dez stared at her, surprised. "I don't know. I just did. I tried not to think about it."

"But did you ever want to quit?"

"Quit? Quit being a cop? No, it's the only thing I know how to do."

Jaylynn burst out into a mirthful laugh. "What do you mean? You know how to do a *ton* of things."

That response flustered Dez, and now it was her turn to look away from the steady eyes. "Not anything that's a profession."

"Oh, give me a break. You can build stuff, you get along with people, you follow directions well, and you're an excellent teacher.

Hell, you could run a paint company. You're very smart, Dez. There's a million professions for you. You've been a patrol cop for all this time. Have you ever thought of promoting?"

Dez pressed back against the cool rock. "Sometimes."

In an excited voice, Jaylynn said, "Why don't you take the sergeant's exam then? It's coming up in a couple months again." She sat up and shifted almost a quarter turn so that she could look over her left shoulder and face the dark woman.

"I don't know. Sergeants have a crappy job."

"You'd be a great detective. Why haven't you applied for vice or homicide or something like that?"

"How did this suddenly get to be all about me?" Dez grumbled.

For some reason that made Jaylynn laugh out loud. "You are such a character."

"What's *that* supposed to mean?"

"You just crack me up." She grinned and then impulsively said, "You make me happy."

Next thing Dez knew, Jaylynn was again nestled in her arms, this time twisted more on her side, her cheek pressed into the chest of the tall cop's green sweatshirt. Dez slowly brought her arms up and gathered the woman tighter to her. She felt a wave of protectiveness wash over her and then realized she was helpless before this bundle of energy. She could no sooner resist her than she could stop breathing. And much as she might hate the uncertainty, she was going to have to do something about it. She sighed and in a soft voice said, "You make me happy, too."

****

Some time later, the two women made their way off the rocks, across the pebbly beach, and back through the forest. It was not nearly as warm under the cover of trees, so Jaylynn unfolded the blanket and draped it over her shoulders.

Dez said, "You look like you're in a blue cape."

"Just call me Superman," Jaylynn said.

"I'm pretty sure Superman's cape was red."

"You think so?" she asked as she thought for a moment. "It couldn't possibly have been this warm."

"Bet that old rag won't let you fly though."

Jaylynn cheerfully trudged up the stone stairs to the truck and stood inspecting the blue material. "I think this blanket has gotten a little dirty today," she said as she refolded it.

"It'll wash," the bigger woman said in a grouchy voice as she stepped up into the truck.

There she goes, thought Jaylynn, *back to being a woman of few words.* She crawled up into the cab and watched Dez out of the corner of her eye as she started the truck up.

Dez looked over and caught her staring. "What?"

Jaylynn hastened to shrug and say, "Nothing," with a hint of innocence in her voice. Inside she was smiling to herself and wondering how to get her companion to extend the day with her.

In a noncommittal voice, Dez said, "Back to Duluth?"

"What do *you* want to do?"

Dez looked away and out the side window. She didn't want the morning to end. *I don't want to go home.* She hadn't wanted to leave the rocky promontory they'd been on. "Are you hungry?"

Jaylynn giggled. "Do fish have fins?"

Dez couldn't help but chuckle. She relaxed as she backed out of the parking space. "Then I guess the question is do we go north or south?"

"Which direction will yield the closest food?"

Dez grinned. "Hmmm..." She thought for a moment. "Two Harbors is south and has some restaurants. Beaver Bay and Silver Bay are north and they do, too. Beyond them there are some neat towns, and there's always Grand Marais, but that's a bit of a drive."

"Sounds good to me."

Dez frowned. "You want to go to Grand Marais?"

"Yeah. Let's head that direction. If you don't mind, that is."

"No, I don't mind at all." Dez threw the truck into gear and peeled out of the parking lot, accelerating to 50 and then easing into a steady speed. She heard a click and saw Jaylynn unbuckling her seatbelt.

Jaylynn moved over toward Dez and fished around in the cushions of the bench seat to find the middle lap belt. Shyly, she said, "I'm gonna sit here by you, okay?"

"Sure."

Jaylynn pulled the center belt around her waist and snapped it together, then let her hands drop to her lap. They drove along up the road like that for some time, following a string of vehicles, before Dez finally mustered up the courage to take her right hand off the wheel and reach out. Jaylynn promptly opened her hand and laced their fingers together.

At the same time that she was flooded with warmth and a buoyancy she wasn't used to, Dez found herself worried about the teenage emotions that kept rising in her unbidden. She felt like a fool, like a sheepish, daffy, lovesick teenager. It was embarrassing. She snuck a dubious look out of the corner of her eye, and her companion seemed to have the same bashfulness adorning her face. Her eyes did not veer away quickly enough, and Jaylynn suddenly turned and looked up at her, catching her unguarded gaze.

The smaller woman asked, "Are we going to talk about what's happening?"

Dez knew immediately what she was referring to, but she hesitated. She turned her eyes back to the road. "No." She paused and took a deep breath. "I mean yes. Just—just, not right now. Is that okay?"

She watched Jaylynn look down at their hands, and then the hazel eyes were looking up at her, full of trust and hope. "Can I ask why?"

Dez didn't answer right away, but when she did, she chose her words with care. "Let's just enjoy the day for right now."

"But we *will* talk?"

Dez nodded. "Soon."

Jaylynn lifted their hands out of her lap. "Is this okay?"

With a big smile on her face, she said, "Yes, it's more than okay. Please—stay right where you are." She leveled her blue eyes on the rookie and was rewarded with a smile, and then Jaylynn leaned her head against her shoulder.

It felt very right. It felt like home.

Chapter
30

Dez and Jaylynn ate omelettes and hash browns in Grand Marais at a funny little café called Gwen's Goodies. In addition to the old-fashioned chrome-trimmed booth in which they sat, they were surrounded by art supplies, stationery, and art pieces: sculptures, mosaics, paintings, clay pots. One entire wall was covered with artwork Grandma Moses could have done. Upon another wall, a variety of Amish quilts were displayed. Over their table hung a four-foot-tall paper-maché mask. Celtic music warbled in the background. The small restaurant was an explosion: wild colors, the sound of pennywhistles, and the smell of butter and cinnamon. Jaylynn loved it.

The tall woman sat slouched in the booth, her hands in her jacket pockets, gazing across the room out the café's bay window. The sun shone brightly through the window, and across the road she could see piles of rocks bordering a finger of the lake that pointed toward them.

Jaylynn said, "A penny for your thoughts."

Dez's head swung toward her, crystal blue eyes coming to rest on the rookie's face. Jaylynn was once again startled at the intensity of her companion's gaze. She couldn't help but smile.

"I wasn't thinking of anything much...just how my dad used to take my brother and me out walleye fishing when we were little. Not up here, but at a smaller lake."

"Do you just have one brother?" Jaylynn asked. "No sisters?"

She nodded and pulled her hands out of her pockets. "Yup."

"You never talk about him."

Dez shrugged and sat up taller. "Not much to say. We're not close."

Jaylynn paused, considering whether to ask the next logical question. Instead, she said, "Where does he live?"

"Eden Prairie."

"That's not far to travel. Wish my family lived so near. And I always wished I had a brother. Is he older or younger than you?"

"Younger, by four years."

Jaylynn paused a moment, worried that she'd start treading on thin ice, but she went ahead. "At the hospital, you know when you got shot, I got the impression that your mom is a doctor."

"Yup. Ophthalmologist."

Jaylynn nodded. "I see. Is she married to that Mac?"

This clearly startled Dez. She jerked up from her slouching position in the booth and leveled an intent stare at the rookie. "Of course they're not married. Why would you say that?"

Jaylynn set her fork down and pushed her plate away. She wiped her lips with the napkin and said, "That night—at the hospital—it was clear to me that they care about each other."

"He was my father's best friend. That's it."

"Dez," Jaylynn said gently. "It's been a lot of years since your dad died. Your mom has moved on, I think."

"With Mac? I don't think so. You're wrong." She crossed her arms over her sweatshirt and glowered at her with a face so cross that Jaylynn would have laughed if the topic had not been so obviously painful.

Jaylynn sat quietly thinking back to the scene in the hospital room on the Fourth of July. She had no doubt that Mac MacArthur and Colette Reilly were more than just friends, but she didn't understand why Dez not only did not know that, but was also so against it. *Yet another mystery to unravel.* She wondered how many secrets and old wounds this woman before her harbored.

The waitress appeared to ask if they needed anything more, and when both women shook their heads, she set the check face-down on the table and cleared their plates away. Dez picked up the ticket, glanced at it, and rose, tossing a sheaf of bills on the table.

Jaylynn opened her mouth to speak, but before she could say anything, Dez said, "I got that—don't worry about it. C'mon."

The rookie slid out of the booth, wincing at the change in her companion. She followed Dez by an eight-foot-tall display of Mary Engelbreit items, between two racks of stationery, and past a shelf full of art supplies. When they got out to the sidewalk, the taller woman strode toward her truck.

Jaylynn caught up with Dez and grabbed her hand, halting her. "Dez! Look at me."

The tall woman raised blue eyes full of misery.

"I didn't mean to upset you."

Mutely Dez nodded, but it looked to Jaylynn like she was on the verge of tears.

"There's no hurry, is there? Can we walk over there by the water?" The rookie pointed across the road to where the long jetty extended out to the sea. She kept hold of Dez's hand and pulled her along behind her, across the street, down a short walk, and then onto the pebbly beach. The wind whipped her hair to the side, and she felt the warmth of the sun as it shone down brightly upon them. As the two women drew close, two gulls took flight and flapped above them before retreating to a safe distance. Jaylynn stepped around a dead bass, its flesh mostly picked away by the birds, and she kept a tight hold on Dez's hand, which felt cold in her grip.

Once they were far away from the street, and the restaurant appeared as small as a tiny wooden block in the distance, Jaylynn stopped and looked up at the person she'd been dragging along behind her. Still holding her hand, she asked, "Remember that conversation we had walking around the lake? That one about practicing talking about stuff?"

Dez nodded.

Jaylynn gave her a little grin and said, "You've been shirking your training in that area. So out of the blue you get a little heavy weight and you can't lift it." She made a tsk-tsk sound with her tongue, and with her free hand shook her finger in the air. In a kind voice, she said, "You know what happens when an athlete dogs it in practice?"

Dez didn't respond in words, but a line of furrows appeared on her forehead, and she looked away out to sea.

"Um hmm. I know you know. Extra drills. Extra training until you're on top of your form." She reached up and cupped Dez's cheek in one hand, bringing the other woman's face back so they were eye to eye. She let her hand drop. "You can't run away from this, Dez, and you don't need to. Come here."

Dez let Jaylynn lead her another twenty paces until they came to a large chunk of driftwood wedged deep into the sand. Between two branches, there was just enough space for one person to sit.

"Here, sit down and take a load off," Jaylynn said, the double meaning not missed by Dez. She started to sit on the log, but the rookie said, "Wait a minute. I think *I* should get the tall seat for once." She sat and pointed down, "You get to sit in front this time."

Dez lowered herself onto the warm sand and nestled her hips back against the partly buried log. Jaylynn splayed her legs out on either side of her, and the big cop leaned her head back until it came in contact with warm solidness. She felt the rookie rest her forearms on her broad shoulders and then a tickle of breath in her ear said, "You don't even have to look at me—just start talking."

Dez was at a loss as to what to say, where to start. She had not been involved in her mother's life—or Mac's, for that matter—for nearly seven years. Mac had retired five years earlier at 55, and she so very rarely saw him. For all she knew, perhaps they *were* together. She didn't remember very much about their visit during that one long night she had spent at the hospital after being shot. She wished she did, but from the moment of the bullet's impact until the next morning, everything was fuzzy.

She sat up tall and reached to grasp Jaylynn's forearms, pulling the tawny limbs down, and then crossed her own arms over the top of them. The smaller woman shifted until she was pressed tight against the muscular back, her chin resting on Dez's left shoulder, and her arms around a warm neck.

In a hoarse voice, Dez asked, "Are you comfortable?"

"Yes, I am," a soft voice said in her ear.

"Okay. Then what do you remember about my mother's visit to the hospital that night?"

Jaylynn considered for a moment. "Are you asking me to tell you every little detail I can remember, or do you want to know why I think Mac and your mother are lovers?"

A snort of laughter erupted from Dez. It occurred to her that Jaylynn didn't mess around skimming the surface of tough subjects. Just then she peered around Dez's shoulder and tried to see in her eyes. "Hey, hey!" Dez said. "You're supposed to stay on your side of the couch, Dr. Freud." She felt Jaylynn laughing behind her. "Yes, I want to know why you think they're lovers."

She heard the rookie take a deep breath and then say, "Body proximity, eye contact, affectionate touch."

Dez wanted to mention that with the exception of the eye contact, right now anyone observing the two of them would assume they were lovers—and *they* weren't—but she held her tongue.

Jaylynn went on, "Do you recall what you said to your mother?"

Dez paused, then shook her head and waited.

"If I remember correctly, it was something like, 'Why are you here, Mom? You don't even like me anymore.' As soon as you said that, she teared up, and Mac stepped in close, a little behind her. His arm had been across her shoulders, but he let it drop around her waist—practically around her whole middle—so that his hand came to rest like this..." Jaylynn's hand caressed down Dez's front until she laid it flat against the reclining woman's stomach, just below her left breast.

Dez drew in a sharp breath.

Jaylynn said, "See? That's kind of an intimate touch, and he wouldn't have done that—under those circumstances especially— unless they had a high level of trust in one another. And from your mother's demeanor, her manner, she doesn't let just *anybody* touch her."

"Like mother, like daughter, huh?"

Jaylynn laughed. "You could say that."

Dez thought about what Jaylynn had explained. It did make sense. She remembered that all through her teen years she had wanted Mac to take her father's place, to leave his wife and come live with her family. But it wasn't until she was 22 that he and his wife had divorced, and then so soon after that, she and Mac had their falling out. Her mouth dropped open, and she stared out across Lake Superior in wonderment. After a moment, she said, "Shit, I think I just figured something out."

"What?"

Jaylynn pressed a slightly chilled face against her neck, and Dez felt a thrill of electricity course through her body, which she tried to disregard. "I always assumed that my mother called up Mac and outed me to him out of spite. But what if she and he were seeing each other and I became a topic of conversation between them? Maybe it was a natural thing for her to confide in him about me, since she knew he cared about me. Then what if he started acting so distant with me because he was just being protective of their relationship as well as my feelings, like maybe he didn't want to interfere with my life?" Dez knew Mac had never been the type to horn in on anyone's business, not in his work life and not in his personal life. He had, in fact, always let her work through her troubles her own way and had been quite supportive of her.

"Why don't you ask him?" Jaylynn asked.

"Easier said than done."

"Call him up on the phone. Send him a letter. Just start something. You'll never find out otherwise, and aren't you incredibly curious? I know I am."

Dez couldn't keep from grinning and was glad the rookie couldn't see the goofy expression on her face. "Yeah, I guess I am. It's probably time to bury the hatchet anyway—for sure with my mom."

"She loves you a lot, Dez. I could see that in the hospital room. When you said that to her, I could tell her heart just about broke. I hope you can sort things out with her—and with your brother. Why don't you two get along?"

"He took Mom's side."

"What does that mean?"

"Let me see. He told me I was being pigheaded and mean, and he said I was a jerk for upsetting her about Mac and also about my lifestyle, and then he said I could just butt out of his life until I saw fit to treat her better." Jaylynn was very still and didn't speak for so long that Dez finally said, "What? What are you thinking?"

"To be honest, I was just realizing that this is the stuff family feuds are made of and that I hope, hope, hope that my sisters and I never go through this. What's your brother's name?"

"Patrick."

"And you haven't seen him for seven years?"

Dez shrugged. "About that."

"Oh, Dez. He was right about one thing. You are the most pigheaded woman I've ever met."

"Hey!" she protested, as she held back her desire to burst out laughing. "I'm sure Dr. Goldman would never be so judgmental."

"But she's not your friend, you fool. I will say one thing for you though: you've got endurance."

"And *you* said I was doggin' it earlier."

"Truer words were never spoken! You're going to need lots and lots and lots of practice at this, Miss Grin-and-Stuff-It. But your exercises have gone quite well today, don't you think?"

"Yeah, not bad." She got to her feet and brushed the sand off the back of her jeans, then reached down and took Jaylynn's hand to pull her up. Still holding the smaller woman's hand she pointed out to the end of the jetty and said, "Let's walk all the way out there, okay?"

Jaylynn nodded, and they strolled along the pebbly beach, hand in hand, in the warm sunlight.

****

Two meals, a large snack, and several hundred miles later, they finally returned to St. Paul. It was full dark, and the early September sun had long ago set. Dez pulled the truck into the parking lot at the precinct and wheeled over to Jaylynn's Camry. Before they came to a stop, the rookie had unhooked her seatbelt and scooted over to the other side of the truck. She sat there awkwardly when the truck halted in front of her car. "It's been quite a day," she said.

"Yup."

"See you Wednesday?"

"For sure."

"Thanks for lunch, Dez."

"To which of the three meals are you referring?" she asked with a smile.

"I don't think you can call the cupcake a lunch."

"Oh, that reminds me..." Dez rooted around behind the seat and dug her jacket out, and after some more searching, triumphantly pulled something up. "Here you go," she said as she handed it to her partner. "You can have it for a midnight snack."

In the darkness of the cab Jaylynn felt the mashed cupcake still folded up in the crinkled cellophane. In a wry voice she said, "I'll treasure it always." She opened the truck door, which flipped the overhead light on, and as she slid out, she caught and held dark blue eyes. Standing hesitantly in the open door, she looked up at Dez. She didn't want to leave, didn't want the night to end, but her courage failed her.

"Good night, Dez."

"'Night, Jay."

Jaylynn slammed Dez's truck door shut and stomped over to her car, realizing with every step that she was mad at herself for being such a coward. It took her a few seconds to find the pocket of her jacket where the keys were. She unlocked the Camry door, gave a little wave and got in, setting the mashed cupcake on the passenger seat. The car was musty and warm and smelled faintly of mint. She didn't know why—she hadn't had anything minty in there that she could remember. She backed up out of the space and headed toward home. Smacking the wheel with the palm of her hand, she frowned. *Why did the day have to end already? And why wasn't I able to summon up the courage to talk to Dez, to tell her how I feel?* The thought that she might not get another chance like today filled her with despair.

Halfway down Lexington, she looked in the rear view mirror and saw the lights of a big vehicle tailing her. Squinting from the bright lights shining in through the back window, she questioned whether it was Dez's truck, but decided the big cop wouldn't follow that close. She came to Como Boulevard and maneuvered down the empty street around to the alley in back of the house. The truck stayed right behind and pulled in next to her.

Before Jaylynn could get out of her car, a tall dark form was opening her door. "Hey," said a gruff voice.

"Long time, no see," Jaylynn said as she emerged from her car and stood with her right arm resting on top of the open doorframe.

Something made of soft fabric was thrust against her chest, and she reached up to take it with her left hand. Dez said, "You forgot this again."

Jaylynn ran her hand over it for a moment before it registered: her U of M sweatshirt. "Possession is nine-tenths of the law," she said in a cool tone. "You've had it so long, you should keep it." She didn't know what was wrong with her, why she was being so brusque. She handed it back to Dez and smacked shut the Camry door.

"Jay." The voice was so soft she barely heard it. "Please?"

Startled, the rookie turned and looked up at the outline of her partner. Though moonlight reflected off the dark hair, she couldn't see her face in the shadows. She did, however, feel the hand that came to rest on her shoulder, and a fierce truth flooded through her. She needed to know...and she wanted to know *now*, today, right this moment: *Is this a one day thing? A one-time occurrence? What was today all about?* With a sigh she said, "We need to have that talk, Dez."

"I know."

In a peevish tone she said, "Do we have to have it here in the alley, or can we go inside where it's comfortable?" Acutely aware of the warm hand pressing lightly on her shoulder, she fumbled with her keys. When she looked up at the taller woman, her eyes had adjusted some to the darkness, and now she could see pale, smoldering eyes burning into her own. She met the gaze and didn't flinch. Everything around her narrowed, telescoping into the face before her, until all she could see were indigo eyes and all she felt was the slow beat of her heart, the rhythm picking up as those eyes drilled into her.

Dez bent her head ever so slowly, eyes never wavering, giving Jaylynn every opportunity to withdraw. Instead, the shorter woman met the gaze, unflinching, and tipped her head back until she connected with lips she found surprisingly soft. She dropped her car keys and brought her hands up to Dez's middle, feeling the ridges of ribs under the worn cloth of the green sweatshirt. She slipped her arms around the taller woman as the hand on her shoulder shifted to encircle her in a tight embrace.

The kiss was intense and overpowering, leaving her gasping for air. She leaned her forehead against Dez's shoulder, gulping, and said in a muffled voice, "Wait. Wait a minute." She could hardly tear herself away, but after a moment, she did. She let her arms drop and backed up two steps, still out of breath, and bumped against the Camry. She choked out, "*Don't* do this if you don't mean it." She took a deep breath and then bent to pick up her keys. When she rose, she saw the tall woman twisting the sweatshirt in her hands.

"I mean it," the husky voice said.

Jaylynn stood uncertainly, then whirled and headed toward the house. She reached the back gate and turned. "Well? Are you coming?"

Dez hesitated for only a moment before moving across the cement in slow strides until she caught up. "Will I be disturbing your roommates?"

"No. Tim's car isn't here, so he's gone. Sara must be gone too because the house is dark. Come on."

They made their way into the house through the kitchen back door, the hinges creaking as the smaller woman shut it. "Are you hungry?" Jaylynn asked in a quiet voice as she slipped her jacket off and tossed her keys on the table.

"Not really." Dez slouched by the back door, her hands in her jeans pockets and Jaylynn's sweatshirt tucked under one arm.

The rookie opened the refrigerator door, which cast a stream of light in the darkened kitchen. She grabbed a plastic pint container of orange juice and shut the door. Turning, she looked at Dez standing in the shadows. "Let's go up to my room."

They passed through the dining area and into the living room, which was illuminated by one dim lamp. They started up the steps and Dez ran her hand over the smooth wood of the banister. It was the first time she had ventured upstairs since the night of the attack, and as they climbed up the staircase, she looked at the walls. She saw a *Zorro* movie poster on the landing, the black-clad hero standing with his sword drawn and the beautiful Catherine Zeta Jones next to him. Dez said, "Hey, that's new. I loved that movie. She was *great*."

Jaylynn peered back at her quizzically. "Why do you think that's new?"

"Oh. Well," she said, taken aback. "I suppose it could actually be months old, but it wasn't there when I was up here last August. I remember all the other ones you have, though."

Jaylynn gave her a funny look. "Actually, we just got it a few weeks ago."

"Where did you get all those posters?"

"Sara gets them at the video store where she works. She can get practically anything."

At the top of the stairs, Jaylynn went into the only room Dez remembered with any clarity. The tall woman hesitated in the dark doorway, still twisting the sweatshirt in her hands, until Jaylynn turned on a table lamp between the couch and bed. It shed a pale glow that barely illuminated the room. Dez's eyes swept the room, noticing that everything was completely different from the last time she had been upstairs. She said, "Wasn't this Sara's room?"

"Yeah, but we switched. She couldn't face it after what happened." Jaylynn reached over and turned on a pole lamp next to the bed. The bright light made Dez squint. Jaylynn frowned and switched off the glaring light. She set the orange juice container on the table next to the dimly glowing lamp. She sank down, angled into the corner of the couch, feet curled underneath her, and patted the cushion beside her. Dez sauntered in, tossing the gray sweatshirt at the other end of the couch. She sat gingerly in the middle of the sofa, unsure and confused. In fact, she realized she felt a little panicky.

Jaylynn picked up the juice and offered it to her, but Dez shook her head and said, "No thanks."

The rookie twisted the cap off and took a sip and then set it back down. "What's the matter?" When the shy woman shrugged, she said, "Come here," and when Dez didn't move, an exasperated Jaylynn said, "I won't bite, and I won't make you do anything you don't want to. Please. Come here, Dez."

With her head down, Dez scooted over. Jaylynn reached for her companion's hand and was surprised to find that it was cool. "Hey! What happened to my furnace?"

Dez looked down, embarrassed, and said, "My hands get cold when I'm nervous."

"Why in the world are you so nervous?" Another shrug. In a kind voice she said, "I'm the same person I was when we sat on the rocks earlier. The same one from the beach. The same one who sat next to you—or slept on you—in the truck for what, 400 miles? Why are you all of a sudden afraid of me?"

"I don't know."

Jaylynn squeezed the large hand and rubbed it a little to warm it up. She pulled the fingers open, and ran the palm of her hand over Dez's palm feeling the calluses there. "You have great hands, you know." Right after she said it, she realized how it sounded, and blushed crimson red. This got a smile out of Dez. Jaylynn said, "Shame on you. You know that's not what I meant—I meant that your hands are nice. I mean, they're strong. They're beautiful."

"They're too big."

"You'd look sort of silly with *my* little hands on your body. These are just right for you. I like them. I like how I feel when they touch me."

Now it was Dez's turn to blush.

"Uh oh, your hands are going cold again. No more compliments for you." Jaylynn reached over and took another drink of the orange juice. "Sure you don't want some?"

"I'm sure." Dez was also sure that if she ate or drank one single drop of anything, she'd be sick. What was she thinking when she had followed the younger woman? She hated how things usually went when she acted impulsively. And yet—she *was* glad to be with Jaylynn. Maybe she wasn't ready to open up, but still, she didn't want to leave. She fumbled for words, something, anything to talk about, but nothing occurred to her.

Several tense seconds passed and then what came out of her mouth next surprised her as much as Jaylynn. "What I said that day in the 7-11 when I got shot? It was true." Dez took a sharp breath and, aghast, bit her tongue.

Now it was Jaylynn's turn to hold her breath as she studied her partner's face, which was blushing the brightest color of scarlet that she had ever seen. In her kindest voice, she said, "I thought so."

She paused. "I'm surprised you remember. You were kind of out of it."

"I remember."

"I wasn't actually sure you were talking to me."

"I was." Dez put her head down. "I am."

Jaylynn reached up and pulled the long dark tresses back and let her palm rest against the blushing woman's neck. With the other hand she gently turned Dez's chin until she faced her and looked her in the eye. "The feeling is so totally mutual."

Dez looked into smiling hazel eyes. She said, "I'm sorry I'm so slow."

Jay shrugged. "You've made me wait a long time, but I think it's been worth it."

Uncertainty hit Dez again, and she shivered. "How do you *know* that? How can you be so sure? We haven't even—you know—slept together."

"Yes, we have. What about at Luella's? What about last night in the truck?" She didn't mention their first night together, the one that had turned so traumatic.

"Don't be silly. That was different. It's not the same as being, you know—intimate."

Jaylynn stifled the urge to laugh, which was difficult since she was filled with so many contradictory and uncontrollable emotions that she almost felt the need to get up and run screaming jubilantly throughout the room. Instead, she said, "I think I'll feel the same way—even more intensely after *that* intimacy."

"But how do you *know*?" Bitterly Dez said, "It's not like I have a good track record. Everybody who's ever slept with me has ended up not liking me in the long run."

"What—a cast of thousands?"

Dez looked down. "Well, no. Three."

"They were idiots." Jaylynn let her hand drop from the pale face to rest on her thigh. "Desiree Reilly, I've been riding with you off and on for what—eight, nine months? I've seen you at your absolute worst and I still like you. Shouldn't that give you a clue?"

Dez considered that. "There's an awful lot of unknowns here, Jay."

The rookie rolled her eyes. "You worry too damn much."

"Guess it comes with the job. Sometimes it's like a heavy weight I can't toss off."

"Sorry, but I'm afraid *I'm* one heavy weight you aren't gonna be able to toss off so easily. Please—why don't you shut up and kiss me like you did in the alley?"

"Wait a minute. I haven't done this for a very long time. What if—"

"Oh, please!" Jaylynn said, laughing. "It's like riding a bike. You won't have just *forgotten*."

"What if someone comes down the hall?" Dez nodded toward the open door.

Jaylynn sprang up from the couch and closed the bedroom door. "There. Is that better?" She stood in the dim lamplight with her hands on her hips and a smirk on her face. "Should I put the desk chair in front of it just to be safe? Maybe we could drag the couch over in front of it?"

Dez groaned and shook her head.

"Will you *stop* worrying then?"

Dez nodded and reached her hand out. "Okay. Come over here."

Jaylynn was across the room like lightning. She stood before her partner and then eased down onto the couch by kneeling on either side of Dez's legs, lowering herself onto muscular thighs.

"You're lucky you're still young and limber," Dez said as she wrapped her arms around the smaller woman's waist. "That'd kill my old knees."

"Yeah, you're *so* ancient." Jaylynn cupped the dark head in her hands and met blue eyes. She arched an eyebrow. "Is this okay? There really isn't any hurry, you know. We should take things slow 'til it feels right to you."

One dark eyebrow arched. In a mocking tone, Dez said, "Go for it."

"All right, but just stop me any time you want, okay?"

Soft lips came together, shyly at first, and then more insistently. After a moment, Jaylynn broke the kiss and pressed closer to Dez, taking the opportunity to slip her arms around the tall woman's shoulders. She felt the bumpy texture of the couch against her forearms and the now very warm hands pressing against her back. Tucking her head against Dez's collarbone, she nuzzled at her neck, smelling the sweet scent she knew so well. "You smell incredibly good."

"How is that possible?" Dez asked in a low voice. "I haven't even had a shower since yesterday."

"I don't know why, but you just smell edible to me." She pressed her nose into the dark hair and inhaled. "You smell great."

"So do you," Dez countered gruffly as she pressed her lips against the side of Jaylynn's neck. "And you taste good, too."

A quiet whimper emerged from Jaylynn, and suddenly she was breathing fast. "Oh, Dez. You don't even know how sweet you are."

With a soft groan, Dez wrapped her arms tightly around her and stood up.

"Dez!"

In three steps they were at the edge of the bed, and Dez dropped them gracefully down onto it. They landed on their sides, still holding each other tightly.

Jaylynn said, "Pretty good for a decrepit old woman. It's not like I'm light as a feather."

"That was fun," Dez said, laughing.

"You could have warned me."

"What? And ruin the surprise? No way." She nuzzled Jaylynn's neck. In a soft voice she whispered, "You don't know how long I've wanted to do this."

"Why didn't you *say* something?"

"Get real. After what happened that first time?" She slid one leg between Jaylynn's and moved as close as she could. "Jay, I thought I had—well, totally and completely blown it. I don't know how you stuck it out all this time."

"But couldn't you *see* how I felt? Couldn't you feel it?"

Dez drew her head back and gave her a quizzical look. "What do you mean?"

"Well, apparently everyone but the blind has been able to tell how I feel about you."

"Meaning who?"

"Try Luella, Crystal, Vanita, Julie. Oh, and of course there's Sara, but she's had inside information. And Tim and Kevin, and Shayna—oh, and my mother definitely caught on, too."

"How do you know this?"

"Half of 'em *told* me. How else?"

In an indignant tone she said, "Good God! Is everyone we know privy to our relationship?"

"Dez! It's not my fault. If all of them could read it in my face, then why didn't you?"

"I'm glad no one read *my* face." Jaylynn burst into giggles. "What?"

"Try Crystal and Luella, for sure. Julie, too. And I'm sure Luella keeps Vanita up-to-date. And then there's Shayna. And Cowboy."

"Well, I'll be damned." She pulled the giggling woman closer. "So how come *you* couldn't tell about *me*?"

"Just because you felt one way about me or maybe were attracted didn't mean you wanted a relationship. Lucky I'm more patient than I look," Jaylynn said. "I—I just wasn't sure—you hide things well, you know."

"It's been harder lately."

"What do you mean by that?"

Dez ran her hand along Jaylynn's hip. She didn't quite know

how to explain, but she took a shot at it. "I let you in too much. I started to rely on you too much."

Jaylynn reached up to stroke the pale cheek. "I don't understand. How can you care about anyone too much? There's no too much about it. It's pretty simple. You either care or you don't."

"Yeah, that's a good theory," Dez muttered.

"Now that's *not* a theory—it's a fact. Trust me." Instead of replying, Dez leaned in for a kiss. "Wait," the rookie said, startling her partner as she hovered over her.

Alarmed, Dez froze. "What?"

Jaylynn half sat up, her elbow under her head, and in a very serious voice said, "I thought you didn't date cops." She blanched when Dez rolled away and onto her back, then held her breath and closed her eyes, swearing silently to herself.

As Dez stared up at the ceiling, she said, "It doesn't matter. At this point in our relationship, it appears that we're skipping right over the dating part."

Jaylynn laughed in relief. "You goofball, you may not have realized it, but every day with you has been a date."

"I don't think so," Dez said sheepishly. "I'm usually much nicer to my dates."

"Now who said you had no sense of humor?" Jaylynn leaned over the prone woman and put a hand on her stomach, stroking softly through the material of the sweatshirt and grinning when she felt Dez's breath catch. She let her hand drift higher until she was stroking the tight skin at her partner's collarbone, then stroking downward over the tight muscle of her chest. Dez shifted and moved closer until Jaylynn could feel the warmth of her breath and then a tender touch on her face as the taller woman lifted her head up off the bed and studied her intently. Jaylynn felt soft cotton under her hands as she slid up against Dez's body, then ducked her head gracefully. She sought out the red lips below, gentle at first and then deepening into a solid contact that made Jaylynn dizzy with longing and elation.

When they came up for air, Dez said, in a husky voice, "I guess I'll have a new rule. I'll only date *one* cop, but that's it. After that, I draw the line. You're the only one that got in the door in time, and now it's closing."

Breathlessly Jaylynn said, "For someone who had no idea what to say a little while ago, you sure are talking a lot."

Dez reached out and put her hands over the back pockets of Jaylynn's jeans and pulled the smaller woman up on top of her, in the process getting her hands up under Jaylynn's shirt. She captured soft lips again. Her hands wandered up the skin of the silken back, thumbs stroking a line along Jaylynn's midsection. She felt the smaller woman shiver and arch upward.

Jaylynn said, "I want to feel your skin against me." She pulled at Dez's sweatshirt until it came off over the bigger woman's head.

"Yours, too." Dez pulled off the polo shirt, and found—yet another t-shirt. "Good God! How you could've been cold all day with all these layers on is beyond me."

Jaylynn shut her up with a kiss.

Unclothed from the waist up, they reveled in the touch of warm skin rapidly heating to the touch. Jaylynn slid to her side to give her hands free rein to touch her partner. She laid her head on Dez's chest and let her right hand run from shoulder to breast to abdomen.

Jaylynn whispered, "You have no idea how much I wanted to touch you, especially the night of the bodybuilding show. I wanted to feel these muscles *so* bad."

Dez answered by rolling the rookie over on her back and easing herself gently over the smaller woman's frame. She traced a trail of kisses down Jaylynn's neck, stroking her abdomen, caressing breasts until Jaylynn thought she would explode with the pleasure of it. She clutched at the broad shoulders and then felt a rush of cool air as her jeans were unbuttoned and slipped off. "Off with yours, too," she whispered as she fumbled at the zipper on Dez's jeans. She couldn't help the sigh of contentment that escaped when the denim against her legs disappeared and suddenly she felt the heat of limbs tangled with hers.

Strong hands stroked across her stomach, over her hips, across her whole upper body and then along the inside of her bare thighs. Elation swept through her as she savored a gentleness that, for some odd reason, she hadn't expected. She completely lost track of where she was, focusing solely on the tension at her center as the heat grew and expanded in response to Dez's tender but insistent touch. She felt lips against her neck, and she clasped the tall woman tightly until she moved closer and closer to an explosion of lights and feeling. The intensity was so powerful that the sensations pounding through her body caused every muscle in her legs and hips to tighten and tremble in repeated waves. Through rasping breaths, she held on to the woman in her arms until the tidal wave washing over her began to abate.

"Geez, Dez," she wheezed. "You certainly seem to have remembered plenty of bike riding techniques." She gulped in air and gradually relaxed as Dez leaned over her and continued to stroke her body with deft hands.

In a low voice, Dez said, "You don't have any idea how beautiful you are, do you?"

"Oh, come on, you crazy woman."

"And," she said, "you're cute when you're embarrassed."

"I can only think of one way to shut you up." Jaylynn pulled the dark head toward her and covered the smiling mouth with her lips. After moments of exploration, they came up for air, and she said, "It's my turn now."

"I thought you just *had* your turn," Dez commented dryly.

"No, it's my turn to make *you* squirm."

"Somehow that doesn't sound very romantic."

"I'll work on it. Roll over, Miss Big Mouth Cop."

Laughing, Dez obeyed, moving upward so she lay nearer the headboard. She pulled a pillow under her neck as the smaller woman straddled her, kneeling on either side of the lean hips.

Jaylynn said, "Okay now, let's see a nice lying double biceps pose."

"I don't think that's in the routine."

"Put it in," she said with fake menace.

So Dez brought up her arms and flexed both biceps, looking first to the left, then to the right in the soft lamplight.

"Not bad," Jaylynn said as she reached down to palm each of the bulging muscles. Quietly she said, "I still can't believe how soft and cuddly you are when, from a distance, you look like so many angles and cuts." She leaned forward slowly and buried her face in the inviting neck below, nipping lightly with her teeth. When warm hands gripped her hips, she slid forward and shifted her legs until she lay atop the taller woman. She found herself clutched tightly as she ran her hands and mouth over as much of Dez as she could reach. It didn't take long to find all the spots that pleased the other woman most, and she stroked and kissed at the soft skin in place after place until she heard a tortured whisper in her ear, "Please. You're killin' me."

Jaylynn chuckled. She couldn't help but grin as her hands caressed her lover's legs. She found herself enfolded in strong arms against a wide chest. Hearing the pounding of the big woman's heartbeat in her ear, she concentrated on the pleasure she hoped to bring. Before she knew it, Dez was clutching at her powerfully and gasping in her ear. She gripped the rookie as she trembled convulsively, and then, when the shuddering subsided, she opened her eyes.

Jaylynn gazed nervously into bright blue eyes. "Back in the saddle again?"

"Okay, okay. You were right," Dez said gruffly. "But that was definitely more fun than any bicycle I ever fell off."

"I'll take that as a compliment."

They lay tangled together for a few moments as their heartbeats gradually resumed normal levels. Dez hugged Jaylynn tightly and closed her eyes, relishing the comfort of the moment. Then she sighed. Guarded eyes flicked open to search out Jaylynn's face. In a low but nervous voice, Dez said, "Should I go home now?"

Jaylynn blinked in disbelief. "You're joking, right?"

"Well, I—I mean, do you want me to go—"

"What? Are you nuts? Of course I don't want you to go." She reached up to the top of the bed and pulled the covers down.

Breathlessly Dez said, "Wait a minute, you can't seriously be cold."

"I will be soon. Here, slide over." She wrestled the covers out from under the two of them and slid her legs under.

Alarmed, Dez said, "You gotta be kidding. I'll roast."

"Yeah, yeah. Here, just pull the sheet up. I'll pull all the blankets over on me." Jaylynn sat up to arrange the bed. She stretched to click off the bedside lamp, the skin on her back and torso taut and smooth, and then when the room went dark, she snuggled up next to her still very warm companion. "I don't want you to leave. Please don't go—ever—okay?" When Dez didn't answer, she asked, "Will you hold me?"

Dez reached out and folded her into a scorching embrace and they lay quietly delighting in the closeness. After a while, Jaylynn glanced at the bedside clock. "Wow, can you believe it's already one o'clock?"

"It seems more like five a.m.," Dez said sleepily as she settled in closer to her companion.

"Not really."

"Maybe not to you, the one who got to sleep all over the north roads of Minnesota." Dez yawned. "But I haven't slept more than two hours at a time for days."

"Why?"

"Don't know. I never sleep well. But you won't believe how tired I am now." Her voice faded and her eyes closed. Jaylynn watched as the drowsy woman took a deep breath, exhaled, and then slept. She smiled, warm and content, and then eased over onto her side facing away from Dez. Her partner tightened her grip and tucked her legs up behind the rookie's until they lay spooned together, a strong right arm gripping Jaylynn's middle.

The joy that coursed through the younger woman kept her awake for several minutes. She took a deep breath, thinking that she had waited her whole life for this—not just making love, though that had been absolutely wonderful—but for this joining with the dark woman of her dreams. Always in the dreams there was a distance, a remoteness to her Hero. But with Dez lately, she had felt a burgeoning closeness that exhilarated her. This tall, complicated person who now held her so protectively in her arms had opened up, unfolding like a flower, in ways she had hoped for all her life.

With a contented sigh, she closed her eyes and pressed her right forearm against the arm around her middle. She must have fallen asleep shortly after, but she opened her eyes some time later. The LED on the clock read 2:20. Wondering what had wakened her, she lay listening for a moment until she heard a familiar tread on the stairs. There was a tap on her door, and in the moonlight streaming through the window, a head poked in.

"Spsssss. You awake?"

"Shhh." Jaylynn sat up, arranging the sheet, and put her finger to her lips. She made a motion to Sara indicating that she'd be right out, and the other woman disappeared from the doorway.

Jaylynn extricated herself from her lover's grip and padded across the floor. She grabbed an emerald green robe from the back of the door and slipped it on before taking a quick glance back. In the soft moonlight she saw dark hair fanned out on the pillow and it made her smile. She was still smiling when she descended the stairs and entered the kitchen to find Sara rooting through the refrigerator.

The brown-eyed woman looked askance at her over the fridge door, a sly grin on her face. "Sorry to barge in on you. Please tell me I didn't imagine one tall policewoman in your bed?"

Jaylynn blushed, but she kept on grinning. "Nope. That was definitely not your imagination. We've had quite the day, to say the least."

Sara smiled. "Hmmm. Guess I knew that was coming. Sorry to interrupt. Ever since you left the message on the answering machine, I've been dying to find out what happened between the two of you." She grinned wickedly at her red-faced friend as she collected an armload of items out of the fridge and kicked the door shut with her foot. "You want a sandwich?"

"Sure. I'm starved."

They stood assembling sandwiches while Jaylynn told her roommate about the events of the day. By the time she had finished the narrative, the two were sitting at the table downing milk and eating turkey and tomato sandwiches.

Sara said, "Where do you go from here then?"

Jaylynn looked thoughtfully across the kitchen table. "I guess that's up to her."

Sara gave her a puzzled look. "What does *that* mean? Isn't it up to the both of you?"

Frowning, Jaylynn said, "I know exactly what I want, and I can only hope she wants the same, but it's up to her. I learned my lesson already not to rush things. I'm just letting it happen however it goes." She popped the last crust of bread into her mouth and drank the final dregs of milk. "I can't believe how tired I am. But I'm glad I ate something. I was hungry." She rose and picked up her plate and glass.

"Good night, my friend," Sara said warmly. "You know I'm hoping and praying this all works out."

"I know you are. You're the best."

They smiled at one another. Jaylynn set her dishes in the sink, left Sara sitting at the table, and headed back upstairs. She crept into her room and slipped out of her robe, hanging it back up on the door hook, and slid into bed next to her toasty partner. She turned on her side, her back to the warmth, and felt an arm go around her and pull her close. She laced her fingers with Dez's and they shifted until every surface of their bodies that could touch was in contact.

Relaxing, she closed her eyes, and then heard a sleepy whisper, "Guess I should have taken you up on your offer to drag the couch over in front of the door, huh?" Jaylynn snickered. "You were gone a long time."

The smaller woman patted her own stomach with their intertwined hands. "Had to get a snack."

"Mmm...figures. Good night, love."

"Sleep well," Jaylynn replied, warmth and happiness flooding through her. She had waited so long, but finally, she was home.

Chapter
31

Dez awoke gradually in much the same position she'd been in when she'd fallen asleep, though she was no longer holding hands with the sleeping rookie. Jaylynn lay on her side facing away from her, the blonde head tucked under the bigger woman's chin. Dez marveled at how every angle, every curve of their bodies fit together perfectly. She glanced over at the bedside clock and was surprised to see that it was nearly ten a.m. For once, she'd actually gotten a whole night's sleep. She only remembered waking once, attempting to escape a dream of fire and screaming. The woman in her arms had soothed her, even in sleep, reaching back and stroking her thigh until she shook awake and realized she was safe.

Her left shoulder felt stiff, but she didn't want to move for fear of awakening her partner. Gently bringing her free right hand up to the hip lying pressed against her, she touched the silky skin from waist to thigh, her hand sliding back up to rest on the soft hip. A sense of disbelief washed over her. *I'm in love with this woman. I can hardly comprehend this, but last night she let me know she loved me, too. I can barely believe it.* She swallowed and drew in a long, slow breath, which she let out gradually.

She looked around the room. It seemed much larger in the daylight than it had in the dim lamplight of the night before. Two walls had two casement windows each, which were covered with peach colored blinds, and plenty of light slanted in through the slats. Next to the closet door sat a huge bookshelf overflowing with books. Three Monet posters hung on one of the walls, and a framed Georgia O'Keeffe print hung above the bed. A cinnamon brown circular rug covered the center of the floor, bordered by the bed on one wall, and the bedside table and couch next to it.

At the other end of the room, next to the door, was a large modular computer desk where a monitor, tower, and printer rested. Above it, hanging from the wall, was a four-by-five foot corkboard. Half of it contained cards and notes and various lists. The other half was covered with newspaper clippings.

Dez squinted, then rose up on her left elbow. She realized that the clippings were all articles about her. The one of her in Jaylynn's arms at the 7-11 looked new, but some of the others were old and yellowed, including the first write-up she'd ever gotten in 1993 when she had pulled two kids from a burning house. Though it was too far away to see clearly, she knew there was a fuzzy photo of herself on that one.

As she stared across the room at the news articles, the figure in her arms shifted and brought her hand up to grab Dez's. The rookie groaned and rolled onto her back. She opened her eyes to look up at her partner. Her white-blonde hair was tousled, but the unlined face looked rested and at peace. In the luminous sunlight, the hazel eyes appeared brighter than usual, and upon seeing them, a faint hint of recognition, of déjà vu, flowed through Dez. She frowned.

A tentative hand reached up and stroked her cheek, and a cheerful voice said, "Hey, what's wrong?"

Again Dez was struck by the familiarity of that face, of those hazel eyes. She'd known Jaylynn for over a year, yet she didn't feel she had ever truly looked at the woman. Now, holding the smaller form in her arms, her face inches away, she was acutely aware of how attractive she was. And not only that, but of something else, too, something intimate and almost recognizable that she had known forever and ever. At the same time she felt a buoyant elation, she also experienced a contradictory sense of grief and loss. The paradox confused her. She cleared her throat and in a low voice said, "Nothing's wrong. As usual, I'm just my same old grouchy self in the morning."

"I don't usually get to see you early in the day." Jaylynn snaked warm arms around the muscled torso and shifted, rolling the bigger woman over, disarranging the covers, until Dez lay on her back with two hazel eyes peering down into her face. "But I could get used to this."

"You could, could you?" Dez pulled the covers back up over the two of them and let her hands stroke the smooth shoulders, back, and hips in firm, languid motions. "It sure looks to *me* like you've been used to seeing me first thing every morning."

A puzzled look creased Jaylynn's brow. "What do you mean?"

Dez looked across the room and nodded toward the corkboard. "What's that supposed to be?"

Jaylynn shot a look over her shoulder. Once she figured out what Dez was referring to, she let out an embarrassed laugh. "Ah, my wall of fame. I forgot all about that." She lowered her head until her lips brushed the collarbone below her. "All I can say in my own defense is that it pales in comparison to the real thing, but it was the best I could do for a long time."

"I see," Dez said, arching one eyebrow and giving her partner just the faintest wisp of a smile. "How long have you been keeping this news and photo archive?"

Jaylynn nestled into Dez's arms and put her head on the wide chest. "I think it's been over a year now. Since last September, I guess."

"How in the heck did you get those old ones?"

Jaylynn blushed and met her eyes sheepishly. "I swiped 'em from some folders I found packed away in that old gray filing cabinet down in the roll call room. I didn't think anyone would care. There's a ton of old junk in there."

"But why?"

"Dez, I know it sounds impossible—maybe weird—but I fell in love with you the first time I laid eyes on you. One look...and that was it for me." She paused, struggling for words, and beginning to blush. "I couldn't help it. You didn't return phone calls. You were distant at the precinct. But I had to get close to you. I don't know why. I can't explain." She broke off obviously flustered.

"Guess I should be flattered."

"Or you could call me crazy," she said, her body tense and uncertain.

Dez lay there with the smaller woman looming over her, a concerned look on the face staring down at her. She tried to think when it was that she could say she had fallen in love with Jaylynn, but everything blended together. It was as if she had been a dead thing—cold and numb and in the dark—and then suddenly, inexplicably, a golden ray of sunlight had blazed through a portal to illuminate everything for her. But when exactly that happened she could not say. One moment she was isolated and outcast; the next, she had a constant companion who cared for her, who saved her from herself. "You're about the farthest thing from crazy I've ever met," she said, her voice low and husky. She tightened her grip around the slender waist, and felt Jaylynn relax against her, the blonde head tucked into her neck. "What happens now?"

"Breakfast?"

Dez smiled, nodding her head. "Hmm. Shoulda known that would be your first thought."

"Aren't *you* hungry?"

"Yeah, I guess I am." She lay there stroking smooth skin with her fingertips. "I should probably go home."

"Why?"

Dez sighed and looked across the room. "Don't wanna wear my welcome out."

A sharp bark of laughter burst from Jaylynn. "You wouldn't

wear your welcome out if we were handcuffed together."

With one eyebrow arched, Dez said, "That could be arranged."

Dez felt the body against her tremble with laughter, and then in a serious voice, Jaylynn asked, "Do you want to do something together today, maybe?"

There was no maybe about it. Dez knew she would be content to lie in bed all day holding Jaylynn. The need to be close to her was so strong it was a gnawing ache.

When she didn't answer right away, the woman in her arms let out a gust of air, as though she'd been holding her breath, and then pulled away and peered intently at her face. "It's okay if you'd rather not—"

"Wait," Dez said. "I didn't say that. I was just thinking about details. You know, things like needing some clean clothes and wanting a shower and a toothbrush—"

"That's no problem." Without warning, Jaylynn rolled away and out of bed. She padded across the room, her skin tawny in the strong morning sunlight. Dez admired the strong thighs, the swell of hips, the slender waist and shapely shoulders. She watched as Jaylynn rooted around in a desk drawer and pulled something out. "Ah ha, thought I had one here," she said. She slapped the drawer shut and then grabbed the green robe off the back of the door and returned to sit on the edge of the bed, the robe across her lap.

Dez marveled that Jaylynn wasn't at all self-conscious sitting before her with no clothes on, her hair uncombed, and goosebumps on her arms. The younger woman handed her a narrow package, which Dez realized was a toothbrush. "Here," she said. "Just take my robe and go shower—straight ahead, second door on the left down the hall. Meanwhile, I'll round up some clothes you could wear."

Dez started to pull the covers back, but inexplicably, she found herself blushing. She reached for the robe, but Jaylynn gave her an amused look. As though she could read her mind, the rookie said, "You're not going shy on me now, are you, Desiree?" When Dez gave her a wry grimace, she giggled and asked, "Shouldn't *I* be the shy one? I've seen *almost* every inch of you at the bodybuilding show." She grabbed the covers and slid in on her side, pressing up to the toasty alabaster skin. "I *love* how warm you always are."

Dez set the toothbrush aside and enfolded the snuggling woman in her arms, feeling a lump rise in her throat. Awash in feeling, she ran her hand through the short blonde hair, her pulse quickening. She swallowed. "It'll be interesting," she said, "to squeeze into whatever you want me to wear."

"You act like you're an elephant." Smiling eyes twinkled at her. "You probably haven't noticed, but your hips are smaller than mine. And maybe your shoulders are broader, Miss Body Building Queen, but I have plenty of XL sweatshirts. So go get in the shower and I'll dig you up something."

They disentangled, and as Dez stepped out of the warm covers, Jaylynn slapped her on the butt. "Nice tush," she said as she held the toothbrush package out. Blushing, Dez snapped it up and then slipped into the robe, which was tight across the shoulders, to say the least. She pulled the tie around her and knotted it in front. "What if one of your roommates—"

Jaylynn waved at her. "Don't worry about it. Just go down the hall. No one will come in. I'm sure neither of them is even up yet. Towels are in the linen closet in there, and the white blow dryer is mine if you want to use it. There's probably five different kinds of shampoo in the shower—just take your pick."

Dez moved to the door and cracked it open, peeking down the hall. She glanced back to see the smirk on Jaylynn's face, and swung the door wide and stepped resolutely out into the hall.

She unwrapped the toothbrush, brushed her teeth, and hung the purple brush in the rack with half a dozen others. When she got done showering, Dez wrung the water out of her hair, which was thick and tangled, but she didn't have a brush. She dried off, slipped the emerald robe back on, and padded back to Jaylynn's room carrying the damp towel with her. She found her partner lounging under the covers again. "Hey, lazybones!"

Jaylynn stuck her tongue out. "I'm just trying to keep warm. *You* weren't here, so what else was I supposed to do?" She reached for a pile of clothes next to her on the bed, and slid them toward the edge. "Why don't you grab that blue brush on the dresser and come here. I'll brush your hair."

Dez did as she was told and came to sit before the smaller woman.

"You have such beautiful hair," Jaylynn said quietly as she combed out the black tangles.

Dez closed her eyes and reveled in the sensation of the brush and warm hands against her damp head and neck.

In a dreamy voice, Jaylynn said, "I used to dream about this when I was a kid."

"Brushing women's hair?"

The rookie stopped abruptly. "Yeah, something like that." She set the brush down on the bed and pulled the long dark hair to the side, revealing an ivory smooth neck. Bending her mouth to the skin near the dark hairline she ran a line of kisses down the graceful neck to the top of the green robe. Dez's breath caught, and she felt shivers course through her body. She twisted to face Jaylynn, found velvety lips and lost herself in a kiss.

The kiss ended leaving them both breathless. Jaylynn smiled widely, revealing flashing white teeth. "You taste good. No fair. You've brushed your teeth." She picked up the hairbrush and quickly arranged the damp tresses into a French braid. "How's that?"

Dez ran her hands over the top of her head. "Good."

"All right. Now let me go get cleaned up." Jaylynn slid out from under the dark woman and was pulling the green robe away before her feet even hit the floor. "My turn. Lemme have the robe."

"I can see that sharing clothes with you is gonna be an experience," Dez said as she let the shorter woman tug the robe down off her shoulders. As Jaylynn put the robe on, Dez swung her legs off the side of the bed and sat on the edge, reaching into the pile of clothes to grab a navy blue sweatshirt. She pulled it on over her head. When her head popped through the neckband, she found Jaylynn watching her, the emerald robe around her shoulders but still open. Jaylynn stepped closer, and Dez slipped her hands inside the robe and pulled the rookie to her. She pressed her lips against the silky skin at Jaylynn's breast and tightened her hold.

Next thing she knew, Jaylynn had pushed her back onto the bed and was kissing her in earnest. Dez crushed the warm body to her, carried away, her heart thundering. As they broke apart for air, Dez both felt and heard the giant rumble that emanated from the waist pressed against her. They laughed and relaxed. "Go on," Dez said. "Your stomach is asserting itself again. Go hop in the shower and then we can get some food in you."

Jaylynn rose, blushing, and rearranged the robe. "Okay, I'll hurry."

While she was gone, Dez finished dressing in pink cotton underwear, dark blue sweatbottoms, and a pair of athletic socks. She paused for a moment and marveled at the response Jaylynn brought about in her. She hadn't expected to feel this way, this passionate hunger that robbed her of all sense and swept away every thought from her mind except for the need to touch and be touched. She had never felt this connection, this kind of rapport before. It was as if she and Jaylynn were totally in harmony, like a finely tuned guitar. One strum, one touch resulted in a rich and vibrant sound and feeling. Both gave her shivers and sent a thrill of happiness through her.

She laced up her own hightops and realized Jaylynn had been right. Everything fit fine, though the sweatpants were a little short. She pressed her hands against her damp hair and arranged a few tendrils off her face. Moving over to the window near the foot of the bed, she pulled the blinds open and looked out.

The sun was heading high in the sky. It shone brightly over the back of the house and glared off the chrome on her red truck. In the far corner of the backyard a shed listed slightly to the left, its white paint cracked and peeling. The last of the wilting tiger lilies struggled valiantly to remain upright, but the early autumn weather had taken its toll. The grass was still a verdant green and looked like it could use one final mowing before winter.

Dez crossed her arms over her chest and watched two squirrels streak across the grass to scramble up the black walnut in the middle of the yard. It occurred to her that things were happening awfully fast all of a sudden. Two days ago she and Jaylynn had been circling one another warily, as if uncertain about the other. Yesterday the barriers had begun to crumble, and last night... *Well, so much for barriers.* Today had already started out on a good note, and she wondered how long it could last. She didn't want to delude herself. What she wanted from Jaylynn and what she might actually get could be miles apart. And yet...something in her told her to trust. That recurring and familiar sense of déjà vu washed over her. She could not have explained her faith in the rookie to anyone, not even to Jaylynn, but at a purely instinctual level, something in her cried out to depend upon what she felt and upon what the younger woman professed to feel.

She moved away from the window and sat down on the bed. The water clunked off down the hall, and she heard the whir of the hair dryer. In short order, a whirling bundle of energy returned to the room and buzzed around, pulling out clothes and chattering away. Dez watched her dress in a white Police Academy sweatshirt, jeans, and running shoes.

Jaylynn brushed her hair back, then said, "Ready for something to eat?"

Dez nodded and rose from the bed. Jaylynn reached for her hand and pulled her down the stairs to the quiet kitchen. She was appalled at Dez's boring choice, but the big cop insisted on having oatmeal, though she did grudgingly accept two pieces of lightly buttered toast. Jaylynn sectioned a grapefruit and they ate that, too, then they sat at the table looking expectantly at one another. The kitchen clock ticked away, displaying the time: 11:15.

"What next?" Jaylynn asked.

Dez brought her large hands up from under the table and stretched them out to take the smaller woman's hands in her own. She squeezed, her thumbs pressing into palms, and said seriously, "These clothes are nice and everything, but—" she cleared her throat and looked out the window.

Jaylynn frowned at her, puzzled. "But what?"

Dez returned her gaze to the concerned eyes before her, a

funny look on her face. "But to be honest, I'd like to go back upstairs and take them off." A pleasant shade of crimson started at her neck and rose as she saw understanding wash over Jaylynn's features. The younger woman broke out in a grin and stood, leaving their dishes on the table. Still holding one of Dez's hands, she pulled her to her feet and up the stairs to her room.

****

The two women spent the afternoon making love and talking, with Jaylynn running downstairs twice to bring up food to munch on in bed. Soon it was late afternoon. The sun had ceased to slant in through the blinds. Dez lay on her back against a pillow, Jaylynn cradled contentedly against her chest with their legs entwined. She reached a hand up to brush the blonde hair out of the younger woman's face. The hazel eyes opened slowly. Dez watched as Jaylynn's eyes went from hazy to intent. "What?" Dez asked.

In a soft, almost inaudible voice, Jaylynn said, "I'm not sure you understand how I feel about you." Dez waited, watching the hazel-eyed woman struggle to put something into words. "This is not lust—well," Jaylynn's face colored sweetly, "I'm not denying the lust, but how I feel is more than just an incredible attraction. Nothing like this has *ever* happened to me before. Do you understand?"

Dez nodded slowly.

"Dez, I don't want to scare you off..."

She reached out and cupped Jaylynn's face in a big hand, her thumb stroking a tight circle on the soft skin. She waited.

"I want you...forever. You probably think that sounds crazy, huh?" Serious eyes and a worried face looked up at her partner.

Shyly, Dez said, "It's not just physical for me either. I feel the same way. I—I—well, I can't explain it," she finished awkwardly.

In answer, the smaller woman snuggled more tightly against her, burrowing her face into the ivory neck. After a few minutes, Jaylynn whispered, "The worst time of my life was when you wouldn't speak to me. You don't know how much that hurt. Please...please don't let that ever happen again."

In a husky voice, Dez said, "I won't. I promise."

They lay there for several minutes, not moving, not talking, before Dez looked over at the bedside clock. "It's nearly five. I should probably go home."

Jaylynn raised her head and gave Dez an alarmed look. "I hope you're not serious."

"We're closing in on 24 hours in bed. We gotta work tomorrow. Don't you want to get up and get ready?"

"What's to get ready?"

"You know—laundry, shopping, cooking, whatever."

Jaylynn rolled off the broad chest onto her back and gave a big sigh. Looking up at the ceiling she said, "I don't want to do any of that. I just want to lie here with you for the rest of our lives."

Dez laughed, making a strangled noise. "Short life. You'd run outta food pretty soon. Then all hell'd break loose."

Jaylynn moved onto her side and propped herself up on her elbow to survey her partner. With a very cranky look on her face, she said, "I *don't* want you to leave."

Dez rolled on her side to face her companion so that they were nose to nose. With her left hand she feathered her fingers along the warm, silky side until she shivered. "Then come with me," Dez said. She leaned in and kissed Jaylynn for added emphasis. She was rewarded with an immediate flashing smile.

Jaylynn said, "Are you saying I could come over to your place and stay the night?"

"Sure."

Jaylynn was out of bed in a shot. She pulled on her clothes, which had been tossed haphazardly on the couch. Dez laced her fingers together and put her hands up behind her head as she watched the smaller woman move around the room collecting clean clothes and stuffing them into a small duffel bag. She sorted through the stack of CD's under the bedside table and grabbed two to put in the bag. Jaylynn tossed the bag over on the couch and came to sit on the edge of the bed.

Amused, Dez said, "I don't think I've *ever* seen you get ready for anything that fast."

"You've had a good effect on me. Come on. Get your clothes on, Miss Slowpoke."

****

Later, undressed again, they held one another in Dez's bed. Jaylynn reclined comfortably, her knees drawn up slightly, and her blonde head cushioned on a pillow against the bed's maple headboard. Dez lay on her stomach with her head resting on the rookie's abdomen, her hands tucked under the other woman's lower back. She was very nearly asleep when her partner's voice rumbled in her ear. "They're not going to make us change shifts or stop riding together, are they?"

Dez opened her eyes, but didn't move her head. "I thought about that, too," she said in a low voice. "I don't know."

"Is there some policy about this?"

"Not really, but there's always the sexual harassment policy."

"What?" Jaylynn asked, surprise in her voice.

"Technically speaking, as your FTO, I supervise you. You could consider this harassment if you wanted to file a suit saying I took advantage of you." She lifted her head and found the startled hazel eyes above her. With a smirk she went on, "If you're sleeping with me for a passing recommendation, you already had it."

"Very funny."

"There's the flip side, too. If any of the other rookies wash out, they could say you got preferential treatment."

Jaylynn thought for a moment. "I don't think any of them are going to wash out." She looked at Dez. "Hey, they're all gonna make it, right?" Her eyes narrowed, and she poked her companion in the side. "Dez!"

Dez lifted her upper body on her elbows and scooted herself up until she lay next to Jaylynn. She snuggled closer until her dark head nestled into the crook of Jaylynn's neck. The smaller woman put an arm around her shoulders and pulled her closer. With a sigh of pleasure, Dez wrapped her arm across the rookie's middle, feeling the taut muscles of her stomach and the silky warmth of Jaylynn's skin. "Neilsen is the only one I am concerned about."

"Why?"

"Besides the fact that he's an asshole?"

Jaylynn gave her a look. "You're still remembering that one little altercation, right?"

"Of course. But besides that, he's already pulled his gun far too many times. Drives like an idiot. Talks big. Pisses citizens off. I'd like to smack him."

"You *have* smacked him."

"No, I mean *really* smack him. He's a jerk. Shouldn't be a cop. I'm sorry, but Alvarez and I talked about this. He's not sure what he's gonna do, but I'm recommending to the Lieutenant that Neilsen not pass probation. Maybe he'll get enough support from other FTO's, but it isn't coming from me."

"Hmm." Jaylynn looked down at the dark head in her arms and brought her hand up to absentmindedly stroke the pale white cheek. "Can I ask you something else?"

"Um hmm."

Jaylynn took a deep breath and pulled Dez as tightly to her as she could. Her fingers feathered across the warm arm against her abdomen, and she said, "Do you remember when we first met?"

"You mean last summer or later at the precinct?"

"At the house that night."

"Yeah, why?"

"What do you remember?"

Dez closed her eyes and thought about the scene that night in the darkened house: the screams, the low laughter of the big man with the knife. She remembered her own fear as a sick feeling in the pit of her stomach—and an overwhelming desire to get in that house for reasons she couldn't understand. She'd tossed aside protocol and gone in alone without backup, something she didn't usually do. Once she got up the stairs, everything was a jumble of physical action, of shouting, of pure exhilaration as she beat down the two assailants. She'd felt so alive, adrenaline coursing through her veins like electricity.

And then, she had looked up and felt one moment of jolting connection. Her eyes had met those of the blonde woman, and she'd felt that strange recognition which she didn't understand at the time. She knew now she had made a big mistake in disregarding that link. "Why do you ask?"

"Just curious."

Dez rolled from her side to her back and then inched over so that her whole right side was touching Jaylynn. She found the smaller hand and laced their fingers together. "I remember you."

Jaylynn paused. "What does that mean?"

"I can't explain it. I tried to ignore it. I've fought it." She looked over at Jaylynn and saw the puzzled look on the rookie's face.

"Why is that?" Jaylynn asked.

"Why is *what*—why can't I explain?"

Jaylynn turned on her side toward her. "No, you fool. Why have you been fighting it? I gave in at the hospital the night of the attack—within minutes."

"Guess you don't have the endurance I do," Dez said in a low, grudging voice.

"Yeah, right." Jaylynn scooted up on her hands and knees and moved over the big woman, straddling one lean leg. Looking down into unflinching blue eyes, she lowered herself until her warm torso touched an even warmer stomach and chest, melting into her partner as strong arms wrapped around her middle and stroked her back. With her face tucked into the crook of the pale neck she whispered, "You're a very good lover, Dez."

In a low voice, the big cop responded, "You're not so bad yourself."

The rookie laughed outright. "Woman of few words, you crack me up." She shifted a bit to the side, and let herself relax upon her partner, nuzzling her face into her neck again. Jaylynn wanted to say how much she loved her, how for the first time ever, she felt complete, but she held back. She didn't know if Dez was ready for that. She lifted her head and gazed into serious blue eyes, feeling her breath catch. A smile worked its way across her face, even though she tried to suppress it, and Dez gave her a questioning look.

Stroking Jaylynn's back, Dez said, "What? What are you thinking?"

Jaylynn grinned. "I'm just very happy, that's all. You make me happy." Dez's arms tightened around her, and she felt entirely safe and protected.

"I'm glad." An impish grin spread across her face, and Jaylynn admired the even, white teeth.

"You should smile more often, Dez. You're really beautiful." Then Jaylynn laughed to see her partner blush.

"I bet you say that to all the girls," Dez growled.

"Nope. Only to you." She moved up onto her elbows and leaned in for a kiss, which quickly kindled rising excitement for both of them. Their bodies melded together into a tangle of warmth and desire, and for a little while, all thought vanished of anything other than the wild hunger for one another.

****

Dez lay on her right side, left arm around the body in front of her, and her legs tucked in behind the rookie's. She let out a contented sigh.

Jaylynn craned her neck around, trying to see her partner. "What was the big sigh for?"

"I don't know. Maybe you're wearing me out...you're a lot younger you know."

"What?" Grinning, she turned over to face the smiling woman and reached over to brush the long dark hair off Dez's face. "You've barely got four years on me."

"I can tell math is not your strong suit, Jay. I'm almost thirty."

Jaylynn laughed, a deep throaty sound that vibrated against Dez's chest. "I plan to get back at you big time, too."

"What's that supposed to mean?"

"When you turn thirty, it'll be payback time. And I'm not *that* bad at math. I know exactly how many days it is until your birthday. And you, Oh Ancient One, are only four years and nine months older than me. That's nothing. When you turn seventy-five, I'll be almost seventy-one, so big deal."

Dez lifted her gaze to meet the hazel eyes glittering before her, and said, "I hope I know you when I'm seventy-five."

"Why wouldn't you?" Jaylynn asked, exasperation in her voice. She let her hand slide along Dez's thigh, feeling the strong curve there.

The tall woman shrugged and looked away. "I don't know."

Jaylynn snuggled closer and hooked her arm under Dez's neck, wrapping her arms around her partner. "Fifty years from now, I hope we are curled up together like this on this very bed."

In a dry voice, Dez said, "I'm pretty sure we'll need a new mattress by then."

Jaylynn reached down to tickle her. "Very funny, you smart aleck." She poked at the muscle in Dez's stomach, causing the bigger woman to double over and squirm away.

"Hey!" Dez said in a mock-threatening tone. "You better not start anything you can't finish."

"I told you," Jaylynn said, "I never start anything I can't finish." She shrieked with laughter and made another grab for Dez's stomach, but just then a series of thumps sounded on the floor.

Dez froze. "Uh oh, it's Luella." She stared for a split second at Jaylynn, then leapt out of bed. "She'll be on her way up here!" In four long strides she was across the room to the bathroom grabbing her red robe off the back of the door. "Lucky she's slow on the stairs." She slipped on the robe and tied it in front. "I'll go see what she wants."

She went out to the kitchen and opened the door. The silver-haired woman's head was just appearing as she tenaciously climbed the stairs. Dez realized it had been several days since she'd talked to her landlady, and she was suddenly glad to see the plump woman. Smiling, she stood in the doorway, pulling the red robe closer around her.

"Thought maybe you up and skipped town, Dez," Luella said as she rounded the newel post. She trained warm brown eyes on her tenant and shuffled toward her.

"Nah, just busy."

"I don't smell a single cooking odor from your place, so I thought maybe you two would like to come down for vegetable beef soup and sandwiches." Dez's mouth opened, but nothing came out. Luella grinned at her, white teeth sparkling. "Well—her car's out front. You should've hid it if you didn't want me to know."

Just then, Jaylynn, barefoot and dressed in sweatbottoms and a t-shirt, squeezed into the doorframe next to Dez. "Hi, Luella," she said, the warmth evident in her voice. "I would love to come down for dinner. Wouldn't you, Dez?" She looked up at her red-faced companion and grabbed hold of a red-clad forearm.

Dez stammered, "Sure...yeah, okay." She looked down at her robe. "Let me go, ah—finish changing." She turned abruptly and fled, leaving Jaylynn and Luella looking at one another, amusement etched in their faces.

Luella said, "Looks like patience paid off, as usual."

Jaylynn nodded. "Yup."

They shared a conspiratorial grin, and Luella said, "Now just stay after her. She's a tricky one, that one is, but she's really a mushball at heart."

Jaylynn giggled. "So I've gathered."

From the other room a testy voice called out, "You two can stop talking about me as if I can't hear 'cause I can."

"Good thing," Luella said in a loud voice. "So you'll know we're on the way downstairs to talk some more about you where you can't hear." She grabbed hold of Jaylynn's hand and pulled her toward the stairs.

"Oh, no you don't," Dez said as she burst into the kitchen dressed in jeans and a sweatshirt.

"My, my," Luella marveled, "she's dressed already. That girl does do everything fast, doesn't she?"

Jaylynn gave her a sly look as she rounded the newel post and said, "Well, not exactly *everything*." She tossed an evil grin back at Dez who was once more coloring up quite nicely.

In her best menacing voice, Dez said, "You two better not gang up on me again." She was answered by two smirks. "Oh, no," she grumbled. "I'm toast."

"You can say that again," Luella said. She and Jaylynn looked at one another and burst out laughing, and the three of them made their way downstairs to the warmth and happiness of a shared meal.

And coming soon from
Quest Books

The riveting sequel to *Gun Shy*

Under the Gun

Under the Gun is the long-awaited sequel to the bestselling novel, *Gun Shy*, about St. Paul Police Officers Dez Reilly and Jaylynn Savage. Picking up just a couple weeks after *Gun Shy* ended, the two partners are adjusting to their relationship, but things start to go downhill when they are dispatched to a double homicide—Jaylynn's first murder scene. Dez is supportive and protective of Jaylynn, and things seem to go all right until their nemesis reports their personal relationship. When the brass restrict them from riding together on patrol, a chain of events is set in motion that results in Jaylynn getting wounded, Dez being suspended, and both of them having to face the possibility of life without the other. They face struggles—separately and together—that they must work through while truly feeling "under the gun."

Another Lori L. Lake title
available from
Yellow Rose Books

Ricochet In Time

Hatred is ugly and does bad things to good people, even in the land of "Minnesota Nice" where no one wants to believe discrimination exists. Danielle "Dani" Corbett knows firsthand what hatred can cost. After they suffer a vicious and intentional attack, Dani's girlfriend, Meg O'Donnell, is dead. Dani is left emotionally scarred, and her injuries prevent her from fleeing on her motorcycle. But as one door has closed for her, another opens when she is befriended by Grace Beaumont, a young woman who works as a physical therapist at the hospital. With Grace's friendship and the help of Grace's aunts, Estelline and Ruth, Dani gets through the ordeal of bringing Meg's killer to justice.

Filled with memorable characters, *Ricochet In Time* is the story of one lonely woman's fight for justice—and her struggle to resolve the troubles of her past and find a place in a world where she belongs.

Available at booksellers everywhere.
ISBN: 1-930928-64-5

Coming in 2003
from Lori L. Lake and
RAP

Different Dress

Different Dress is the story of three women on a cross-country musical road tour. Jaime Esperanza is a gaffer/electrician and roadie. The headliner, Lacey Leigh Jaxon, is a fast-living prima donna with intimacy problems. She's had a brief relationship with Jaime, then dumped her for the new guy (who lasted all of about two weeks). Lacey still comes back to Jaime in between conquests, and Jaime hasn't yet gotten her entirely out of her heart.

After Lacey Leigh steamrolls yet another opening act, a folksinger from Minnesota named Kip Galvin, who wrote one of Lacey's biggest songs, is brought on board for the summer tour. Kip has true talent, she loves people and they respond, and she has a pleasant stage presence. A friendship springs up between Jaime and Kip—but what about Lacey Leigh?

It's a honky-tonk, bluesy, pop, country EXPLOSION of emotion as these three women duke it out. Who will win Jaime's heart and soul?

Jumping Over My Head

Something a little different from novelist Lori L. Lake. Here is a book of short stories written about ordinary people with uncommon—and also universal—problems.

A mother and daughter having an age-old fight. Small children bullied on the playground taking back their power. A father trying to understand his lesbian daughter's retreat from him. A frightened woman attempting to deal with an abusive partner. An athlete who misses her chance—or does she? An elderly couple stalked by an old woman. These stories and more are told in Jumping Over My Head & Other Stories.

Vagabonds...A Letter From Father...Mouse...Afraid of the Dark...Everything You Learn in Kindergarten Can Ruin Your Life...The Jungle Garden...Busy-body...Defending Angels...Propane...Strange Inclinations...The Big Eddy...My Lifesaving Journal...Jumping Over My Head

Thirteen stories about characters dealing with life and loss. The collection has been described as a series of mini-novels, with each story being odd and quirky, as though slightly off-kilter at the beginning and regaining stability by the end.

Other titles from
Quest Books

Vendetta
By Talaran
ISBN 1-930928-56-4

Blue Holes to Terror
By Trish Kocialski
ISBN 1-930928-61-0

Staying in the Game
By Nann Dunne
ISBN 1-930928-60-2

Murder Mystery Series: Book One
By Anne Azel
ISBN 1-930928-72-6

High Intensity
By Belle Reilly
ISBN 1-930928-33-5

Shield of Justice
By Radclyffe
ISBN 1-930928-41-6

Available at www.rapbooks.biz
and booksellers everywhere.

Lori L. Lake lives in the Twin Cities area with her partner of two decades. She spent over ten years apprenticed to the craft of writing short stories and didn't realize until recently—on the verge of her fortieth birthday—that novel writing was her true creative form.

In real life, Lori works as a supervisor in a government office. In her off hours, she is a writer, editor, and housework avoider. She enjoys music, playing guitar, weightlifting, hiking, the movies, reading, her nieces, nephews, and godchildren, sports not involving water or horses, and cracking bad puns.

Ricochet in Time and *Gun Shy* were her first published novels. *Under The Gun*, the sequel to *Gun Shy,* will be published in summer 2002. Her fourth novel, *Different Dress* will be published by Renaissance Alliance Publishing, Inc. in 2003, as well as a book of short stories entitled *Jumping Over My Head & Other Stories*. She is at work on her fifth and sixth novels. Further information about Lori L. Lake can be found at her website at http://www.LoriLLake.com.

Printed in the United States
43030LVS00004B/145-171

9 781930 928435